THE OTHER
LOLA

ALSO BY RIPLEY JONES

Missing Clarissa

THE OTHER LOLA

A Novel

RIPLEY JONES

WEDNESDAY BOOKS
NEW YORK

Published in the United States by Wednesday Books, an imprint of
St. Martin's Publishing Group

THE OTHER LOLA. Copyright © 2024 by 3BD Holdings, Inc. All rights reserved.
Printed in the United States of America. For information, address St. Martin's
Publishing Group, 120 Broadway, New York, NY 10271.

www.wednesdaybooks.com

The Library of Congress Cataloging-in-Publication Data is available upon request.

ISBN 978-1-250-34046-7 (trade paperback)
ISBN 978-1-250-80198-2 (hardcover)
ISBN 978-1-250-80199-9 (ebook)

Our books may be purchased in bulk for promotional, educational, or
business use. Please contact your local bookseller or the Macmillan Corporate
and Premium Sales Department at 1-800-221-7945, extension 5442, or
by email at MacmillanSpecialMarkets@macmillan.com.

First Edition: 2024

10 9 8 7 6 5 4 3 2 1

for Andrea M., with gratitude

Each detective, alone in the woods, must take her clues, and solve her mysteries herself.

—Sara Gran

THE OTHER LOLA

THE
RETURN

LOLA was gone before she ever went missing. Mattie's always known this, marrow-deep. Lola and her haunted cat-green eyes. Lola and her cloud of black hair, dense as night. Lola, the most beautiful person Mattie's ever known: keeper of secrets, teller of stories, barrier between Mattie and the harsh unfeeling world.

That Lola was born with one foot out the door.

Even as a child, Mattie knew.

But what Mattie has still, will have forever, is the before time. Summer nights, the woods behind the house alive with coyotes singing down the moon. First a single yip, and then the chorus. The thrumming frogs in the neighbor's pond falling silent. Windows open to the piney dark.

And Lola, slipping through Mattie's bedroom door sometime before dawn silvers the edges of the mountains. Coming home in the thick wolf-hour dark from wherever it is she goes, smelling of cigarettes and vanilla and something sweetish and musky that Mattie will recognize years later as weed. Crawling into Mattie's bed, under the covers, curling herself snail-tight against Mattie's back, inhaling the hay-sweet warmth at the nape of Mattie's neck. Whispering *You know I'll never leave you behind here when I go, Mats* into Mattie's sparrow-boned shoulders.

Mattie will carry that promise a lifetime long. Lola's humid body, her hot, whiskey-scented breath. Her long arms flung out, her legs kicking restlessly as Mattie holds perfectly still so as not to disturb her.

Lola muttering in her sleep as the stars wink out one by one, the sky lightens, the sun climbs over the mountains to wheel its way through another day.

But no matter how hard Mattie fights to stay awake, to bind Lola to the real and breathing daylight world—in the harsh light of morning, Mattie wakes again alone, the night before as blurry and wondrous as a dream.

And then, five years ago: the morning Mattie woke and knew Lola was gone for good.

And now: The girl who came back yesterday, the girl who says she's Lola, is somebody else.

It's not possible.

But it's true.

Lola's mouth, but full of lies. Lola's laugh refracted through another throat. Her eyes are the same green, but they're layered with different secrets. Stories Lola never would have told.

Mattie knows where the girl detectives live, and Mattie is going to make them help.

Their addresses are online, pictures of their homes plastered across hateful troll-filled forums and comment-thronged web articles.

Pictures of the girls themselves: the tall one, all angles and elbows and disordered hair, head down and one bony arm thrown up as she tries to evade the cameras outside her apartment building. The pretty one, trying to hide her sweet face behind movie-star sunglasses, her bright gold hair stuffed under a hat.

They're teenagers. They should be safe, their lives lived behind closed doors. But after what they did last year, they're everywhere. There's nowhere they can hide.

Mattie finds their class schedules—pathetically easy, since they all go to the same school. And then Mattie keeps looking, building a case. Finds their parents' workplaces, the license plate number of the pretty one's car. That's easy. Anyone could do it.

But Mattie isn't anyone. Mattie is patient, and persistent, and spends a lot of time alone online.

Mattie can find things no one else could.

The pretty one's ex-boyfriend, on a basketball court in North Carolina.

The tall one's girlfriend, smiling in the autumn sun on a leaf-strewn college lawn.

The cemetery in New York where her father is buried.

The cemetery in Mexico where her grandparents are buried.

Nobody in this world can keep a secret, if the right person knows how to look.

In the old Lola's bedroom, the other Lola is singing. Mattie puts a few things in a backpack, pulls on warm clothes. Out the front door into the sheeting rain without a goodbye.

Mattie doesn't talk to *her*.

In the old Lola's bedroom, the new Lola hears Mattie leave. The new Lola watches Mattie trudging down the long driveway, head bent. A flash of unease crosses the new Lola's perfect face.

Mattie doesn't trust her.

Mattie has good reason not to trust her. She is a liar, and a thief, and a lot worse than that.

The new Lola has no plans to go anywhere, now that she's here.

In the old Lola's life.

With the old Lola's new credit card in her wallet.

The old Lola's mother in her pocket.

The old Lola's brother willing, at least for now, to believe her.

Mattie will have to be persuaded.

But that's a problem for tomorrow.

For today, the new Lola sits on the old Lola's bed. She pulls the old Lola's diary out of the old Lola's dresser drawer.

Five years that diary lay concealed, undiscovered by the old Lola's own family.

Five minutes the new Lola had stood in the old Lola's room. Looking at the pictures on her walls: gloom, gloom, and more gloom. The clothes on her hangers: black, black, and more black. The books on her shelves: *Kurt Cobain: Journals. The Unabridged Journals of Sylvia Plath. Anne Sexton: A Self-Portrait in Letters.*

This girl kept a diary; there's no doubt about that.

I'm here, thought the new Lola. *I'm her. Where did I hide it?*

Her eyes had landed on the heating vent, held to the wall with a single loose screw that came away with a twist of her hand.

That was all it took to give her the old Lola's memories.

As if it were her fate to come here, to be this girl.

No fate but what we make, the other Lola thinks.

It's hard to have much pity for that missing girl, who sat in this princess's jewel box of a room, in this palace of a house, and chose to wrap herself up in darkness. But the void the old Lola left is a blank place, a workshop, an open door.

And now?

It's easy enough to come back. To walk into this house and see where the old Lola failed. Where her edges didn't fit. To smooth herself into a shape that slots into the void the old Lola left, and then remake it. A gentler, more pliable version of the girl who left for good all those years ago. A light, gentle Lola whose mother will want to keep her, not hide her away in shame.

The new Lola has valuable skills. She can feign softness, hiding what's hard beneath. She can smile sweetly. She can ask for nothing in a way that makes other people want to give, and give, and give.

It's easier than you think to be a girl everyone wants to love.

All you have to do is lie.

The old Lola's mother is so overjoyed to have the daughter she always wanted that she asks no questions.

The old Lola's brother—he's not so convinced. There's something reserved about him, a thread she'll have to unspool to keep herself safe.

And Mattie will be a problem.

But the new Lola didn't get to where she is without taking a few risks.

Settling in, the new Lola opens to the first page of the old Lola's diary. Humming "Heart-Shaped Box" to herself, she begins to read.

Day 0: Friday

THE UNINVITED GUEST

DESPITE her singular accomplishments in the field of cold-case resolution, Cameron P. Muñoz, ex–teen podcaster extraordinaire, nationally recognized amateur sleuth, and locator of the most famous missing girl in Washington State, would herself admit she's not the most perceptive person in the world.

But even she knows that someone's following her home from school.

She refused a ride home from her best friend and fellow onetime investigator, Blair—a refusal she's already regretting, as the looming December clouds are threatening downpour.

And now she's got a stalker.

Again.

Great.

In the first months after Cam and Blair broke their small hometown's legendary missing-girl story, reporters clouded around them like a swarm of summer gnats. Cameramen set up camp in Blair's cul-de-sac. Journalists lurked in the bushes outside Cam's apartment.

Both of them had to change their phone numbers.

Both of them had to change their phone numbers again.

Because everybody was calling: journalists, pundits, talk-show hosts. People from the internet who wanted their story, wanted their methods, or wanted them dead. Cam learned quickly to stop googling her own name, out of sheer horror at what she found: page after page of threats and recriminations and theories and lies.

> you are o ugly how do you look at yourselves
>
> if u hate the cops so much dont bother calling them when i rape u
>
> shld both just die so i don't have to listen to them talk anymore wtf
>
> Obviously, these idiots should have considered the possibility that one of the I-5 corridor's many serial offenders is responsible for this heinous crime
>
> verbal diarea,worthless. why do u hate white people anyway racist bitchs

Et cetera, and much worse.

Like, a lot worse.

Cam-doesn't-think-about-it-ever worse.

The kind of worse that she filed in a black hole inside her head and left there.

But that was a year ago. Since then, thankfully, most of the world has moved on. There's always a dead-er white girl with a more spectacular demise and better hair. Cam hasn't had to run from a reporter in months.

She's out of practice, and she's no track star like Blair.

Whoever this is, she'll have to face them.

A block before the front door of her building, she stops short and turns around.

The person behind her freezes, staring at Cam like a stunned deer.

Whoever they are, they're no reporter. They look about ten years old. Skinny and furtive, dressed in a knitted grandpa cardigan with leather elbow patches darkened by damp and a pair of too-large men's trousers cut off above the ankles and a wool newsboy cap.

What the hell? Cam thinks.

"Cameron Muñoz," the urchin says.

"What," Cam says warily.

"I'm Mattie," the person says. "You have to help me find my sister."

Oh.

That explains it, then.

"Not on your life," Cam says, and turns back around.

The pitter-patter of feet behind her. Bony fingers grasping at her elbow. Cam jerks her arm away from Mattie's hand.

"*No,*" Cam says again.

"Please," Mattie says. "I'm not some rando. I'm a freshman at Oreville. I know all about you. Nobody else can help me. You found that girl Clarissa. You and Blair. You found her when the police didn't do anything. That's why I need your help."

That's when the rain starts, a downpour that cuts through fabric like an icy knife.

"*Please,*" Mattie begs.

Cam does recognize this urchin. Huge sad eyes in a pinched white face, scurrying past her in the halls of Oreville High.

Mattie is already wet through to the skin.

"I'll give you five minutes," Cam growls, stomping the rest of the way home down the watery sidewalk. Mattie freezes for a moment, as if unable to believe the plea really worked, and then runs after her.

Cam's mom, Irene, is still at work. Cam offers up a silent

prayer of thanks. Irene is a tolerant person under most circumstances, but Cam has no desire to explain a sopping child dripping rainwater all over the kitchen floor.

"Your lips are turning blue," Cam says. "Stay here. I'll get you dry clothes. If you touch anything, I'll kill you. And I know how to hide a body where it will never be found."

This isn't at all true, but Mattie nods, teeth chattering.

Cam doesn't want to turn her back on this weirdo.

But she also doesn't want this weirdo to go into hypothermic shock in her apartment.

That will be hard to explain to Irene.

Cam gathers up a towel from a pile of what she's pretty sure is clean laundry on the living room floor and a sweatshirt from a pile of what she's pretty sure is clean laundry on her bedroom floor. Her pants will be far too long for her mystery guest, so she filches a pair of sweatpants from a pile of what she's pretty sure is clean laundry on Irene's bedroom floor.

Mattie hasn't moved, standing stiffly in the kitchen and shivering so violently Cam worries her odd visitor will fly apart at the seams.

"Here," Cam says, handing over her bundle. "Bathroom is down the hall. You want something warm to drink? Tea? Coffee?"

"C-c-coffee," Mattie says, and takes the clothes. "Can you call Blair?"

"No," Cam says, and turns to the coffeepot.

Ten minutes later Mattie is sitting across from Cam at Cam's kitchen table, engulfed by Cam's sweatshirt, skinny ankles sticking out from Irene's sweatpants, wet clothes tumbling in Cam's dryer.

Mattie takes a sip of coffee.

Cam's interviewed enough people to see that now that Mattie's here in front of her, Mattie has no idea where to start.

But Cam's not about to lend a helping hand.

When the coffee is gone, Mattie leaves.

End of story.

Cam's middle-aged black cat, Kitten, wanders into the kitchen, lashing his tail and eyeing the refrigerator. He gives Mattie a long, suspicious look, then turns his accusing gaze to Cam as if demanding to know what she's thinking bringing a damp stranger into the sanctity of his demesne.

You and me both, buddy, Cam thinks.

"Start talking," she says.

"I want to talk to Blair too."

"You are in no position to make demands," Cam says.

"Please," says Mattie for a third time. The line of Mattie's mouth is resolute.

Small as her uninvited guest is, Cam realizes, it will not be as easy to get Mattie out of her house as she hoped. She is a warrior of the mind, not the body.

She glances at the window, gives herself the satisfaction of imagining hauling it open, dragging Mattie from the chair, and giving Mattie a good solid push.

His mind apparently made up about the visitor, Kitten takes a flying leap into Mattie's lap, settles in, and starts to purr.

"Traitor," Cam says, and texts Blair.

"All right," Blair says. "Start from the beginning."

She came when Cam texted. She always does. Though Cam's message made absolutely no sense.

And now that she's here, she's even more confused.

It is extremely Cam to collect a scrawny nonsense-spouting stranger off the street, and it is equally Cam to make Blair come over and help her deal with it.

Cam's always been there for Blair too, so at least it's an even exchange.

But Blair never asks Cam to do anything that out of the ordinary.

So maybe it isn't.

"Make it fast," Cam says. "I don't know when Irene is coming home, and I do not want to explain you to my mother."

"My sister is Lola Brosillard," Mattie says as if Cam and Blair should know who that is.

"Who?" Blair asks.

But, Cam thinks, the name is familiar. All that time she spent online, looking for Clarissa.

Lola Brosillard.

"Your sister ran away," Cam says, remembering. "Three years ago?"

"Five. And my sister *went missing*," Mattie says. "She didn't run away." Mattie looks down at the coffee cup. "Lola's six years older than me. She got in trouble a lot," Mattie says to the mug. "Sometimes she would disappear for two or three days. But she always came back. She promised me she'd always come back, and she did."

"What kind of trouble?" Blair asks.

Mattie grimaces. "Sometimes shoplifting. Dumb stuff, though, nothing big. A couple times she got caught drinking in public. I know what it sounds like. But she's a good person. She just doesn't like doing what other people think she should."

"And then she went missing?" Blair asks.

"One night the summer after her sophomore year Lola and my brother, Luke, had a party at our house. Our mom was out of town, and they were supposed to be watching me. I never minded when they did stuff like that, though. Lola would let me stay up late and watch scary movies. And she'd buy me ice cream." Mattie smiles at the memory. "After their friends left, Luke and Lola went to bed. I was already asleep. My brother had a dream that somebody was in the house, a stranger. Except it wasn't a dream. In the morning, Lola was gone. The glass in the patio door was shattered, like someone had tried to break in from outside. Ruth—our mom—got home right after Luke woke up, and she called the police. They came, but they didn't do much. Just took pictures of the door and wrote a report. Nothing was stolen, so I don't think they really cared."

"Your *sister* was gone," Cam says incredulously. "They didn't notice?"

Mattie shifts in the chair. "She ran away a few times before," Mattie says. "Ruth called the police the first time. They found her at her boyfriend's house. It wasn't a big deal, but Ruth kind of lost it. I was in the other room when the cops brought her home and Ruth wouldn't stop screaming at her. 'How could you do this to me, how could you embarrass your family, how will I show my face in town.' That kind of stuff. After that, she stopped calling the police when Lola left."

"But she called the police this time," Blair says. "Why?"

"The window was broken," Mattie says. "She probably needed the police report for the insurance company."

"She didn't tell them your sister was missing?" Blair asks in disbelief.

"I did," Mattie says. "Because of the window. And Luke's dream. It felt different than the other times. I knew she hadn't run away."

"Different how?" Blair asks.

Mattie frowns. "Just . . . different."

"Then what?" Cam asks.

"They didn't believe me," Mattie says simply. "The cops put it in their report, but I could tell. And Ruth yelled at me afterward for dragging our family business out where other people could see it, and Luke told Ruth to leave me alone, and then we never talked about it again. And Lola didn't come back. So I was right, but nobody cared."

Cam stares. "Your sister didn't come home and you didn't *talk* about it?"

"I called the police again a week later," Mattie says. "But they don't listen to little kids. Ruth wasn't worried about it. Luke was her favorite; he still is. Ruth and Lola fought all the time. I mean, *all* the time. About everything. Lola's clothes, Lola's friends, Lola's attitude. You know how when you're a teenager, you're supposed to be mortified by your parents? With them, it was the other way around. Ruth didn't want people to see her and Lola together in public. This one time, Lola dyed her hair red—like, fire-truck red—and Ruth just screamed at her when she saw it. 'You're making yourself ugly on purpose to humiliate me,' stuff like that."

"That sounds horrible," Blair says. "I would've run away from that too."

"But she didn't," Mattie says. "I'm telling you, that night was different. I know she didn't run away on her own, because she never came back. She *promised* me she would never leave me alone with Ruth."

"You think someone kidnapped her?" Cam asks.

"Why else would someone break into the house and not take anything? Why else wouldn't she come home?"

"Who would do that?" Cam asks.

"I don't know," Mattie says.

"What about the other people at the party?" Blair asks. "Did they see something?"

"Luke gave the police their names," Mattie says. "And the cops interviewed them. At least they did that much. Everybody left around two in the morning. When they went home, Lola was sitting on the patio looking at the stars."

"You saw the police report?" Blair asks.

"I interviewed them too," Mattie says. "After I called the police the second time, and realized they weren't going to help."

"You tracked down your sister's friends and interviewed them?" Cam asks.

"I was young, not stupid," Mattie says defensively.

"I didn't mean that in a bad way," Cam says. "It's impressive."

Mattie stares at Cam suspiciously before deciding Cam's not joking.

"What about her stuff?" Blair asks. "Like her wallet? Or her phone?"

"I never found them," Mattie says.

"The police didn't think they were stolen?" Blair asks.

"They thought she took them with her. She had a credit card our mom gave her, but nobody used it after she disappeared."

"And the police . . . dropped it?" Cam asks, still disbelieving.

"Maybe if Ruth had told them to look for Lola, they would've. But like I said, I think she was relieved Lola was gone. I think she'd be happier if I ran away too." One hand rises unconsciously to touch Mattie's own raggedy close-cropped hair. "I'm the one who did all kinds of things to try and find her. I set up search alerts on Ruth's computer until she made me turn them off. I emailed people who run missing-persons websites. My brother helped me make posters and put them up all over town."

"Your mom didn't help with the posters?"

"No," Mattie says flatly.

Now Blair remembers. Leaflets fluttering from telephone poles. A dark-haired, broody-looking, beautiful girl, unsmiling in her photograph.

HAVE YOU SEEN LOLA?

She'd been a kid then herself. She'd wondered where the girl had gone, who'd taken her. She remembers the shivery feeling she got between her shoulder blades, understanding that whatever happened to missing girls, it wasn't good.

"I watched all the footage from our security camera from that night and days before and after. However Lola left that night, she didn't go out the front door. But the camera only covers the driveway and the front porch." Mattie pulls a notebook out of the backpack, shows it to Cam and Blair. It's thick, every page covered with tiny handwriting, stuffed with dog-eared printouts. "You can read all my notes," Mattie says.

"That's all right," Cam says quickly.

"What about your dad?" Blair asks.

"He lives in Hawaii. He left Ruth for his secretary when I was five. We don't hear from him much. Ruth got all his money in the divorce because he cheated on her, and he's still pissed."

"But Lola disappeared," Cam says.

"I don't think he cared by then," Mattie says.

Blair thinks of Clarissa's parents, locked away forever in the same house she'd lived in.

Of Clarissa's dad, his haunted, broken face.

Of all the people who'd missed her, searched for her, kept her memory alive, in all the long years between when she'd disappeared and when Cam and Blair, against all odds, had found her.

But if what Mattie's saying is true, this other girl vanished, and nobody cared enough to look.

It happens; Blair knows this. Learned this again last year, thinking about all the other missing girls who weren't like Clarissa: weren't white, weren't pretty, didn't have the kind of lives that made for splashy magazine profiles full of glamour shots. Girls who went missing like a stone sinking into dark water, without a ripple to mark the place where it had gone under.

Still.

Not even her own *parents*?

She swallows hard.

Jesus, she thinks. *Poor Lola.*

"Your brother?" she asks.

"He doesn't know anything," Mattie says. "He couldn't re-member what the person who took her looked like in his dream. I asked him if Lola had any enemies, but he said nobody they knew would want to hurt her. Him and Lola are—were—really close. Almost as close as me and Lola. They're fraternal twins."

"If Lola disappeared five years ago, why are you coming to us now?" Cam asks.

"Because three days ago a girl walked into a police station in eastern Oregon and said she was my sister," Mattie says.

"What?" Cam asks in astonishment.

"I think you might've buried the lede a little there," Blair says dryly.

"She told the cops she had been kidnapped from our house five years ago by people who had been watching our family," Mattie continues, ignoring the interruption. "They were plan-ning to hold her for ransom. Once, she tried to run away when they stopped for gas, and they chased her down and almost killed her. They kept her drugged and drove her around the country and eventually she got Stockholm syndrome and didn't know how to get away from them. Finally they left her in a basement in an abandoned house in this random tiny town in Oregon and after five days she figured they weren't coming back. So she es-caped and found the police.

"Ruth drove me and Luke down there right away. It was an eight-hour drive, but when we got there, this girl was sitting there waiting for us. Totally calm. Ruth lost it. She was hyster-ical. Crying, screaming. 'My baby' this, 'my baby' that." Mattie scowls. "That was a big show for the cops. Luke went into the bathroom and puked. Everybody's freaking out all over the place, the secretary's crying, Ruth's crying, Luke's crying, the girl starts crying, this cop in a *cowboy hat* keeps trying to hug us all—it was a circus."

"It seems normal to get emotional during a reunion like that," Blair says carefully.

"I didn't," Mattie says. "Because she's not Lola."

Cam and Blair stare at Mattie, speechless.

"She . . . What?" Cam says finally.

"I knew it the second I saw her," Mattie says. "I never saw that girl before in my life. I don't know who she is or what she wants. She says she's Lola. My mom and brother say she's Lola. She *looks* like Lola. But she isn't."

Cam's mouth is hanging open slightly. Blair's sure she looks just as astonished.

"But . . ." Blair says. "No offense, but that's insane."

Mattie nods. "Exactly. A bunch of people followed Lola around when she was fifteen, kidnapped her, drove her around for five years, and just *left*? No way."

"I didn't mean—" Blair tries to assemble a coherent response. "She has to be your sister. Right? Why on earth would someone impersonate your sister five years after she disappeared? How did she get to Oregon? Why would she make up a whole story about being kidnapped? How would she even know Lola was gone in the first place?"

"I don't know," Mattie says.

"What about your brother?" Cam asks.

"My brother doesn't believe me either," Mattie says. "He says I was so young when Lola disappeared that I don't remember her as well as I think I do. He says I'm having a hard time accepting the truth, because it was so hard for me when she left. And that she only seems different because of what she went through."

"That sounds a lot more likely than some girl with a secret plan who happens to look exactly like your sister lied her way into your family five years after she went missing," Cam says.

"Her story can't be true," Mattie retorts, flushing angrily. "Why didn't the kidnappers ever ask us for ransom? Why did they hang on to her for five years and then leave her behind for no reason? None of it makes sense. Ruth buys it, but she'll believe anything she hears on Fox News. Evil terrorists stalking families for no reason and kidnapping their kids is the kind of thing she thinks happens all the time. She probably thinks they were drag queens trying to sex traffic Lola."

"That's a fake story made up by bigots," Cam says.

"I know that," Mattie says, irritated. "That's my point."

"But you said your mom fought with Lola all the time," Blair says, redirecting quickly. "Now she's happy Lola's back?"

"She's happy she can pretend this girl is her daughter," Mattie says. "This girl wears pretty dresses and says she's so happy to be home and tells Ruth what a great mom she is. The real Lola never would have done any of that."

"Make her take a DNA test, then," Cam says.

"I thought of that already," Mattie says. "I said she should take one when we went to the police station and met her. Ruth told me I have a morbid imagination and want everyone else to be as miserable as I am. I can steal strands of her hair from the bathroom or whatever, but I'm not old enough to get a credit card or bank account on my own, and even if I was I don't have three hundred dollars." Mattie pulls out a cell phone. "Look at this picture."

Cam and Blair look. The photo is a close-up candid shot of a teenage girl. Her face is turned toward the camera, but she's looking at something behind whoever took the picture. Her eyes are huge, a startling shade of green that makes Blair think of beach glass. Her hair is a dense black cloud, her skin even paler than Mattie's winter-white face. Her mouth is open slightly, as if she was in the middle of saying something when the shutter closed.

"She's beautiful," Blair says.

Mattie nods. "That's my sister. Now look at this one." Mattie swipes through pictures, holds out the phone again. Another close-up shot, but this time the girl has her face turned partly away, as if she doesn't know her picture is being taken. Her hair's a few shades lighter, but her eyes are the same glass-green, her skin a matching cream. Her cheekbones are a little sharper, her face a little less rounded. She's older than the girl in the first picture by a few years.

"This is her now?" Cam asks.

"That's not my sister," Mattie snaps. "That's *her.*"

"The hair is different," Blair says neutrally.

"Lola dyed her hair," Mattie says.

"So maybe she stopped," Cam says.

"The hair doesn't matter," Mattie says angrily. "I'm showing you that it's *not her.*"

Cam glances at Blair. "It sure looks like her," Cam mutters.

"It's hard to tell for sure," Blair says tactfully. "The pictures are at different angles. What about the police? Did they try and find the kidnappers?"

Mattie gives Blair a world-weary look that says *You too?* as loud as spoken language. "She didn't give them anything to go on. She says their faces are a blur and she had no idea they'd taken her for so long. Ruth took her to a psychiatrist the day after she got back. The shrink says she has 'trauma-induced amnesia' and she might not ever remember anything. Very convenient for her."

"Mattie," Blair says gently, "your sister might have changed a lot in five years. You just told us yourself that she ran away a lot, got in trouble—"

"You're just like the cops!" Mattie says angrily.

"That's not what I meant," Blair says. "You're right, the kidnapping story is wild. Maybe it is a lie—because Lola doesn't want to tell your family what she was really doing. Maybe she just wanted to come home, and didn't know how else to do it. Lying about where she went doesn't mean she's someone else."

"Your mom thinks it's her," Cam says. "Your brother thinks it's her. Right?"

Mattie scowls. "I don't know what my brother thinks. He won't talk to me about it. He told me to drop it and be glad she's home."

"If he thought this person was pretending to be Lola, why wouldn't he say something? You said they were close. Why would he go along with an impostor? How would he not know she's a fake?"

"I don't know," Mattie says. "I don't know, all right? All I know is, that girl isn't my sister. I can feel it. She looks like Lola, but it's not her. I know how it sounds, but you have to believe me. I know Lola better than anyone else."

Blair, looking at Mattie, thinks: *That's what you've been telling yourself for years. That's what's kept you going.*

That doesn't mean it's true.

Still—

What a story.

"Fine," Cam says. "Let's say you're not making this up, and some random Lola doppelgänger found your family five years after your sister ran away—"

"Went missing," Mattie corrects fiercely.

"Went missing," Cam corrects, enunciating the words sarcastically. "Why come to us? What are we supposed to do about it?"

"I need help," Mattie says. "I'm only fourteen. I don't have a driver's license. I have to live in the same *house* as this girl. You can ask questions. Talk to people. Nobody in my family knows you, so they'll tell you things they won't tell me. You found Clarissa Campbell. You can help me find my sister. She's somewhere out there, and she needs me. You have to help me find out who this other girl is, and what she wants. You have to help me get rid of her."

"We—" Blair begins.

Mattie steamrolls over her. "I've listened to your podcast about a thousand times. If I could do this myself, I would. Believe me. But I need someone this girl doesn't know. Someone who can go around and talk to Lola's old friends again. Find out where she is and why she can't come home."

"What if she's dead?" Cam asks calmly.

"Cam!" says Blair.

Cam ignores her. "What if you're right? What if this girl isn't your sister and your real sister is dead?"

Mattie's face is resolute. "I'm not afraid of the truth. Anything is better than living in a house with—*that*. Anything is better than not knowing."

"We tore up our whole lives looking for Clarissa," Cam says, as fierce as Mattie. "We got sued. We got stalked. We hurt a lot of people. We got hurt ourselves. Why should we go through anything like that again for you?"

"Cam," Blair says again. "She doesn't know about all that."

"They," Mattie says.

"They who?" asks Blair.

"Me," says Mattie. "Not she. They."

"Got it. Sorry," Blair says.

"I know what happened to you," Mattie says. "I didn't want to ask you to do this. My family has a lot of money, but I can't pay you. I don't get an allowance. I understand why you don't want to help me. But I can't do this alone. Ruth is having a welcome-home party on Sunday." Mattie almost spits the word "welcome." "Just family, but you can come. I'll tell her that you're peer mentors from school. I've already planned it out. See what you think. If you decide I'm crazy then, I'll leave you alone. I promise. *Please.*"

"No," Cam says at the same time as Blair says, "We'll think about it."

"We'll *think* about it?" Cam repeats.

"Cam, can we have a moment?" Blair asks.

"No moments," Cam says again. But Blair's already halfway out of the kitchen.

Cam gives Mattie a murderous look and follows Blair into her room.

"What the hell, Blair?" she hisses before Blair's even closed the bedroom door. "This kid is nuts. They think a person who looks exactly like their sister—who their *mom and brother* think is their sister—isn't really their sister based on, like, vibes? They haven't seen her in five years! Of course she's different!"

"Maybe," Blair says. "I'm sure you're right. But what if it's true? At least, some part of it?"

"Blair, come on. There's no way—"

"What if there is?" Blair grabs Cam's hand. "What if there's something? What if—what if something bad happens because we didn't help them? Come on, Cam, aren't you bored? Don't you miss having something to do? Something meaningful?"

"No," Cam says.

"We solved a *murder,* Cam! We brought closure to all of Clarissa's friends and family. We did something totally amazing, just you and me. Don't you want to feel like that again?"

Blair's talking fast, and her eyes are bright.

Cam hasn't seen her this excited since—

Since they found Clarissa.

Blair's been her friend through everything. Through all the worst things Cam's done.

And everything bad that happened last year is Cam's fault. All of it.

Which means she owes Blair, big-time.

Cam's not sure why, but Blair wants this. Wants Mattie's

ridiculous story to be real. Wants the two of them to follow it and see where it leads.

Cam can say no to Mattie.

She can't say no to Blair.

No matter how badly she wants to. No matter how loud her instincts are screaming at her to push Mattie out the front door and never think about them again.

"I'm not making another podcast," Cam says. "Ever. About anything."

"Mattie's not asking us to make a podcast," Blair says. "They're asking us to go to a party."

"That's not all they're asking us, Blair," Cam says. "Come on."

"I know," Blair says. "But aren't you curious? If they're making all this up for some reason, don't you want to know why?"

"If they're making all this up, they need a therapist," Cam says. "Not us."

"Just come to the party with me," Blair says.

Cam studies Blair's face. Something changed for Blair in Cam's kitchen. Somehow she went from just as incredulous as Cam to trying to sweet-talk Cam into humoring a delusional fourteen-year-old.

"You've been listening to too many true-crime podcasts," Cam says.

Blair rolls her eyes. "I didn't even listen to the one we made."

"You didn't?" Cam asks in surprise.

"I hate the sound of my own voice," Blair says. "Come with me to this party. It'll be weird. But it could be fun."

"Fun," Cam says sourly. "Sure."

"Please."

"Fine. Just the party," Cam says, her heart heavy in her chest.

Blair's whole face lights up. "Just the party," she agrees, too fast. "That's it."

Cam's not fooled. She knows she's giving in to a lot more than a party.

She lets Blair tell Mattie yes.

Lets Blair have the delight of watching Mattie's face transform with a disbelieving smile.

"Thank you," Mattie says. "I can't pay you," they say again, the grin vanishing.

"We don't care about that," Blair says.

Mattie stands, gently tilting Kitten out of their lap. They gather up their notebook and their backpack.

Cam retrieves Mattie's still-damp clothes from the dryer, puts them in a grocery bag. "You can give the sweatpants back later," she says, grumpy. She doesn't want a "later" with Mattie.

The rain hammers against the kitchen window.

"Um, so," Mattie says, glancing outside. "I sort of walked here."

"I'll give you a ride home," Blair says. "Come on."

"Here we go again," Cam says after the door has shut on Blair and Mattie's backs.

Kitten squeezes his eyes shut and purrs.

MEREDITH PAYNE-WHITELEY ENTERS THE CHAT

Blair's senior year so far has been calm. Track meets and homework. Family dinners, the same every night: Mom's Stepford-wife cheer, Dad's eternal just-got-home-from-a-long-day-at-the-office grumpiness. Her younger brother, Scott, leaves appalling messes in their shared bathroom no matter how many times Blair complains about it and falls madly in love with a new girl every six to nine days, which Blair can track by the level of his cologne usage.

Last year is something they don't talk about, in true Johnson family fashion. No complex emotions are to be discussed, let alone displayed, in the Johnson home. And her parents blame Cam for the whole mess anyway: the lawsuit, the reporters banging on their door for months, Blair's dad's colleagues who stopped talking to him because his daughter's podcast accused a pillar of the community of being a sexual predator. (The fact that his daughter's podcast was correct did not enter into their excommunication process.)

Blair knows she should be grateful. Her parents have every reason to be pissed with her for all eternity. But something stings about her family's willingness to attribute everything the podcast accomplished to someone else.

Because, though the podcast was Cam's idea, Cam could never have pulled it off without Blair. Blair's the one who got Clarissa's family and friends to talk. Blair's the one who steered the madcap engine of Cam's brain. Blair's the one who figured out what was really going on with Clarissa and her teacher, and Blair's the one who came to the rescue when Cam got herself imprisoned in a basement and almost murdered.

She doesn't want her parents to hate her. She doesn't want anyone to hate her. But she sure would like some credit.

Last year, she realized for the first time that she might not be the most boring girl in the world. That she might have something worth saying. Last year, hundreds of thousands of people hung on her every word.

This year?

Crickets.

This year, she's back where she's always been. Good old Blair Johnson. Not the smartest, not the prettiest, but such a *nice* girl.

And she hates it.

Which is why, when her phone rang last week with an area code she didn't recognize, she answered the call.

"Blair Johnson?" said the voice on the other end of the line. A woman's voice, clipped and assured, with a trace of an accent Blair couldn't place. "This is Meredith Payne-Whiteley, with CMA. Do you have a few moments to chat about your career?"

Blair had had to google "CMA"—Creative Management Agency—after she hung up, and then she had to google "creative management," and then she had to google "literary agent." She'd spent most of the call making bewildered noises of assent as Meredith Payne-Whiteley explained to her, Blair Johnson, that she, Meredith Payne-Whiteley, would like Blair Johnson to put together a book proposal. (Blair had also had to google "book proposal.") That she, Blair Johnson, had *unlimited creative potential* and *an incredible market foothold* and a *major platform waiting to be leveraged.*

Blair hadn't understood a whole lot of what Meredith Payne-Whiteley said, other than something about a lot of money and a plane ticket to New York to *develop some ideas in person for a new project.*

"But I don't have any ideas for a new project," Blair had blurted.

"That's part of my role," Meredith Payne-Whiteley said smoothly. "We'd be a team, Blair. I'll support you every step of the way. And with your reach, there's plenty of material you can tackle. We can look for a cold case that would be a good market fit—something with a high-concept twist to intrigue a jaded audience. Something we haven't seen before, something attention-grabbing. Of course, serial killers always do quite well."

"What about Cam?" Blair asked.

"My understanding is that you were the primary content creator," Meredith Payne-Whiteley said. "I've worked with creative teams before, but I'm not sure that's the right step forward here."

Blair doesn't have to google "primary content creator" or "creative teams" to get Meredith Payne-Whiteley's drift.

Which is why she's kept the call secret from Cam.

And why the secret is eating through her.

She can't possibly say yes to Meredith Payne-Whiteley.

The podcast was Cam's idea. More importantly, Cam is her best and oldest friend. Cam would never forgive her for going it alone with another dead girl. For shutting Cam out of a world she created and invited Blair into.

And Cam's right. A lot of things went wrong last year. A lot of bad things happened. Blair thinks of Cam's pleading face in her bedroom while Mattie sat in the kitchen. She's pushing Cam into something she doesn't want to do, and Blair knows it.

But she can't possibly say no to Meredith Payne-Whiteley either.

Because when is she ever going to get another chance like this? All she's ever wanted is to be a writer. Meredith Payne-Whiteley is holding her biggest dream out to her on a platter, saying *take what you want, it's yours* in her brisk, authoritative voice.

Blair's not like Cam. Cam is brilliant and confident and fearless and has had her entire career track planned out since she was ten years old. She's so sure of herself she only applied early decision to MIT and didn't bother with a backup.

Blair has no doubt she'll get in. They don't make brains like Cam's very often, and people tend to notice when they do.

Blair, on the other hand, has never been able to imagine life beyond high school as anything other than a vague blur. She hasn't applied to the college of her dreams. She hasn't applied to college at all. The writers she loves best didn't go to fancy schools. They went around the world and had adventures. Or they survived wars. Or they had complicated love affairs with lots of different people at once. Or they were heiresses with interesting friends and laudanum habits.

They most certainly did *not* take Introduction to Creative Writing with a bunch of other eighteen-year-olds from good homes.

Cam's been getting letters from places like Stanford and Caltech since she was a freshman.

Even after the podcast, nobody's courting Blair.

Blair knows her parents love her, but sometimes she wonders if her future is just an afterthought for them. Her two older brothers are at the University of Washington, where her parents met when they were students there themselves. It's a given that Scott will go to UDub too. The Johnson family assumption is that Blair will go first to community college, polish up her GPA, and eventually transfer to the Johnson alma mater once she has her AA.

UDub is a Johnson family tradition, and Blair knows her parents don't have the money for an out-of-state school, let alone a private one. Their plan for her is a perfectly acceptable one for someone who doesn't have another, bigger, secret goal, a goal she hasn't shared with anyone other than Cam.

It's not Blair's parents' fault that her brothers have overshadowed her for her entire life.

It's not her parents' fault she hasn't ever told them what she really wants.

Maybe it *is* their fault, though, that they've never asked.

Blair's been putting off the question of her future for a long time. But as her senior year progresses, her future is looming ever closer. Cam can tell Blair about multidimensional theories of space-time until Blair's ears fall off, but in this dimension time progresses in a relentlessly orderly fashion.

In six months, Blair graduates. Her future will have arrived whether she likes it or not.

And now: this thing with Mattie.

Dropped into her lap as if Meredith Payne-Whiteley herself sent it express.

The perfect opportunity.

Another missing girl.

Another mystery.

And talk about a *high-concept twist*. Mattie's theory that the returned Lola isn't their sister doesn't make any sense.

But *something* happened to Mattie's missing sister in the last five years.

And something made her come back.

Blair knows there's a story there. She's sure of it.

But for some reason, Cam's fighting her. It's as if Cam's somehow guessed her secret. As if Cam's trying to keep her from the thing she wants most.

Blair doesn't get it. Cam was the one who wanted to find Clarissa in the first place. Cam's the one who had to talk Blair into joining the search. And now that they have another mystery handed to them gift wrapped, Cam wants to bail?

Which means, Blair decides, that for now she's on her own. Once Blair makes some progress, she'll have no trouble getting Cam back on board.

She'll tell Cam about Meredith Payne-Whiteley.

She'll tell Meredith Payne-Whiteley she and Cam are a team.

She'll tell her parents about her dreams. And when Meredith Payne-Whiteley gets her a book deal, they'll know she's serious.

But first, she needs something to show for herself. That's all. She's not doing anything wrong.

So why does she feel so bad?

———

BAD DREAMS

When she was younger, Cam used to get in trouble in math.

Seventh grade, pre-algebra, Mr. Rosen. The most irritating teacher Cam's ever had, which is saying a lot. On the third week of class he returned her homework—her beautiful, perfect homework with its tidy lines of solved equations—with *REDO* scrawled across the top in ugly red letters.

"These are all correct," Cam said, appalled.

"You need to show your work, Cameron," said Mr. Rosen, with a sanctimonious twitch of his mustache.

"That is my work," Cam said.

"The *steps,* Cameron," Mr. Rosen said, his voice dripping with stagy disappointment.

"What steps? There are no steps," Cam said.

Mr. Rosen leaned in. Up close, his breath smelled of stale coffee and condescension. "Cameron," he said. "Did your father help you with this?"

Cam blinked. "Not fucking likely," she said.

Irene got called into the principal's office over that one—Mr. Rosen was quick to injury and keen on respect for elders—where she had to explain that no, it was not fucking likely that Cam's father had helped her with her math homework, considering he'd been dead for nearly a decade, and no, she, Irene Muñoz, was not helping Cam with her math homework either, and perhaps the problem here was not for once the admittedly big mouth of her daughter but rather the patently inferior quality of the instruction she was receiving.

Cam was quietly transferred into Mrs. Litow's eighth-grade algebra class.

A week later, she was quietly transferred into Ms. Ritter's tenth-grade trigonometry class.

And nobody doubted Cam was doing her own homework

after that, although Mr. Rosen still gives her filthy looks on the rare occasions they cross paths.

Cam despised—still despises—Mr. Rosen, but she hadn't understood what he was asking. Not then, and not for a long time. Not until she realized years later that for most people, the movement between an unsolved problem and its solution didn't happen in their heads. That the beauty of a perfect language describing the interaction of bodies and time and space was as opaque to other people as, say, Shakespeare was to her.

Shakespeare, she thinks, doodling in the physics textbook Irene ordered for her online. Shakespeare, and talking about her feelings. Physics, at least, is not a problem. Oreville High doesn't offer AP Physics C; she's doing it as an independent study, fording her way through particle systems and linear momentum on her own.

But linear momentum is not helping her understand the kinematics of human interaction.

Why Blair has been acting so weird the last week, for example.

Even Cam can tell Blair has a secret.

And for the first time in the entire history of their friendship, Blair's not telling her what the secret is.

But Cam has a secret too.

Cam's secret? Being imprisoned in a basement and threatened with a gun and almost getting her best friend and her mother killed along with her has kind of messed her up.

And being relentlessly harassed by the entire internet on top of her mother, her journalism teacher, her best friend, and her best friend's entire family being relentlessly harassed by the entire internet has messed her up more.

And the fact that all of it is her fault?

That's messed her up most of all.

Cam and Blair haven't talked about it. Not head-on. They've

saved unhinged screeds from the worst of their hate-emailers in case somebody comes after them in real life. They've commiserated over the persistence of certain reporters. They've expressed relief the lawsuit fell through before either of their families was bankrupted.

But they haven't *talked* about it.

Cam doesn't know *how* to talk about it.

She has no idea if Blair is still mad at her, and she's too terrified to ask.

She can't ask her own mother.

Because what if she does ask, and they say yes?

What would she do then?

Cam hasn't told Blair about her nightmares.

She hasn't told Sophie, her girlfriend.

She didn't want to tell Irene either, but it's hard to hide the fact that she wakes up screaming in the middle of the night at least once a week when she lives with her mother in an eight-hundred-square-foot apartment.

She hasn't told Blair or Irene about her panic attacks. Thankfully, they don't happen that often, and they haven't happened around other people—yet. But they descend on her without warning and transform her from a perfectly functional human being with an exceptionally functional brain into a shattered wreck, trembling and sweat-soaked.

And she hasn't told Blair that her nightmares got so bad over the summer that Irene frog-marched her to a therapist. The therapist was called Dr. Bird and she looked like one: a frowsy, diminutive white woman with a thatch of disordered, dull-brown hair dressed in a dull-brown skirt and a dull-brown sweater that engulfed her like a nest. She cocked her head and looked at Cam with her round, dull-brown eyes and asked Cam how her dreams made her *feel*.

"How do you think they make me feel?" Cam shouted. "How would *you* feel if you were dumb enough to get trapped in a basement, you pigeon?"

The rest of Cam's first therapy session had not gone much better. Cam waited in the car, seething, while Irene had a hushed conference with the therapist. On the drive home Cam told Irene she was never talking to someone as stupid as Dr. Bird again. Irene didn't say anything for a while, and Cam knew she was trying to work out how to talk Cam into going back.

"She thinks you have PTSD," Irene said finally.

"You don't say," Cam said.

"It might help you a lot to talk to someone, Cam," Irene said.

"I talk to you."

"No, you don't. And I meant someone who can support you better. Someone objective. Even if you don't want to talk about what happened, she can teach you tools that will help you cope with—"

"Please don't make me do that again," Cam said.

Irene didn't like it, but she didn't push.

Cam's nightmares got better on their own.

Mostly.

And now: this thing with Mattie.

Dropped on them like a falling piano.

And Blair wants to stand directly underneath it.

Cam's sitting at her desk, looking idly out at the familiar view: the scabby patch of winter-depilated grass in front of her apartment building; the park across the street, where a tall blonde lady is walking a little three-legged dog in a festive neckerchief; the lone streetlight flickering in the descending twilight.

Kitten is asleep in Cam's unmade bed, his paws twitching as he runs after dream mice. Irene's home from work and clanking around in the kitchen, which means she's cooking, which means dinner will be either spaghetti with red sauce from a box or spaghetti with white sauce from a box.

Cam might be unforgivable, but at least she is warm and cozy and working through scientific problems of great difficulty with the powers of her formidable brain.

In six months she will be free of Oreville and far enough away from Blair and Irene that she can't ruin their lives any more than she already has.

She will be free at last of her guilt, surely, and the people she loves will be safe.

The last thing she wants is another missing girl.

But the one thing she can't do is say no to Blair.

Dear Mats,

I'll never send this. You don't know the whole story, and I guess it works better for me that way. But I know you have a lot of questions.

Why did I do it? Where have I been?

What else have I done?

There are some things a person can't explain entirely. Even when I was a child, I always wanted to be someone else. It didn't take me long to learn that most of what other people see as us is what we choose to tell them. Not just with our stories. With our bodies, our clothes, our smiles, our eyes. I learned early on that the rules are only there for people who follow them. There are a thousand other ways, over and around, for people who don't want to go through.

You're different; I know that. You want me to be the person you remember, and I'm not. You believe in true things that stay that way. You believe in a straight path through to the end. But what happens when you get there? What if the end you find is just another beginning? Just a thread from a tapestry so large you can't even find your own place inside it? What if there's no such thing as the end at all? *The end* implies a storyteller, someone who knows what's happening and what's to come. Someone in charge. Someone with the answers, even if the characters can't see the arc they're living. I understand why you want to trust that something can be true or false, that everything in our lives is moving forward toward a purpose. But Mattie, hear me out. What if you're wrong, and none of this means anything at all? What if the only true story about you is the one you choose to live?

It's a funny thing to say, but: I really like you.

I probably won't ever know what you think of me, although I can guess. That's how it goes. And I might not get to know who you'll become when you grow up. If you'll be like me—well, that's unlikely. If you'll be like Luke—no, that's unlikely too. You won't be like Ruth; that's not a question. I think you'll be exactly like yourself. Unpredictable and fierce. Determined. Devoted to the truth. I don't know if I'll be around long enough to see it. I guess you never know.

Big dreams have small beginnings. Maybe I can teach you that much, while I'm here.

Love,
Lo

Day 2: Sunday

Party Time

CAM has no idea how to dress for a family gathering to celebrate the unexpected return of a possibly fraudulent prodigal, so she wears the same thing she always wears: faded old jeans more hole than denim, a pilled sweater, and a new raincoat that Irene got her for an early Christmas present. The winter weather in northwest Washington is not generally conducive to chic ensembles.

Blair has done her best, as she always does. Under her shapeless winter puffer, she's wearing a blue dress that sets off the color of her eyes. She's put on mascara and lip gloss, and her hair is curled.

Blair's cranked the defrost in her ancient Ford Focus, but the windshield is a steamy mess anyway. The wipers screech back and forth at a frantic pace, no match for the pouring rain. Blair hunches over the steering wheel, peering out at the road.

"Is this a metaphor?" Cam asks from the passenger seat.

"Is what a metaphor?" Blair's distracted, trying to read the house numbers. It'd been dark already when she dropped

Mattie off on Friday afternoon. She can't tell in the rain-soaked gray afternoon light which driveway is the right one.

"You can't see where you're going," Cam says.

"I can see," Blair says, against the evidence.

Last year, Cam would've argued. Obviously Blair can't see. This is a matter of fact, not opinion, and Cam's whole life up until Clarissa revolved around the immutability of the provable.

This year, she doesn't push it. *Facts,* she has learned, do not always figure into human relationships. She doesn't want to argue with Blair—not about Mattie, and not about something as dumb as Blair's field of vision in inclement weather—because Blair almost stopped being friends with her last year when she got too fast with the facts, and losing Blair is one of the most terrifying things she can imagine.

Cam doesn't know what it is that Blair's keeping back from her. Did she do something bad again without knowing about it? Is she supposed to apologize? For what? Does she have to ask Blair what she did? Is Blair sad about something else? What could Blair be sad about?

Cam knows Blair's been in touch with her ex-boyfriend, James, who graduated last year and is now playing basketball across the country at Duke and doing whatever else it is that James does. Beer drinking, Cam thinks. James is playing basketball and drinking beer. Does Blair miss this? How could anyone miss a person who plays sports with a ball and drinks beer? Does Blair want a different boyfriend? James always wore a lot of cologne. Does Cam need cologne? Does Cam smell bad?

Cam surreptitiously sniffs her sweater. It smells like the biodegradable laundry detergent Irene buys in bulk at Costco. No, Cam decides, she doesn't smell bad. The problem is something else. Maybe Cam is—

"Here we are," Blair says in relief, putting on her turn signal. "Look, we're right on time."

"We don't have a plan," Cam says as Blair crunches down the long gravel driveway. "No way is the mom going to believe we're Mattie's—"

And then she sees the house at the end of the drive and stops short.

Mattie's house is a monster, architectural angles sprouting out of the ground like a colossal fungus, self-conscious gravel landscaping features scabbing over the denuded earth—one of the countless fungible McMansions that've sprouted like weeds on the outskirts of humble Oreville thanks to tech money. All those rich white idiots thronging to the peninsula, buying up land that rightfully belongs to the Coast Salish people with their millions of dollars that rightfully belong to real working people.

This is not a line of thought Cam would've spent much time on before last year either, but Sophie is an ecofeminist socialist abolitionist and has had a marked effect on her politics.

Mattie's terrible house looms over them like a bad idea.

"Wow," Blair says, parking her car in the immense circular driveway, where it stands out among the luxury vehicles like a parakeet in a raptor exhibit. "I guess we have motive for kidnapping."

"Or for coming home," Cam says.

"This much money would be hard to walk away from," Blair agrees.

"Maybe Mattie's lying about the whole thing," Cam says, eyeing the house.

"Why would Mattie lie to us?"

"Maybe they want to be podcast famous too. Maybe they think the world still cares about us enough to pay attention."

"Maybe the world *does* still care about us enough to pay attention," Blair counters.

That's worse, Cam thinks.

Cam heaves a sigh and gets out of the car, her heart sinking. Blair's already scurrying toward the front porch as fast as she can, her puffer held awkwardly overhead to keep off the rain. Cam trudges after her. The massive front door swings open, Mattie peering out at them with wide eyes. Someone, presumably their mother, has put poor Mattie in a pink dress with a protuberance of ruffles at the collar.

Cam, who understands very well the utter indignity of such a horrifying costume, does not laugh. She can tell from Blair's expression that Blair is thinking the same thing.

"Come in," Mattie whispers, smoothing their palms down the front of the dress as if they're trying to make it disappear.

Mattie leads them through a cavernous foyer, past a formal living room with vaulted ceilings and skylights and pristine furniture that looks as though it's just been unwrapped, down a long hall lined with oil portraits of people Blair assumes must be family members, to an open-plan kitchen and family room the size of a hospital lobby where fifteen or twenty white people are already gathered, leaning on the immense marble-topped island that divides the space and waving around crystal glasses full of champagne. A handful of small children dodge in and out between adult legs. A brown woman in an actual maid's uniform is circling the room with a tray piled with hors d'oeuvres on tiny china plates, neatly evading the children.

"Oh my god," Blair says.

"Sorry," Mattie says.

A regal-looking woman in a natty black-trimmed pink wool skirt suit and pearls is holding court in front of a huge fireplace, where a gas fire burns prettily.

And next to her is the girl.

Lola.

She's wearing a long, modest, rose-pink dress that drapes gorgeously over her enviable form. Heavy dark hair falls nearly to her waist in waves. Her skin is flawless porcelain, her cheekbones sharp as the razor edges of the Olympics silhouetted against a sunset. She's laughing at something someone's said to her, her head thrown back to show the elegant line of her white throat.

"That's her," Mattie says unnecessarily.

There's no one else at the party close to Lola's age, Cam notes with interest. Nobody who looks like a friend. The guests are all adults and toddlers.

One of the little children, dressed in a sailor suit, his mouth smeared with hors d'oeuvre, catapults across the white carpet.

"Brandon," snaps the woman next to Lola. "We do not *run* in Aunt Ruth's house."

Her voice is savage, pitched to carry. A man drinking beer out of a can across the room leans away from his circle of jolly uncle types whose bellies strain against their button-downs.

"Aw Ruth," he says. "He ain't doing nothin'. C'mere, Bran." He holds one hand out to the sailor suit, who reels away, shrieking.

Ruth looks after the child with a predatory gaze. "I do not want *stains* all over my *carpets*, Stephen," she thunders. "I just had them all *redone*."

"And that's our mom," Mattie says. "Mine and Luke's mom," they add.

"Oh, wow," Cam says. "Let's go meet her."

"Cam, should we think of an angle—?" Blair asks. But Cam's already marching toward Ruth and Lola with an expression of resignation, like she's walking to her own execution.

Mattie scrambles after her. Blair, filled with misgivings—Cam is perhaps not the best hand to lead with when playing out their investigation—follows.

"Hi," Cam's saying loudly, sticking her hand out at Lola. "You must be Lola. Mattie's told us *so much* about you."

Up close, Lola is so stunning that Blair's nerve fails her totally. Her uncanny green eyes are amused as she daintily shakes Cam's outstretched hand. "Thanks so much for coming," she says, her voice low and musical. "Are you friends of Mattie's?"

"I'm Cam," says Cam. "This is Blair. We're Mattie's Big Sisters. At school. Since you're Mattie's big sister at home."

Ruth's head swivels on her long, stalklike neck. Her blond hair is arranged in a kind of stiff halo that moves along with her head. She stares at Mattie. "You didn't tell me you were in an after-school program, Matilda," she says accusingly. Ruth's beautiful too, but not all of her heavily made-up face moves when she talks, and her neck looks about twenty years older than the rest of her.

Contouring, Blair thinks. *That is a lot of Botox and a lot of contouring.*

"You didn't ask," Mattie mumbles at the floor. They seem painfully uncomfortable, though whether it's because of Lola, their mother, or the combined forces of both, Blair can't tell.

"You picked a gem," Lola says, smiling at her sibling with real warmth. Mattie won't look up.

"Mattie is very intelligent," Cam says staunchly. It's the highest compliment Blair can imagine her giving.

"Lola is already a wonderful mentor to her *sister*," Ruth says, with a hard cold emphasis on "sister."

Mattie flinches.

Blair suddenly has an idea of how much it must've cost Mattie to bring her and Cam here, to show them the inside of this house, their mother, their perfect sister. The categorical humiliation of the awful, misgendering dress.

Cam's wrong. Mattie doesn't want fame. Mattie wants to find their sister. There's no way they would have exposed all this to Cam and Blair otherwise.

But now that she's here, Blair's sure that this Lola *is* Mattie's sister. How could a stranger possibly fool all these people? Especially the dragon-eyed Ruth?

This girl went somewhere, Blair thinks. *She went somewhere, and then something happened that made her come back and lie about it.*

Why?

Lola gives Ruth a strange, freighted look that Mattie doesn't catch and rests one hand on Mattie's shoulder protectively. Mattie flinches again but then settles, wild-eyed and bristling, like a feral animal that knows it's been trapped.

"It's good for *them* to have more friends," Lola says, with her own emphasis on the "them."

Ruth looks briefly pickled.

Lola smiles at her, radiant and guileless, and Ruth can't help it: She smiles back. Lola turns back to Blair and Cam. "Have they talked your ears off about classic noir yet? I've been on a Chandler kick because of them." She laughs, bright and lovely. It's impossible to look away from her perfect face. "Mattie, I'm so sorry. You're right here, and I'm talking about you like you're in the other room. Do Blair and Cam know about—"

"Oh, DAAA-yid," sings out the sailor suit. "Cousin Jesse called you a butthole, Daa-yid."

"You're a butthole, Brandon," sobs Cousin Jesse, yanking his clip-on bow tie from his neck and flinging it to the ground in a rage. "You, you, you."

Ruth's head swivels again. "STEPHEN!" she barks.

"C'mon," Lola says smoothly. "Let's go outside. Brandon!"

she calls to the sailor suit, who's grinning evilly and advancing on a wailing Cousin Jesse. The sailor suit turns, sticky mouth dropping open, to gaze up at her in rapt adoration. Lola holds out her hand. He runs toward her and takes it in his own filthy one. Cam shudders.

"Want to go outside with us?" Lola asks Mattie.

"Yes," Cam says.

On the far side of the living room, a pair of French doors open out onto a colossal terrace and a pristine swath of lawn. Lola leads Brandon toward them. Cam, Blair, and Mattie follow. Cam catches the other guests' eyes snapping toward her and Blair. Cam does not look down at her decrepit Converse, held together at the toes with duct tape. She is not going to let rich people make her feel self-conscious.

Blair, she can tell, is not immune to the smell of money moving through the room either. Her shoulders are drawn in, and she keeps touching her hair, which the humidity has stripped of its hot-iron curls.

Cam resists the urge to scratch her armpits and hoot like a monkey. She wishes Mattie had never found them. She wishes she had never heard of Clarissa Campbell. She does not like these stupid adults or these dreadful children in their snap-on bow ties. She does not like Lola. She does not like mystery. She wants to go home to her own shabby kitchen, Irene cursing under her breath at the stove and then digging out her phone to order pizza instead, tea steaming comfortably on the weathered table in chipped thrift-store mugs with corny slogans like FIFTY AND LOVING IT or, Irene's favorite, WORLD'S #1 DAD.

Cam runs a hand through her hair, which she cut herself last week with a pair of kitchen scissors and which, she knows without checking a mirror, is sticking straight up in the back, because it always does. Maybe she'll get Irene to shave her head for her.

Lola opens the French doors enough for Brandon to barrel through, shrieking with glee. Cam, Blair, and Mattie slither through after them and Lola shuts the doors tight against the chilly air.

Once they're outside, they can see what was invisible from the living room: a young man in his late teens or early twenties whose face is a careworn carbon copy of Lola's and who is smoking what even Cam recognizes as a joint.

"Hey, Luke," Lola says. He looks up at them, registering his younger sibling and small cousin—who is barreling toward a mud puddle in the broad expanse of the yard with reckless abandon—with slow-moving alarm.

"*Shit*," he says, a cloud of smoke escaping from his mouth. He pinches out the joint between his thumb and forefinger, stowing it in his pocket.

"You're good," Lola says. "They wouldn't notice in there if you came in on fire. Ruth's got the cavalry out."

"That bad, huh?" Luke says.

"I wouldn't want to be Uncle Stephen," Lola says merrily. "These are Mattie's friends from school."

"Cam," Cam says curtly.

"I'm Blair," says Blair, with less attitude and more warmth. She's looking at Luke in an appraising sort of way.

Cam looks at him again.

Is he hot?

Oh no, Cam thinks. *He* is *hot.*

Blair is touching her hair again. This could be bad.

Brandon is bathing himself in puddle water, screaming wordlessly with transcendent joy. The front of his sailor suit is covered in mud.

"Should we . . ." Luke says, gesturing vaguely.

Lola's grin is infectious. "Uncle Stephen's the one who let him have four pieces of cake," she says. "And I want to see what the little monster does to Ruth's carpets."

Flicker-quick, she's a completely different person than the demure, humble Lola at Ruth's side: funny, sly, mischievous, feigning wide-eyed innocence with a sultry wink for the lucky few in on the joke. Luke is laughing. Even Mattie can't hold back a faint twist of a smile, gone so fast Blair wouldn't have seen it if she hadn't been looking at them.

"You must be so happy to be home," Cam says to Lola. "I can't imagine what it must've been like."

"Mmmm," Lola says. And like that, she's someone else again. Shy, reserved, unwilling to talk about herself.

"Kidnapping," Cam persists. "You must have been so scared."

"I don't remember much," Lola says.

"Five years is a lot to forget," Cam says in disbelief.

"You writing a book?" Luke asks. Blair flinches. Cam doesn't notice; her attention is focused on Lola.

"And then you escaped," Cam says.

"I've been very lucky," Lola says. Her gaze goes distant, as if she's pondering the great mysteries. Her dreamy green stare lands on Brandon, who is industriously lathering his once-blond hair with mud. "I met him for the first time today," she says. "All of them. My little cousins."

"Now what?" Cam asks bluntly. "What are you going to do next? Live here forever? Don't you have to get a job or something?"

"She's only been back for a few days," Luke says, moving in to protect his sister. "Right now, we're happy to have her home."

Luke's eyes are deep, haunted hollows. His nails, Blair notices, are bitten to the quick. She has never seen a less happy-looking person in her life.

And he's looking at Lola like he's afraid of her.

Afraid of her? Blair wonders. *Or afraid of what she'll say?*

"But when you were in this *van*—" Cam begins, relentless. The patio doors swing open again, and Luke's panicked, bloodshot eyes move toward someone coming out onto the terrace.

"Oh, no," he says. "Lo, did you invite Becca?"

"No," Lola says.

The white girl walking toward them is about Lola's age, small and curvy and solid. Her short hair is dyed black, her eyes ringed with heavy eyeliner, her ears studded with piercings. A silver barbell bristles in her lower lip.

"Lola?" she says in disbelief. "Are you seriously—oh my god, *Lola?*"

Lola's composure falters. Her eyes widen, and she takes a step back. "Becca," she says. "I'm sorry I didn't invite—"

"You're *sorry?*" The girl's voice is climbing to a frenetic pitch. "You disappear for five years and all you can say is you're *sorry? Where have you been?*"

"Becca, you shouldn't be here," Luke says helplessly, reaching out for her.

"Did you know?" she screams at him. "Did you know? Did you know all this time and not tell me? Is that why you stopped talking to me?"

"No, Becca, I swear—" Luke babbles.

Becca falls to her knees, sobbing, never taking her eyes off Lola's face.

"You're dead," she wheezes, her voice giving out. "You're dead, Lola."

"I'm sorry," Lola says again, her face pale with panic.

Luke drops to his knees next to Becca, heedless of the wet concrete, whispering in Becca's ear. She looks away from Lola with a wrenching sob, buries her head in his chest. His arms steal around her as she shudders. Adults pour out onto the patio, Ruth marching at their head like a general.

"Lola!" Ruth barks. "What is the meaning of this?"

"I didn't invite her!" Lola cries.

"Sorry I showed up to ruin your perfect new life," Becca snarls.

"Becca," Luke says desperately. He's still holding her, but now he looks like he wants to shake her. "We'll talk, okay? I'll—we'll talk. I'm sorry, I should've—listen, maybe right now isn't the best time for this—"

"Not the best time? Is that seriously all you have to say for yourself?" Becca shrieks.

Blair looks at Cam, who's watching the astonishing scene with big eyes. Mattie looks just as stricken. *Somebody should do something,* Blair thinks. But who? And what?

"I'm calling the police now," Ruth says loudly.

"Don't do that, Mom," Lola says, the mask snapping back into place so seamlessly Blair wonders for a second if it ever faltered. "It's my fault. I'll take care of it."

"We agreed this party was a *celebration,*" Ruth says. "Of your *new start.*"

Luke is pulling Becca gently to her feet, one arm still around her shoulders. He whispers something into her ear again. She pushes him away, still crying. "Get off me," she mumbles. "Don't you dare touch me." But the fight's gone out of her. She looks like someone who's just been in a car accident, stunned and disoriented.

"Everything's fine, Mom," Luke says, loud enough that they can all hear him. "Just a misunderstanding. She's going home now. Right, Becca?"

"How is she here?" Becca's voice cracks. "How did she get here?"

"Everything's been so crazy," Lola says, her voice light and even. "I'll call you this week. We can catch up. I promise."

"Catch up," Becca spits, the words ugly. "You ruined my life, and you want to *catch up*? You're both—" She's breathing hard, but she's stopped crying. "There's something wrong with both of you. *Both* of you. How you can just—"

"Becca," Luke says. He reaches for her.

She slaps his hand away. "Forget it. Forget I was ever here. That's what you're both good at, isn't it? You're right. I shouldn't have come here. I don't ever want to see either one of you again." She turns and stumbles toward the door. Luke gives the assembled partygoers a helpless half shrug and turns to follow her. Becca looks up, sees his reflection in the patio doors as he moves toward her.

"Stay away from me!" she screams without turning around, and she breaks into a run. Cam and Blair can hear the thump of her booted feet as she moves through the house and then, more distant, the slam of the front door.

"Bet that was bad for the rug," Cam mutters under her breath.

The adults stand around them in a stunned silence.

"Sorry, everyone!" Lola says brightly. "It's been a strange few days. It's freezing out here. Why don't we all go back inside? Luke, can you help corral the kids? Uncle Mark, your glass is empty—let's get you something to drink. Aunt Brenda, can you ask Maria to check the fridge? I think we might need to get more beer out of the garage."

The spell of Becca's dramatic departure is broken as Lola briskly delegates tasks. The adults stir, chatter among themselves, trickle slowly back indoors with toddlers in tow. Cousin Brandon lets out a wail from his mud puddle.

"Aw, *shit*, Bran," Uncle Stephen says, catching sight of his child. "You had to go and—" He strides over to the puddle, hauling out his offspring by the scruff. Brandon's wails intensify as Stephen half drags, half carries him across the patio, muttering invectives.

"*Not* through the house," Ruth snaps. "Take him *around*."

Uncle Stephen looks mutinous, but he drags Brandon shrieking off the patio and toward the side of the house. Ruth marches after them to supervise their movements.

"Mattie? You coming inside with your friends?" Lola's paused in the doorway, flashing her movie-star smile at the three of them.

"That—what *was* that?" Cam asks. "What just happened?"

"Why didn't you tell Becca you were home?" Mattie asks accusingly.

The mask is back in place. Lola looks untroubled. "It's an emotional time," she says. "I haven't told a lot of people that I'm home."

"Why did she think you were dead?" Cam asks.

Lola turns that serene green gaze on Cam with mild reproach. "Everyone thought I was dead," she says. "I have to get back to my party now. Nice to meet you."

"Nice to meet you," Blair says faintly, watching her go.

When Lola's back inside and the doors are closed behind her, Blair turns to Mattie. But Mattie's already talking before Blair can open her mouth.

"See?" they say eagerly. "See what I mean? You'll help me, right?"

"See what?" Cam counters. "All I saw is an entire roomful of people—your *relatives*—and your brother and your mother—who think that girl is your sister."

"Becca was her best friend!" Mattie protests. "If that was Lola, why didn't she call Becca as soon as she got back?"

"Her best friend, who *also* thought she was Lola," Cam says.

"But she didn't—"

"Your brother didn't call her either!" Cam interrupts. "Your sister was just returned to her family after she escaped a bunch of kidnappers! Probably she's been busy the last couple of days!"

Mattie glares at Cam. "It's *not her*," they say.

"You keep saying that," Cam says. "But you haven't shown us a single thing that gives us a reason to believe you."

"Cam," Blair says.

"Cam, what?" Cam snaps. "Come on, Blair! You saw the same thing I just saw!"

"There's this kind of bird that lays its eggs in the nests of other birds," Mattie says. "It pushes one egg out when the parents aren't looking, and lays its own, and flies away. Its egg hatches first and knocks all the other baby birds out of the nest. The parents think the chick is theirs. It eats all the food the parents bring for their own babies."

"You think your sister is going to push you out of a tree?" Cam asks.

"The parents don't even know it's not theirs!" Mattie yells. "Nobody knows! But I'm telling you, that girl is not my sister, and if you won't help me, I'll find somebody who will!"

"I think we should all take it down a notch before Ruth really does call the cops," Blair says. "Mattie, do you have any kind of proof that that's not the real Lola?"

"Cuckoo chicks don't look like the baby birds they're replacing," Cam says. "By the time they leave the nest, they're bigger than their host parents."

"Jesus, Cam," Blair says tiredly. "You know everything."

"How do you know anybody is the person you love?" Mattie asks. "How do you know Blair is Blair?"

"Because that *is* Blair," Cam says.

"That's what I mean," Mattie says helplessly. "You just *know*. You know it's her, the same way you'd know if it wasn't."

"The odds of someone who looks exactly like Blair—" Cam begins.

"Let's say we say yes," Blair says, cutting her off. "Let's say we agree to help you. Where would you tell us to start?"

"Blair," Cam says, just as tiredly.

"Talk to Darren," Mattie says immediately. "He was Lola's boyfriend. He was really nice. He used to bring me lollipops from the gas station every time he came over. Once I fell down outside and he spent all this time bandaging up my knee. He was great."

"He's not here?" Cam asks.

"*She* didn't call him either," Mattie says.

"Why not?" Blair asks.

"You'd have to ask her," Mattie says. "Maybe she's afraid he'll know she's a liar."

"Does he know Lola's back?" Cam asks, interested despite herself.

"I don't know," Mattie says. "I haven't talked to him."

"Since when?" Blair asks.

"Since Lola got kidnapped," Mattie says.

If he was such a great guy, why didn't he stick around? Blair wonders. But she doesn't say it. "Do you have his number?" Blair asks instead.

"Blair," Cam says.

"No," Mattie says. "But I know he's a park ranger in Olympic National Park. I google him every few months."

"Blair," Cam says again. "It's raining even harder now. Can we go home?"

"I don't want anything to do with this," Cam says in the car.

"I know," Blair says. "But you have to admit, *something* is going on there."

"Something that's none of our business."

"Clarissa was none of our business," Blair says without thinking.

"Yeah," Cam says. "And look where Clarissa got us."

"It wasn't all bad," Blair counters.

"Yes," Cam says fervently. "Yes, it was."

Cam scowls out the window at the sheeting rain.

Blair considers her next angle of attack.

"Don't you want to know where she was?" Blair asks.

"No," Cam says.

"Or why she came back?"

"Money," Cam says.

"What if Mattie's in danger? Wouldn't it be our job to protect them?"

"No," Cam says.

"Come on," Blair says.

Why is Cam fighting her so hard? Cam can't possibly know about Meredith Payne-Whiteley. Finding Clarissa was Cam's idea. She was the one who dragged Blair into it.

What's changed? Why is she so resistant now?

"You think the brother's hot," Cam says.

"He's not hot," Blair says, blushing. Cam rolls her eyes. "Come with me. Talk to Darren. One more conversation."

"No."

"I'm going to talk to him."

"Why?"

"Why not?"

"Because!" Cam shouts, exasperated. "Because that kid is crazy! That's their sister! They're in denial!"

"Why, though?" Blair asks.

"I don't know!" Cam says. "I don't know, and I don't care!"

Blair stays quiet. She eyes the speedometer. If she slows down just a bit, she can prolong this car ride without Cam noticing. Let the silence do its work.

"I don't want to talk to somebody's stupid boyfriend!" Cam says.

Blair says nothing.

"I don't care where that girl went!" Cam insists.

Blair nods, keep her mouth shut.

"I don't care if her best friend showed up and flipped out!" Silence.

"Are you seriously going to interview this boyfriend without me?"

Blair flicks her gaze to the rearview mirror, meets Cam's eyes, says nothing.

"What's he going to tell you? He's not going to tell you anything!"

Silence.

"The not-talking trick doesn't work on me!" Cam yells. "I know what you're doing! I'm not that gullible!"

"I know," Blair says.

Silence.

"*One* conversation," Cam says. "And then when it turns out to be nothing, we drop it."

Blair smiles.

"Wipe that smirk off your face."

"It's not a smirk," Blair says innocently. "Something's stuck in my teeth."

"*No podcasts.*"

"No podcasts," Blair says.

"You're a monster," Cam says.

"I know," Blair says again.

"What's a Chandler?" Cam asks. "Lola said Mattie's into Chandlers."

"He was a noir writer," Blair says. "He invented one of the most famous fictional private investigators."

"So Mattie's into detective stories," Cam says. "You two have so much in common already."

Blair, having won the battle, will not be distracted by stray shots fired. "Do you want to call Darren, or should I?"

"Are you kidding?"

"I'll do it," Blair says.

SOPHIE OFFERS COUNSEL

Cam video-calls Sophie after Blair drops her off at her apartment. It's almost midnight on the east coast, but Sophie never seems to sleep.

To her relief, Sophie answers right away.

"Hi, sweetheart. Hi, Kitten."

Sophie's in her dorm room, lying across her floral-print bedspread in a vintage dressing gown Cam knows she probably scored in some out-of-the-way upstate thrift store whose location she's unearthed through careful research and guards with her life. Her dark hair is piled on top of her head in an elegantly messy topknot, and her brilliant turquoise cat eye is immaculate.

Since she's left Oreville, Sophie's style has changed. She wears neon eyeliner and brighter colors: pink and coral, rose and gold, jewel-bright hues that pop against her brown skin. In the selfies she sends Cam she's often added nods to her Filipina mom: a vibrant satin bolero with rich embroidery along the placket, a sheer gold alampay, a vintage kimona hand-painted with huge pink peonies. Cam thinks she looks like a movie star.

Now, her heart gives its inevitable lurch at the sight of Sophie's beloved face. Sophie is so beautiful! Sophie is so stylish! Sophie is so smart! Sophie is so cool! Sophie is her *girlfriend*!

"Is your roommate there?" Cam asks.

"No, thank god. She's at a Kool-Aid keg event for on-campus Christians."

"What?"

"I can't tell if the Kool-Aid drinking joke is deliberate," Sophie says. "It seems in bad taste for the followers of the Lord."

Sophie's roommate, Zoë Bavelle, is a real bitch. Spawned from a rabidly wealthy evangelical megachurch franchise family, she pitched a fit when she found out she'd have to share with Sophie. Whether this outrage was due to Sophie's being a lesbian, biracial, on scholarship, an aspiring underground abortion provider, or some combination of the above remains unclear.

At Vassar, Sophie has also become a literal card-carrying Communist (she sent Cam a laminated membership card of her own, which Cam gave to Irene, who hooted with glee), a labor organizer, a Land Back activist, an abortion fund volunteer, and a contender for the throne in both the women's center and the LGBTQ+ center despite being only a freshman. Cam is in firm support of Sophie's worldview, which she finds perfectly reasonable, but she does sometimes wish her now extremely overbooked girlfriend was a bit easier to pin down for video calls.

"How's lacrosse?" Cam asks. This is a joke. Sophie would not set foot on a lacrosse field if all the scions of all the megachurch fortunes in the world paid her to do so.

"Cutting," Sophie says. "How's orbital mechanics?"

"Dynamic," Cam says. "Do you feel like giving me advice?"

"Uh-oh," Sophie says.

"Just you wait," Cam says. "You're not going to believe it."

Cam tells Sophie about her visit from Mattie. Mattie's story. The party. "And Blair thinks . . . I don't know what she thinks. But she wants us to interview Lola's boyfriend."

There is a prolonged silence in Poughkeepsie.

"Cam," Sophie says finally.

"I know. Believe me. I don't want anything to do with it. But Blair won't let it go."

"Have you told Irene?"

"Are you kidding?"

"What about Mr. Park?"

"Mr. Park would tell us to drop it. Or he'd tell Irene. Or Blair's parents. Or, I don't know, the police."

"He wouldn't tell the police," Sophie says.

"Is that supposed to be helpful?"

"Don't be so impatient. I'm thinking. Why is Mattie so sure this person isn't their sister?"

"It's a 'feeling' they have." Cam makes scare quotes with her fingers around "feeling."

"But what about proof?"

"No telltale birthmarks, if that's what you mean. Not that anybody other than Mattie is looking for them." Cam shakes her head. "The whole family believes this girl is the real Lola. Her friend who crashed the party believes this girl is the real Lola. There's nothing Mattie can show us to say that she isn't. Just this . . . feeling."

"We all know how you feel about feelings." Sophie grins.

Cam scowls.

"But you're right. Five years is a long time," Sophie says. "Especially at that age. And especially if she was really kidnapped. It's no wonder she seems like a different person."

"You don't have to convince me," Cam says miserably. "But for whatever reason, Blair believes Mattie."

"She thinks the sister is a fake?"

"I don't know if she thinks that," Cam says, "but she thinks there's more to the story."

"Well, sure," Sophie says. "The kidnapping is pretty farfetched. But that doesn't mean it's not her. And it definitely doesn't mean that whatever really happened is any of Blair's business."

"That's what I said."

"But she won't listen to you?"

"Blair's on a tear."

"She really thinks the sister is an impostor?"

"She thinks there's something to what Mattie says."

"But even if some random person looks so much like the missing girl that she could fool Lola's own family, which is a stretch, why would anyone *do* that? How would this girl even know Lola was gone in the first place?"

"The mom didn't get the police involved when she disappeared, but Mattie did their best to publicize it," Cam says. "It's not like Clarissa, though. No magazine stories or anything like that. And the family's superrich. It seems a lot more likely that the real Lola came home because she got tired of being broke. Maybe she has a trust fund or something."

Ask Mattie about trust fund, Cam notes to herself in her brain, and then realizes what she's doing.

Remembers the notebook she carried around last year when they were looking for Clarissa.

Remembers where those kinds of questions got her.

"Money would be a good motive for kidnapping," Sophie says.

"As far as Mattie knows, nobody asked for ransom."

"Why else would you kidnap someone and keep them alive for that long?"

"Torture, I guess," Cam says.

"I think that happens on TV a lot more than it happens in real life. Does she look tortured?"

"She looks like she spent the last five years at a spa," Cam says.

"Do you want my honest opinion?"

"That's why I called you."

"That's not why you called me," Sophie says, laughing. "You're going to do whatever you want, no matter what I say."

"You think this is a bad idea," Cam says.

"I mean . . ." Sophie pauses. "I was going to try for diplomacy, but—"

"It's me," Cam says.

Sophie smiles at her. Cam's heart flip-flops in her chest. "It's you. Cam, this is a terrible idea. You can tell Blair I said that."

Cam puts her head in her hands. "How many times can one person get sued for libel?"

"I don't think there's a limit," Sophie says.

Cam groans. "Why is Blair so obsessed with this?"

"Have you asked her?"

"No," Cam says miserably.

"You have to talk about—"

"I know. I don't want to talk about my feelings."

"Well, then," Sophie says.

"What if she stops wanting to be my friend?" Cam asks in a small voice.

"Oh, Cam," Sophie says. "Blair's not going to stop wanting to be your friend. She loves you."

"I don't know about that anymore," Cam says. "Let's talk about something else."

"You wanted to talk about this," Sophie says patiently.

"I changed my mind. I want it to go away."

"You can't make things go away by not talking about—"

"I know," Cam says. "Let's pretend I can for a minute."

"Okay. I'm changing the subject now, although I want it noted for the record that *you* called *me* to talk about this. I wish you were here," Sophie says.

Not, Cam notes, *I wish I was there.*

Which is fair. Cam wouldn't wish Oreville on her worst enemy, let alone someone she loves.

"I wish I was with you too," Cam says. "I can't wait to see you at winter break. Check out those lacrosse muscles."

"Pervert," Sophie says affectionately, flexing one arm. "It's only two weeks. Don't do anything crazy until then. Promise me."

"I promise."

"And make Blair be careful."

"Blair is the careful one."

"Just promise me."

"I'll try."

"I love you," Sophie says.

"I love you too."

Cam feels obscurely better when she hangs up.

Sophie is right. Helping Mattie is a terrible idea. She will go talk to Darren the boyfriend with Blair, and she will make sure they don't offend him so much that he tries to sue them, and then when he has nothing to tell them she will convince Blair to drop it.

And in two weeks Sophie comes back to Oreville, and next year Cam will go to MIT, and Cam and Sophie will take turns visiting each other every weekend—it's only six hours from Cambridge to Poughkeepsie by train, Cam's already memorized the route—and Blair will travel around the world and become a famous author and drop in on them from time to time, and Irene will be rich and never have to worry about money again or go to work if she doesn't want to, and Mattie will—Mattie will patch things up with Lola and leave Cam and Blair alone.

Everything is going to be fine, Cam thinks, determined to believe it.

"That's right," she says out loud, scratching Kitten behind the ears. "And they all lived happily ever after."

Kitten yawns and bites her hand.

Day 3: Monday

MEREDITH PAYNE-WHITELEY SITS RIGHT UP IN HER CHAIR

BLAIR has a phone call to make before she picks up Cam on the way to school.

But her heart is thumping so loud in her chest that she's worried Meredith Payne-Whiteley won't be able to hear her voice.

Her thumb hovers over the new contact in her list, trembling.

Come on, Johnson, Blair thinks.

What if Mattie's story sounds stupid, or Blair can't describe it the right way, and Meredith Payne-Whiteley thinks she is an idiot? What if Blair's wrong, and it's not a good story at all? What if she *is* an idiot? What if Meredith Payne-Whiteley tells her to never call again and hangs up on her? What if—

Blair's thumb twitches so violently that it taps her screen. And then the phone is ringing.

She's calling Meredith Payne-Whiteley whether she wants to or not.

"Good afternoon, CMA," says a smooth voice on the other end of the call.

"H-hi," Blair says. "This is Blair."

Oh my god, you are *an idiot,* she thinks as the words leave her mouth. *Hi, this is Blair?* Like a kindergartener? Why didn't she say "Good morning, can I speak with Ms. Payne-Whiteley" like a normal adult human being?

"Blair!" says the voice with sudden warmth. "Of course. Meredith's just gotten out of a meeting. I'll put you through."

Blair is so astonished she can't reply.

"Good morning, Blair," says the crisp voice of Meredith Payne-Whiteley. "What can I do for you?"

"I think I have a story," Blair says, finding her voice at last.

Meredith is silent through Blair's long, rambling explanation of Mattie's visit; their plea; the strange, surreal welcome-home party; the sailor suit. When Blair finishes, Meredith is silent for a long moment more.

She hates it, Blair thinks. *I'm babbling. I sound like a fool. She hates it, and she hates me.*

"Blair, this is incredible," Meredith Payne-Whiteley says. "This girl really is an impostor?"

It's a better story if she is, isn't it? "Mattie's completely certain," she says.

"You think she killed the biological sister?"

"I—uh—could?"

"You're making recordings?"

"Not—um, not yet," Blair says.

No podcasts, she promised Cam.

What if Meredith Payne-Whiteley wants another podcast?

"I'm sure you're thinking about doing another podcast," Meredith Payne-Whiteley says. "But let's make sure our planning here is impeccable. You already have your market edge. We don't want to rush into anything potentially viral when we don't have linked properties to promote. I want you to move quickly but carefully—let's start with a book proposal, and then we can build out additional planned content when we're ready to shop."

"You're absolutely right," says Blair. Meredith Payne-Whiteley definitely *sounds* absolutely right, even if Blair didn't understand much of what she said.

"Wonderful," Meredith Payne-Whiteley says, with absolutely no change in her intonation. "I'm so glad we're on the same page here. Why don't you send me material as you develop it, and I can provide guidance."

"That sounds great," Blair says. She's pretty sure she understands what she's agreeing to, at least.

"I'm thrilled," says Meredith Payne-Whiteley.

"Me too," Blair says.

"More soon," says Meredith Payne-Whiteley.

"Yes," Blair says. "Lots more."

Shit, she thinks.

What is she going to tell Cam?

What is she going to tell *Mattie*?

What did you already ask Darren? she texts Mattie.

Mattie's response is almost immediate.

I haven't talked to him since
I was 9

But he told me the same
story as everybody else. That
he left at 2 and Lola was fine

I can show you my notes

Sure

Has he seen Lola since she
came back?

No

Are you sure?

She never leaves the house.
She doesn't have a car yet

Ruth is talking about buying
her a BMW

Jesus

Yeah

Has she talked to him?

I don't think so

She doesn't know he exists

Right, Blair thinks, thumbs hovering over her phone. Because Mattie thinks this Lola is a fake. And a fake Lola would have no idea who the real Lola's friends were.

But Lola hadn't looked like she didn't recognize Becca at her party.

She'd looked like she was afraid of her.

I think Luke called Darren
after the party

I heard him telling someone
about it but I couldn't
understand most of what he
was saying

Because he was in his room
and I didn't have time to get
a glass

?

You know to put against the
door

OK right old school

So Darren knows she's back

ITS NOT HER

Right sorry

I mean that someone is back

That people think is Lola

I think so

And he hasn't tried to talk
to her

I don't think so

Interesting

We'll ask him why

Record it

We can't without asking
him

It's not legal

I don't care

I'm not going to record him
Mattie but I promise I'll tell
you everything he says

. . .

. . .

. . .

fine

———

SCHOOL

High school is boring; high school is the same as it has always been and always will be. "Be strong, saith my heart; I am a soldier; I have seen worse sights than this," Irene often quotes when Cam complains. To which Cam always replies, "*I'm* a pacifist, and I'd rather not go."

But Cam knows if—when—she gets her acceptance from MIT, they'll still check up on her for the rest of the year. Ensure she commits no felonies, flunks no AP exams, amasses no tardies.

She could pass all her classes in her sleep, except maybe Journalism, where Mr. Park brooks no dillydallying. But outright truancy is frowned upon, even for the intellectually superior. As much as she would like to skip the rest of the year, including her own graduation and up until the moment she gets on the plane to Boston, she is tethered to a respectable attendance record.

But it's not easy. And this year, her beloved Journalism is a shark-infested harbor in which to seek port. It's her last class of the day again, and once again her only class with Blair. But this year, unlike last year, Journalism is full. This year Journalism had a waiting list. Everyone, it turns out, wants a piece of Cam and Blair's magic. Or, more likely, their unwilling fame.

Mr. Park, at first thrilled by Oreville High's sudden enthusiasm for his life's work, caught on quick. The first week of class, he banned questions about Cam and Blair's podcast. The second week of class, he banned questions about any lingering cold cases awaiting potential teen sleuths. The third week of class, he threw up his hands and shouted that for this year's project they would put together a school newspaper, so help him god, and it would feature absolutely zero unsolved mysteries, disappeared girls, serial killers, or podcast elements.

Clarissa wasn't murdered by a serial killer, Cam thinks dourly. But she would've been more famous if she had been. And if Cam and Blair had tracked down and defeated a real live serial killer—perhaps confronted him in his torture lair, surrounded by the heinous implements of his dark craft, at great peril to their own lives, et cetera—they would never have to work again.

In addition to giving her PTSD, Cam reflects, the last year has also made her rather cynical.

She still finds Mr. Park a great comfort; he remains the smartest adult she knows, except for maybe Irene. But this year everything is different, and not in a good way. This year, unlike last year, Cam comes to class on time. She sits in the back with Blair and keeps her mouth shut. She doesn't steamroll other people with her (correct, obviously) opinions, and she doesn't shoot down anyone else's ideas.

She doesn't *have* any ideas.

She doesn't *want* any ideas.

Maybe she should have taken Woodshop.

If Mr. Park misses the old Cam, he hasn't said anything. But Cam has looked up from her desk more than once, where she's dutifully outlining potential puff pieces for the future *Oreville High School Star,* and found his sharp dark eyes on her and his expression thoughtful.

Today, Mr. Park is in fine form.

"Stories!" he shouts from the front of the room, cutting through the post-bell chatter with an authoritative boom. "Where are we at for stories, people?"

Next to Cam, Matt and Miles murmur to each other. They're back this year too. Like Cam and Blair, they've decamped to the back row. Cam feels almost fond of them, as though they've all been through the wars together.

They did end up completing their Area 51 documentary last

year, which they screened on the last day of school. It was two hours and thirty-seven minutes long and consisted primarily of spliced-together YouTube footage. Cam isn't sure if they uncovered any conspiracies, since she fell asleep five minutes in.

"We're almost done with our piece about teenage social media influencers," Matt—Miles? Cam still can't remember which one is which—says.

"Thank you, Miles," Mr. Park says. "As you know, winter break is our deadline for the first issue." He gives Mattmiles a pointed look. They nod. "We will also want to consider a reasonable *length* for our pieces," Mr. Park says.

"But length isn't really an issue, since the paper will be online-only," Miles—Matt?—says in a surprisingly clear voice. Their status as Journo veterans has stripped away the worst of their shyness.

"My dear Matt, we must consider the needs of our readers as well as the capacities of our platforms," Mr. Park says. "Two thousand words. Maximum. Got it?"

Mattmiles looks dismayed, but they nod.

Jenna the irritating sophomore, who is an irritating junior this year, waves her hand frantically from the front row. The corner of Mr. Park's mouth twitches as he surveys the room, clearly hoping to call on someone else. Even Mr. Park, whose ass is being kissed, thinks Jenna the irritating junior is a kiss-ass. But there are no other takers. With Cam so quiet, Jenna has stepped into the role of Most Annoying Brownnoser with aplomb.

"Yes, Jenna?" Mr. Park asks. "How are you coming along with the website?"

Jenna has undertaken the task of coordinating with the school administration to set up the new site for the *Oreville High School Star*. Since she will probably end up becoming a high-school administrator herself, given her general temperament and love of bureaucracy, this is an excellent role for her. Nevertheless, she has proven herself to be a top-tier coder; she's building the website from scratch, alone.

"We'll be ready to launch, sir," she says proudly. "You have my word. As you know, the code that generates the website is stored and tracked with the Git version control system and hosted by GitHub. But working manually within Git can be intimidating for non-natives, and we don't want to have to worry about merge conflicts, so I'm building an editing interface that will allow—"

"Starship *Oreville Star* is nearly ready to launch. Great news, Jenna," Mr. Park interrupts firmly. "And?"

"I finished my editorial about the issue with dress codes," says Hannah, a freshman. Their hair color has already cycled through neon orange, electric blue, and, briefly, an unfortunate green that made them look moldy. They sport a daily uniform of shredded jeans and a green army jacket festooned with slogan buttons.

"Oreville doesn't have a dress code," Cam says, unable to help herself.

"Lucky for you," Jenna mutters. Jenna is not the world's biggest fan of Cam and Blair's unexpected success.

The freshman turns pink. "Dress codes are sexist, and I think we should take a stand," they say tremulously.

"But there isn't—" Blair kicks Cam's ankle, and Cam subsides.

"Great, Hannah," Mr. Park says smoothly. "Do you have a critique partner? Who else is ready for feedback?"

So it goes until the bell rings, liberating Cam and Blair from Mr. Park's scrutiny before either one of them is forced to confess they have written absolutely nothing for the debut issue of the *Oreville High School Star.*

"What should we do our piece on?" Blair asks Cam for the thousandth time on the way to their lockers.

"Ugh," Cam says. "I don't know. How America's obsession with true crime has exacerbated privileged white women's racist paranoia and increased the ongoing criminalization of already marginalized people rather than addressing the root causes of interpersonal violence, like poverty, inequality, and systemic racism?"

"That sounds like something Sophie would say."

"It is something Sophie said."

"We should write about something we would say," Blair says.

"Do you think Sophie's wrong?"

"No," Blair says, dialing her combination. "I guess we're kind of experts now."

"We don't have to work together," Cam says, watching Blair carefully slot her textbooks into her orderly locker. Cam's own locker looks like a site requiring FEMA involvement. At the least, a biohazard warning.

"What do you mean?" Blair asks, straightening up. "You don't want to work together?"

"I didn't say that," Cam says. "Just, if you want to do your own thing, I won't be mad."

Blair narrows her eyes. "Cam, what are we really talking about here?"

"The newspaper," Cam says.

Blair looks at Cam for a minute. Cam doesn't blink.

"We don't have to decide this second," Blair says. "We still have a couple of weeks until it's due. Want to come over later and plan what we ask Darren?"

"Darren who?"

"Cam," Blair says. "You said you'd go talk to Lola's boy-friend with me."

"I'm having regrets," Cam says.

"Don't you want to know what happened to Lola? Where she went?"

"Remember what happened last time we did this?"

"That was different."

"Different how?"

"Clarissa was dead," Blair says. "Someone in town killed her. We're not doing anything dangerous this time."

"That's what we thought last time."

"What's gotten into you?" Blair asks. "The podcast was your idea, remember? You had to convince me. You were the one who wanted to solve crimes and get famous. Why don't you want to help Mattie?"

"I don't know," Cam says, looking past Blair down the hall. "I'm busy this year. Did someone fill the drinking fountain with dish soap?"

Blair looks. "I believe they did."

"Solve that mystery," Cam says.

"Want to come over later?" Blair presses.

Cam won't meet her eyes. "I have to do physics."

"You do physics every day."

"Physics requires a lot of upkeep."

Blair gives up. "Okay," she says. "But—come with me to talk to the boyfriend."

"Why are *you* so into this?" Cam asks. "Your life got just as messed up as mine did last year."

Now it's Blair who won't quite look Cam in the eye. "I feel bad for Mattie," she says. "I want to help them."

"Uh-huh," Cam says. "Sure. See you tomorrow."

And she's off, her overloaded backpack slung over one skinny shoulder, her back crooked against the weight.

Blair watches her walk away.

"See you tomorrow," she says.

But Cam's too far to catch it.

Blair sighs and digs her track shoes out of her locker.

Day 4: Tuesday

Irene is in a terrible mood

THE next morning, no one is living happily ever after in the Muñoz household. Cam is filled with anxiety about Blair's new obsession. And Irene is in a terrible mood, which she attributes to finally quitting smoking two weeks ago. The morning terrible mood, however, has become such a fixture of their lives in the last fourteen days that Cam almost wishes Irene would take her filthy habit back up again.

And now Cam is brimming over with what is not exactly a *lie* but is definitely a piece of information she should not be withholding from Irene.

But if Cam tells Irene about Mattie—

Don't even go there, Cam thinks.

There's nowhere to go, she tells herself. She will talk Blair out of this madness.

Somehow.

"Where the *fuck* are the coffee filters?" Irene growls, slamming around the kitchen.

"We're out," Cam says. "But I made a fresh pot with the last one."

"Oh," Irene says. She looks around, as if searching for something else to get mad about.

"I can go to the grocery store on the way home from school if you give me some cash," Cam offers.

"You hate going to the grocery store."

"Maybe it's time I pulled my weight around here," Cam says.

To her relief, Irene hoots with laughter. "That'll be the day," she says, chortling. She pours herself a cup of coffee and puts two slices of bread in the toaster. "Get any exciting mail lately?"

"It's not the Dark Ages, they don't *mail* you," Cam says. "They update your online portal with your admission status."

"My humblest apologies. Any online portal updates?" Irene says.

"Not yet," Cam says. "I'm not worried."

"I imagine not," Irene says.

"What are you going to do without me next year, anyway?"

"Rattle around the house like a lost sock," Irene says contentedly.

"Socks don't rattle."

"A fine point. Drape myself around the house like a lost sock."

"Really?"

"No," Irene says. She fiddles with her toast plate. "Brad and I are talking about taking a vacation."

Brad is her mother's new-ish boyfriend and the impetus behind Irene quitting smoking. He and Irene went to high school together and were inadvertently reconnected when Cam and Blair almost destroyed his life by featuring him on their podcast. He lives out in the county, where he operates a gun range for a living and, as it turns out, forages for mushrooms and other wild foods and researches permaculture in his spare time. For a quiet loner who could comfortably arm a small citizens' militia,

Brad is surprisingly wholesome. Irene has even intimated she might take up jogging.

Cam is agog. "A vacation?"

"You know, that thing where you stop working for a while and lie around in the sun," Irene says.

"I don't like to be hot."

"You can vacation in Antarctica, then, and Brad and I will go to Mexico."

"You never took *me* to Mexico."

"You just said you don't like to be hot. Anyway, we never had the money. But if I don't have to feed you anymore, all kinds of possibilities open up. We have family there, actually, although I haven't been in touch with them in years."

"Really?"

"You've got a whole bunch of great-aunts still running around. And I think some cousins in Mexico City."

Cam considers this. "What if I don't get a scholarship?"

"Then I don't go on vacation."

"I'll take out loans."

"You'll have to," Irene says. "But I'll help as much as I can. You know that." An expression crosses Irene's face that Cam can't read. "I'm sorry, Cam."

"For what?"

"That we don't have more money."

"Why are you sorry? You work all the time. It's not your fault psychiatric nurses in rural inpatient hospitals are unappreciated and underpaid in the United States."

"You sound like a union organizer," Irene says affectionately. "Making your old lady proud."

"How is work, anyway?"

"Work is work. We have a new patient who's a real sweetheart."

Kitten waddles into the kitchen and winds his way around

Irene's ankles, meowing hopefully. Irene pushes him gently away with her foot. He falls to the ground dramatically, staring up at Irene with immense, reproachful eyes.

"The cat is not a football, Mother," Cam says.

"I barely touched him."

"You still have to go to jail for a thousand years. Put a couple slices in for me? What's the story with your new patient?"

Irene drops in two more pieces of toast. "She's a few years older than you, but she's had a rough go of it."

Irene is careful never to share identifying details about her patients, but she will occasionally discuss them with Cam in general terms. She is matter-of-fact about their illnesses, as if depression and mania and delusional behavior are ordinary things that might go awry with a body, like a bad flu or a broken leg. Cam finds Irene's pragmatism comforting. Her own brain moves so fast she sometimes wonders if she is predisposed to going a bit haywire herself.

Irene butters Cam's toast for her, passes Cam a plate, joins her at the kitchen table.

"How long does she have to stay for?"

"Depends," Irene says. "Insurance, for one thing." Irene has nothing good to say about the private insurance system, thanks to a combination of her lifelong communism and many years of working in health care. "But hopefully we can get her stabilized and back into outpatient in a couple of days. She was doing really well in group therapy, but she was at a party over the weekend and something happened there that triggered her."

Cam freezes. "Party?"

"Yeah, she ran into some old friends. You know, sometimes when people have a big traumatic event in their past, seeing people from that time can bring it up. Anything can, really, if the trauma was significant enough." Irene eyes Cam. "But this girl has done a lot of work in recovery. Got herself into ongoing outpatient therapy, found a support group, built a routine, set goals for herself."

Cam is well aware Irene is telling her this because Irene is trying to convey a message. A special therapeutic message for her, Cam, a person who has experienced what Irene would describe—what a lot of people would describe—as a *big traumatic event*. Irene is catapulting HIPAA into the sun in order to transmit this missive to her daughter: Bad things happen, they mess people up, those people take steps and find their way out.

Outpatient therapy.

Support groups.

Rallying in the wake of something cataclysmic.

Exactly what Cam should be doing for her own recovery.

And all she can think is *What are the odds?*

Oreville is a small town. How many troubled girls a few years older than Cam could possibly have experienced triggering events at parties with people from their pasts on the same weekend?

Cam keeps her eyes on her toast. Irene can read her like a book.

"Support group?" Cam says. Too casual. And when Irene takes the bait, her stomach lurches.

Something like guilt.

Something like longing.

A feeling she couldn't name if she were ten thousand times the writer Blair is.

"The hospital sponsors all kinds of support groups," Irene says. "It's helpful for a lot of people, even when individual therapy isn't successful."

Cam wants to barf. "The hospital sponsors the groups?"

"Sure," says Irene. Cam can tell: Irene thinks her message is getting through. "The schedules and locations are all online. You don't have to register or anything. You can just show up.

They're all free and anonymous." Irene glances at the clock, digs around in her bag, comes out with a couple of twenties.

Act normal, Cam thinks. "That was a peace offering," Cam says. "I didn't mean it about going grocery shopping."

All kinds of support groups.

The schedules and locations are all online.

When Becca gets out of inpatient, Cam and Blair can find her.

And if Irene ever finds out what Cam is thinking about—telling Blair what Irene has told her, let alone hunting down one of *Irene's patients*—

Irene laughs, oblivious. "Too late, now you're committed. I'll text you the grocery list."

"Put coffee filters on it."

"Is Blair picking you up, or do you want a ride to school?"

Normally, Cam enjoys riding with Irene, who drives like a Formula 1 champion and cranks fun old dad bands like Nirvana. But she is concerned that prolonged exposure to Irene's uncanny Cam-antennae will reveal her secrets.

And now she really needs to talk to Blair.

"Blair," Cam says.

"Okeydoke," Irene says, blowing her an air kiss. "I'll be home late."

"Date with Brad?"

"Fourteen-hour shift, Little Miss Nosy."

"Don't make me give you a curfew," Cam says.

Irene rolls her eyes. "Have a good day at school."

"Always," Cam says, which Irene knows is not true.

"Chin up," Irene says. "Not much longer in the trenches."

Cam salutes, and Irene's out the door.

Cam slumps in her chair.

Is she really going to do this?

Is she seriously going to tell Blair what Irene has trusted her with?

Irene, who's trying to help her get better?

Blair, who's obsessed with a story Cam wants nothing to do with?

"Shit," Cam says aloud to the cat. Kitten has recovered ably from his own recent traumatic event and is purring next to the refrigerator, eyes crossed in expectant ecstasy.

Kitten is getting older. One day, Cam thinks dispassionately, Kitten will die. Not that that has anything to do with any of this. But it will be sad.

Who knows how much future any of us have? Cam could lose Kitten, her beloved Kitten, at any moment. She could lose Irene. She could lose Blair. Anything could happen to any of them, the light of their being snuffed out as easily as a candle flame, and Cam will be powerless to stop any possible end: illness, accident, a man with a gun.

Cam's throat constricts and the edges of her vision go dark. Suddenly she is back in that dimly lit basement, the smell of laundry left too long in the washer filling her nostrils, her heart rabbiting in her chest, a sour taste in her mouth. She can't breathe and she can't move, she is trapped alone in the dark as Clarissa's killer moves toward her, gun trained on her chest. Panic floods her veins and drowns her lungs and she can't move, she can't *move*—

Cam cries out in terror. Kitten, startled, leaps to his feet and flees the kitchen with a loud thump. *Kitten,* Cam thinks. *I'm in my house. I'm in the kitchen of my house. I'm not back there. I'm not back there. I'm not back there.*

The terror leaches out of her slowly, leaving her muscles so shaky she can barely sit upright in her chair. She folds her arms on the kitchen table and rests her forehead on her forearms and then, to her absolute shame, she starts to cry. A moment later, she feels insistent paws on her thigh. Kitten has returned to investigate the scene. With an awkward, hitching leap, he worms his way onto her bony lap and settles across her thighs, purring like an ancient outboard motor. Cam strokes his hard little skull with one hand and wipes her nose with the back of the other.

"Let's pretend that didn't happen," she says to the cat, mostly to test whether she can talk like a normal person. Her voice is faint and high-pitched.

Great, she thinks. *Just great, Muñoz. Stellar work all around.*

She takes a deep breath and tries again. "Let's pretend that didn't happen," she repeats. This time, her voice is firmer. "That *didn't* happen," she says. Better still.

Except that it did happen.

And it's probably going to happen again.

Cam pushes that thought aside. *No,* she thinks angrily. *I don't want it to happen again. I will stop it from happening again. I am going to think about other things now.*

So: Back to the matter at hand.

Irene's told her something she shouldn't, and now Cam has a way forward through the mystery of Lola.

Blair wants to know what happened to Lola. Blair is her only friend.

And maybe, deep down, Cam kind of wants to know what happened to Lola too.

Cam makes up her mind.

Come get me? she texts Blair. I have something to tell you.

"What are the odds!" Blair shrieks in the car. "She's Irene's *patient*?"

"I know," Cam says. She'd washed her face before Blair pulled up outside her apartment, but she checks in Blair's rearview mirror again. Her eyes are a little red around the edges, but she just looks sleepy. Not like someone who had a full-blown panic attack in the perfect safety of her own kitchen.

"We have to interview her! We have to get into the hospital!" Blair's so worked up, she almost takes out a mailbox.

"Eyes on the road!" Cam squeaks. "We can't go to the hospital."

"Why not?"

"Because Irene works there," Cam says. "First, they'll fire her, and then she'll kill me. And they're not going to let us walk into the psych ward anyway."

"But we have to find a way to talk to her," Blair says.

Cam grimaces.

This is it.

This is the line, and she is crossing it. Again.

"I think I know how," she says. "Irene says she'll go back to her support group once she gets out of inpatient. There aren't that many, and their locations aren't secret or anything. We can figure out which one is hers and talk to her afterward."

Blair is radiant with excitement, which almost makes the betrayal worth it.

"Cam, you're amazing," Blair says. "Does this mean you're in? Like, all the way in?"

"I guess," Cam says, before she can think about it.

"I knew it," Blair says, triumphant. "Let's start with Darren, since Becca's still in the hospital. Mattie doesn't think he's been in contact with Lola at all since she came back. Which is totally weird, right?"

"How do you know what Mattie thinks?"

"We text," Blair says. She catches Cam's expression out of the corner of her eye. "I can make it a group chat."

"Mattie likes you more. They feel safer talking to you."

"True," Blair says. She's not joking, which hurts.

"We'll just ask Darren a few questions," Cam says.

"Yeah, sure," Blair says blithely. "If you get a bad feeling, we can totally walk."

But Cam knows Blair too well to be fooled. Blair's the one driving this car now, and she's not going to stop until she gets where she wants to go.

Blair's all in, whatever comes next.

Which means, like it or not, Cam's all in now too.

COFFEE WITH DARREN

Blair starts by calling the Olympic National Park Visitor Center. "Darren?" says the ranger who answers the phone. "Sure, you're in luck. He just came in from the backcountry. Hold on a sec."

Darren has a nice voice when he comes on the phone, deep and reassuring and friendly. Blair can imagine him talking small children into appreciating the wonders of lichens.

She and Cam had worked out her story in the car on the way to school.

More accurately, she had worked out the story, and Cam had supplied commentary.

"But that's *lying*," Cam had said.

"Not exactly lying."

"It is exactly lying."

"He's not going to talk to us if we tell him the truth."

"Then maybe we shouldn't talk to him."

"Lying never bothered you when we were doing the podcast," Blair said.

"That's not true," Cam said, stung. "We didn't *lie*."

"Cam, we lied constantly."

"Not *constantly.*"

"Well, we lied. Do you want to help Mattie or not?"

Cam had dropped it. And now, Blair tells Darren her story. She and Cam, Mattie's school mentors. Mattie has mentioned Darren frequently. Mattie pines for role models.

"Aw, Mats," he says with real warmth. "How's she doing?"

"They," Blair says. "They're, uh, not so great. That's why I called you."

"Not so great?"

"You know about this whole situation with their sister?"

Darren is silent for a moment. "Yeah," he says cautiously. "I heard about that."

"Cam and I haven't been mentoring Mattie that long. We think it would be good for them to talk to someone who's known them for a long time. Someone who was there when— you know. In the past."

"That was a bad time for me too," Darren says, still hesitant.

"Mattie needs you," Blair says. This, she is aware, is a horribly manipulative thing to say, but she also knows it will be effective. Solving mysteries requires occasional moral compromise, she tells herself, but it doesn't make her feel like any less of a creep.

"You should talk to an adult," Darren says.

"You are an adult," Blair says.

"I haven't seen Mattie in years."

"But they haven't forgotten you. You mean a lot to them," Blair says ruthlessly. "We're trying to help them move on. Adjust to having Lola back. Just meet us for coffee after school. Me and Cam. Mattie doesn't have to be there."

"I guess I could come into town this afternoon," Darren says reluctantly.

"Great," Blair says.

"Just coffee."

"Just coffee. And then we'll leave you alone."

"Wow," Cam says when Blair hangs up. "You can be kind of evil."

Cam's lunch tray sits in front of her, mostly untouched. But that doesn't mean anything, since lunch today is a light brown something, possibly chicken-adjacent, in a dark brown something, possibly meant to be sauce. Blair wouldn't eat it either.

"That wasn't evil," Blair says, taking a bit of her peanut-butter-and-jelly sandwich. Her mom has packed a lunch for her every day since she started kindergarten; Blair's long since given up trying to get her to stop. Despite the setting, the scene, Blair thinks, is familiar in a way that is comfortable and thrilling. Blair and Cam, solvers of disappearances and now reappearances. It feels good to be doing something again.

Something that is bigger than her own ordinary life.

Something worth writing about.

"'Mattie needs you'?" Cam is looking at her with a frank, appraising expression. Blair finds she doesn't like it much.

"It worked," she says. "He'll meet us after school."

"What about track?"

"I'll skip."

"You never skip track."

"This is important, Cam."

"All right," Cam says. "We should think about what we want to ask him."

In person, Darren matches his voice. He's tall, broad, bearded, a guy who looks like he knows his way around an axe. He's wearing outdoor-person clothes, high-end but well-worn. He wipes his boots diligently at the entrance to the café, hangs his dripping rain jacket carefully on the back of his chair. His big hands dwarf his coffee mug. They are clean but scarred, his fingers callused. He radiates competence. If it was the end of the world, Blair thinks, she would want to be in this guy's apocalypse pod.

"I'm still not sure what you want to talk to me about," Darren says. "If there's anything I can do for Mattie, I'll try."

"It's sort of about Lola," Blair says, feeling her way forward.

"Lola," Darren says. His expression is carefully neutral. "Wow. I haven't thought about her in—years."

"How long were you her boyfriend?"

Darren looks mildly alarmed. "Oh, uh," he says. "Boyfriend is maybe a strong word. You know."

"I don't know," Blair says.

"We hung out for a couple of years," Darren says, shifting in his chair.

"What was she like?"

"I thought you wanted to talk about Mattie."

"Just for context," Blair says. "She's so important to Mattie. We're trying to understand their dynamic."

Darren thinks about this. "I don't know if Lola was the best role model back then," he says finally. "But Mats worshipped her. And Lola adored Mattie. It was kind of the three of them against the world. Luke and Lola were so protective of Mattie, Lola especially. But I guess you know all that."

"Protective?" Blair asks. "Why did Mattie need protecting?"

"Ruth's not the easiest person," Darren says. "She wasn't, anyway. I don't know what she's like now."

Blair thinks of the Botox, Mattie's pink dress. "I don't think she's changed much."

"Why wasn't Lola a good role model?" Cam asks.

Darren shifts again. "She, uh . . ." He looks down at his coffee cup, as if he's hoping it will answer the question for him.

"Mattie said Lola sometimes had parties," Blair prompts.

"Yeah," Darren says. "We were all kind of—young. Young and dumb. I'm sober now," he adds hastily. "That's all in the past. Got my five-year chip and everything." He takes out his key ring and shows them.

"Cool," Cam says flatly. Blair kicks her ankle under the table, nodding supportively at Darren.

"That's very impressive," Blair says.

Five years, she thinks.

That means Darren got sober right after Lola disappeared.

Why? How can she work the conversation around to that night without scaring him off?

"She must have known a lot of other partyer types?" Blair says, tilting the sentence into a question so that it doesn't sound like an accusation.

"Lola? She didn't have too many friends, to be honest," Darren says.

"So she wouldn't have known . . ." Blair is trying to think of how to phrase the question.

Did Lola know bad people?

Did Lola do bad things?

Did Lola know the kind of people who would have stolen her away?

"But she had a lot of parties?" Blair tries.

"You know how it is," he says. "Ruth was gone a lot. Big empty house, no parents around. People kind of showed up. But Lola wasn't close to most of them."

"Who was she close to?" Cam asks.

"Me," Darren says. "Mats. Luke." He starts to say something else, and then he stops. "That's it," he says.

"Becca?" Cam tries.

Darren glances at her. "Becca who?" he says. His confusion is not convincing.

"Becca who was there the night Lola disappeared," Cam says.

"Oh, *Becca,*" Darren says. "Right. Her. Yeah. Uh, no, I don't think they were close. She's not going to tell you anything that will help Mattie." He fidgets with his key ring.

"Mattie was really isolated," he says suddenly. "I felt so bad for them. I don't know what Ruth was like before, but I think the divorce really screwed her up. Not because she loved him so much, but because she's so big on appearances. When Lola was Mattie's age, Ruth put her in beauty pageants, tried to get her in TV commercials. Lola hated all that shit. It messed with her head. She didn't want Mattie to go through the same thing. Mattie's never been into, you know." He clears his throat. "Girl stuff."

"Girl stuff?" Cam asks sarcastically.

Darren looks embarrassed, gestures vaguely with one broad hand. "I'm not real smart about gender, okay? But it makes sense that they're not a girl. And Lola was a total goth. Dyed her hair black, big eyeliner, crushed velvet, that whole thing. She was always trying to get me to listen to weird old bands from the nineties."

"Not anymore," Cam says.

Darren freezes. "You saw her?"

"Ruth had a welcome-home party," Blair says. "Mattie invited us."

Darren swallows. "I see. How did she seem?"

"Fine," Cam says. "Considering what happened to her."

"Right," Darren says. "The kidnapping. I heard about that too."

"From Mattie?" Cam asks.

"No," Darren says. "I told you. I haven't talked to Mattie in years."

"Then where?" Cam asks.

Darren's eyes slide toward the door. "Around," he says. "How you hear stuff."

"It doesn't seem like either Ruth or Lola have told anyone outside the family that Lola's home safe," Cam says.

"I don't remember who I heard it from," Darren says.

"You weren't at Lola's party," Blair says.

"Ruth wasn't my biggest fan," Darren says. He's trying for sardonic, but there's something else underneath. Blair is pretty sure it's fear.

"Why not?" Cam asks.

"I told you," he says. "I was a different person then. Me and Lola—it was like darkness just kind of followed her around. She was already like that when I met her. But I'm sure Ruth knew we partied. It didn't stop Ruth from going away all the time, but it didn't make her like me."

"Do you know who might have kidnapped Lola?" Blair asks.

Darren sits up in his chair, alarmed. "What? Of course not. You think I would've kept that to myself?"

"Why haven't you gotten in touch with her?" Cam presses. "You must be so happy she's back. You can pick up where you left off."

Darren is shaking his head. "No way," he says. "Like I said, we weren't—she wasn't anything—I mean, sure, I liked her a lot, okay? But that was kid stuff. A long time ago. I grew up. I have a serious girlfriend. We're engaged. I got a real job and everything. I should've been there for Mats and Luke after Lola disappeared, I know that. But you have to understand, I was a different person then. I'm not going back. Look, the park service has a couple programs for kids Mattie's age. I can maybe pull a few strings to—"

"Mattie doesn't think the girl who came back is really Lola," Cam interrupts.

Darren lifts his head and looks at Cam directly.

Cam meets his stare head-on.

"I'm sorry," he says. "How did you say you know Mattie again?"

"An after-school pro—" Blair begins, but Cam cuts her off.

"Last year we did a school project about a cold case in Oreville and helped the police solve the murder," Cam says. "Mattie came to us because of that. They think the girl who came back is someone else, and they want us to find out where the real Lola is."

"*Missing Clarissa?*" Darren says. "Jesus Christ. That was you? Are you recording this?"

"That's illegal," Cam says.

"You should've told me that from the beginning," Darren says. He stands up, pulls on his raincoat. His hands are shaking. "This is messed up."

"We're not recording you," Blair insists. "We're not making a podcast, I swear. We're just trying to help Mattie—"

"You lied to me," Darren says. "You keep my name out of this, you understand? Whatever the hell you're doing."

"Wait!" Blair pleads.

"What do you think happened to her?" Cam yells after him as he stalks away from the table. "Where do you think she went?"

But he doesn't turn around. The coffee shop door swings closed behind him with a final thwack.

"Thanks, Cam, that went well," Blair says with a sigh.

"What did you think was going to happen?"

Blair shakes her head. "Did you see his face when you said Mattie thinks the girl who came back isn't Lola? He *knows* something, Cam."

"He knows you lied to him," Cam says.

"I only sort of lied to him. But he definitely lied to us."

"Maybe he didn't lie to us," Cam says, looking at Blair. "Maybe he left a lot out."

Blair's stomach twists. "Let's talk to Luke. Find out if he's the one who's been in contact with Darren. And why."

"*Are* you making a podcast?" Cam asks.

"What? No! Of course not! I wouldn't do that without telling you!"

Cam looks at Blair for a long time. "I can't help you with this anymore today," she says finally. "I have to study."

"Physics," Blair says.

"Yeah," Cam says.

"Cam—" Blair stops, unsure of what it is she even wants to say. Cam waits. When Blair doesn't say anything else, Cam picks up her bag.

"Want me to drop you off?" Blair asks.

"I'll take the bus."

And then Cam too is gone.

Blair ignores the feeling in her stomach. Digs out her phone. Hey, she texts Mattie. Does your brother have a job?

CAM CONDUCTS INDEPENDENT RESEARCH

Once she's home, Cam realizes she forgot to go to the grocery store. She sticks her head in the refrigerator, knowing ahead of time what she will find there: the end of a stick of butter, a half-full carton of orange juice, a couple of Brad's hippie IPAs, and a jar of brine in which a single pickle at least as old as Kitten bobs forlornly.

It would not be *ethical* to spend the grocery money Irene gave her on takeout, but it would be *convenient*. And her ethics are already on shaky ground these days. She might as well be a well-fed reprobate.

She calls her favorite Thai restaurant, orders shrimp pad thai for herself and a drunken noodle for Irene to eat later.

"Anything else?" the friendly woman who answered the phone asks her.

"Do you have coffee filters?" Cam asks hopefully.

"Sorry?"

"Never mind," Cam says. "That's all, thank you."

Kitten follows her into her room. She belly flops onto her bed, opens her computer. Kitten clambers onto her butt, where he settles in to biscuit-making.

"Ouch," Cam says companionably as she types Lola's name into a search engine.

Lola Brosillard does not have a Facebook or a TikTok or a Twitter, but she does have an Instagram, and it is not set to private. Her last update is from five years ago. Three days before she disappeared, she posted a blurry nighttime shot of what looks like trees, with a blurry white smear in one corner that could be someone's arm.

Then, nothing.

Presumably, her kidnappers did not allow her access to social media, but Cam wonders why she hasn't posted now that she's back. Perhaps her trauma has erased all memory of her passwords; perhaps "Hey guys, been a while, I was being driven around the country in a van by lunatics" makes for an awkward status update.

Still, it's interesting.

Discuss Lola social media with Blair, she notes to herself in her imaginary book.

If she's going to do this, she should start keeping a real one.

If.

"Who am I kidding," she says to Kitten.

There's no *if* here. If there was an *if,* she wouldn't be looking at Lola's Instagram.

Blair's right. Cam wants to know where Lola went too.

Cam scrolls idly through Lola's feed. She liked to photograph forests and mountains. A lot of nighttime pictures, similar to the last one she posted: indistinct figures holding beer cans aloft, lit cigarettes dangling from their mouths, campfires an orange blur against the textured dark.

Occasionally, she'd geotagged campgrounds. Lola liked to go deep in the woods; Cam recognizes places from the heart of Olympic National Park. West and then farther west, toward the ocean, where the trees are vast and old and draped in sheets of low-hanging moss, and the dark places between them hold old secrets and older stories. Or out at the edge of the Pacific itself, stony gray beaches that make you think you've reached the end of the known world.

Darren's a park ranger now. Did he take her out there? Or was Lola the one who wanted wilderness first?

Cam rolls off her bed, dislodging an indignant Kitten, and digs through her bottom desk drawer, flinging aside ancient calculus tests, an obsolete graphing calculator she'd filched from the Oreville lost-and-found as a freshman, ink-sticky ballpoint pen caps, and a Canadian ten-dollar bill.

At the bottom, she finds what she's looking for: her Clarissa notebook, only half-full.

She looks at it for a long time.

And then she opens it to a blank page.

Talk to Blair social media she writes, and then she returns to her bed and adds the names of the campgrounds Lola tagged, though she's not sure how much this will help them. Ruby Beach, Rialto Beach, Heart O' the Hills, Sol Duc, Kalaloch, Mount Angeles.

Mount Angeles! Sophie says in her head. *Settler name!* Cam smiles, her heart surging with a wave of love.

The few pictures with Lola in them are mostly selfies, taken at odd and often unflattering angles. Lola was so beautiful she didn't feel the need for vanity, maybe. Or maybe she didn't care. Luke and Lola, cheeks smashed together, gazing up at the camera. Luke looks stoned and considerably happier than he did at Lola's welcome-home party. One of Lola and Darren that she'd snapped while they were kissing.

Cam almost looks away, as if she's spying on something private.

Which, actually, she is.

Past Darren doesn't smile. His face is set and serious, almost cruel. In one picture he's wearing a leather jacket, straddling a motorcycle. He looks more like a junior member of a biker gang than a future forest ranger.

Does he look like someone who'd know kidnappers? Cam's not sure how you tell.

Ask Blair Darren scary??? she writes.

She looks at Darren's picture, thinking.

Mattie had told them Lola said her kidnappers planned to hold her for ransom, but no one had ever demanded money from the family. But all that means is that Mattie doesn't know, not that the request had never come. What if the kidnappers *had* asked for money, and Ruth had never told Mattie or the police, because she'd never paid it?

What if Darren had wanted more than just Lola? What if he'd wanted the Brosillards' money?

Or—

Cam thinks it through. Ruth and Lola, at constant odds. Maybe Lola didn't want to live in that house anymore, but didn't want to give up the easy life either. What if Lola had hated her old life so much she'd arranged the kidnapping herself? Maybe she'd talked Darren into helping her. Planned to use her mother's ransom to start over somewhere new. But Ruth never paid, and Lola was left dangling.

And then, when she couldn't make it alone anymore, she'd come back. If she admitted to what she'd done, she'd be in trouble. If she'd had a hand in staging her own kidnapping, that might explain why she'd left Mattie behind and lied to them once she returned. Cam hasn't known Mattie for long, but she can easily imagine how devastated they would be to learn that freedom mattered more to their sister than her loyalty to them. Maybe Lola was never the devoted protector Mattie remembers.

And if Darren helped her—well, neither was he.

But if he'd helped Lola run away, why didn't he run with her? Did they plan to meet up somewhere later? Did something go wrong?

Or is Lola's impossible story actually true?

Just how rich are *the Brosillards?* Cam wonders. Rich enough to make the risk of kidnapping Lola worth it?

She searches for "Lola Brosillard missing person." There's almost nothing. When Mattie said that Ruth didn't spread the word about her daughter's disappearance, they weren't kidding. Cam finds the mention she vaguely remembered, in which Lola is a footnote to a three-year-old article about the anniversary of Clarissa's disappearance. The only other hit is a profile on a missing-persons website that looks like it's run out of somebody's house. There are three photos and a terse summary of her disappearance.

NAME: Lola Marie Brosillard
MISSING SINCE: July 16, 2017
MISSING FROM: Oreville, WA
SEX: F
RACE: White
AGE: 15
HEIGHT AND WEIGHT: 5'6", 115 lbs

DISTINGUISHING CHARACTERISTICS: White female, long wavy hair dyed black. Natural color is dark brown. Green eyes. No tattoos or other identifying scars, marks, etc.

DETAILS OF DISAPPEARANCE: Brosillard disappeared from own residence in Oreville, WA on the night of July 16, 2017. Fraternal twin brother last person to see her. Possible abduction. Further details are unavailable in Brosillard's case. Reported missing by mother Ruth Brosillard AM July 17.

INVESTIGATING AGENCY: Hoquiam Police Department

NOTES: Any information submitted on this disappearance will be passed along to Brosillard's sibling

Mattie, Cam thinks. This is Mattie's work. Reaching out to strangers, desperate for clues. For anything. Cam's heart feels creaky. What would she do, in Mattie's position? What if something happened to Irene? To Sophie?

Cam pushes the thought away and turns her attention back to the website. Two of the pictures are pulled from Lola's Instagram, but the other one must have been her school photo. She's staring unsmiling into the camera, her green eyes wide and surrounded by a thick rim of eyeliner. She looks stoned and sad, like her brother.

Beneath the scowl and tough makeup, she's a dead ringer for the Lola Cam and Blair met on Sunday. Her cheeks are rounder, the lines of her face softer, but her eyes are the same.

What are the odds Mattie's sister had a doppelgänger? The odds, Cam thinks, are vanishingly small.

If the Lola who left is the Lola who came back, what story is she hiding? And why?

The doorbell rings.

Kitten protests again as she gets up, but thumps off the bed and follows her to the door. He winds around her legs hopefully as she buzzes the deliveryperson into her building and retrieves her noodles. She is careful to tip generously. Irene might be irritated Cam used their grocery money for takeout, but if she finds out Cam stiffed the driver, she'll be livid.

"Not for cats," Cam tells Kitten, holding the heavy paper sack aloft. "Cats don't eat noodles."

Kitten meows loudly, unconvinced.

Cam puts Irene's noodles in the fridge and transports her own back to her bed and laptop. Kitten trails after her, sulking.

"I don't know what else to look for," Cam says aloud, pushing Kitten's insistent head away from her takeout. She googles "Lola Brosillard rich." "Lola Brosillard Darren." "Lola Brosillard conspiracy." "Lola Brosillard Sasquatch"—which pulls up, incredibly enough, the Clarissa Sasquatch abduction forum. *Missing Clarissa,* Cam notes, failed to quench it. If anything, the Sasquatch theories are even more fervid than they were before the podcast. At least someone got something out of the mess she made of last year.

Finally, at a loss, she tries the Brosillards' address.

And then she sits straight up, dislodging Kitten once again.

With Lola's home address, she's able to find out how much Ruth pays in property tax every year. She learns that Ruth was granted a permit to remodel her kitchen in 2018 (not too distracted by grief, apparently), where Ruth's property line lies, and that Ruth is not permitted to drill a well but luckily is connected to the county water system.

She has multiple photographs of the exterior of the Brosillards' home, a rough floor plan, and the names of every person who lived there before the Brosillards did.

And she knows that Ruth owns the house outright, that she purchased it in 2013 for 9.6 million dollars in cash, and that its current value is estimated at $15.5 million.

"Holy shit," Cam breathes.

Mattie had said Ruth got all their dad's money in the divorce.

But they hadn't said it was ten-million-dollars-cash-for-a-house kind of money.

Maybe they don't know.

Maybe Ruth never told them.

Maybe they've never looked.

But if Cam can find that out with a five-minute Google search, so could anyone.

Cam grabs her phone, dials a number that's been saved there unused since last year. And then that pleasant, familiar voice at the other end: "Reloj here."

"Hi," says Cam. "It's Cam."

Silence.

"Cameron? Cameron Muñoz?" Cam tries. Has he really forgotten her? How insulting.

"There's only one," Officer Reloj says cautiously. "What can I do for you, Cameron?"

He's Detective Reloj now, Cam remembers. And maybe he'll eventually be Sheriff Reloj. Clarissa made him a big star.

"Congratulations on your promotion," Cam says. "Do you have your own office now?"

"Thank you," Detective Reloj says. "I do."

"Nice view?"

"Of the parking lot."

"That's exciting," Cam says. "Listen, I have some questions about a missing person."

"Absolutely not," Detective Reloj says immediately. "No, no, and no, Cameron."

"We're not making a podcast," Cam says truthfully. "It's for school."

"That's what you said the last time."

"That was for school."

"You're not helping yourself here, Cam. I'm going to hang up now."

"No!" Cam protests. "It's not a real missing person. She came back. So there's nothing to solve. I promise."

Another, longer silence.

Technically, Detective Reloj owes his career boost to Cam and Blair. Cam knows it is not tactful to point this out unless there is an emergency. But she knows Detective Reloj knows he owes them too.

"Which case?" Detective Reloj says warily.

"It happened here in Oreville five years ago. Lola Brosillard was a teenager who disappeared from her house in the middle of the night."

"Sure, I remember that one. That was my first year on the job, but I didn't have anything to do with the case. Sorry, Cam. Can't help you."

You're not getting out of this that easy, Cam thinks.

"The police dismissed Lola's disappearance because the mom didn't make a fuss and because Lola had a history of running away," Cam says.

"I told you, I wouldn't know anything about that."

"Sounds like the last time the police ignored a girl's disappearance because she had a history," Cam says.

This is a low blow. Blair would be proud.

"Now come on," Detective Reloj snaps. "The Brosillard case was nothing like Clarissa's."

"Why not?"

"Clarissa liked to break into golf courses at night, not shooting up her—" Detective Reloj stops himself short, but it's too late. Cam pounces.

"Lola was doing *heroin*? Did the police think that had something to do with her disappearance? Why wouldn't they pursue the case?"

Detective Reloj sighs mightily. "If you were to search the public record, you'd find that the boyfriend was arrested for possession. More than once."

"How would it be public record? They were minors."

Another, eloquent silence.

"Darren wasn't a minor? He was over twenty-one and dating a fifteen-year-old? Gross."

"You're the abolitionist," Detective Reloj says mildly.

"I didn't say you should put him in jail for being gross," Cam says. "I just said he was gross." Darren hadn't seemed gross in the coffee shop; before he'd realized who they were, he'd seemed like the kind of guy you'd want to go hiking with, if you were a person who liked to go hiking. Still. He'd been out of high school, dating a sophomore girl at least six years younger than he was?

No wonder the mom hated him, Cam thinks.

Ruth hadn't struck Cam as being the most open and supportive of parents, but even Irene would most likely have something to say about Cam bringing around a twenty-one-year-old hard drug user at the tender age of fifteen.

Although, knowing Irene, she would've followed Darren around talking loudly about harm reduction and the importance of informed consent and equitable power dynamics until he fled the country to escape her monologue.

"Well, if that's all," Detective Reloj says.

"No! I'm not done. Don't hang up. Please. Did Lola get arrested too?" Cam asks.

Silence.

"Lola *was* a minor," Cam says. "So you can't tell me. But the police already knew who she was, which is why they didn't believe she was kidnapped. So she must've been."

Silence.

"The family is really wealthy," Cam says. "And Lola

was—is—beautiful. And the police still didn't do anything when Lola disappeared. So they *really* didn't believe she was kidnapped. Or care."

Silence.

"Even if Lola got arrested herself, Ruth could've bailed her out easily," Cam continues, thinking out loud. "And she's the type who would've. For appearances. If she thought her daughter had been kidnapped, she would've made the police do something about it."

Silence.

"Did she even fill out a missing persons report?"

"She reported the break-in," Detective Reloj says.

He's only confirming what Mattie's already told them. Cam still finds it hard to believe.

"Did she really not tell the police her *daughter* was missing?"

"She mentioned it, once they arrived. But she didn't seem worried. The police talked to Lola's friends, but there was nothing to go on."

"She was *fifteen*. She *disappeared*," Cam says in disbelief. "She was *gone*. In the middle of the night."

Detective Reloj clears his throat. "This wasn't another Clarissa, Cam. That girl ran away."

"Then who broke into the house?"

"As a general rule, inviting recreational drug users into a domicile is not beneficial to home security," Detective Reloj says primly.

"The police judged a teenage girl and ignored her disappearance because a few times she made bad decisions and maybe her mother covered it up," Cam says. "Understood. But then she came back a couple of weeks ago. And she said she was kidnapped."

"I heard about that."

"The police in Oregon aren't trying to find the people who took her?"

"Kidnapping a minor and transporting them across state lines is a federal crime," Officer Reloj says. "The local police would pass the case on to the feds."

"Did they?"

Silence.

"Blink once for yes, twice for no," Cam says.

"Cam, what does this have to do with school?"

"They didn't believe her," Cam says. "You think she ran away, and the police in Oregon didn't believe the kidnapping story."

"Are you recording this conversation?" Detective Reloj asks in sudden alarm.

"That's illegal," Cam says.

"Are you?"

"I wouldn't do that to you, Detective Reloj."

"Sure you would."

"I'm turning over a new leaf. Who was the detective who worked the original case? That's not a secret, is it?"

This silence lasts longer than all the other silences put together. Cam has to check her phone to be sure Detective Reloj hasn't hung up on her.

"Tom Bradshaw," Detective Reloj says finally. "He retired two years ago."

"Do you have his phone number?"

"Cameron."

"Okay, okay," Cam says.

"How's Annie Oakley doing these days?"

"Who?"

"Your sharpshooter friend. Blair."

"She's good," Cam says. "Everybody's good."

"Please don't get yourself in trouble again," Detective Reloj says.

"I swore off trouble," Cam says.

"But if you do get into trouble, you call me."

"I'm not going to get in trouble."

"Promise me, Cameron. No more charging into armed killers' houses."

"I didn't know you cared, Detective Reloj."

"Promise me."

"I promise," Cam says.

"Good girl," Detective Reloj says.

DAY 5: WEDNESDAY

BLAIR'S BOOK PROPOSAL:
A BIT OF LIGHT STALKING, WITH SUBTERFUGE

Dear Meredith Payne-Whiteley,

As you know, this is my first book proposal. So in all honesty, I'm not entirely clear what I'm doing here, or which parts of this will be interesting to you.

All of it is interesting to *me,* because it's my life. I guess you'll have to help me sort out what belongs in a book and what should stay in my head.

I skipped track practice again to pursue a lead. I like track practice—running in circles is the only time I feel like a normal person, which tells you a lot about me—but Mattie told me Luke only has two shifts scheduled this week, and the other one is on Saturday, which is too long to wait. You said to move swiftly. And I can sometimes be impatient. Not as impatient as Cam, but still impatient.

No, I did not tell Cam I skipped. Yes, by "pursue a lead" I mean "stalk Mattie's brother at his part-time job," but this is my book, so I get to frame the narrative in a manner I find suitable.

Do you think people who write about true crime are presenting an objective narrative?

Please.

I'm seventeen years old, and *I* know there's no such thing as objectivity.

Luke works at the fancy seafood restaurant in the harbor. In Oreville, there's only one. It's the kind of place your parents take you when they want to tell you they're getting a divorce and your prom date takes you when he wants to be sure you'll give it up.

I've never been there personally.

And I didn't go in blind. *You're like Philip Marlowe,* Mattie said when I asked them what Luke's into. Doing the research. I've only read one Chandler novel, and from what I remember, Marlowe researches little and gets beat up a lot. Mattie told me Luke's into whales, sailing, weed, and reading. I don't know anything about sailing, I don't smoke weed, and whales I'm not so sure about.

But reading, I can do. I sent Mattie into Luke's room to text me a picture of his bookshelves. And on my way to the restaurant I stopped by the bookstore to find one of his favorites (I guessed by the number of creases on the spine—maybe I have a future as a PI after all).

So that's how I ended up at Luke's restaurant on a slow Wednesday afternoon, with a copy of Nick Pyenson's *Spying on Whales* tucked under my arm.

I doubt you've ever been to humble Oreville, Meredith, so let me set the scene for you.

Our harbor is the part of town that would be featured on postcards, if anybody made postcards of Oreville. Pretty wooden sailboats bob in their slips, along with a handful of less-picturesque fishing boats and a few flashy new speedboats.

If you stand facing the water, the horizon behind you is ringed with mountains and trees and more mountains, and past the shelter of the harbor's stone breakwater (I had to look up the word "breakwater") the Straits stretch all the broad blue way to Canada, which you can see sometimes in the summer on clear days.

This isn't summer, and clear days are a long way off. In December, the sky comes all the way down to the treetops, and you can barely see past the edge of the jetties (I had to look up the word "jetty" too).

Luke's restaurant, like I said, is what passes for fine dining in Oreville. It sits at the edge of the water, with big picture windows looking out on the view. I showed up right after school—early enough in the day that there was hardly anyone else eating there. A middle-aged woman in a pressed white shirt leaned heavily on the hostess stand, looking bored. She didn't look any less bored when she saw me, but she did seat me by a window, which was nice. Outside, a couple of seagulls the size of cats battled over a french fry. Behind them, the water was socked in with fog.

Luke had the same uniform as the hostess. He looked the same way he looked at Lola's party: tired and sad and kind of stoned. The circles under his eyes are hollowed so deep they seem permanent.

He's cute despite all that, objectively speaking. As a writer, I notice detail.

Objectively.

"Can I start you with something to drink?" he asked. And then he saw the book where I had left it conspicuously face up on the table, and his whole face changed. Like somebody turning the lights on in a darkened house.

"I *love* that book," he said.

"I just started it," I said.

That was the last entirely truthful thing that came out of my mouth for a while.

And then I said, "I'm thinking about majoring in marine biology," which is not a lie, since I *was* thinking about it at the moment I *said* I was thinking about it, although what I know about whales could fit on an index card. (They are big, they live in water, some of them have teeth, and some of them have that other stuff that works like a strainer.)

And then I said, "Wait, have we met? You're Mattie's brother, right?"

"I thought you looked familiar," he said. "Sorry about that party. My family is . . ." He waved one arm vaguely.

"Whose isn't," I said. That made him laugh.

There was no one else in the restaurant, so we started talking about other things: yes Oreville is so boring (that much is true), yes at least it's beautiful (also true, once you get outside the city limits), yes omg I've always *dreamed* of sailing!!!! (I get seasick on the ferry), there's a *Deep Water* rerelease at the Oreville independent movie theater??? No way!!!! Of course I want to see it! (I have lived in Oreville since kindergarten and had no idea we have an independent movie theater, and I also kind of hate Ben Affleck movies, but it's all for the Cause, right?)

And that's how I ended up with a date with Luke Brosillard for Friday night.

For investigation only. I swear.

And I *will* investigate. Because he offered to pick me up, but I said my parents are strict about boys (this is not true at all; I don't think my parents would notice if I was dating forty people at a time, as long as I showed up each night at family dinner) and why don't I pick him up instead.

Which means I can get back into that house.

To investigate.

The beautiful green eyes of Luke Brosillard have nothing to do with anything. I am an undercover agent, working on my book proposal.

I had no idea I was such a good liar.

Maybe that's not a good thing for my conscience, but it's a great thing for my story. Meredith, you would be proud.

Cam, maybe not so much.

But I just want to see Lola's room, and then I'll leave Luke Brosillard alone.

Unless you tell me not to.

Sincerely,
Blair Johnson

PAINTING TIME

"So," Irene says.

School's out, and for once Irene has an afternoon off. She's in their small living room, trying out paint swatches on the landlord-cream walls.

Cam's sitting on their cozy old sofa, sock feet tucked up underneath her, going through AP practice exams.

"The dark blue," Cam says without looking up.

Irene's been talking about repainting the living room since Cam acquired language. The paint-swatch trials of years past are hidden behind crammed bookshelves and dusty milagros and a battered poster of Poly Styrene, Irene's idea of home decor.

"Not enough light in here," Irene says, dipping her brush in a can of sunny yellow. "But I was going to ask you about winter break."

Cam looks up from her laptop. "What about it?"

Irene eyes the daffodil-colored streak she's made.

"Looks like the inside of a Burger King," Cam says.

"Why is this so hard? It doesn't look this hard on the internet."

"People on the internet are rich," Cam says. "And have a lot of free time. And personal assistants."

"Personal assistant," says Irene. "Now there's an idea."

"Not me," Cam says.

"No," Irene agrees. "I'd need someone competent. Is Sophie coming home for break?"

Cam gets the silly look that always comes over her whenever she talks about Sophie. "Yeah," she says. "On the nineteenth. She has all of January off too, but she'll only be here a couple of weeks. She's volunteering with a Land Back collective fighting that pipeline."

Irene looks thoughtfully at her sample-size mossy green. "I could put her in touch with some explosives guys," she says. "Although it's been a while."

"I know Sophie is willing to go to prison," Cam says, "but I would prefer she didn't."

Irene smiles her private anarchist smile to herself. "Give me a few minutes alone with her anyway," she says. "Things are good with Sophie, then?"

"She's all the way across the country," Cam says. "I wouldn't call that good."

"You'll be out there soon enough. Heard anything yet?"

"Um," Cam says.

"*Cameron P. Muñoz.*" Irene drops her brush with a wet smack. "When were you planning on telling me?"

"They updated my application portal this morning," Cam says.

"Good news?"

"Full ride," Cam says.

"Holy shit!" Irene shouts. "Cameron!" Irene scrambles for the couch, grabs Cam up in a bear hug, nearly knocking Cam's laptop to the floor. Cam squeaks in protest and then submits to her mother's embrace.

When Irene finally pulls away, her face is wet.

"Are you crying?" Cam asks. "Don't cry!"

"I'm so proud of you," Irene says, wiping her eyes with the back of one hand. "I can't believe what kind of a kid I raised. Look at you. My brilliant terror."

This display of emotion is so out of character for Irene that Cam is at a loss how to respond. She lurches off the couch, stumbles to the bathroom, and reemerges with a handful of toilet paper, which she thrusts at Irene. Irene blows her nose with a loud honk, restoring something of a sense of normality.

"Get yourself together, woman," Cam says, trying for stern humor. Irene laughs and then starts sobbing again. Cam stands there in horror, arms dangling, until she lunges forward and hugs her mother again. Irene clings to her.

"I wish your father was here to see this," Irene wails into Cam's shoulder. "He would be so proud of you. I'm so proud of you. I'm proud enough for both of us. Look at you! My magnificent child!"

Cam makes what she hopes is a soothing noise and pats

Irene on the back as if Irene is a colicky infant Cam is trying to burp.

At last, Irene squeezes Cam tight one last time and releases her. Blows her nose again with her sodden handful of toilet paper. Takes a deep breath and shakes her head.

"Good god," she says in wonder at her own outburst.

"Good god," Cam agrees uncertainly.

"We should celebrate," Irene says briskly. "I'll take you and Blair and Sophie out to dinner. How does that sound?"

"Olive Garden!" Cam says happily.

"I was thinking somewhere a bit fancier," Irene says, laughing. "Maybe that place in the harbor."

"Endless breadsticks are plenty fancy," Cam says.

"It's your party," Irene says. "Have you told Sophie?"

"I haven't talked to her," Cam says.

Irene gives her a sharp look.

"It's fine," Cam says. Irene waits. "It's weird," Cam allows. "She's so far away. She has this whole new life I don't know anything about. She's busy all the time. Like, *all* the time. We don't talk as much. But only because she's so busy. There's nothing wrong or anything."

When Sophie first left for school, she and Cam talked every day.

Then, once every few days.

Then, once a week.

Now, less. Cam was surprised Sophie answered her call on Monday, and she hasn't heard a thing from Sophie since.

But only because she's so busy, Cam thinks firmly. Which she's just said out loud to Irene. As if she's trying to reassure herself.

If something were wrong, Sophie would tell her. Wouldn't she?

Except, if she and Sophie never talk, when would Sophie say that?

"Distance is hard," Irene says, watching her daughter. Cam would not be a difficult person for Irene to read if Irene were as perceptive as a refrigerator, and Irene is a lot more perceptive than an appliance. "Especially when so much is changing for Sophie. It's not easy to give someone the space to grow when they're already so far away."

"Do you think Sophie needs to grow?" Cam asks.

"Of course. You do too."

Cam sits back down on the couch. Irene sits next to her and puts her arm around Cam's shoulders. Cam leans into her mother. This is a lot of emotion for one day, but maybe it's allowed, given the circumstances.

"Do you think Sophie has to grow—" There is something stuck in Cam's throat. She clears it irritably. "Do you think we're going to—"

For some reason, she can't get the words out.

"I don't know," Irene says matter-of-factly. No matter how many emotions Irene displays at once, she will never lie to make Cam feel better. Instead of making Cam sad, this makes her feel safe. "You might both need to grow in different directions. Or you might change in ways that make your relationship stronger. But whatever happens, Cam, both you and Sophie will be all right. You're both very special people."

"Sophie's the most special person I've ever met," Cam says.

"I know. But she's not the last special person you'll meet."

"I don't want a different special person," Cam says.

"That's an important place to start," Irene says. "But you're allowed to change your mind one day. And so is Sophie."

"I don't want Sophie to change her mind!"

"I know, sweetheart. But you can't choose how other people

feel. You can only choose what you do about it. Talk to Sophie when she's here. Ask her what she needs."

"I'm really bad at that," Cam says.

"You don't practice very often," Irene says. Irene clears her own throat. "You know, you're almost an adult. And I know her family's strict."

Sophie's dad is white, ex-Navy, met Sophie's mom when he was stationed in the Philippines. Cam knows enough about him to hate him with all her heart, though she's never met him and probably never will.

"Her family's homophobic," Cam says. "And her dad makes her go to church all the time."

"I'm saying, Sophie's welcome to stay here as long as she wants," Irene says. "And I trust you to be safe when I'm not around."

"Are you planning to skip town?"

"I could stay with Brad for a few days if you, uh, wanted privacy."

"Privacy?"

"With *Sophie,* Cameron. I am asking if you would like to have a few *overnights* alone with your girlfriend."

Cam blinks. "Is this The Talk? Are we having The Talk right now?"

"I already tried that with you last year, remember? You said you knew all about sex with women."

Cam covers her ears with her hands. "This ends now! Now!"

Irene grins, back on solid ground at last. "Don't come crying to your mother if you get the clap one day."

"I don't think they call it 'the clap' anymore," Cam says. "But thanks."

"For the STI advice?" Irene cackles.

"For the offer," Cam says. Cam takes a deep breath. Her throat is still strangely tight. Perhaps she is coming down with something. "I would like that. If Sophie wants to. Have some time. Alone. With Sophie. With me. Us."

"We can play it by ear," Irene says, ruffling Cam's hair affectionately.

"How's your patient, by the way?" Cam asks. Her heart thumps loudly enough that she's sure Irene can hear it.

"Which patient?"

"That new girl you told me about."

"She's doing great," Irene says. "She was released this morning. She'll be back in outpatient therapy this weekend." Irene pauses for emphasis. "Support group," Irene says.

"Support group," Cam says.

"Helpful," Irene says.

"Happy ending," Cam says.

"It's not an ending," Irene says. "It's a beginning."

"Right," Cam says. "A beginning."

Dear Mats,

It's funny all the things you can learn about a family by paying attention. All the secrets that fall into your lap when you put your ear to the wall in the quiet of your room. You know all about that, don't you? All those mystery novels on your shelves. I don't have to be a therapist to figure that one out.

There's so much I didn't get to see of your life. So much I missed. As hard as it is for me, I know it's so much harder for you. I know how badly you needed the girl who disappeared. Even though—forgive me—you hardly knew her. When I said there's a simple trick to becoming the girl everyone wants you to be, I didn't tell you about the flip side: how easy it is to see the girl you want in someone who is another person completely.

I think you're going to have to learn that the hard way.

You will. And I don't think you know this yet, but you're going to be okay. You don't need that girl as much as you think. It doesn't feel good now, and it might not feel good for a long time. But you'll be okay in a way I never will. Not because of the choices I've made, but because of who I am inside. Not because of what I've done. Because of what I am.

All those long years wandering, and they brought me back to you. Searching for something, someone—when home was right here all along. Don't take it away from me yet, Mats, I'm begging you. I haven't earned it, you'd say. I don't deserve it, you'd say. Are you sure? Is that really how it works? The world for you is fixed at the moment your sister disappeared.

What if it was bigger?

Love,
Lo

DAY 6: THURSDAY

BLAIR'S BOOK PROPOSAL:
MEETING NOTES ON A CLANDESTINE
CLIENT CONSULTATION

Dear Meredith Payne-Whiteley,

Cam's started a notebook again. It's the same notebook
she used when we were looking for Clarissa. Is that
too heavy-handed a through line from Clarissa's story
to Lola's? What happens when something isn't heavy-
handed, it's just real life? Irene's always yelling at the
news on the rare occasions she watches it when I'm over
at Cam's. "The writers for this season should be fired!"
she says. And then she starts talking about the death of
irony.

Anyway.

Cam told me about her call with Detective Reloj. And then she showed me the list of questions she
started in her notebook of missing girls.

The big one:

Is Darren scary?

He didn't scare us in the coffee shop. But when Cam

told me how much Ruth's house cost, I asked the same question.

Mattie doesn't remember him that way. Mattie remembers him as someone who brought them lollipops.

Mattie doesn't know that he was also the person bringing their sister drugs.

"You're going to tell them, right?" Cam asked. We were in the car on the way to school this morning.

"That Darren might've had a motive to hurt Lola?" I asked.

"That Darren was giving her heroin, Blair," Cam said.

I love Cam. If that wasn't clear. But she sees the world her own way. It's kind of like black and white, but only Cam has the color chart. So only Cam knows which thing is the right thing to do, and which one isn't.

"I can't tell Mattie their beloved sister was shooting up!" I said.

"You have to," Cam said.

That's the other thing about Cam. She's right a lot of the time.

Maybe even most of the time.

But doing the right thing is usually the same thing as doing the hard thing. And, as I'm learning, I'm not always great at either one.

"I will," I said. "Soon."

"All right," Cam said, flipping through her notebook.

If Cam says she's going to do something, she does it. It doesn't ever occur to her that other people might not mean what they say, which is kind of a relief.

"Ask Mattie if Lola had—has—a trust fund." She

closed her notebook. "That's the last thing on my list for now. I think we should think about whether the kidnapping might've been real, but fake," she said.

"What do you mean?"

"Maybe Lola set it up with Darren. Or maybe it was all Darren's idea. Mattie said there was no ransom request, but there might've been one they didn't know about. For all they know, Ruth *did* pay somebody off back when Lola disappeared. Maybe Ruth knew Lola or Darren was behind it, and that's why she didn't want the cops involved. Too messy. Or too embarrassing."

"Or this girl was behind it," I said.

"You mean, this girl kidnapped the real Lola five years ago for money, and then came back and is pretending to be her for more?"

"It's possible," I said.

"It's possible," Cam agreed. "Or . . ."

"Or what?"

"Mattie said Ruth took Lola to a psychiatrist, right?"

"Who diagnosed her with trauma-induced amnesia," I said, remembering.

"Right," Cam said. "Maybe she *does* have amnesia. Maybe whatever happened to her was so bad that . . . You know."

"Ugh," I said.

I watch movies; I read books. I don't need to imagine the kinds of things that happen to girls who go missing. I know the girls who vanish on the page—white, pretty, from good homes, girls like Clarissa with perfect teeth and impeccable résumés—are the least likely girls to be disappeared in real life. I know that in real life, serial killers target women who are already so vulnerable few people will think to look for them when they vanish for good.

That doesn't mean someone very bad couldn't have happened to Lola. Someone who did something so terrible her own brain rewrote the story of her missing years.

I could tell from Cam's face she was thinking the same thing.

"Yeah," she said.

"Do you think Mattie—"

"No," Cam said.

"Maybe that's part of why they're so insistent this girl isn't their sister," I said. "Because they can't bear to think what might've—"

"Yeah," Cam said.

"*Ugh,*" I said.

"You know that corny old show Irene loves about the FBI agents who are trying to prove aliens are real?" Cam said thoughtfully.

"Sure," I said. Irene is fanatical about that kind of thing. I've probably seen parts of at least a million movies about aliens and asteroids and spaceships accidentally traveling to alternate horror dimensions in all the years I've been spending the night at Cam's. Cam never makes it through the whole movie without yelling about which parts of the science don't make any sense. "That's not how gravity works! Asteroids don't spin like that! There's no sound in space!" That kind of thing.

"There's an episode about this guy who's an air force pilot and the military makes him fly an alien spacecraft they got hold of somehow," Cam said. "But then he freaks out, so they wipe all the spacecraft-flying memories from his brain. When they send him back home, his wife thinks he's a different person. She doesn't have anything to prove it, she just knows."

"Cam," I said. "Do you think Lola had her memories wiped after she piloted an alien spacecraft?"

Last year Cam would've gotten all pedantic on me and spent ten minutes explaining the mechanics of alien spacecraft flight. This year, she just laughed. "No, of course not. I don't even know why I thought of that. I guess because the whole thing is so far-fetched it seems like bad science fiction. And because it's not very nice to think about what could've really wiped Lola's brain, if that's what happened."

"No," I agreed. "It's not."

"But," she said. "Last year, I would've said it's impossible to know something is true without being able to prove it. This year . . ." She shrugged.

"You think Mattie's right? That Lola is some kind of—I don't know—evil twin?"

"I mean—it's not possible. Right? Even the pilot's wife was wrong. It *was* him. But he was different. She knew he was different. I know, I know—" She held up a hand to stop me from interrupting. "It's a dumb TV episode. I'm just saying, maybe Mattie *does* know something. Maybe they know something without even knowing that they know it."

"Or maybe they didn't know their sister as well as they thought," I said.

"They're not going to want to hear that," Cam said.

"No," I said. "They're not."

Cam's face was turned away from me. I knew she was thinking about Clarissa.

If one missing girl turned our lives upside down, what would a second one do?

I don't know yet, Meredith. Maybe you have some ideas.

I waited for Mattie outside their third-period class. "Come eat lunch with me in my car," I said. "I have a few things to tell you."

I didn't tell them about the drugs.

I didn't tell them about Detective Reloj.

I did tell them about my date with their brother.

Which I sort of hadn't mentioned to Cam.

"Undercover," they said. "Cool."

"It's not weird?"

"It's perfect," they said. "See if you can get into her room." They paused. "This is for the investigation, right?"

"What do you mean?"

"Never mind," they said. Another pause. "Girls think my brother is hot."

"He's nice," I said, hoping I wasn't blushing. "But that's not important. I want to look around. Ask a few questions."

"I can get her out of the house," Mattie said.

"How?" I asked.

"She's been after me since she got here to spend more time with her. I'll ask her to take me shopping for gender-appropriate clothing." Mattie made scare quotes with their fingers around "gender-appropriate." "Since Ruth won't buy me anything I like. She'll lose her mind."

"Is that safe?"

"What's she going to do, cut my throat in Swain's?"

Mattie took a bite of their sandwich. "She keeps trying to butter me up," they said through a mouthful of cheese and bread. "Follows me around the house if I'm not in my room. Trying to talk to me."

"About what?" I asked.

"Anything," Mattie said. "How my day was." They snort. "Like she cares. But she's not trying that with my brother. Or with Ruth. I don't know why."

"Maybe she likes you," I said without thinking.

Mattie turned in the passenger seat to stare at me, their eyes flat and hard.

"She doesn't know a thing about me," they said.

I thought it best to change the subject fast, and did. "Did—does—Lola have a trust fund?" I asked.

Mattie thought about this for a minute. "I don't know," they said. "I don't have one. I don't think. My brother might. He's the only one Ruth likes. Him, and the new Lola."

"Does *she* have a trust fund?" I asked.

Mattie snorted again. "She has one of Ruth's credit cards," they said. "The next best thing. You think this girl's after money?"

"Don't you? It would make sense," I said.

Mattie shook their head and took another bite of sandwich. "That's the problem," they said. "None of this makes sense."

It doesn't make sense, if Lola was acting alone.

Or if a fake Lola came along out of nowhere to replace her.

What does make sense? If Lola and Darren cooked up some kind of wild plan. Fake a kidnapping, demand ransom. Lola would have a way to escape her crappy home, and enough money to start over somewhere else.

It's hard to imagine even the most resourceful fifteen-year-old could've pulled something like that off on her own, but Darren was an adult. He could've helped her. Hidden her for a while. If Ruth never paid up, maybe he helped her out until she was old enough to get a job of her own. The police weren't looking for her. Her own mother wasn't looking for her. She could've stayed under the radar for five years, as long as she cut off contact with her family.

But what if something went wrong? What if Darren backed out? Maybe Darren lost his nerve, or Lola did. Maybe life without the cushion of Ruth's money got too tough.

So Lola came back. Ready to turn over a new leaf.

There's one big problem, Meredith, and I'm sure you can see it as well as I do.

If that's what happened, if their sister just walked away from them without looking back? It's going to tear Mattie apart.

Sincerely,
Blair Johnson

Day 7: Friday

BLAIR'S BOOK PROPOSAL:
SOME MINOR HOME INVASION AND
A HOT DATE WITH LUKE BROSILLARD

Dear Meredith Payne-Whiteley,

The third time's the charm; for once, I didn't have any
trouble finding the Brosillards'. Luke answered the
door, coming out onto the porch and starting to shut it
behind him, but I was prepared for that.

"Can I use your bathroom before we go?" I
asked.

I don't think he wanted to say yes, but he couldn't
really say no. He opened the front door again, and I
followed him into the huge entryway. He pointed me to
a guest bathroom, stocked with hand towels folded into
perfect triangles and enough scented bath soaps to open
a booth at the farmers' market.

I checked the cabinet behind the heavy mirror. A
half-empty sleeve of cotton makeup pads, a tube of
Neosporin, and a fancy tin of lavender-scented French
throat lozenges that looked like something somebody

had brought back from a trip and not known what to do with.

What did I think I was going to find in a guest bathroom's medicine cabinet? Lola's prescription drug stash? A bloody knife? I closed the door, flushed the toilet, ran the taps for a moment. Looked in the cabinet under the sink. Nothing but Costco toilet paper.

Oh look, the rich are just like us, I thought.

Luke was waiting for me right outside the bathroom door. I jumped.

"Sorry," he said.

"No worries," I said. "Is Mattie home?"

"They're out with Lola," he said.

I knew this, but he didn't know I knew it. "Things are going better with Mattie and Lola?" I asked. He was beelining for the front door, but I was determined to weasel my way into a look around the rest of the house.

"Everything's fine," he said. "It was a shock for Mattie when Lola came back, is all."

"I didn't really get to see this place at Lola's party," I said as he led me down the hall.

"It's kind of ridiculous," he said, embarrassed. "I should move out, but I don't want to leave Mattie here alone."

"It's so clean."

"The cleaning lady comes twice a week, but Ruth always cleans before she gets here."

"Why?"

"So the cleaning lady doesn't think we're dirty," he said.

And then he finally smiled at me, a wry,

self-deprecating grin that brought a light to his eyes and made my stomach flip like a hooked fish.

"Ruth always does what?"

Ruth's voice boomed in the empty house. Luke and I both jumped; we hadn't heard her coming.

Ruth was dressed more casually than she'd been at Lola's party: pale pink button-down blouse, untucked; tailored jeans; incongruous fluffy slippers on her stockinged feet. But her makeup was as immaculate as it had been on Sunday, her hair a smooth, polished mass.

I'd never known before I encountered Ruth Brosillard that a person could be dressed in perfectly ordinary-looking clothes and somehow I'd still know their outfit cost more than some people make in a month.

Maybe not more than my dad makes, but definitely more than Irene.

"Cleans," Luke said, flushing. He looked between me and his mother.

Trapped, I thought with triumph. *Try getting me out of here now, Luke Brosillard.*

I put on my best Girl Scout act. "Ms. Brosillard," I said warmly, extending my hand. "It's so nice to see you again. I was just saying what a lovely home you have."

Ruth eyed me top to toe, her laser gaze snagging on my own jeans, which looked as cheap as they were next to hers. But the "lovely home" had penetrated her defenses.

"Thank you, dear," she murmured, grasping my fingers as one might a wet dishrag and giving them an unconvincing shake. She knew she'd seen me before, but she didn't remember where, and she was unwilling to let go of the upper hand by asking. I pressed my advantage.

"I would *love* a tour," I said, turning to Luke.

Ruth glanced at my feet. "We don't wear shoes in the house."

"Of course," I said. "The new carpets." I slipped out of my shoes and tucked them next to the front door.

"We should really get going," Luke said. "The movie."

"Just a peek," I said, gazing at Ruth with big doe eyes. "I am in *awe* of your sense of *style,* Ms. Brosillard."

"It's a lifelong process," Ruth said, warming to me visibly. "Luke, show her the salon, at least."

I made a show of checking my phone. "We have lots of time," I said. "The movie doesn't start for another forty minutes."

Luke clearly did not want to show me anything, but he knew when he was defeated.

"You must be so happy to have Lola back," I said.

They both froze. Ruth turned her head to look at me, the immovable plane of her face frozen into a rigid smile.

"We've been very lucky," she said mechanically.

"I actually write for the *Oreville High School Star,*" I said, which was not technically untrue. "I would love to interview you for the paper. I can't imagine what your family has been through. I think you would be a wonderful example of courage and resilience for our readers."

"Uh, I don't—" Luke began next to me. Ruth cut him off without even looking at him.

"That's sweet of you," she said in a voice that suggested she had checked her new carpets and realized I'd tracked dog shit all over them. "But we are a *private* family, and we value our *privacy.*"

"Maybe I could talk to Lola?" I tried.

"I'm on my way out," Ruth said to Luke, ignoring that completely. She gave me a tight little smile, which was probably the best she could do with all that Botox. "You two have a *wonderful* time."

She turned her back on us and trotted away in her silly slippers. A moment later I heard a door slam, and then the sound of an electric garage door opening.

"Oreville doesn't have a school paper," Luke said.

"It does now!" I said brightly. I cocked my head at him, a study in dim-bulb innocence. "Oh my gosh, I'm sorry! I didn't mean to be nosy. It's so hard not to be, like, totally fascinated by your sister! What an amazing story, right?"

"Right," Luke said. "You ready to go?"

"Tour!" I said with manic cheer. I put one hand on his arm, leaned in slightly, widened my eyes. That always used to work on James when I was trying to get him to do something he didn't want to do, like pay attention to me. It worked on Luke like a charm.

"Of course," he said, smiling down at me. "The speedy version."

He towed me at a rapid clip through the parts of the house I'd already seen: the kitchen, the living room, the long art hallway. "Are those your relatives?" I asked breathily, gazing up at the oil portraits. "That's so cool. Your family must have so much history."

Luke smiled again. "Ruth took a bunch of old pictures she bought at an antique store to this guy who had a booth at the mall," he said.

I dropped the dipshit act. "Wait, really?"

"Yeah," he said, laughing. "I think he charged her by the yard. He must've been over the moon."

"No way," I said, laughing too. "That's amazing."

"That's Ruth," Luke said. "Want to see the library? She bought all the books by the yard too. You can order them by color depending on your decor scheme."

I gave him doe eyes again. "Can I see your room?"

"Uh," he said, blushing violently. "Okay."

Cute. Not a Casanova, our Luke, whatever Mattie says. I had no idea shyness could be so appealing.

Unlike the rest of the house, carefully curated as a magazine set, Luke's room felt like a person lived in it. It was big and bright, with a ten-million-dollar view of the water beyond a line of trees, but the furniture was old and cozy-looking, the bookshelves stuffed with books whose spines were so cracked he'd obviously actually read them. A big model of a three-masted sailing ship stood on a battered oak desk. I leaned over to look at it, careful not to touch it.

"I did that with my dad when I was a kid," he said.

"You put this together? The detail is incredible." Cloth sails billowed in an imaginary wind. Dozens of lines of string ran from each mast to matching wooden pins along the rails. Each board on the deck was hammered down with tiny nails. There was even a little wooden lifeboat.

"It's a beginner's kit," he said. "Everybody starts with the *Terror,* but I never put together another one after this. My dad had to do all the knots in the rigging. I was about seven."

"You were a terror?"

He smiled, his eyes on the model. "*Terror*'s the name of the ship. She was a warship first, and then converted for polar exploration. You know about the Franklin expedition?"

"No," I said. "But I assume they all died?"

"Good guess," he said, laughing. "That was usually how it went. A bunch of unprepared white men go somewhere cold, get stuck, eat the dogs, get scurvy, die horribly. The Franklin expedition didn't have dogs, so they ate each other before they died horribly. Polar exploration was my dad's thing. He was obsessed with all those guys."

"Why?"

"Their dauntless bravery," Luke said dryly. "They weren't all white, actually. Matthew Henson was a Black man who dragged Robert Peary's sorry ass all the way to the North Pole. He did all of the work—learned dogsledding, learned Inuktitut, made friends with the Inuit and learned how to survive from them. When they came back to the United States, Peary got all the credit. He said Henson was nothing more than his valet."

"Nice guy," I said.

"They were all assholes," Luke said. "Even the ones who survived. Ruined their families' lives. Just to plant a flag in some snow nobody had ever touched before."

I don't think we're talking about polar explorers anymore, I thought.

"How old were you when your dad left?" I asked.

He reached out, touched the loose edge of one sail. "Eight. He never finished the rigging," he said.

"I'm sorry," I said.

"He's not," Luke said. He touched the sail again, and now I saw that the corner was discolored and grubby.

As if a child had worried at the unfinished place over and over again.

Mattie's room was next to Luke's. They had the same view, the same old sturdy furniture. From before their dad left, I guessed. From their life before Ruth collected her cash winnings and reinvented herself as a multimillionaire. Mattie's walls were covered with posters from old black-and-white mystery movies: *The Thin Man, The Big Sleep, The Maltese Falcon.*

"Mattie didn't tell us they were into all this stuff," I said.

"They got obsessed with detective movies after Lola—went away," Luke said.

"I guess you don't have to be a shrink to figure that one out." I took another step into Mattie's room, scanning the titles on their shelves. All classic crime: Raymond Chandler, Dashiell Hammett, Patricia Highsmith. Some names I didn't recognize: Dorothy B. Hughes, Margaret Millar, Eleanor Taylor Bland.

"You're both big readers," I said. "Lola too?"

"She was when she was younger. Lola always said—" Luke bit down on the words. I turned to look at him.

"Lola always said what?"

"She always said Mattie was smart enough to do anything they wanted. They never forget anything. And they notice everything," Luke said.

"I believe it," I said, casual. And then: "What do you think happened to your sister?"

Luke started. "What do you mean?"

"Do you buy this kidnapping story?"

"Why would she lie?"

"I don't know," I said. "I don't know her at all." I weighed my options. "Has she talked to you about what happened?"

"Ruth sent her to a psychiatrist. It's normal for traumatized people to forget things."

"Yeah, but have *you* talked to her?"

"My family doesn't really do talking," Luke said.

"Mine either," I said. "But you know Mattie doesn't think it's her, don't you?"

"Yeah," he said tiredly. "Mattie's made that clear."

"And you?"

"What do you think?" He looked at me. "That's insane. Of course it's her."

"Right," I said. "You and Lola must be close."

"We were," Luke said.

"I never knew anybody who had a twin. Is it true you feel it when the other person gets hurt?"

"No," he said flatly.

"I heard sometimes twins make up their own language."

"Lola wanted—wants—to be a writer," he said. "But I've never been good at languages."

"What about Darren?"

"What about him?" Luke's face was blank.

"Did you keep in touch with him afterward?"

"No," Luke said.

I tried again. "Where do you think she went?"

"To tell you the truth," Luke said, "I'm trying not to think about it too much."

"Mattie's having a hard time with it," I said.

"I know," Luke said, relenting. "Lola's changed a lot."

"You don't think she was kidnapped," I said, watching him.

"I don't think it matters," he said. "If she doesn't want to talk about what happened, that's up to her. The important thing is that she's back." He forced a smile and changed the subject pointedly. "You know, it's cool what you guys are doing. You and your friend."

"What do you mean?"

"Mentoring Mattie. They need it. I'm not much

help," he said. "It's why I'm still here, living in this
loony bin. The second Mats graduates, I'm out."

"What about now?" I asked. "Lola's back. You
could move out."

He looked at Mattie's posters. "Yeah," he said dully.
"Sure. I love Mats, I'd do anything for them, but—
you know, our family is messed up. Lola was the one
they were closest to, and the way Mattie sees it, Lola
abandoned them like our dad. And now she's back like
nothing ever happened. I don't blame Mattie for being
pissed at her."

"And you?" I asked. "Are you pissed at her?"

He looked at me, his face blank again. "I stopped
expecting anything from my family a long time ago," he
said. "We're going to be late for the movie if we don't
leave now."

I drove Luke to the movie.

It turns out that before *Deep Water* was a movie
about Ben Affleck killing his wife's boyfriends it was a
documentary about a man who entered a solo sailboat race around the world in 1968. But he wasn't
prepared to sail across the open ocean, and his boat
wasn't good enough. Rather than drop out of the race,
which he knew he wouldn't survive, he faked elabo-
rate entries in his ship's log that said he'd gotten much
farther than he had. He kept another logbook, full of
his theories about the cosmic beings who controlled
human destinies.

And then he disappeared.

His empty boat was found adrift nine days after the
date of his last log entry.

Maybe you knew all that already.

I didn't.

Luke took my hand at the end of the movie when I cried and let it go when the lights came up. I went to the bathroom and washed my face. What if you already know you'll fail, but you've told too many people to back out? What if you're just crazy? What if you're so good at fooling people, at making them think you have everything under control, that nobody notices you're drowning until it's too late?

In the bathroom mirror, my eyes were still red.

When I came out, Luke was on his phone in the theater lobby. He was hunched over, as if he was trying to hide from someone. His voice was low, but I could hear him. "I can't talk right now," he said. "You shouldn't even be calling me."

I should've said something. I shouldn't have slowed my walk toward him, to give myself more time to eavesdrop. Should, should, should. What would you have done, Meredith? You would've listened too.

Luke was silent for a long moment. Whoever he was talking to must've had a lot to say. I couldn't see his face.

"Of course I don't fucking know what she wants!" he shouted into the phone. I jumped. And then he saw me. "I have to go," he said, and hung up. "Sorry," he said to me.

"Who was that?"

"My aunt Maisie. She wants to know what Ruth wants for Christmas." He smiled wryly. "Like anyone knows what Ruth wants. You okay?"

"Yeah," I said.

"You don't look okay," Luke said.

"I'm fine."

I drove him home. We didn't talk.

I turned my engine off in his driveway, and neither one of us said anything or moved for a moment.

"That was heavy," I said. "But really beautiful. Thank you."

"I think about doing that sometimes," he said. "Just taking the boat out one day and . . ." He trailed off.

The sailor in the movie had wanted to die, that was the thing. It hadn't just been the pressure. He could've called it off, his whole charade, but he didn't. At some point he'd gone into the water of his own volition.

Did Luke want to die? I didn't know if that's what he was telling me, or if he was trying to say something else. His face was impossible to read, turned away from me in the dark.

Mattie had plenty of reasons to be mad at Lola.

Did Luke?

If Lola faked her own kidnapping, did Luke know? Did he guess? Why hadn't he said anything, if he did? Did he help her? If they were so close, why didn't he run away too?

I am in way over my head, I thought for the first time.

"I've never been sailing," I said.

"Really?" The weight in the air lifted, carried away by the sudden warmth in his voice. "You've lived here your whole life, and you've never been sailing?"

Sailing is for rich people, I thought but didn't say. "Does the ferry count?"

"No," he said. He was smiling now. "The ferry definitely doesn't count. What are you doing on Sunday?"

"Wait, do you seriously have a sailboat?"

"Sure," he said. "One more thing my dad left behind." He said it easily, but I could still hear the pain buried deep beneath the lightness.

"You know how to sail?"

"Of course," he said. "You know who's a great sailor, actually, is Mattie. We used to go out on the water together all the time. I think they were an old sea captain in a past life."

"I can see that," I said. "You know, it's funny that your sister—Lola—wants—to be a writer. I've always wanted to be a writer too."

I don't know where that came from. I mean, I know where it came from. I don't know why I said it. I guess I wanted him to think of me as someone who could do something special. Someone larger and more interesting than the person I actually am.

He reached out, touching my jaw gently and tilting my face toward his. I thought my heart was going to stop. His eyes were huge, the irises clear even in the dark. "I bet you tell a good story," he said, and then he leaned in and kissed me softly on the cheek. "Sunday?"

"I'll pick you up again," I said. My voice was steady, but my hands were shaking.

"See you," he said. He opened the car door, ducked out easily, loped toward his mother's dream palace.

I heard the front door shut, but it was a long time before I started the engine again and drove away.

Of course I don't fucking know what she wants.

Meredith, I think I'm in trouble.

Sincerely,
Blair Johnson

IRENE HAS A DINNER GUEST

In the early weeks of Irene and Brad's relationship, Irene had sat Cam down for a Family Conversation about Boundaries and how Brad was of course not a Replacement for Cam's dad and Cam should always feel Safe and Comfortable in her own home and if Cam had any problems with Irene Seeing Someone then Cam should always feel welcome to—

"Are you serious?" Cam interrupted Irene's anxious monologue. "I've been wishing you would get laid for a *decade*! I don't care if he moves *in* with us!"

"I have gotten laid *occasionally* in the last decade," Irene said with great dignity.

"It didn't make you any less insufferable," Cam said. "Brad must have some incredible D for you to be this relaxed."

Irene laughed so hard she almost fell off the couch, Kitten fled the chaos grumbling, and that was the end of that palaver.

Irene works too much to have Brad over more than once or twice a week. But Irene is also a prickly person who values her time alone, and Cam does appreciate the pleasingly womb-like nature of their shared apartment, repellent to all outside forces, so this works out for them both.

Maybe not so much for Brad, who, even Cam can tell, is absolutely smitten, but who cares what Brad needs.

And, Cam has to admit, Brad is an eminently suitable boyfriend.

Sure, he never left Oreville. He doesn't have exciting stories of battling cops in the streets at massive protests, or squatting in derelict Brooklyn warehouses, or playing legendary punk shows in the East Village the way Irene does. He doesn't have fancy clothes or fast cars or any of the other things boyfriends have on television.

But he does have a Northwest Man vibe going—five o'clock

shadow, chiseled cheekbones, massive biceps, flannel shirts—
that Irene seems to enjoy, though Cam is not the best person to as-
sess the appeal of such a masculinity. He is smart and thoughtful.
He is good at fixing things. He lets Blair drive out to his gun range
and practice her aim for free anytime she wants. He has placidly
allowed Irene to steer his politics so far to the left of communism
they have fallen off the map altogether. And he is an incredible
cook.

Cam asked him once where he learned.

"YouTube," he said bashfully.

"See?" Cam said, turning to Irene. "There's no reason *you*
can't watch videos."

"Don't bother your mother," Irene said to Cam, and to Brad,
"Don't undermine my parenting, and get back in the kitchen."

"Yes, ma'am," he said, and did.

Tonight he is roasting a sheet pan (his gift to the Muñoz
home; pre-Brad, Irene did not own so much as a saucepan) of
vegetables and salmon, with a salad of winter kale from his old
friend Jenny's garden. Poor Brad; whenever he comes over, he
has to bring all the groceries too. Irene is on the couch, drinking
red wine out of her WORLD'S #1 DAD mug and watching what
she refers to as her "stories."

Cam has been enlisted to chop apples and red onion for the
salad while Brad keeps an eye on the oven (Cam, while well-
intentioned and eager to learn, has a tendency to burn things).

"First the vegetables, see," Brad explains. "Then, at the last
minute, you add the salmon—it barely needs any time at all,
not even ten minutes at this temperature, if you want it to—"

"Mm-hmm," Cam says dreamily.

Brad laughs. "You're not paying attention. You should be.
Chicks dig good cooks."

"What?"

"Never mind. What are you thinking about?"

"College," Cam says. "I got in."

"Not bad," Brad says, opening the oven a crack and releasing a hot blast of wonderful smells.

"Wow," Cam says. "*Wow*. That's amazing."

"Very simple," Brad says modestly. "Anyone can roast vegetables."

"Irene can't."

"She can now that she has a sheet pan," Brad says.

"She doesn't know how to turn on the oven," Cam says. "Or where to purchase actual food."

"Stop talking shit about your mother, Cameron!" Irene yells from the living room.

"Stop talking shit about your mother, Cameron," Brad says.

"Leave me alone, or I'll put you in another podcast," Cam says contentedly.

This whole feeling—the warm good-smelling kitchen; winter rain battering against the snug steam-fogged windows; the nonsensical background chatter of Irene's inane TV show; the banter; their small, shabby, dear apartment—

This, she thinks, is a special kind of happiness. Special and new.

"My heart is big," Cam says.

Brad reaches over and grabs her in a one-armed hug. Cam leans in to his side.

"Don't tell anyone," Brad says, "but I'm glad you did put me in a podcast."

"Irene is too," Cam says. "Since, you know. Now she gets to bang you after all these years."

"Not big on having feelings, the Muñoz women," Brad says with a small, private smile. "But not very good at hiding them either."

"Asshole," Cam says affectionately, ducking his hug. "Go back to your arsenal in the woods."

"Who'll feed you then?"

"That's enough!" Irene yells.

"No eavesdropping!" Cam and Brad yell together.

Cam briefly considers telling Brad she is having problems with Blair. He is a solid sort who has survived many difficulties, including dating her mother; he would be likely to have good advice.

But if she tells Brad about Blair, she will have to tell Brad about Lola. Cam knows Brad cares about her, but he is also loyal to Irene. He would never let something so serious stay secret, not after what happened last year.

Which is an excellent argument, Cam thinks ruefully, for not letting something so serious stay secret herself.

What happened last year was bad.

But it also brought her mom and Brad together, which is good.

Cam still wakes up screaming in the night: bad. Panic attacks: bad. Clarissa is dead, and nothing will bring her back: bad.

Cam and Blair pulled a lot of ugly secrets out into the light of day: Good? Bad? Who knows. The fallout is still ongoing. The legal proceedings, she's been told, may take years. Not everyone who should be punished will be, and a lot of people who did nothing wrong, who were hurt themselves, will have to live with the consequences of harm they did not cause.

That's bad.

But here is Brad, humming to himself as he pulls out the sheet pan and turns sweet potatoes and beets and parsnips with a fork. The salmon gleams a rich, glorious rose-pink on the counter, waiting for its time in the oven. Irene will never admit it to Cam—or Brad, for that matter—but Irene is in love, and Cam is pretty sure Brad knows it.

That's good.

"Things are so complicated," Cam says out loud.

Brad closes the oven door.

"It's just olive oil and garlic, really," he says. "Nothing to it."

Dear Mats,

Of all the places to have a revelation, the Oreville Swain's General Store wouldn't have been first on my list. But I guess they come when you least expect them. That's why they're called revelations, not scheduled events.

You're fighting me the whole way. Everything nice I'm trying to do for you, every kindness I extend. I'm getting tired of it, Mattie Brosillard. Who else in that house is on your side? Ruth's a monster. Luke's a fool. Your friends can't be around all the time, turning up rocks with you and looking under them for what crawls away from the light. It's just you and me at the end of the day, Mats. Cut me a break.

I asked you in the flannel shirt aisle if you remembered the day Darren drove the two of us out to the hot springs. The long, twisting road made you carsick, so I let you sit up front. That time of year, the parking lot was empty. We were completely alone. Didn't see a single other person for two days. The hike along the Elwha River, straining at its banks. How we rested at the overlook before the slow climb; how it felt to come to the springs at the end of it, steaming pools dotted throughout the forest like a scene in a fantasy novel. You'd never seen anything like it. You stayed in the water for hours, refused to come out until after we'd set up the tent, cooked dinner. After sunset the sky cleared as if by magic. No moon, a night wild with stars. You insisted on sleeping outside, but it started raining at four in the morning and you crept into the tent like a drowned rat, laughing. You were so happy that weekend. I've never seen you that happy.

I don't remember that, you said. Your hand was on a red-checked flannel I knew you didn't want. You wouldn't look at me. I kept talking, and you still wouldn't look at me.

You can't meet my eyes when you lie. Interesting.

Of course you remember. It happened. You were there.

How did the first lie feel? Did it sit heavy in your mouth? I think it came easier than you'd like. You're more like me than you're willing to admit to yourself, but I can see you realizing it. Trying to push it away. But it's settling in you, the knowledge. I'm not the girl who left you.

But that doesn't mean I'm not your sister too.

Love,

Lo

Day 8: Saturday

CAM PAYS A VISIT

CAM wakes up thinking about drugs.

Detective Reloj let slip that Lola was using heroin. According to Irene's television stories, people who use drugs often end up around people who are doing bad things, or are prone to doing bad things themselves, or go through drug withdrawals without telling their doctors while also suffering from obscure illnesses, thus complicating their medical diagnoses in a dramatic fashion. Surely these plot staples have at least a minimal grounding in fact.

But Cam herself doesn't know anything about drugs, let alone why someone would want to do them.

Irene smokes pot occasionally when she thinks Cam is asleep, but Cam feels that pot is maybe not the same thing as heroin. And she can't ask Irene why people do drugs without Irene wanting to know why she wants to know, and she can't tell Irene why she wants to know without telling Irene about the new investigation, and if she tells Irene about the new investigation Irene will lose it, and Cam will be confined to her quarters on bread-and-water rations for the rest of her sorry existence.

So Irene is out.

Sophie is attending a private liberal arts school, where presumably many people do drugs. But Cam can't bear the thought of Sophie not answering if she calls. Or the worse thought that Sophie is now taking drugs herself, along with all the other things she could potentially be doing at a private liberal arts school and not telling Cam about, starting with heroin and ending with, say, orgies with the lacrosse team.

So Sophie is out.

Blair used to drink beer sometimes when she was dating James. Beer is not *drugs,* which, as far as Cam knows, Blair does not do. But this new, secretive, mystery Blair could be inhaling methamphetamines every weekend without telling Cam about it, and Cam would have no idea. (Inhaling methamphetamines? Smoking them? Making them into soup? Cam does not know how one ingests methamphetamines in the first place.) If Blair has become a drug expert, Cam doesn't really want to know.

So Blair is out.

Who do I know who knows about drugs? Cam thinks.

And then she remembers the obvious.

Cam hasn't kept in touch much in the last year with Clarissa's best friend, Jenny Alexander, though she knows Brad spends a lot of time with her. But back when Cam and Blair were in the thick of things, fighting off reporters, trying to get back to their normal lives, Jenny sent her a message Cam hasn't forgotten: Anytime you need to talk, I'm here.

Apparently, she'd meant it. Because a phone call later, Cam's sitting on Jenny's quilt-covered sofa, with Jenny's huge dog, Baskerville, half in her lap and a mug of Jenny's tea in one hand. The tea is as good and comforting as it was a year ago.

Jenny's hair has grown out a bit and sticks out from her head in a fuzzy halo. She's wearing a much-patched pair of overalls over an old wool sweater with darned elbows. Just sitting next to her on the couch makes Cam feel calmer.

I want to know why a person does drugs is what Cam means to say. But when she opens her mouth, that's not what comes out.

"I'm having really bad dreams, and I think my girlfriend's going to break up with me," she blurts.

"Oh, honey," Jenny says. She leans over Baskerville and grabs Cam tight. Suddenly, Cam finds herself crying. Why is she crying? She hates crying! Cam bawls on Jenny's woolly shoulder like a toddler while Jenny rubs her back in gentle circles and the dog wriggles around in search of a lap.

"You're safe here," Jenny says. "Just let it out."

Cam's tears at last subside, and she sits back, mortified and dripping snot. Jenny hops up, goes into the kitchen, comes back with a roll of paper towels.

"Sorry," she says, handing them to Cam. "That's all we've got. Ellie says Kleenex are an environmental catastrophe, but I got her to compromise on paper towels—you know how hard it is to cook without paper towels?—she won't buy them herself, but she stopped yelling at me for bringing them home. My little eco-terrorist, that one. You know she used to be in one of those groups that U-lock themselves to logging road gates to try and block old-growth clear-cuts? Well, that was all before your time."

Jenny chatters on lightly, giving Cam time to blow her nose with a vigorous Irene-like honk, blow it again, scrub her face dry, compose herself.

"Thanks," Cam says. "Sorry. I hate crying."

Jenny smiles at her from the other end of the couch, where she's resettled herself. "Happens to the best of us."

"It doesn't happen to *me*," Cam says in disgust.

"Want to talk about it?" Jenny asks.

"Maybe later. What I meant to ask you is, why do people do drugs?"

Jenny is taken aback. "I wouldn't recommend it," she says. "If you're thinking about—"

"Not for me, I promise," Cam says. "I'm trying to understand someone else."

"Do you want to tell me who?"

"No," Cam says.

Jenny frowns. "Is someone in danger, Cam?"

"No. Maybe. I don't know," Cam says. "This person isn't using drugs anymore. I don't think."

Jenny gives her a look that bears a discomfiting resemblance to Irene's patented *Excuse Me, Cameron P. Muñoz?*

"Is this for a podcast?"

"No," Cam says immediately. "I swear. Not a podcast. Never again."

"Does Blair know you're here, Cam?"

"No," Cam says. "Blair's being . . . It's complicated. I don't want to talk about Blair either. We're looking into something for a, uh, friend. Sort of."

"Ooookay," Jenny says. "You want to tell me what kind of drugs we're talking about here?"

"Heroin," Cam says.

"And how old is this person?"

"Fifteen. But not anymore. In the past, when the person was using the drugs, the person was fifteen."

"Cam," Jenny says.

"It's for a good cause," Cam says. "I know you don't have any reason to believe me. But after last year, I never want to be famous again. I'm just trying to help out a friend. Who isn't the person who was on drugs," she adds hastily. "The friend is fine. Maybe not fine. But not on drugs."

Jenny shakes her head. "All right," she says slowly. "People don't generally start using heroin as teenagers if all is well in their lives. Obviously. Maybe there was a situation the person was trying to escape, or feelings they were trying to numb."

"Like maybe they were being abused?"

Mattie would've told them if they thought Lola was being abused, but Mattie wasn't with their sister all the time. It's hard to imagine wholesome park ranger Darren doing anything to hurt someone else, but it's also hard to imagine him as a drug dealer, or a person who might fake his teenage girlfriend's kidnapping for cash. He was definitely at least one of those things, even if he's changed since.

And if there's one thing Cam's learned in the last year, it's that people aren't always what they seem.

But Jenny is shaking her head again. "Cam, hold up. Forget it. I'm not going to do this with you," Jenny says. "I'm not armchair diagnosing a teenager I don't know. If you think somebody is being abused, you need to get help. Real help."

"Fair," Cam says.

"Cameron, do you think someone is being abused?"

"Not now," Cam says. "Not anymore."

"Cam—"

"I promise," Cam says. "I would get real help if I thought something bad was happening. Can I ask why *you* did drugs? You weren't much older than fifteen when you started, right?"

Jenny thinks about this for a while. "Once when I was in rehab," she says finally, "I met this girl who got drunk for the first time at someone's pool party when she was eleven or twelve. She said she was floating on her back in the middle of this swimming pool, looking up at the moon, feeling the best she'd ever felt in her whole life, thinking, *This is what I want forever.* She said that was the night she fell in love."

"With who?" Cam asks.

"With getting wasted," Jenny says.

Cam waits for the revelation. "And?" she says, confused.

Jenny laughs. "And that's it. That feeling. Nobody fully understands how addiction works, but in my experience, there are people who feel that bliss, and people who don't. And if you do—that's bad luck, honestly. You can spend the rest of your life chasing that feeling and never fully catch it again. But once you've been there, it's hard to let go. That's how it was for me, even before Clarissa disappeared. And afterward, I wanted to forget I was a person. I wanted to erase everything I'd ever been. I was so ashamed of who I was that I couldn't look in a mirror."

"Huh," Cam says. She looks down at Baskerville, pets his large soft ears. He emits a pleased groan-whine.

"In Buddhist cosmology, there's a realm that belongs to hungry ghosts," Jenny says. "The ghosts are beings eternally tormented by desire. What the ghosts really want are things like love, acceptance, community. But they don't know how to find those things, or those things have been taken away from them, so they try and fill their empty bellies with fancy cars, or sex, or alcohol, or shopping—whatever calms the hunger for a moment."

"Drugs," Cam says.

Jenny nods. "Drugs. But none of those things are real nourishment, right? So the ghost is always hungry, and feeding the ghost becomes an endless loop of suffering."

Mattie hasn't said anything about the returned Lola using drugs, but they didn't say anything about the old Lola using drugs either. Then again, that's not the kind of thing you tell your younger sibling. If Mattie didn't know Lola was doing drugs, they wouldn't know if she'd stopped.

The returned Lola doesn't look like a person who's stuck in a loop of suffering, that's for sure. She looks like a person who smiles all the way to the bank.

Mattie thinks the new Lola doesn't act like the old Lola.

What if that just means she got sober?

"Does your personality change when you stop using drugs?" Cam asks. "In general," she adds hastily.

"It can," Jenny says. "It doesn't always."

"But, *in general,* if a person is using drugs, and then they stop using drugs, they might act really different? They could seem like a different person altogether?"

Jenny eyes her. "*In general,*" she says, "that could *generally* be true."

"Is that because getting sober fixes all your problems?" Cam asks.

Jenny laughs out loud. "Getting sober is when your problems really start," she says, chuckling.

"But you're not on drugs anymore," Cam says, confused.

"Exactly," Jenny says. "And once you're not on drugs anymore, you have to deal with your*self.* With the ghost. Everybody wants a tidy ending, right? 'I was in the closet, and I was sad and lonely, and then I came out, and now everything's perfect.' 'I did a bunch of heroin, and I was sad and lonely, and then I got clean, and now everything's perfect.' But that's not how it works at all. You're still the same person, with the same traumas, the same coping skills—which may or may not be good ones—the same problems. The same hungry ghost, if that's how you want to think about it, and now the ghost doesn't have anything to eat.

"When I got clean, I was just as big of a mess as when I was using. And on top of everything else, my feelings were *right there.* Everything I'd been using to get away from landed on me all at once, and then I had to deal with it. I still have to deal with it, every day. Being sober is the hardest work I've ever done."

Cam considers this.

Did her life change after she came out? Not really, since the people closest to her—Irene and Blair—already knew she was gay.

Yes, totally, because now Sophie is her girlfriend, and Sophie is incredible and amazing and life-altering.

But Cam is still Cam. Cam still does reckless, stupid things and runs over other people's feelings and makes mistakes and is obnoxious sometimes.

So is she the same, or different?

Is this what Jenny means?

And what, if anything, does this tell her about Lola?

"So if a person got sober, they might still act the same as before?" Cam asks.

Jenny only raises her eyebrows.

"You can't tell me about someone you don't know," Cam says. "Message received."

"Now, do you want to talk about why you really came here?" Jenny asks.

"No," Cam says sullenly.

"I used to have awful dreams too, after Clarissa disappeared," Jenny says.

"You did?" Cam looks up. "What about?"

"They weren't subtle, let's put it that way," Jenny says. "Like *The Silence of the Lambs,* but all the chopped-up girls had her face. It got so bad I was scared to fall asleep." Cam shifts uncomfortably. "Not a great way to live," Jenny says. "That's a big part of why I started using."

"Did it work?" Cam asks.

"For a while," Jenny says. "But then the nightmares started back up, and on top of that I had a drug problem. I wouldn't say hard drug use was an ideal solution."

"Irene sent me to a therapist," Cam confesses.

"Did that work?"

"I wouldn't say it was an ideal solution."

Jenny smiles. "Don't give up so fast," she says. "It can take a long time to find the right therapist."

Cam does not want to spend a long time finding the right therapist. She does not want to spend a short time finding the right therapist. She wants to stop dreaming about Clarissa, and she wants Sophie to call her back, and she wants Blair to stop acting weird, and she wants Mattie to go away, except now she's curious about Lola's deal, so she wants to know the answer to the mystery of where Lola went with no disruptions to her daily life or physical safety.

Baskerville gives her a mournful look.

"None of this is easy," Jenny says, as if she can see directly into Cam's skull. "What happened to you was really traumatic."

"Nothing happened to me," Cam says.

"Cam, you could've died. Blair and Irene could've died. And I heard about the online stuff. People were sending you death threats. That's a lot for anyone to deal with."

"Blair doesn't have nightmares," Cam says.

"You don't know that."

Right, Cam thinks. *Because Blair doesn't tell me anything anymore.*

Not that *she's* told Blair about *her* nightmares.

But that's different. Right?

"Wait, how did you know about the death threats?" Cam asks.

"Oops." Jenny looks embarrassed. "Uh, Brad may have mentioned it."

Great, Cam thinks. Irene's talking to Brad instead of Cam about the nightmarish messages people have sent her family over the last year. Just add that to the list of Terrible Things No One Is Talking About.

"She doesn't want to stress you out any more than you're already stressed," Jenny says. Is Jenny psychic? "She needed someone to vent to, Cam. It's not your fault."

"It *is* my fault," Cam says. "That's the thing. All of this is my fault. If I hadn't started that stupid podcast and dragged Blair into it, none of this would've happened."

"No, it's not," Jenny says. "Cam, you didn't kill Clarissa. None of this is your fault."

"I—" Cam stops, trying to find the right words. "I wish it had never happened," she says. "I wish none of this had ever happened. I wish Clarissa got to live her life."

"You and me both," Jenny says. "But it did happen. And you and Blair found out the truth. You helped the people who loved her find a way to end that story. Nothing will ever bring her back. But after all that time wondering, I know what happened to her. Brad knows what happened to her. We know that she didn't leave us on purpose. Her parents got to bury her. What you and Blair did is huge, Cam. I never thought I'd get to have that kind of relief."

"Relief?" Cam asks.

"If you never know whether what you're grieving is really gone, it's easy to get stuck," Jenny says. "It's like living in a waiting room. I was sure Clarissa was dead, but I didn't *know*. No matter how much work I did, how much of a life I built for myself"—Jenny waves a hand, encompassing her house, the dog, the garden, her girlfriend—"that uncertainty was always festering somewhere deep inside. Knowing what happened doesn't make what happened any easier. But it's helping me make peace with it."

"Did you make peace with it?" Cam asks.

"Ask me again in another year," Jenny says.

Cam wonders what Sophie would say, and her heart contracts. Something really smart about how finding Clarissa doesn't balance out Cam and Blair inserting themselves into someone else's story and making a public spectacle out of it.

She wants to tell Sophie that her heart hurts, and she doesn't know what to fight when the answer is everything, and she doesn't know how to fight when it feels like she does everything wrong.

But Sophie is three thousand miles away.

And now Cam's crying again.

Jenny hands her another wad of paper towels and sits quietly with her while she sobs. With anyone else—Irene, Blair, Sophie—especially Sophie?—this would be unbearable, but something about Jenny makes Cam feel okay.

If there is a list somewhere of people Cam is cool with breaking down in front of, Jenny's is the only name on it.

"Sorry," Cam says again, snuffling.

"Don't apologize for having feelings," Jenny says. "Not to anybody."

"Sorry," Cam says automatically, and then she laughs, and Jenny laughs too.

Cam mops her face, laugh-crying. "Shit!" she says. Baskerville tries to eat one of her paper towels.

"None of that, old man," Jenny says firmly. Baskerville gives her a look of mournful admonition.

"You should be a therapist," Cam says. "I would go to you for therapy, if you were a therapist."

"That's a very nice thing to say, but I'd be an awful therapist," Jenny says. "I always tell people what to do and get mad when they don't listen."

"I think I might need someone telling me what to do," Cam says.

"That's not therapeutic," Jenny says, laughing. "That's a dictatorship. But I'm always here if you want to talk, Cam."

"Me too," Cam says. "I don't have any good advice for you, though."

"You never know," Jenny says. "And you can keep me apprised of the hip activities of queer young people."

"I think we make a lot of TikToks, but I'm not very au courant," Cam says. "I could ask Sophie."

"Sophie's the girlfriend? Want to talk about her?"

"Irene says we might be growing in different directions," Cam says to Baskerville. As if she and Sophie are plants. Cam is a cactus: spiky, sturdy, and unpleasant, with the occasional blossom.

Sophie? Sophie's a dahlia. Bright and blazing and gorgeous.

"It happens," Jenny says. "Give it time. You know what they say about the things you love. Let them be free and flap around a little. If they come back, blah blah blah."

"I don't want anything I love to leave me," Cam says.

"I know the feeling," Jenny says.

A great melancholy descends. Cam and Jenny are quiet for a long moment.

"I had panic attacks for a while too," Jenny says conversationally, breaking the silence. "Pretty bad ones."

"Huh," Cam says. As if she doesn't know what Jenny's getting at. As if her own face isn't as easy to read as a newspaper headline. Not for the first time, she curses her utter lack of a poker face.

"They don't just go away," Jenny continues. "You have to put in some work."

"Like what?" Cam asks. "I mean, not that I'm having—not that I—"

Jenny doesn't bother to let her finish. "Therapy," she says, relentless.

"I don't want to talk about—"

"There are techniques you can learn to manage them, even if you don't want to do traditional talk therapy," Jenny says, cutting her off briskly. "Breathing exercises. Mindfulness. Support groups." Irene, Cam remembers, said basically the same thing. Are Jenny and Irene in some kind of Cam group chat? Cam considers this very real possibility with horror.

"Just saying," Jenny says. "All right, I'm done. But you can always talk to me."

"Okay," Cam says. "Thanks." She does not feel grateful. But she knows Jenny is trying to help, and that Jenny has been through a lot herself, and here Jenny is now, on the other side.

Maybe Jenny has a point. Even if she is in a chat with Cam's mother.

Cam stops petting Baskerville. He pushes his nose into her hand and sighs with such reproach that Cam and Jenny both laugh and the heaviness lifts.

"All right, that's enough of the sad shit," Jenny says. "Tell me. Is it true Irene's totally whipped?"

Day 9: Sunday

BLAIR IS EXPOSED IN A LIE,
PART ONE

BLAIR'S never been sailing before, and she has no idea what to wear. The sky outside her window is threatening, and her phone tells her the temperature is only a sliver above frigid.

Maybe she'll get hypothermia on Luke's boat, and the two of them will have to take off their clothes and huddle in a foil blanket together as a lifesaving maneuver.

Blair Johnson, Blair Johnson tells herself.

Still, a girl can dream.

It's hard to dress warmly and look cute. And what about shoes? Do you need special shoes for boats? Hasn't she read that somewhere? She doesn't have special shoes for a boat. She has her running shoes, her warm but ugly winter boots, and various flats and heels that are barely suitable for walking down a sidewalk in this weather, let alone sailing the high seas.

Luke saw her look cute at Lola's party and at the movie, she reasons. He knows she cleans up well. Freezing to death is unattractive, despite the potential for foil-wrapped hypothermia rescue scenarios.

Hideous puffer jacket and hideous-er boots it is.

The drive to the Brosillards' is familiar now. Blair allows herself to briefly indulge in future speculation on the way: herself, a year from now, expert sailor and madly, mutually in love with Luke Brosillard, her first book about to publish to universal acclaim . . .

Except what is her book going to be about?

And if she's still in Oreville in a year, that means she'll still be living with her *parents*.

Doing what?

Fighting her brother for the bathroom?

Watching him go to high school every morning?

Smiling cheerfully at the dinner table after a long day of . . . work? In a . . . restaurant?

Luke is rich. Luke could sail her to a magical tropical island, and they could live in a beautiful hut by the sea and go swimming every day and eat whatever it is that people eat on magical tropical islands, all expenses paid by the Brosillards.

Bananas, perhaps.

Maybe Luke will sail her to the magical tropical island of free money today, and then she won't have to deal with telling Cam about Meredith Payne-Whiteley.

Or Mattie.

Or Luke, for that matter. Because what is she going to say to him?

Hi, so I sort of lied to you from the beginning, and originally I only got you to ask me out because I'm trying to find out what happened to your sister, but now I think I might have it pretty bad for you even though we've only hung out once?

Who was on the tropical island first, colonizer? Sophie says in her head.

Blair releases her tropical island into the gloomy December atmosphere with a sigh.

She's always let other people make decisions for her. But now that she's trying to make decisions for herself, she's not turning out to be much good at it.

Mattie answers the door, shutting it behind them and stepping out onto the front porch. "You didn't get in her room, did you?" they hiss.

"Hi to you too," Blair says.

"Did you try?"

"It wasn't that easy," Blair says. "I couldn't ransack your house while your brother was standing right there."

"What do you think you're going to find on the boat?" Mattie asks. "*She* doesn't sail."

"I didn't know that."

"You would've known if you asked me," Mattie says. "This isn't about her. This is about my brother. You're going on a *date* with my *brother*."

"It's not a date," Blair says weakly. "Did Lola sail?"

"She got seasick. Don't change the subject. You *like* him."

"I barely know him," Blair says.

"Girls always like my brother," Mattie says wearily. "They think they can fix him."

"What girls?" Blair asks. "Does your brother have a girlfriend?"

Mattie gives her a look of utter disdain. "You can't, you know."

"Be his girlfriend?"

"Fix him."

"I'm not trying to fix anyone," Blair says.

"Everybody loves a project," Mattie says disgustedly.

The door opens again behind them, and Luke peers out. Blair's stomach lurches as his clear green eyes meet hers.

"Hi," he says. "Is this a private conference?"

"I was saying hello," Mattie says. "To my *mentor*."

"Did you want to do that inside?" Luke asks mildly. "It's sort of cold."

Mattie huffs, stomps past him into the cavernous foyer. Shoulders hunched up to their ears, hair sticking up, oversized men's clothes dwarfing their small frame—for the first time, it occurs to Blair how much Mattie resembles Cam in temperament and sheer pigheadedness. Though Mattie's street-urchin aesthetic has an air of careful cultivation about it, whereas Cam's mismatched old clothes convey more of a distracted-genius-indifferent-to-fashion message.

Maybe that's deliberate too. Blair's never thought about it.

Luke winks at her. Luke and Blair follow Mattie into the kitchen.

"I'm getting the rest of my stuff together," Luke says. "Be right back."

He disappears down the hall, and Blair and Mattie stare at each other in the immense, sterile white room.

You could do surgery in here, Blair thinks. Did the cleaning lady come today? Or is this how it is all the time?

She wonders if Ruth cooks. Ruth doesn't look like someone who rolls her sleeves up often.

Blair breaks the silence first. "I'm sorry," she says, though she's not totally sure what she's apologizing for. "I'll try to get into Lola's room next time."

"She's always in it," Mattie hisses. "That was the whole point of going shopping with her. I spent two hours with her and you didn't do anything."

"I'm sorry," Blair says again. "How did the shopping trip go? Did she say anything useful?"

Mattie glares out the bank of kitchen windows. It is, Blair notes, starting to rain.

So much for that tropical island.

"It was fine," Mattie says.

"Fine?"

"She ate it up," Mattie spits. "'This sweater is perfect for your style, these pants are so cute, oh my god you look like Humphrey Bogart in *The Big Sleep*, want to watch it later?' She thinks she can butter me up. But she can't. It's not going to work. She can fake being nice to me all she wants, but I know what she really is."

"Fake being nice?" Blair asks. "What if she's just . . . nice?"

"How can she be nice? She's a liar. She's a fraud. She's trying to get something from us, and I don't know what it is or why she's here!"

"Right," Blair says.

"She can fake all this stuff she knows about me—"

Mattie stops.

"All what stuff?" Blair asks.

"Nothing," Mattie says.

"Mattie."

Mattie's jaw works. "She talked about something that happened with me and Darren and Lola before she was kidnapped. Just the three of us. We went to these hot springs Darren and Lola loved. I don't know how she knows. But she can't fool me. You have to find out how she knows. It could tell us who she is. What she did with my sister."

Mattie's expression is a study in misery.

Blair thinks again about what it's like for them in this house.

Ruth, cold and often cruel.

Luke, caring but unable to help—and, Blair admits to herself, perpetually stoned.

And now Lola. Whether she's the real Lola or a fake, she's the only person in Mattie's life who's trying to build a relationship with them.

Blair doesn't want to push Mattie. Not here, not now.

But why would a stranger do that?

Why would someone who isn't Mattie's real sister care?

How would she know about something that happened years ago, when Mattie was the only other person there?

"You don't believe me," Mattie says.

"Of course I believe you," Blair says.

Mattie shakes their head. "I knew it," they say.

"Knew what?" It's Luke. Mattie and Blair both jump. He's wearing a heavy jacket that looks official, waterproof, and extremely expensive, and a waxed-canvas duffel bag is slung over one shoulder. A wool watch cap is pulled low over his ears. Blair can tell from where she's standing that it's cashmere.

I am way out of my league, she thinks. *On all sides.*

"Knew I picked the wrong essay topic," Mattie says, without missing a beat. "Blair had Mr. Stone for freshman English too. She was giving me advice."

"He's a softie," Blair says. "He'll like whatever you write about, as long as you work in something he said in class like it's a really brilliant observation."

"Great idea," Mattie says, their voice flat. "Thanks, Blair." They give their brother an inscrutable look and march off in the direction of their bedroom.

Luke watches them go, his expression quizzical.

"If you ever figure out what Mattie actually means when they say something," he says finally, "definitely let me know."

"Deal," Blair says. Their eyes meet again.

Blair feels like a traitor. But she likes the way Luke's looking at her. Her phone buzzes in her pocket, but she ignores it. Their eyes hold and the moment thickens, gains weight.

If Blair takes one tiny step forward, she'll be close enough to kiss him.

Her phone buzzes again. She reaches into her pocket and thumbs it to silent.

"You ready?" Luke asks.

"Ready as I'll ever be," Blair says.

They're on their way to the harbor when a torrential down-pour loosens itself from the leaden sky. Blair turns her wind-shield wipers all the way up.

Luke slaps his forehead with one hand.

"I'm an idiot," he says. "I meant to bring an extra jacket for you. I took all the foul-weather gear off the boat to get it cleaned last month and I haven't put it back yet. Do you have a raincoat?"

"Not with me," Blair says. "Which makes me the idiot."

"Not an idiot," Luke says, smiling at her from the passenger seat. "An optimist."

As if it's heard him, the rain stops as suddenly as it started. "See?" Blair says.

"Still, you should have one," Luke says. "It's going to rain again. This is Washington."

"My house is on the way to the harbor," Blair says. "I can run in and grab something."

"Probably a good idea," Luke says. "Sorry."

"No worries," Blair says, turning off from the harbor road. "It'll take five minutes, tops."

But it won't take five minutes, tops, she realizes as she pulls into her driveway.

Because Cam's standing on her front porch, her mouth open in an almost comical O of astonishment as she clocks Blair be-hind the wheel and Luke in the passenger seat.

Astonishment that's turning to anger.

"Ah, shit," Blair says.

———

BLAIR IS EXPOSED IN A LIE,
PART TWO

Blair hasn't been answering her phone all morning, which is a problem, because Cam's almost certain she's figured out where Becca will be this afternoon. Becca is an unlikely candidate for Gambling Addiction, Living with Cancer, or Family of Alcoholics. Disordered Eating, maybe.

But Substance Abuse and Trauma, which meets Sunday afternoons and Thursday nights near the harbor, seems a sure bet.

Cam doesn't want to go alone. Mattie doesn't have a car, or a driver's license. It's not like she can ask Irene for a ride. (*Hey, Irene? So I totally abused the information you gave me in confidence to support me in seeking help for my own problems because I want to confront a vulnerable person about a highly traumatic experience—oh, did I mention Blair and I are investigating another maybe-missing girl's sort-of disappearance?* No.)

And this whole thing is Blair's deal, anyway.

So where is she?

Cam's stewing in her room. Kitten snores thunderously at her side. He gets this occasional rattling wheeze she doesn't like the sound of.

It's not nice to think about Kitten getting old. He's been a part of her life for almost as long as she's been sentient. And before she met Blair, he was her best friend.

Her only friend, but who's counting.

Cam remembers what happened the last time she considered Kitten's mortality. *Stop thinking about this,* Cam thinks. The last thing she needs is another panic attack.

She scratches Kitten under the chin. "You're fine," she says to him. He grumbles in his sleep, flexing one paw.

Think about something else, Cam thinks. What else is there to think about? Physics? Lola? No, not Lola.

Sophie.

I miss you so much, she texts Sophie, not really expecting a response. But her screen lights up seconds later.

I miss you too. How are
things with Blair?

                                     She's still being weird

About this missing girl?

                                     Honestly, I don't know

Cam watches the telltale dots forming and disappearing, thinking of Jenny.

What would Jenny do? Jenny would talk about her feelings. Before she can regret it, she types, Is everything okay with us?

What do you mean?

                                     Come on Sophie you know
                                     what I mean

No, Cam, I don't know what
you mean

                                     Are we still

                                     You know

Together????

                                     Yes

Of course we're still together
Cam

Why would you think we're
not together

You're never there

. . .

. . .

I know

I'm sorry

My world here is so different

There are so many things to get done

But nothing changes how I feel about you Cam I promise

Things will be better next year when you're out here

Did you hear from MIT yet

I got in

Full ride

CAMERON MUÑOZ WHEN WERE YOU GOING TO TELL ME

OMG OMG OMG OMG OH MY GODDDDDDDD

CAM I'M SO PROUD OF YOU

CONGRATULATIONS!!!!!!!!!!!!! !!!!!!!!!!!!!!!!!!!!!!!!!!!!!

Sophie I really love you

I really love you too Cam

We'll talk for real when I'm back for break

I miss you

I have to run I'm so sorry!!!!!
CONGRATULATIONS

> love you too Sophie

> What should I do about Blair
> though

> Sophie?

> Are you there?

Cam's own girlfriend has left her on read.

She resists the urge to throw her phone at the wall. Irene can't afford to buy her a new one.

"That's what I get for talking about my feelings," she says to Kitten. Kitten does not express interest in further discussion.

Still, it was not an entirely pointless exercise. She doesn't feel reassured, but she does feel somewhat lighter.

She is not crazy.

Blair *is* being weird.

Sophie *is* being distant.

At least it's out in the open now, even if nothing has been resolved. And at least the whole exercise didn't turn her into a sobbing, shuddering mess. Small victories.

For once, it isn't raining, and Blair's house isn't all that far away. Cam could do with a walk. She gives Kitten a kiss on the top of his head to convey her appreciation for his ongoing loyalty.

"I don't know what I'd do without you, old man," she says.

Kitten opens one eye and looks up at her. He is, she notes, drooling on her bedspread. "See you soon," she says. He opens the other eye, looking hopeful. "No snacks," she adds. "Sorry."

Cam stuffs her raincoat, notebook, and water bottle in her

backpack. What else should she bring, if they're really going to go on a Becca hunt? She has no idea what she might need. Maybe Blair will know. Blair knows a lot more than Cam does about talking through feelings.

Normally she does, anyway. Lately, Cam's not so sure.

The walk to Blair's is as refreshing as Cam had hoped. The air is cool, with the rich, peaty, rain-heavy scent of Washington in winter. Cam is no fan of Oreville, but she can still appreciate the peninsula's wild beauty.

Maybe someday she and Sophie will end up in their own cabin in the middle of the woods, like Jenny and her girlfriend. Cam can't hammer a nail straight, and Sophie will be too busy for carpentry, but perhaps Jenny can build it for them.

And the idea of a cabin in the middle of nowhere—Sophie laboring tirelessly alongside their First Nations neighbors toward a more just future, Cam solving the Beal Conjecture and securing its concomitant million-dollar prize—does have a certain appeal. Sophie will demand she reparate the million dollars, which is perfectly sensible, but she will first set aside a small amount to send Brad and Irene to Mexico, all expenses paid. And take Kitten to the finest veterinarians in all the land, so he can live forever.

"And they all lived happily ever after," she says to a crow pecking at a McDonald's bag in the middle of the shoulder as she passes. The crow hops twice and gives her a knowing look.

But when she gets to Blair's, there's nobody home. She rings the doorbell twice to be sure.

She pulls her phone out again. Blair hasn't read any of her messages.

"Where *are* you?" Cam asks aloud.

Which is when she hears the familiar froggy rattle of Blair's engine.

Blair, turning into her driveway. Reachable at last.

And not alone.

Cam sees who's in Blair's passenger seat.

"Blair Johnson, you are kidding me," Cam says.

And sees Blair clearly mouth the words *Ah, shit* behind the windshield when her eyes meet Cam's.

AN AWKWARD REUNION OF GREAT MINDS

"You did not," Cam is already shouting as Blair turns off the engine, so loud Blair can hear her inside the car. "You did *not!*"

"Oh my gosh," Blair babbles to Luke. "I am such a space cadet. I, uh, made plans with Cam for today! I totally forgot!"

"She seems kind of pissed," Luke observes neutrally.

"She's a passionate person," Blair says. She unbuckles her seat belt, opens the door. "This will just take a minute," she says to Luke.

"I can't believe you!" Cam is already at her door, on the verge of dragging her out of the car by her elbow.

"Cam, I can explain," Blair says. "We're—I'm—" She escapes the car, shutting the door on a bemused Luke.

"*You're on a date with Mattie's brother,*" Cam snarls, blotchy with fury. "What are you *doing*? Does Mattie *know?*"

"Yes," Blair says.

"You *both* knew and you didn't *tell me?*"

"It's not like that—" Blair tries, her cheeks bright with embarrassment.

"No? What is it like, then? Tell me, Blair, because I'm very interested in hearing *what it's like.*"

Luke has gotten out of the car. He comes around the front to where Cam is shout-whispering at Blair.

"Hey, it's Cam, right?" he says easily. "You and Blair are helping Mattie out at school."

Cam snaps her mouth closed on whatever she was about to say to Blair.

"Yes," she says savagely.

"That's so cool," Luke says.

"What?" Cam asks.

"That you're doing that," he says in the same placid tone. "I'm really grateful. They need that. I'm sorry to screw up your afternoon."

"*What?*"

"I badgered Blair into coming sailing with me. I didn't know you already had plans." A fat drop of rain hits him in the middle of the forehead, and then another. He gestures at the sky. "This is crappy weather anyway, even for me. We can take a rain check." He gives a rueful grin at his own bad joke.

"I'm so sorry," Blair says, unsure of who she's apologizing to.

"Oh, it's *fine,*" Cam says stagily. "Don't let *me* get in the way. I'll just *walk* back home now."

"No, don't do that," Luke says.

Blair marvels at his approach; he is utterly serene in the face of Cam's fury. Maybe Blair should start smoking pot.

With no one to combat, Cam deflates slightly.

"Why don't you drop me off at home, and you guys can go do your own thing," Luke says to Blair.

Without waiting for an answer, he walks back around to the passenger side of the car and gets in.

"That's my seat," Cam says.

"I'm sorry," Blair says again.

"I have something important to tell you," Cam says. "We have somewhere important to go."

"Now?"

"I'm not going to tell you in front of *him,*" Cam says.

"Let me drop him off," Blair says, trying for Luke's casual ease.

Cam huffs noisily, but clambers into the back seat without another word.

A painful silence reigns as Blair ferries Luke back to the Brosillards'. Sheets of rain shiver across the road, and Blair has to turn her windshield wipers all the way up.

"Don't get out, it's pouring," Luke says when they're in front of the house. He touches Blair's arm, smiles. "I'll call you."

And then he's gone.

Cam gets out of the back, stomps around to the passenger seat, slams the door, makes a production out of shaking rain from her wet hair.

"Where am I going?" Blair asks.

Wordlessly, Cam pulls out her phone, sends Blair the location tag for Becca's support group. She turns to look out the window, not sure she can trust herself not to cry, not sure if she can live with herself if she does and Blair sees it. Cam has had about enough of feelings for one week.

"I'm sorry," Blair says for a third time. "I should have told you."

"You don't say," Cam says. She blinks hard several times to check for tears. Nope, she's okay.

She looks at Blair, who's staring ahead at the water-slicked road. To Cam's surprise, she really does look sorry.

"Are you *dating*?" Cam asks. "That was fast."

"No!" Blair says. "No. I don't think so. We only hung out once. I promised Mattie I'd try to get into Lola's bedroom and look around. I got . . . carried away."

"Why didn't you tell me?"

"I didn't think you'd go for it."

"I wouldn't have," Cam says.

"That's why I didn't tell you."

"You really like him," Cam says. It's not a question.

"I barely know him," Blair protests.

"Come on, Blair. I've known you since you were twelve."

Out of the corner of her eye, Cam sees Blair's hands tighten on the steering wheel.

"You're right," Blair says. "I really like him."

"More than James?"

"Oh, James," Blair says philosophically. "James is a child. Luke is an adult."

"He doesn't look like much of an adult to me," Cam mutters.

"James is the past," Blair says.

"Do you still talk to him?"

"Not really. He sends me these plaintive text messages sometimes at like four in the morning. But I expect he's just drunk."

Sophie never sends me plaintive text messages, Cam thinks.

Then again, Sophie is not really the plaintive drunk-texting sort. And if she were, Cam probably wouldn't like her. Much to think about.

"Blair, you can't date Luke," Cam says. "What if he killed his sister?"

"What?" Blair exclaims. "Of course he didn't kill his sister. I think that girl *is* his sister."

"You do?"

"Don't you?"

"You're the expert," Cam says sourly. But then she relents. She can't stay mad at Blair; it's like getting mad at the best part of herself for being upstanding. Even though Blair hasn't been especially upstanding lately. "Yeah," she says. "I think it's her. But that still doesn't explain where she went for the last five years. He could know more than he's telling you."

Blair remembers Luke's phone conversation in the movie theater.

Of course I don't fucking know what she wants.

She sighs.

"What?" Cam asks.

"I heard Luke on the phone with someone," Blair says. "When we were at the movies. He said, 'You shouldn't even be calling me.' And then he said, 'Of course I don't effing know what she wants.' Except he said, you know."

"Fucking?"

"Yes," Blair says. "He said 'fucking.'"

"He said 'fucking' in front of a minor?"

"You leave me the fuck alone, Cameron P. Muñoz."

"Who was he talking to?"

"He said it was his aunt," Blair says weakly.

"His *aunt*?"

"She was calling to ask what Ruth wanted for Christmas. You know, Ruth *would* be hard to shop for. What do you buy a fascist millionaire who has everything?"

"And *you* bought *that*?" Cam is incredulous.

"There's no reason to think he knows anything about what happened to his sister. He was the one who said there was some-one else in the house the night she disappeared. Why wouldn't he say who it was, if he knew?"

"I'm sure you're right," Cam says, heavy on the sarcasm. "But let's pretend just for a minute he was lying. Who would he be talking to? Who wasn't supposed to call him? Why wouldn't he know what Lola wants?"

"He doesn't know anything about what happened to Lola," Blair says. "I can tell."

Cam snorts. "Yeah, since our all-powerful instincts sure helped us out the last time around," she says bitterly.

"Is that what this is about? Last year? Is that why you're so mad?"

"No!" Cam yells. "I'm not mad! This isn't about last year! It's about everyone being a liar!"

Blair's silent for a beat. Then: "Everyone?" she says.

Cam is overcome by the urge to disappear. She buries her face in the sleeve of her grubby hoodie, aware she is being absurd. Like a small child playing hide-and-seek, lying in the middle of the floor with her eyes covered: If she can't see Blair, maybe Blair can't see her.

"Cam, did something happen with you and Sophie?"

"No," Cam says into her sweatshirt.

"Are you thinking about—the basement?"

"No!" Cam yells into a mouthful of fabric.

Blair pulls over, puts the car in park, and turns off the engine. She gently tugs Cam's arm away from her eyes.

"Look at me, Cam," she says.

"No," Cam says.

"Cam?"

"What?"

"There's something else I have to tell you," Blair says.

"No," Cam says. "I don't want to know. I want to go home. I don't want any of this. I changed my mind."

"I need to tell you anyway," Blair says. "A week and a half ago, this lady called me from New York."

And then it all comes out, a mess of words so tangled she can't imagine Cam can understand her. She can barely understand herself.

Cam listens without saying anything as Blair explains that Meredith Payne-Whiteley is handing her everything she's ever wanted, all of it arranged for her on a platter.

The plane ticket to New York, the book proposal, the need for a new project, the whole thing.

All of it for Blair, and Blair alone.

Mattie showing up at Cam's with this incredible story.

Just at the right time.

"I thought it was a sign," Blair says. "Like, how is it possible that this is really happening to us *twice*? In a town the size of Oreville? I thought . . . I don't know what I thought. I thought this was my chance. To be—you know." It's hard to say the words, but she forces herself. "To be a writer."

"Blair," Cam says. "Why didn't you say something?"

"Because the podcast was your idea. I felt like I would be stealing all your hard work. And the longer I took to think about how to tell you, the harder it got. I'm so sorry, Cam. I'm . . . I'm really, really sorry."

"What on earth would I do with a literary agent?"

"What?"

Cam, incredibly, starts to laugh. "I can't believe you thought I'd care. Why would I ever want to write a book? Writing books sounds horrible. You can have this Meredith person. That podcast was the worst idea I've ever had."

"You're not mad?"

"Blair, I almost got you *killed* last year. I got your family sued. I thought you were acting like a freak because *you* were still mad at *me*."

"I've been acting like a freak?"

"A freak with a dirty secret."

"Oh," Blair says.

"Is that everything? You want to bone Lola's brother and you're about to get a bazillion dollars for your first book before you even write it and you're not actually pissed at me?"

"I don't want to bone Lola's brother," Blair says.

"Yes, you do."

"Maybe slightly." Cam snorts. "Fine," Blair says. "Yes. I want to bone Lola's brother."

"For your book."

"Solely for artistic purposes."

"But you're not mad at me?" Cam asks.

Blair turns to face Cam head on. She takes both of Cam's hands in hers.

"Cameron P. Muñoz, I am not mad at you," Blair says. "What happened last year was not your fault."

"Yes, it was," Cam says.

"You're not the teacher who had sex with his students. You're not the person who murdered Clarissa. You're the person who told the truth. What happened in that house was scary, and it was bad. But it was not your fault." Blair looks harder at Cam's face. "You don't believe me," she says. "But it's the truth. Are *you* mad at *me* for not telling you about Meredith?"

"No," Cam says. "Because I got into MIT, and I didn't tell you yet either."

"You *what*? Cam! Cam, that's incredible!" Blair shrieks.

"But it means I ruined your life and now I'm leaving," Cam says.

"That's all you've ever wanted!" Blair says. "The leaving part."

"It means I'm leaving *you*," Cam says.

"Oh, Cam," Blair says, leaning across the center console to wrap Cam up in a bear hug. "You lunatic. I love you."

"That's all the secrets?" Cam says into Blair's shoulder.

Blair releases her, sits back. "I quit track," she says.

"You love track."

"Not as much as I love this. Finding a story."

Cam nods.

"And I lied to Meredith too, sort of," Blair says. "I made her think Lola *is* a fake, because it's a better story."

"That's your problem now," Cam says. "Are you sure you're not mad at me for leaving?"

"Cam, I've known you were going to leave Oreville since the moment I met you. I could never be mad at you for leaving."

"You're going to leave Oreville too, though, right? Want to come with me?"

"To MIT?" Blair laughs. "I don't think I have a lot to offer them."

"You could move to New York and get a fancy apartment and drink whiskey," Cam says. "Isn't that what writers do?"

"Is it?"

"It's what they do on television."

"I think rent in New York is sort of expensive," Blair says.

"But this Meredith person is going to sell your book for millions of dollars. You can have all the whiskey and New York rent you want. I'll come visit you."

"Will you?"

"Of course," Cam says. "Can we go see the dinosaurs?"

"What dinosaurs?"

"At the Museum of Natural History. Irene says they have great dinosaurs."

"It will be my pleasure to visit the dinosaurs with you," Blair says. "You're sure you're not mad about the book? I can tell Meredith Payne-Whiteley to eat a bag of dicks."

"No!" Cam says. "No, don't do that. We have to get you out of Oreville. I don't ever want to come back here for a visit."

"What about Irene?"

"I'll think of something," Cam says.

"Cam, did something happen with Sophie?"

"No," Cam says. "Nothing. That's the problem. She's never there."

"Do you think she's cheating on you?"

"I'm trying not to. Think, I mean. What does Mattie think about being in a book?"

Blair is silent. Cam looks at her.

"You didn't tell them?"

"I'm waiting for the right time," Blair says.

"*Blair,*" Cam says.

"I know," Blair says. "I'll tell them. Hand to heart. Hand to god. Whatever."

"Tell them *now.*"

"Where are we going, anyway?"

"Don't change the subject," Cam says.

"Cam, I'll tell them."

Cam frowns at her. "I think I found Becca's support group," she says. "Blair Johnson, I will help you with this investigation. I will interview Becca now with you. I will look forward to your book. I will even stop arguing with you about Lola's brother. For now. Mostly. But you have to tell Mattie."

"I will," Blair says.

"We can't lie to them, Blair."

"I know," Blair says. "I let this get out of hand."

"Yeah, well, let me tell you from experience," Cam says. "That's not the way you want to do things."

"Are we good? You and me?" Blair asks.

"If Luke Brosillard gives you the clap," Cam says, echoing Irene with great satisfaction, "don't you come crying to me."

"Deal," Blair says, and starts the car.

BECCA HAS A FEW THINGS TO SAY

On Sundays, Becca's support group meets from two to four p.m. in a former real estate office between a weed store and a Domino's Pizza in a strip mall near the water.

Blair pulls into the parking lot at ten to four. They sit in the car, watching the door.

"The weed store is a little on the nose," Blair says.

"If you wanted to rent an office space *not* next to a weed

store in rural Washington, you'd have to leave the state. It's kind of depressing, though."

The office has a hollowed-out look, like a place that's been abandoned for a long time. There are still faded flyers with houses for sale papering the dirty windows. Cam can't see the prices from here, but she can imagine. Everyone wants a piece of the peninsula these days.

But the paint is peeling from the building's exterior wall in long brown strips, and the weed store has bars over all its windows. Rich people buy up acreage in the remote, scenic woods. They don't bother investing in the half-shuttered downtown.

At five minutes after four, a handful of people trickle out the real estate office door.

One of them is unmistakably the girl from Lola's party. She has the same heavy eyeliner, and her short dyed-black hair is tucked behind ears bristling with tiny hoops. Her nails are painted black, her fingers stacked with silver rings. She's wearing another short, stretchy dress over black tights with little cats on them and battered black Doc Martens. She's laughing at something one of the other support-group attendees has said to her.

"That's her," Blair says, sitting up.

"You go talk to her," Cam says. "I'll scare her."

Blair rolls her eyes, but she gets out of the car and walks confidently up to Becca. Cam can't hear what she's saying, but Becca's smile disappears. Becca shakes her head. Blair says something else. Becca looks around and back at Blair, scowling. Finally, Becca follows Blair back to the car.

"This is Cam," Blair says as Becca climbs into the back seat.

"Hi," Becca says curtly.

"Starbucks okay? It's the closest," Blair says.

"No," Cam says.

"Why?" Blair asks.

"They're on strike," Cam says.

"Right," Blair says.

"I like those milkshake things they have," Becca says.

"I don't cross picket lines," Cam says.

"*I'm* doing you a favor," Becca says.

Blair gives Cam a pleading look.

"Blair has to donate to the strike fund," Cam says. "And then donate extra for Becca and me."

"Fine," Blair says. She drives down the street and parks in front of the Starbucks, where a small handful of workers mill around outside with signs.

"I don't know how you live with yourself," Cam says to Becca.

"*Cam,*" Blair says.

Becca gazes at the striking baristas shivering bravely in the freezing damp.

"We can go to that place by the high school," she says, her voice slightly warmer.

"Thank you," Cam says. "Also, I appreciate your—" She has no idea what Blair has told Becca to get her to come with them. "Uh, helping us. With our . . . thing."

"It's cool," Becca says. "Mattie's a good kid."

Blair must've given her the same story she gave Darren, then, Cam thinks, as Blair drives to the next coffee shop.

Inside the café, Becca gives Blair a sly look and orders the most expensive thing on the menu, an extra-large mocha with several flavored syrups and a tower of whipped cream. Cam, ever budget-conscious, orders a small black coffee. Blair goes for a cappuccino. They settle into a booth with their coffees.

"Sorry you saw me flip out at Lola's," Becca says without preamble. "I was having kind of a bad day."

"I could see how you'd be mad," Blair says, feeling her way forward. "You were close, right? And she didn't invite you?"

"She hasn't called me," Becca says. "So I'm not really sure how I can help you with Mattie, if Lola doesn't want me there."

Blair remembers the screaming, sobbing girl she and Cam witnessed in Lola's backyard.

That's more than a bad day, she thinks. *That's something way bigger.*

If Lola ran away, did Becca help her? Or if someone really did kidnap her, does Becca know who? Did she help them? Is she scared she'll get in trouble, now that Lola's back? Is she still in touch with Darren? Did he threaten her?

Blair decides on a version of the truth. "We're worried about Mattie," she says, kicking Cam under the table to warn her to stay quiet.

"They worshipped her," Becca says. "I'm sure they're going through a lot right now. Not hearing anything for so long, and then . . ." She trails off and looks at her mountain of whipped cream.

"They're saying that girl's not Lola," Blair says.

Becca freezes. A slow flush creeps up her neck.

"That's not possible," she says.

"No," Blair says, feeling like a traitor. "I don't think so either. But it goes to show you how upset they are." Becca still won't look up. "You don't know what really happened to Lola, do you?" Blair asks.

"She got kidnapped," Becca says.

"That's what she says happened," Blair says. Next to her, Cam starts to say something. Blair kicks her ankle again, and she subsides.

"You don't believe her?" At last Becca meets Blair's eyes.

"I haven't asked her myself," Blair says. "But Mattie says she's vague on the details."

Becca sucks her lip piercing into her mouth, spits it out again. "Huh" is all she says.

"You were there that night, right?" Blair asks. "The night she disappeared?"

Becca's eyes flick around the coffee shop. "A bunch of people were there," she says. "She was still there when we all left. Whatever happened to her, it happened to her after we were gone."

"That's what you told the police," Blair says.

"Because it was the truth," Becca says.

"Lola was into some dark stuff, right?" Blair asks.

Becca's eyes narrow. "Who told you that? Who have you been talking to?"

"What about you?" Blair asks. "Were you doing heroin too?"

A multitude of emotions flicker across Becca's face, but she stays quiet.

"Were you and Lola close?" Blair tries.

"Why are you asking me this?"

"We're trying to figure out where she went," Blair says. "If something bad happened to her. For Mattie's sake."

"I think it's pretty obvious something bad happened to her," Becca says.

"Or she ran away," Blair says.

"I wouldn't know," Becca says.

"But you were close?"

Becca closes her eyes, breathes in deep and out again, repeats this a few times. As if it's an exercise someone's taught her. Cam remembers what Blair used to tell her last year, about the utility of calming breaths.

Cam opens her mouth. Blair shakes her head. Cam scowls but stays quiet.

When Becca opens her eyes again, they're brimming with tears. "We were really messed up that night," she says. "Darren came over and . . . I don't know, okay? It was a long time ago.

I thought Lola was my best friend, and then I never saw her again. I didn't hear a thing from her for five years. And then she comes back like that? Without a word? I felt like I was losing my mind. If I were Mattie, I'd be freaking out too."

"What do you think happened to her?"

Becca is quiet for so long that Blair's not sure she heard the question.

"I don't know," Becca says. "I thought she was dead. Maybe I'd feel better if she was."

"You don't mean that." That's Cam, unable to hold it in.

Blair knows what Cam's thinking, because she's thinking it too: Clarissa, who disappeared into thin air and stayed missing for twenty years.

No one who loved her knowing whether or not she was still alive.

No one who loved her able to fully let her go.

Whatever else they'd done, Blair and Cam had given Clarissa's friends and family closure.

But what if Clarissa hadn't been murdered? What if she'd run away?

What if she had come back, and hadn't bothered to tell the truth about where she'd been?

What if she'd showed up like nothing had ever happened?

"What about Darren?" Cam asks.

"What about him?"

"Did he think Lola was dead too?"

Becca's expression is unreadable. "Is this some kind of a test? Did he put you up to this?"

"A test of what?" Blair asks, surprised. "Were you and Darren . . ."

She doesn't finish the sentence, but Becca gets where she was going. "Me and *Darren*? Are you kidding?"

"Because he was your best friend's boyfriend?" Blair asks.

"Because he was Darren," Becca says. "He was that guy. You know that guy. Graduated years ago, still hanging around with teenagers. The guy who brings all the drugs, buys everybody booze. Darren was the only thing me and Lola ever fought about."

"Why?" Cam asks.

"Because Darren was a loser," Becca says. And then she puts her hand over her own mouth, her eyes wide. "Please don't tell him I said that," she says. "What does he want? Why did he send you to talk to me?"

"He didn't send us to talk to you," Cam says. "Why would he? Are you still friends?"

Becca is tearing her napkin into pieces, her drink untouched. "We were never friends."

"What about Luke?" Cam asks. "Why didn't you stay in touch with—"

Becca flinches.

Cam sits back. "You and Luke were a thing," Cam says.

Becca stares at her. "That's none of your business," she says, low and harsh.

"But you were," Cam says. Blair tries kicking her again, but Cam's moved her leg out of the way. "You know something about what happened that night, don't you? You and Luke? Did Lola run away? Was Darren—"

"Stop it!" Becca cries. "Just leave me alone! Why are you asking me about this? That was the worst night of my life, okay? This has nothing to do with Mattie. Why are you doing this?" Her voice is climbing to a heartrending pitch. All around them, stroller moms with lattes are turning to look at their table, mouths open.

"You *know* something!" Cam insists. "You know something about where Lola went, don't you? You owe it to Mattie—"

"I don't owe anyone in that family shit," Becca snarls. She

stands up so fast her chair tips backward, hitting the floor with a loud crack. There's not a single person in the coffee shop who isn't staring at them now, and a barista is coming around from behind the counter, walking toward them with a stern expression.

Becca grabs her bag from where it's fallen.

"Becca, please—" Blair pleads. But Becca's already stomping toward the door, slamming it behind her.

The barista has reached them. He's trying for authority, but is thwarted by his wispy facial hair and ill-fitting uniform. "Young ladies," he says.

"We're not any younger than you are," Cam snaps.

"Cam," Blair says, tugging at her arm. "We're going," she says apologetically to the barista, righting Becca's toppled chair. "Sorry about that."

"We're amassing quite a track record of getting walked out on in coffee shops," Cam says in the car.

"You did take kind of a hostile approach," Blair says.

"She knows something!"

"Sure," Blair says. "Something she's definitely not going to tell us now."

Cam's mouth twists, and she looks down at her lap. "Sorry," she says.

"It's okay," Blair says. "You, uh, meant well." She frowns. "But why would she think Darren sent us to talk to her? What did she mean by a test?"

"I don't know," Cam says. "What would he want to test her about? He didn't want to talk to us either. Especially after he realized you lied to him."

Blair doesn't get defensive, which makes her a better person than Cam. Not that this is a surprise. "Darren told us that Becca and Lola weren't close," she says thoughtfully. "But she said they were best friends. So, which one was it? And why would one of them lie?"

"He didn't want us to talk to her," Cam says.

Blair nods. "That's the only thing that makes sense. But why? What does he think she knows?"

"Darren was a lot older," Cam says slowly. "And he went to jail. More than once. What if it wasn't just for drugs? What if he hurt Lola?"

"Maybe," Blair says. "Mattie might not know that, but Becca would. If she and Lola were as close as she says." She shakes her head. "There's something she's not telling us, that's for sure. But I don't know what it is. This whole thing is like something out of a Lifetime movie."

"I'm sure it will be a bestseller," Cam says.

"Maybe," Blair says. "But first we have to get to the end of the story."

"She's afraid of him," Cam says. "She's afraid of Darren."

"Yeah," Blair says. "I think so too."

"I went to see Jenny yesterday," Cam says. "To ask her about doing drugs."

"You're going to start doing drugs?" Blair asks, startled.

"To ask her why people do drugs," Cam clarifies. "She said that people can change a lot when they get sober."

"You think Lola seems different to Mattie because she's not using drugs anymore?"

"Could be," Cam says.

"Maybe Lola didn't tell Darren and Becca she came back because she's trying to stay clean," Blair muses. "But she still knows what they did back then. If Darren set up the kidnapping, she could get him in a lot of trouble if she wanted to."

"You need to find out who Luke was talking to in the movie theater," Cam says. "And if you tell me 'his aunt,' I'm going to let Kitten pee in your car."

"Do you really think he'd lie to Mattie if he knew where Lola went? For five *years*?" Blair asks. "You've seen how he is around them. He loves them."

"You've seen him a lot more than I have," Cam says.

Blair winces. "Fair enough."

"Maybe Luke doesn't know anything," Cam says. "But I bet Darren does. Darren and his perfect new life. Didn't he say he's getting married?"

"Darren has a lot more to lose than Luke," Blair says.

"Yeah, since Luke is an adult who still lives with his mother," Cam says.

Blair ignores this. "If Darren did help Lola fake her kidnapping, and he's scared Lola or Becca might talk, what would he do?"

"We need to find out what happened that night," Cam says. "Before somebody gets hurt."

Day 10: Monday

MS. LACKMANN REVEALS A SECRET

BLAIR and Cam have assured Mr. Park that they are hard at work on their cowritten piece for the *Oreville High School Star*. Which, they have decided, will be a long-form editorial on the widespread cultural effects of America's true-crime obsession. Since, as they pointed out, they are uniquely qualified to cover this topic. (Jenna the irritating junior snorted aloud at this.)

They *will* write this piece.

For sure.

Soon.

Just not right now. Because right now, telling Mr. Park they are still hammering out a draft gives them a perfect cover for dissecting the mystery of Lola Brosillard during group work time.

Cam feels rather bad about this. Between the two of them, they have put poor Mr. Park through so much already. Lying to him is not nice. And they spend enough time together after school to think about Lola in their off-hours.

Still, a true crime that is maybe in the process of occurring is more compelling than the problem of true crime in the abstract, even if this means they are contributing to societal failure.

Plus, Blair points out, they could use their own fixation on the mystery of Lola as further personal experience for their article.

Blair can be quite convincing when she's on a roll.

Cam hopes she is as convincing on the page, if they ever get around to writing what they're supposed to.

"Becca doesn't want to tell us anything else; that's obvious," Blair is saying now. They're hunched together over her desk, pretending to take notes. Or, more accurately, they are taking notes; their notes are just about Lola instead of their assigned task. "And Darren's not going to talk to us again."

"What about Luke?" Cam asks.

Blair chews the end of her pen. "Now it's sort of awkward," she says. "But maybe I can find a way to bring up the night Lola disappeared."

"On your next *date*," Cam says, enjoying watching Blair squirm. "Maybe when he's *naked* he'll be more *vulnerable*."

"Leave me alone," Blair says.

Cam grins at her. "Never," she says. "What about the rest of the people who were at the party? Mattie has all their names."

Blair frowns. "If they had something to do with Lola's kidnapping, she would've recognized them and said something, right?"

"Maybe they saw something and didn't realize it," Cam says. "They all gave the police the same story, but it doesn't sound like the cops got too deep with their questions. Or maybe one of them helped Lola run away."

"If they did, they're hardly going to tell us," Blair says. "We could try calling them, but we don't even know what to ask."

"'Did you by chance notice a sinister van driving away with Lola and forget to mention it to anyone? Or perhaps help your friend fake her own kidnapping in order to hustle ransom money out of her mom?'" Cam suggests.

"Yeah, no," Blair says. "Maybe we're going about this the wrong way. Luke said Lola wanted to be a writer."

"You're the Luke expert," Cam says.

Blair ignores this. "So, where's her writing?"

"What do you mean?"

"Lola was fifteen the summer she disappeared. She would've been a freshman the year before."

"At Oreville," Cam says, realizing what Blair's getting at.

"Somebody must remember her. We could ask Mr. Park if she was in Journo. Or find out who her English teacher was. Mr. Stone only started a couple of years ago, but Ms. Lackmann has been at Oreville forever."

"What do you think her teachers could tell us that Mattie can't?"

"She didn't tell Mattie everything," Blair says. "Mattie was a kid. They didn't know Lola was using drugs."

"Did you tell them about that?" Cam asks.

Blair's mouth tightens.

"*Blair*," Cam says. "You're going to, right?"

"Do you think they need to know?"

"Are you kidding?"

"Mattie's already having such a hard time. How can I tell them that their sister was also a drug addict dating a drug dealer? Everything we find out is like tearing up this image they had of their sister as perfect."

"Mattie was the first person to tell us Lola wasn't perfect," Cam says.

"True. But we know she kept a lot of secrets from them. If she faked her own disappearance, she didn't tell them that. She wouldn't have told her teachers that either, but maybe she told her teachers something she didn't tell anyone else. Or kept a journal. Maybe they remember something that could help us."

"We can't ask Mr. Park," Cam says, shooting a glance

toward the front of the room, where Mr. Park is obliviously marking papers.

His brow is furrowed mightily; his owlish glasses are slipping down his nose. Cam feels a surge of affection so strong it's almost a physical force.

What are we doing? she thinks. *Why are we lying to him? Again?*

Not for the first time, she ignores her better self. "He's going to know we're up to something the second we ask him a question," she continues.

"Anybody we ask is going to figure out we're up to something," Blair says.

"We *are* up to something," Cam says. "But what if we use the truth? A version of the truth, anyway. We can say we're mentoring Mattie and their sister was a big influence. We're trying to find any of Lola's old writing to share with them."

"Why wouldn't they ask Lola?"

"Ruth didn't want people looking too hard at Lola's kidnapping story. It's not like her return was in the newspaper. Her old teachers might not know she's back."

"That's a big 'might,'" Blair says.

"Do you have a better idea?"

"No," Blair says. She glances at the clock. "We've got fifteen minutes left. Let's go talk to Ms. Lackmann after class."

Cam looks down at her notebook, covered with scribbled notes detailing the increasingly dense mystery of Lola.

"True crime," she says. "Poisoning the minds of Americans."

Ms. Lackmann is an ageless white woman who has taught Freshman Comp and Introduction to Shakespeare for longer than Blair and Cam have been alive. (Since Introduction to Shakespeare is the only class on Shakespeare Oreville High has ever offered—and was, in fact, Ms. Lackmann's own creation—it is unclear what relationship to the Bard Oreville students are meant to progress to once their initial encounter has been established.)

Cam never had her, but Blair took Comp as a freshman and Shakespeare as a sophomore, and Ms. Lackmann has remained one of her favorite teachers ever since. She is a universally beloved Oreville institution, famous for pushing even the surliest Oreville miscreants into at least a grudging respect for the powers of Shakespeare, and also for creatively wording permission slips so that even the most Christian-parented students are granted leave to view Claire Danes's breasts in the Baz Luhrmann *Romeo + Juliet* each year.

They find her after the last bell, sitting at her massive old desk in her empty classroom gazing pensively out the window at the lowering December sky. The classroom is exactly as Blair remembers it—windowsills overflowing with plants, walls papered with faded posters from various Shakespeare productions around the world—and Ms. Lackmann is exactly as Blair remembers her, in ostentatiously arty black platform boots and flowy black garments of the sort generally sported by wacky substitute art teachers who like to talk about fermentation and shadow work.

"Blair!" Ms. Lackmann says, with such warmth that Blair feels a pang of guilt she's never thought to drop by Ms. Lackmann's room after school before. "And this is Cam, isn't it? To what do I owe the honor? Am I to be featured on a podcast?"

"Nothing like that." Blair laughs.

Ms. Lackmann winks. "Thank goodness," she says. "I forgot to put on my mascara this morning."

"We have a question for you about a former student," Blair says. "Lola Brosillard. Remember her?"

Ms. Lackmann raises an eloquent eyebrow. "Lola Brosillard,

who disappeared mysteriously? Are you sure this isn't for a podcast, Blair?"

"No podcasts, I promise," Blair says, relieved that this is the truth. Not the whole truth, but she doesn't want to lie outright to Ms. Lackmann if she doesn't have to. "We're mentoring her sibling, Mattie. Like an informal after-school kind of thing."

"I know Mattie," Ms. Lackmann says. "I don't have them this year, though. They're in Mr. Stone's second period."

"But you had Lola?" Cam asks.

Ms. Lackmann's expression is neutral. "I did."

"Mattie really worshipped Lola," Blair forges on. "And we don't know much about her, other than what Mattie tells us. We were wondering—I know this is sort of unorthodox, but do you remember anything about Lola's writing? Anything that could tell us more about what kind of person she was?"

Ms. Lackmann leans back in her chair, giving Blair a long look with her sharp blue eyes. "You know I can't tell you anything confidential about a former student, Blair," she says, and now her voice is not warm at all. "Even if she is missing. And even if it isn't for a podcast." The stress on "isn't" suggests Ms. Lackmann is not buying what Blair's selling.

"No, of course not," Blair says. "Nothing confidential. But maybe you have some of her old assignments, or something like that? Something we could look at?"

Again with that piercing stare. Blair tries not to fidget.

"If I did," Ms. Lackmann says finally, "I certainly wouldn't give them to you."

"Right," Blair says. There is a brief, uncomfortable silence. Then Ms. Lackmann relents.

"She kept an online journal," Ms. Lackmann says. "So I suppose that isn't private."

"An online journal?"

"An Instagram," Ms. Lackmann says, and smiles. "The technology keeps changing, but young people will always find ways to become poets and writers. She was tremendously talented." A shadow crosses her face. "It's devastating, what happened."

"She's—" Cam begins. Blair kicks her ankle.

"Cam looked at her Instagram," Blair says. "She didn't see anything like that."

"She only ever showed me on her phone," Ms. Lackmann says.

"Maybe it was a Finsta," Blair says thoughtfully.

"A what?" Ms. Lackmann asks.

"Never mind," Blair says. "Thank you. That's a big help."

"I hope you know what you're doing, Blair," Ms. Lackmann says.

"What do you mean?" Blair asks.

"You know perfectly well what I mean," Ms. Lackmann says, standing up. "Come and visit me anytime, if you want to talk about something other than my former students. But I'm afraid I have to get home now."

"Yikes," Blair says in the hallway.

"I think she might be onto us," Cam says dryly.

"You'd think she'd want to help us more," Blair says. "Since we solved the last one."

"She's protecting Lola," Cam says.

"Who she thinks is dead. Or missing. Or—something."

"Even dead people deserve privacy," Cam says.

"You didn't think that last year," Blair points out.

"Yeah, and look what happened."

Blair frowns. "I wonder if Lola told Ms. Lackmann anything else."

"About the drugs, you mean? Or if Darren was hurting her?"

"Something like that," Blair says. "Teachers are mandated CPS reporters, aren't they?"

Cam looks away from her, toward the fountain. Which, once again, someone has filled with dish soap.

"This is getting dark," she says.

Blair thinks of Becca's words. *I think it's pretty obvious something bad happened to her.*

"If Ms. Lackmann filed a CPS report, the police would know," Blair says.

"Detective Reloj didn't say anything about that when I talked to him."

"He wouldn't," Blair says. "I doubt he's allowed to. What was the name of the detective who worked the case again?"

Cam flips through her notebook. "Tom Bradshaw. He's retired, but maybe we could find him." But there's no enthusiasm in her voice.

"Is this really okay with you?" Blair asks.

"What do you mean?"

"Cam, I dragged you into all this. You don't have to help anymore if you don't want to."

"Are you kidding?" Cam's angry now. "You think I'm going to let you end up in a basement at gunpoint?"

"I'm not going to end up in a basement at gunpoint, Cam."

"I would've said the same thing last year. Blair, if Mattie's right, and that girl isn't Lola—that means she's *scary*. Or if she *is* Lola, and Darren hurt her back then, or kidnapped her, and is trying to stop us from finding out—I couldn't live with myself if anything happened to you."

"I can drop this," Blair says.

"Don't lie to me," Cam says in disgust. "After everything we've been through? I deserve better than that. You're not going to drop this. And I'm not going to let you do this alone."

Blair squares her shoulders. "Sorry. You're right. Let's go talk to Mattie," she says. "Together."

A BRIEF STOP AT THE BROSILLARDS'

This time, it's Lola who answers the door. She's wearing a soft gray cashmere sweater that brings out the siren green of her eyes. Cam had no idea you could tell a person's jeans were expensive. Except, looking at Lola, she can tell that Lola's jeans are expensive. How? she wonders. How can a pair of pants scream *I'm expensive*? She doesn't know. But she knows Lola's clothes cost a lot.

Maybe that's why you say someone looks like a million bucks.

Lola, she thinks, looks like a million bucks.

"Hi," Lola says. She gives Blair a knowing smile. "You here for Mattie, or my brother?"

Blair blushes a fetching pink. "Mattie," she says.

"That's good," Lola says, standing aside to let them in. "Since my brother's not here."

"Where is he?" Cam asks, trying not to fall over as she pulls her shoes off in the hallway.

Lola is so graceful, it's like she emits a force field that causes Cam to be even clumsier than usual.

Or maybe it's that Cam can't stop staring at her face.

Great, she thinks.

As if one of them sprung on one Brosillard twin isn't enough.

But that's not really what Lola makes her feel. It's nothing like the fizzy, giddy joy that floods through her every time she sees Sophie.

Lola's beauty is almost frightening. Like a tall mountain that would kill you real fast if you fell off it.

Ah, yes, Cam thinks. *Ye olde beauty of mountainous death.* It's a good thing *she's* not the writer.

"I don't know where my brother is," Lola says. "I'm sure Blair has his number, if you want to ask him."

She walks away from them on light feet. Cam, hurrying after her, trips over her own shoes and crashes into the wall.

"You gonna make it?" Blair asks.

"Shut up," Cam says.

Mattie is in their room, hunched over their desk, scribbling furiously in the thick notebook Blair recognizes as their Lola case file. They start at Lola's soft knock on the doorframe, a scowl creasing their features until they see Blair and Cam behind her.

"Hi, Blair. Hi, Cam." They give Lola an irritated look. "I was hoping for some privacy," they say stiffly.

Lola holds her hands up with a smile. "Of course," she says. "But I was wondering if you all might want to do something together."

"Like what?" Mattie asks, bristling.

"We could go get something to eat," Lola says. "I would love to get to know your friends."

"Right," Mattie says. "Your treat. Since you have Ruth's credit card."

An expression of hurt flashes across Lola's face and then is gone.

Either Lola is the best actress Blair has ever seen, or the hurt is real.

Interesting, Blair thinks.

"Okay," Lola says lightly. "I'll leave you all alone." And like that, she's gone, trailing a subtle perfume that smells like summer.

"Shut the door," Mattie says. "I don't want anyone eaves-dropping."

Blair obeys. If Mattie weren't so serious, it would almost be funny.

Because there's one person who Mattie reminds her of to an uncanny degree. The explosive chaos of their room, their untidy laundry piles, their overstuffed bookshelves, their prickliness, their absolute certainty that they're right.

Cam runs a hand absently through her hair. The back is sticking up, the way it always does.

Mattie and Cam even have the same cowlick.

"Did you find something?" Mattie asks.

"Sort of," Blair says. She sits on Mattie's bed. Cam gingerly clears a place on the floor and sits there, looking around at Mattie's noir-movie posters. Blair tells Mattie about their visit to Ms. Lackmann, Lola's writing Instagram.

"I think it must've been a Finsta," Blair says. "We looked at her public one, and there was nothing like that on there. Do you know anything about another account Lola might've had?"

Mattie shakes their head.

"What about a journal?" Cam asks.

"She had one," Mattie says. "She kept it with her all the time. But I never found it after she disappeared."

"Do you think she took it with her?" Blair asks.

"I don't know," Mattie says. "She didn't take anything else."

"You don't know her passwords, do you?" Cam asks hopefully.

Mattie shakes their head. "If she had a Finsta, I don't know anything about it," they say. "I wouldn't know how to log in."

"Mattie," Blair says carefully. "Do you think . . . is it possible that Darren was . . ."

"Darren was what?" Mattie asks.

"Hurting your sister," Cam says, since Blair can't seem to get the words out.

"What do you mean, hurting my sister?" Mattie's confusion is genuine.

"You know," Cam says. "Abusing her."

"No!" Mattie's protest is immediate. "No way! He loved my sister! He was so nice to us! He was the nicest person I knew back then!"

"Got it," Blair says.

"I mean it," they say. "Darren was great. He was special. He never would've hurt Lola."

"But he was—" Cam begins.

Blair cuts her off. "We'll keep looking," she says. "I'm sure you're right about Darren. What about Becca? The girl who showed up at Lola's welcome-home party? Did you know her back then?"

"I remember her from before, but not that well," Mattie says. "She was nice, though. She would always talk to me when she came over. Most of Lola's friends ignored me."

"Were she and your sister close?"

Mattie thinks for a moment. "I think so," they say. "She was over here all the time. But so were other people."

"We talked to her too," Cam says. "But she didn't want to tell us anything."

"You did? What did you ask her?"

"You didn't tell them?" Cam asks Blair accusingly.

"I was going to," Blair says.

"She didn't tell us much, honestly," Cam says. "But she did confirm the drugs. Sort of."

"What drugs?" Mattie asks.

"I, uh . . ." Blair says.

Cam gives her an incredulous look. "I talked to a police

officer we know," she says. "He let it slip that Lola was using drugs. Like, hard drugs. I thought Blair told you."

"I was going to," Blair says again.

"But you told them about the book, right?" Cam asks.

"Book?" Mattie asks.

"*Blair,*" Cam says. Blair is turning bright red. "Blair, you promised."

"*What book?*" Mattie asks.

So Blair tells them. Slowly. Painfully. About Meredith Payne-Whiteley. Her book proposal. Her big idea.

Which is, of course, Mattie's story.

When she's done, Mattie is silent.

"I'm sorry," Blair says. "I should have told you. I should've asked you. In Cam's kitchen. That first day."

"Yeah," Mattie says. Their voice is cold. "You really should've, Blair. Why didn't you?"

Cam doesn't say anything. Briefly, Blair resents her best friend for letting her dangle. But she knows that's absurd.

She doesn't get to be mad at Cam.

She dug this hole herself.

She takes a deep breath. "At first, it seemed like the wrong time. And then, I thought you'd say no. And the further we got, the harder it was to ask you."

"What if I do say no?" Mattie asks. "Are you going to go ahead without me?"

Blair meets their eyes. "No," she says. "If you say no, I tell Meredith to forget it. You have my word."

"But then you won't help me," Mattie says.

"We'll still help you," Blair says. "I mean, I'll still help you. I don't want to speak for Cam."

"That's very generous of you," Cam says.

"I'm sorry," Blair says. "I really, really screwed up."

"Yeah," Mattie says. "You did." They slump in their chair, run one hand through their unruly hair in a gesture that's a precise echo of Cam. "How long have you known my sister was doing hard drugs?"

"A few days," Cam says. "I could've told you that too. I thought Blair did. It might not be important."

"Of course it's important," Mattie says. "How could it not be important? Did you leave anything else out? You found out Lola could fly? You've been filming me this whole time without me knowing it? Ruth paid you to keep me busy? All of this is for another podcast?"

"No podcasts," Blair says. "Hand to my heart."

"It's 'hand to god.' Why should I believe you?" Mattie snaps.

"No podcasts," Cam says. "Unless Blair's making one she hasn't told me about."

"I'm not," Blair says weakly. "I promise. Do you want us to go?"

"Do whatever you want," Mattie says dully.

"Do you mean . . ." Blair shifts on Mattie's bed. "Does that mean I should leave?"

"Write your book," Mattie says. "I don't care. Why should I care? All I want to do is find my sister. You want to sell a book about it, suit yourself. I already told you I can't pay you. So you might as well get something out of all this."

Mattie blinks hard. Cam recognizes a person who is fighting valiantly not to cry because crying is too humiliating to bear in the situation that person finds themself in.

She sees it immediately, because she's been that person herself.

"Blair will show you anything she writes before she sends it to Meredith," Cam says. "She's going to swear in blood. And we're going to help you, the best we can. We don't know anything else that we haven't told you. Or at least, I don't."

"That's all of it," Blair says.

"And we think that Darren might've kidnapped your sister," Cam says. "For the ransom money. But that's just a theory."

Here it is, she thinks. This is the part where she and Blair tell Mattie the other thing they think: that if that's what happened, Lola might've been in on it too.

Despite all the lecturing she's been doing about honesty, the words won't come.

"There was no ransom money," Mattie says.

"That you know of," Cam counters.

"I would've known," Mattie says. "Darren couldn't do something like that. He wouldn't."

"He was a drug dealer, Mattie," Cam says.

"So?" Mattie stands up. "So what? So he brought drugs to parties sometimes, what's the big deal? He shouldn't have gotten arrested. We're not talking about an episode of *Narcos.* I thought you hated the police."

"I do hate the police," Cam says patiently, "but that doesn't mean Darren was a good guy."

"He was a great guy," Mattie says. "He was good to my sister, and he was good to me. He didn't have anything to do with what happened to her. He wouldn't do that."

Cam doesn't know what to say. She looks at Blair, who's looking at Mattie with pity. Cam might not be the most astute person in the world, but even she can work it out.

It's too much for Mattie to admit that their sister's entire life was a secret from them.

That Darren wasn't the gentle, dad-like older boyfriend, bringer of lollipops and mender of scraped knees, that Mattie remembers.

It's too much for them to take in all at once.

And if the girl in the bedroom next door is Lola, if she faked her own disappearance, or is keeping her mouth shut to protect Darren—

It's going to be worse.

And, on top of everything else, Mattie just found out the real reason Blair's helping them.

Cam can't imagine how alone they must feel. How close to the edge. She can't force them into the truth. All she can do is be there for them.

All she can do, now, is stay.

"I don't know who else to talk to at this point," Cam says. That much, at least, is the truth. "I'm not sure we can find out anything you don't already know. But we're going to try. And Blair isn't going to do anything that you're not okay with. Ever. And if you don't believe her, believe me. Because if she screws with you again, I'm going to kill her."

And then, to Cam—and Blair's—relief, Mattie laughs. "I'd like to see that," they say. "Isn't Blair the one who shot the man who killed Clarissa?"

"I'm a master of the ambush," Cam says. "Also, the guy who owns the gun range is sleeping with my mom. I can cut off Blair's supply of small arms at any time. Never make the mistake of underestimating my powers."

Mattie smiles at Cam. A real smile. "You can keep helping me. I still don't have a driver's license."

"Mattie, I'm so so—" Blair begins.

Mattie interrupts her. "Forget it," they say.

"I'll show you—"

"I don't care," Mattie says. "I don't want to talk about your stupid book. How are we going to crack my sister's Finsta? We don't even know how to find it."

Cam, idealess, looks at Blair.

"If that girl is your sister, she's going to be the first person to find out we're trying to get into her old social media," Blair says.

Mattie stares at her. "After all this, you don't believe me?"

"I'm just asking if you're sure you want to do this," Blair says.

"Are you serious?" Mattie snaps. "What do you think?"

"I have an idea," Blair says. "But Cam's not going to like it."

DAY 11: TUESDAY

A DISPLEASING ALLY IS
RECRUITED TO THE CAUSE

IT takes a considerable amount of groveling in the hall outside Journalism to get Jenna the irritating junior tech wizard to talk to them. Cam, happy to have the moral high ground firmly under her own feet for once, insists on Blair doing the dirty work. ("Jenna hates my guts." "She does not." "Blair, I'm not *degrading* myself." "Fine.")

"You want to crack a stranger's social media password why?" is Jenna's response when Blair explains that she and Cam are curious as to how a person would go about doing such a thing. "Is this for a podcast?"

"No!" Blair says. "This is for a hypothetical situation."

They're filing into the classroom. Jenna hovers as Blair and Cam heap their bags on their desks.

"It's for Blair's book," Cam says at the same time Blair says, "It's for our editorial."

"You're writing a book?" Jenna asks.

"An editorial," Cam says. "For this class. As you know. That's what I meant to say."

"What does scamming strangers have to do with true crime's effect on American society?"

"Please?" Blair asks.

Jenna rolls her eyes. "The easiest way would be to guess this hypothetical person's password. But I'm guessing you already tried that, hypothetically."

"How many people can actually guess someone else's passwords in real life?" Blair counters.

"Can't you, like, write an algorithm to do it?" Cam asks.

Jenna gives Cam a look of withering disbelief. "You sure you should be going to MIT? No, I can't, like, write an algorithm to do it."

"Okay," says Cam, unruffled.

"You could try a phishing scam," Jenna says.

"Wouldn't the original account holder still have to be around for that to work?" Cam asks.

"You're hacking a dead person's account?"

"Nobody's dead," Blair says quickly. "Just . . . inactive."

Jenna shakes her head. "You know what? I don't want to know. *I* don't live for attention. *I* don't want to get doxxed and sued."

"So how would you do it?" Cam asks.

Jenna doesn't want to help them, but she can't resist showing off. Cam can relate. "A SIM swap might work," Jenna says. "You call this person's mobile provider and pretend you're them and you lost your phone. The company can port their phone number to a new SIM card, so you get all their incoming calls and texts. Once you can access their authentication texts, you can reset all their social media account passwords. You just need to be a smooth talker with enough personal information to convince the phone company you're that person."

"Jenna, that's brilliant," Blair says.

"It's literally a Wikipedia entry," Jenna says. "Which you would know, if you asked Google instead of bothering me."

"I'm not as smart as you," Blair says piously. Jenna looks slightly less cantankerous.

"Lola disappeared five years ago," Cam says to Blair. "What if her phone number doesn't work anymore?"

"Lola who?" Jenna asks. "Never mind," she amends quickly.

"She could've been on a family plan," Blair says. "Maybe Ruth never deactivated her number."

"Would this SIM card thing work for a phone that hadn't been used in five years?" Cam asks Jenna.

Jenna shrugs. "No idea, but I don't see why not. As long as the number is active."

"It's worth a shot," Blair says.

"Just, like, FYI?" Jenna says with a sarcastic Valley girl inflection. "This would be, like, totally illegal?" She gives Cam a sardonic look. "Not that that's stopped you before."

"Thanks," Blair says.

"Don't mention it," Jenna says. "Like, for real."

At the front of the room, Mr. Park is eyeing them over the rim of his glasses.

"I'm going to my desk now," Jenna sings out. "Thanks *so much* for the *help* with that *thing*, Blair."

Mr. Park's eyes narrow. Blair can see him thinking the obvious: Jenna would never, ever, in a million years, ask Blair for help.

But she can't help herself. She pulls out her phone.

Meet us at my car after school, Blair texts Mattie.

"Blair!" Mr. Park barks. "Phone out of sight or it goes in my desk!"

"Sorry!" Blair says brightly. Heads swivel.

At her own desk, Jenna smiles.

In her pocket, Blair's phone buzzes.

And then it buzzes again.

At last, Mr. Park turns away. Blair bends down, pretending to look in her bag, as she checks her phone.

Two messages.

One from Mattie: OK see you then

And one from Luke: Rain check tomorrow night?

AN INTERVIEW WITH OFFICER MILITIA

Irene's at work, so Blair drives them to Cam's. They pile into Cam's room. Kitten follows, looking interested. Perhaps Mattie or Blair has brought along snacks for cats? No? Are they certain about this?

Blair is the best actor of the three of them, so she pretends to be Lola on the phone. Mattie supplies the relevant identifying details. And it's terrifyingly easy to get the Brosillards' cell provider to port Lola's old phone to Blair's. All Blair needs is a scattering of personal details, provided by Mattie, and a story (lost her old phone years ago, only just noticed all her social media is two-step verified at the old number).

It's not a good story.

But it works.

A single text message lets them reset Lola's password. And they're in.

Lola's secret Instagram has zero followers and few posts. She updated it once every few weeks. The pictures are similar to her public account—trees, the ocean, campfires—but the captions are as long as Instagram allows, sometimes spilling over into the comments.

Blair scrolls through, skimming.

"What does it say?" Mattie asks.

Kitten has given up on snacks, and now he's sprawled across their lap, purring like a small personal thundercloud. Cam is mildly jealous, but can't begrudge Mattie their new best friend. Kitten has an unerring knack for knowing who in a room is most in need of comfort. "Blair, let me read it," Mattie says. "What did she write?"

"Mattie, this is pretty rough stuff," Blair says. "I don't know if you want to see it."

"I don't care," Mattie says. "I can take it. Whatever she says about me."

"It's nothing bad about you," Blair says quickly. "It's just that Lola was definitely really, really sad—oh my god."

"What?!" Mattie and Cam cry in unison.

"I just checked the date on her last post," Blair says. "It's from the night she disappeared." Blair turns her phone so they both can see it.

Another blurry night shot. The caption is stream of consciousness, uncapitalized.

another night the same night as always. when does it get better. does it ever. maybe not for someone like me. darren says i think too many dark things. that i have to look for hope where hope seems absent. i wish i had what he has. to be able to look at the world and see anything other than people dying, animals dying, the earth dying. he says we can take care of each other until the end. he says that's what people do. that's what love is. i wouldn't know, i said, and his face fell. and that's when i thought all i do is ruin everything good. all i do is ruin. all i do is—they're telling me to put it down and join them what am i supposed to say

"All I do is what?" Mattie asks, snatching the phone from Blair.

"That's it," Blair says. "That's the end of the post."

Mattie looks through Lola's Instagram in silence. Their eyes are brimming with tears that spill over as they read, leaving glistening tracks across their cheeks that they don't bother to wipe away. It's like they're in a trance.

"Mattie," Cam says gently. Mattie ignores her. Cam reaches

out and puts one hand on Mattie's shoulder. "Mattie, look at me."

"She was so sad," Mattie says. "I had no idea she was this sad. I should've helped her."

"Mattie, you were a little kid," Cam says. "This is so much bigger than anything you could've helped with."

Cam takes the phone from Mattie's limp hand. They don't protest. Cam looks down at the screen.

Then she looks again.

"Wait," she says. "You can see a person in this last one."

"The one she posted the night she disappeared?" Blair asks.

"Yeah." Cam zooms in. "I can't tell, but is that Becca?"

She hands the phone to Blair.

"It could be," Blair says, passing it back to Mattie. "But we already knew she was there that night."

"Yeah," Cam says, "but look at the time stamp. Lola posted that at three-thirty in the morning. Becca said she left at two."

"She could've posted it after everybody went home," Blair says.

"'They're telling me to put it down and join them what am i supposed to say,'" Mattie reads. "She's talking about her phone! She posted this while someone else was talking to her."

"Maybe it wasn't Becca talking to her," Cam says. "Maybe the picture is from earlier in the night. But if she took the picture when she posted that, Becca lied to us. And Luke lied to the police."

"He could've gone to bed early," Blair says.

"Then why didn't he say that? Why make such a big deal out of everybody leaving at two, when they didn't?"

"Luke would never hurt Lola," Mattie says, ferocious. "Never."

"But—" Cam begins.

"He wouldn't!" Mattie says.

"I believe you," Cam says. "But what if he's covering for someone? Like Darren? Or someone we haven't found yet?"

"Or Lola," Blair says.

"Or Lola," Cam agrees. Mattie starts to protest, but Cam talks over them. "Mattie, I know you don't want to hear this, but we should consider the possibility that the girl who came back *is* your sister. And if she is, she's been lying to everyone too."

Mattie gives her a terrible look. *Et tu?*

"Fine," Cam says. "She's a sociopathic doppelgänger. But we should talk to Becca again. *And* Luke."

Blair flushes. "I'm, uh, seeing him tomorrow night," she says.

"For the investigation," Cam says dryly.

"I can ask him about that night again," Blair says.

"If he lied to the police, I doubt even your feminine wiles are going to get the truth out of him," Cam says. "But if we can prove that Becca was still at the Brosillards' after she said she left, we'll have leverage when we go talk to her again."

"But the security footage *shows* everyone leaving at two," Mattie says, frustrated.

"How many cars?" Cam asks.

Mattie pulls their Lola notebook out of their bag, flips through it until they find the page they're looking for. They hand it to Cam.

"You wrote down the make and color of each car, the license plate number, and the time it left?" Cam asks.

"So?" Mattie is defensive.

"So that's great," Cam says. "That's amazing. But it doesn't tell us who was in each car."

"What was the name of that cop again?" Blair asks. "The one who worked the original case?"

"Bradshaw," Cam says. "Tom Bradshaw. But he's retired."

Blair's already taken her phone back from Mattie to search.

"Look at this," she says, holding out her phone again so they can see it.

Former Detective Tom Bradshaw has his own website. It looks like it was built by a twelve-year-old in approximately 1993: fluorescent green typewriter font against a cobalt blue background, photographs crowded along the edges. The pictures are of American flags and bald eagles. There's one of an older white man, presumably Tom Bradshaw, holding an assault rifle and looking stern.

A cluster of headers across the top of the site read THE FACTS ABOUT ANTIFA, MY JOURNEY TO THE TRUTH, and PREPARATION FOR PATRIOTS (SUBSCRIBE FOR MY FREE NEWSLETER!!!!!).

"This man is going to shoot us if we interview him," Cam says.

"Maybe we should bring Brad," Blair says. "But this is the website of a man desperate for publicity. We could pretend to give it to him. Tell him we're working on another podcast."

"What does Lola's disappearance have to do with this stuff?" Mattie asks.

"Nothing," Blair says. "But he doesn't know that. He'll talk to us."

"I don't want to talk to this dreadful man," Cam says morosely. She waves off Blair's protest. "Call him. But if he starts saying heinous things about trans people or touches his guns, we're out."

"Brad has a gun collection," Blair says.

"Brad's not a Nazi," Cam says.

"I meant we could raid it," Blair says.

Cam makes a strangled noise and falls backward on her bed. Kitten, sensing he is needed, abandons Mattie's lap and clambers onto her chest to knead industrious biscuits.

"That was a joke," Blair says.

"Not funny," Cam says.

"We won't go talk to him in person," Blair says. "Too scary. We'll call him. There's a phone number right here."

"He must really be nuts if he has his phone number on the internet," Mattie says.

"Whatever," Cam says, her voice coming out funny thanks to Kitten's considerable weight. "Give Officer Militia a call. Give him my home address, while you're at it. Tell him Kitten is undocumented."

Blair is already dialing.

Retired Detective Tom Bradshaw answers his phone right away. *Missing Clarissa?* Yes, of course he's listened to *Missing Clarissa*. He found it hampered by wokeness, but can't fault their results. And they're young; they have time to learn the error of their generation's ways. Did they record it in an aquarium, though?

"We're very sorry, sir," Blair says. "About the—wokeness. And the recording quality. You're right, we've learned a lot since then. Do you have time to talk to us for—uh—a new podcast? About another cold case? You do? When is convenient for you? Now? Seriously? Great! Yes, a video call so we can record! What a great idea. Let's switch to video. Just a second."

She props her phone up so that all three of them can see. A few seconds later, Retired Detective Tom Bradshaw's enormous face fills her screen. He is holding his own phone directly under his nose, offering an alarming view of his extravagant nostril hairs.

"Good afternoon, girls!" he bellows. "How can I help you?"

"We're researching a case you worked on a few years ago, and we were wondering if we could talk to you about the particulars," Blair says.

"For a new podcast?"

Blair angles her phone slightly so he can't see Cam's face.

"Yes, sir," she says. "Like I said. We're hoping this one has an even bigger, um, footprint."

"Call me Tom, sweetheart. And I'd be happy to help. I can offer you some pointers on narrative structure. You did pretty good with the first one, for amateurs, but with the help of a real expert—"

Cam makes a retching noise.

"Problem with your signal?" Bradshaw bellows.

"I think so, sir. Tom." Blair pokes Cam in the side. "Anyway, that would be wonderful if you could help us with our new project. Since you have so much to offer. And we really don't know how to do anything at all on our own."

"Yes, yes," Bradshaw agrees briskly. "What's the case?"

Much to Blair's relief, he moves the phone away from his nasal cavity and props it up so that he can stay on camera without holding it. They can see more of what's behind him. He's in an office or living room—wood paneling, an immense American flag hung over a fireplace, a resigned-looking deer head staring into the abyss. Next to the fireplace, a bookshelf is stuffed with pamphlets and papers. Blair is grateful she can't read any of the titles.

"You investigated a kidnapping five years ago," Blair says.

"Ah," booms Bradshaw. "That would be the Brosillard girl."

"You remember?" Mattie blurts.

Bradshaw's face jerks toward the screen again as he peers at them.

"This is M—uh," Blair says. "Our, uh, intern." Better to leave Mattie's identity out of it. If this conversation blows up in their faces, Blair doesn't want Bradshaw to be able to find Mattie afterward.

"Hello, young lady," Bradshaw says.

Mattie winces but doesn't correct him. Mattie, Blair thinks, is used to dealing with people like this in Oreville. She wants to defend them, but she doesn't want to antagonize Bradshaw before they get the information they need. Out of view of the camera, she gives Mattie's hand a squeeze. Mattie squeezes back. Cam opens her mouth. This time, it's Mattie who pokes her in the side.

"Sure, I remember the Brosillard case," Bradshaw says, oblivious to the complex network of decisions unfolding on Blair's end of the call. "That was no kidnapping, though. That girl ran off." He shakes his head mournfully. "See it all the time. Beautiful girl. Led astray. *Drugs,*" he enunciates.

"Right," Blair says.

"I'm an expert," Bradshaw says again. "Nothing gets past me. I'm sorry to tell you girls, but there's no mystery here. Now, if you'd like some *real* ideas for your next podcast, I can talk to you about the war on American values—"

"Right," Blair says hastily. "Of course, sir. Tom. We'd never imagined that you missed anything. Because you're such an expert. It's just that, with the Brosillard case, uh . . ."

Shit, she thinks. Why didn't she consider this? Of course he's not going to listen to them. He's the one who said Lola ran away in the first place. They can't get him to talk without disagreeing with him. And Tom Bradshaw is clearly not a man who tolerates disagreement.

And then Blair is struck with a left-field fit of genius that is either so preposterous Bradshaw will hang up on her immediately or so perfect he will give them everything they need in a gift basket with a bow.

Nothing ventured, nothing gained, Blair thinks, and crosses her fingers.

She lowers her voice to a conspiratorial tone. "The thing is, sir—Tom—she's returned to the family domicile. We've been, uh, tailing her. A lot of suspicious behavior. And what you're saying about a war on American values? We couldn't agree more. The thing is, based on her activities, we think she's been working this whole time with . . ." Blair leans in for the kill. "*Antifa.*"

The effect of this disclosure is immediate and extraordinary.

Cam makes a noise like a steam engine derailing.

Mattie lets their breath out in an explosive snort.

And on the other end of the call, Bradshaw's mouth drops open. He is absolutely rapt.

"Of all the . . . *goddamn.* God*damn.* You're kidding me," he breathes.

"No, sir," Blair says. "She's been under their thumb all along. Antifa." She is working hard not to dissolve into hysterical laughter herself. "We think the party she disappeared from was a, uh, recruitment event. For more antifa. So we need your help to find out who was there."

"Sleeper agents," Bradshaw says, nodding. "Yes. They do that. Infiltration. They could be any one of us."

"Yes, sir," Blair says. "And you're the only one who can help us stop them."

Cam has rolled away from the camera's eye, shaking with suppressed laughter.

Hold it together, Johnson, Blair tells herself sternly. *Get the names out of him, and then you can lose it.*

"There could be sex trafficking," Bradshaw says in solemn tones. "That's often what they're after. Perverse sex."

"We haven't gotten into the details yet," Blair says. "But we have the license plate numbers of the cars who were at the Brosillard place the night the girl says she was kidnapped. We need names to go with the numbers."

Bradshaw nods. "Of course. Goddamn," he says. "Of all the—goddamn. There was no sign of it."

"Like you said, sir, they could be anywhere," Blair says. "Any one of us. They're very good at covering their tracks."

Bradshaw shakes his head sorrowfully. "They want the downfall of America," he says. "The end of freedom. They won't stop at anything less. Hold on a second, girls. Let me check my files. It's possible I kept the information you need when I packed up my office."

He stands up and walks away from the phone. The camera focuses on the deer head, which gazes at them implacably. They can hear several crashing noises from off-screen and a loud curse.

"Oh my god," Cam whispers.

"Shut up," Blair hisses. "I can't laugh yet."

Mattie, she is grateful to note, is staring at her with admiration.

"Unbelievable," they say softly.

After more mysterious background noise—heavy boxes being dragged, perhaps, and a few drawers opening and closing, and a lot of unidentifiable thumping—Bradshaw is back on camera, triumphantly holding up a battered notebook.

Blair arranges her features as best she can into a solemn expression.

"Knew I still had this somewhere," Bradshaw says. He gives the camera a significant look. "Now, girls, I'm going to give this information to you freely, because I believe in justice. These people must be stopped. But you come to me first when you have enough of a case to confront this girl. This is dangerous stuff, you hear me? These people will stop at nothing. *Nothing.* You understand me?"

"Yes, sir," Blair says.

"I want to be a part of this," Bradshaw says. "You need my protection."

"You're already doing your part, sir," Blair says.

"A patriot's part *never stops,*" Bradshaw says, holding up an admonishing finger. "You girls are playing in the big leagues now, you understand? And when you go to the big leagues, you bring the big guns."

"My mom's boyfriend has lots of guns," Cam says brightly.

"Good," Bradshaw says, nodding. "Good. You keep that sensible head on your shoulders, young lady, and you'll get through this in one piece. But I'm coming with you when you—"

"Absolutely," Blair says. "You'll be with us every step of the way. Wouldn't dream of moving forward without you. Um, you have that list?"

Bradshaw nods and reads them a list of names, car models, and license plate numbers. Mattie writes them down in their notebook as he lists them off, their face as grave as a tombstone.

"That's it, then," Blair says. "That's what we needed. Sir, you've helped the side of justice today."

"And you'll call me as soon as—"

"What?" Blair says loudly. "What? I can't hear you, sir. Are you there? I think I've lost my signal." Blair disconnects the call and looks at her phone in dismay.

"Shit," she says. "Now he has my phone number."

But Cam and Mattie are both laughing too hard to reply.

STRATEGY

There's no reason for Cam to go with them when Blair drops Mattie off at home, and it'll be out of the way for Blair to bring Cam back to her apartment afterward. But Cam goes with them anyway, and Blair doesn't protest. She turns the defrost all the way up before her engine's warm, and a blast of frigid air sends them all shivering.

"I hate December," Blair says.

"It's not so bad," Cam says.

"Was he really a Nazi?" Mattie asks.

"Probably," Cam says. "A lot of those guys got radicalized out here during the public park standoffs between the far-right militias and the Bureau of Land Management. Remember the Bundy family? Those guys armed to the teeth and trying to take over wildlife refuges? The Pacific Northwest has been home to people like that since white people got here, basically. Starting with the treatment of Native people, obviously, and then the Black exclusion laws in Oregon and the Chinese Exclusion Act, which expelled a lot of the Chinese people in Washington. You don't have to dig very deep to find a lot of ugly history here."

"We didn't learn any of that in school yet," Mattie says.

"You never will," Cam says. "I learned it from my girlfriend."

Blair catches the look that flashes across Mattie's face from her rearview mirror. "You have a girlfriend?" Mattie asks.

"Sure," Cam says. "I'm gay. Her name is Sophie. Want to see a picture?"

"Yes," Mattie says.

Cam scrolls through her photos, hands her phone back to Mattie.

"Oh, wow," Mattie says. "She's beautiful."

"She really is," Blair says.

"She's the smartest person I've ever met," Cam says. "Aside from me."

"Did you meet her in Oreville?" Mattie asks in disbelief.

"She's in college now, but believe it or not, I did," Cam says. Cam turns around in the passenger seat to examine Mattie. "You never know," she says. "You could meet someone here too. Of, you know, whatever gender you're into. Or not. If you're not into that. That would also be fine. If you're not into, like, things. With other people."

"Okay," Mattie says. "Thanks."

"Blair's not putting any of that stuff in her book," Cam says. "If you wanted to talk about it."

"No," Blair says. "Not going in the book. Of course not."

"Okay," Mattie says again. "I think I'm good for now, but I'll let you know. Do you have time to look at the security camera footage when we get to my house?"

Blair's going to miss family dinner. And she hasn't called home. She'll be in for it.

She finds she doesn't much care.

"Sure," she says. "Cam?"

"Of course," Cam says.

Mattie's house is silent and empty, but a light shines from under Lola's closed door. Beneath the brooding glare of Humphrey Bogart, Mattie pulls out a laptop—the newest and most expensive version of the same model Cam has—and unearths a USB stick from a drawer. They plug the thumb drive into their computer and open their notebook.

"Becca told Tom Bradshaw that she left with somebody called Mark Runslow and his friend Jake Northington. White pickup truck. I think they were friends of Darren's." They consult their notebook. "I called them after Lola disappeared, but they didn't tell me anything. They've all moved away, but my fake Facebook is Facebook friends with them if you want to interview them."

"Your fake Facebook?" Blair asks.

"I keep track of everyone who was there that night," Mattie says. They show Cam and Blair a Facebook page for a Cal Clarken, a computer network engineer who lives in Springfield, Ohio, and has thirty-six friends.

"Where on earth did you get that profile picture?" Cam asks.

"It's Elliott Gould," Mattie says. "From *The Long Goodbye*? You've never seen *The Long Goodbye*? How are you even a detective?"

"I wouldn't say it was a calling," Cam says.

Mattie shakes their head in sorrowful disbelief. "You should really watch *The Long Goodbye*. Anyway, I can message the people who were there. Cal is friends with all of them. Adults will friend *anyone*."

"Let's start with the security camera footage," Blair suggests.

Mattie nods and opens the file.

On their computer screen, a car-filled driveway flickers to life in a silent, eerie, black-and-white movie. Cam leans forward, speeds through the footage until she gets to two a.m, when she lets it play at normal speed.

A few minutes after two, a couple of dark shadows emerge from the house, get into the white truck parked in the driveway. The truck's taillights flare to life. It executes a sloppy multipoint turn and pulls out of view.

"That's the pickup Becca told the police she left in? Both of those people are too tall to be her," Blair says.

Cam speeds ahead again until another car pulls out at 2:15. Three more people, getting into a dark four-door sedan.

"That's Julie Frank, Maureen Pullman, and Jeff Chalstrom," Mattie says, looking at their notebook.

At 2:23, a third car, with four more passengers. At 2:27, the fourth and final car. Five passengers. One of them falls down walking to the car and then turns out, alarmingly, to be the driver.

All of the passengers correspond to the names and cars Bradshaw gave them.

None of them is Becca.

"We should check earlier, just in case," Blair says.

"She said she left with those two guys in the pickup," Cam says.

Mattie rewinds to 1:45. All the cars, back in their places. The driveway is dead still. Mattie rewinds further, and then fast-forwards to after the last car disappears.

Nobody moves in the hour before the white truck leaves.

And nobody moves in the hour after the fourth car drives away.

"Let's check one more time," Blair says.

"I've watched this a million times already," Mattie says. "That's everybody."

But the three of them watch the departures again. Each dark silhouette, each car, until the driveway is empty.

None of the people who left the Brosillards' is Becca.

Not in the car she told the police took her home.

Not before.

And not after.

And no one who leaves the house is Lola.

"She lied," Cam says. "She was still in the house. Unless—"

"Unless what?" Mattie asks.

Cam glances at Blair, who guesses where this is going. Blair's eyes are sad. She gives Cam a nod: *Go ahead.*

"Could somebody drive up to the backyard without ending up on camera?" Cam asks.

"There's no driveway back there," Mattie says. "But they could pull up on the lawn. The camera's only on the front of the house. But why would someone want to—"

They stop.

"Oh," they say.

"Someone who knew the house," Cam says. "Someone who knew where she was, and how to get her out without being seen. And Becca was there." She looks at Blair. "So was Luke," she says.

"He was in bed," Mattie says. "He was asleep. But Darren never left either. Not through the front door."

"Luke asked me out tomorrow night," Blair says.

Cam is looking at her with the most complicated expression

Blair has ever seen on Cam's face. Somewhere between sad and angry and pleading.

"He didn't hurt her," Blair says.

"Of course he didn't," Mattie says. They're staring at the computer screen, oblivious to what's happening between Blair and Cam.

"He might know something," Cam says carefully. "He might remember something from the dream he thought he had. Something about Becca. Or Darren."

"I'll ask him," Blair says.

"But—" Cam says.

"And then we go talk to Becca again," Mattie says. "The three of us."

"When's the next support group meeting?" Blair asks.

"Thursday at eight," Cam says. "It's over at nine thirty."

"I'm coming with you," Mattie says.

"Of course," Blair says. "You can tell your mom you're spending the night at Cam's. Right, Cam?"

"Sure," Cam says. "We'll make it a slumber party."

"Ruth won't care," Mattie says. "She hasn't known where I am since our dad left. But that's nice of you."

Cam and Blair are silent in the car on the way back to Cam's.

Blair stops the car in front of Cam's apartment building. Cam undoes her seat belt, but she doesn't get out.

"I don't think you should do this," Cam says.

"Do what?"

"This date," Cam says.

"Cam," Blair says. "It's fine."

"It's not fine," Cam says. "None of this is fine." Her fingers are knotted together in her lap, twisting. "If you get hurt—"

"I'm not going to get hurt."

"I'll kill him," Cam says simply. "If he touches you, I'll kill him. But it'll be too late. You'll already be—"

"He's not going to hurt me," Blair says. She puts her hand over the tangle of Cam's fingers. "He's not like that," she says. "I promise. Whatever happened to her, it wasn't him."

"You don't know that. If it wasn't him, he *knows* something. You know he knows something. What happens if you piss him off, Blair? What if Mattie's right, and that girl isn't Lola? What if they killed her?"

"Cam, come on. That's crazy."

Cam shakes her head, takes her hands away.

She gets out of the car without saying goodbye. When the door closes behind her, the sound is final.

Blair watches her trudge toward her building, her shoulders hunched.

She doesn't look back.

Blair knows Cam well enough to know that she's crying. Her own heart twists in her chest.

She thinks of Luke's green eyes, his smile.

She thinks of his hands, gentle on her cheek. The softness of his mouth.

She thinks of Meredith Payne-Whiteley, sitting at her desk in New York.

She thinks of how Luke told her he wanted to sail out across the ocean and disappear. To go into that unknown darkness utterly alone.

She thinks of what she'd wanted to say in response:

I'll go with you.

"He's not like that," she says aloud. "Lola ran away, and then she came back. I'm going to find out where she went, that's all. Everything's going to be fine."

DAY 12: WEDNESDAY

PREPARATION FOR AN INTERROGATION

IN the morning Cam is still quiet, and there are dark circles under her eyes, as if she hasn't slept.

"Are you okay?" Blair asks in the car.

"Bad dreams," Cam says curtly.

"Are you not talking to me?" Blair asks.

"I'm talking to you now," Cam says. "Why wouldn't I be talking to you?"

"It's not a big deal," Blair says. "Nothing bad is going to happen."

"I'm not not talking to you. But can we talk about something else?"

Blair turns on her windshield wipers. "I keep forgetting to replace these things. That was really nice, what you said to Mattie last night."

"About the security camera?"

"About how it doesn't matter who they like. Or if they don't like someone. At least, I think that's what you said."

"Oh, that," Cam says. "It was clearer in my head." She

fiddles with Blair's armrest. "Oreville's not the easiest place to be gay. If they're gay. Nonbinary. Queer." Cam looks slightly panicked. "Whatever. I wanted them to know it's cool."

"Yeah," Blair says carefully. "I can't really talk about that, so I'm glad they have you."

Now Cam is actively alarmed. "You can't?"

"Of course we can *talk* about it," Blair says. "But it's not my experience. I can try to support them if they need it, but I think it's better for them to have someone else who's . . ."

"If you say 'unique' our friendship ends now," Cam says.

"I was going to say 'special,'" Blair says with a straight face. Cam socks her in the arm, but gently enough that Blair knows she got the joke.

Blair turns into the high school parking lot, finds a spot.

"How are things with Sophie?" Blair asks, switching off the ignition but not getting out of the car.

"I don't know," Cam says miserably. "I guess when she comes back for break I have to talk about it. But I don't want to talk about it. I want everything to be better."

"How?" Blair asks.

"I don't know. Better," Cam says.

Blair considers and discards several possible approaches before she decides to go straight for the jugular.

"If you have a problem with someone, and you want to fix it, you have to decide first what you want to happen," Blair says. "Then you know what to ask for. You have to be specific. Like, do you want her to text you every night at a certain time?"

"That would be a strange thing to ask," Cam says. "Don't you think?"

"Then something else. You want to FaceTime twice a week? You want her to try to visit more?"

"Sophie doesn't have any money either," Cam says. "How's she supposed to visit more?"

"Cam," Blair says patiently, "I'm trying to give you examples of things you could ask for. You're the one who has to figure out what you want."

"Oh," says Cam. She thinks about this. "I want everything to be better," she says.

"You are impossible, Cameron P. Muñoz," Blair says. "And I say that with great love."

"I know," Cam says meekly. "Thank you for trying. If Luke doesn't turn out to be a serial killer, are you going to bone him tonight?"

"CAMERON," Blair says.

"Don't forget, you still have a curfew," Cam says. "You'll have to bone him fast. Come on, we're going to be late for first period."

Mattie is waiting for them at Blair's locker. Their face is paler than usual.

"Hi," Blair says. "You okay?"

Mattie shakes their head. "This was on my bed last night," they say. They pull a book out of their backpack and hand it to Blair. Cam looks over her shoulder as she examines it.

It's a hardcover copy of a Raymond Chandler book called *The Big Sleep*—an old edition, from the looks of it. The paper is heavy, the print elegant. But nearly every page is marked with ugly words in bloody-red marker.

> Leave it alone.
> Stop asking questions.
> If you don't drop this, you'll regret it.

"What the hell is this?" Cam asks, taking the book from Blair. She turns it over, as if the back of the book will reveal some secret.

"It's mine," Mattie says. "Lola bought it for me." They're trying, Blair can tell, not to cry. "It's my—it was one of my—it meant a lot to me. *She* did this."

"Lo—the girl?" Blair asks, confused. "Did you see her?"

"I told you, somebody left it on my bed. I found it after you left yesterday."

"Why didn't you call me?" Blair asks. "Us?"

Mattie shrugs. "It's not like she was standing next to it with a knife or anything. I'll be fine."

"Mattie, this is a threat," Blair says. "This is serious."

"It's proof," Mattie says. "It's proof that she's not my sister."

"You don't know it was her, though," Cam points out. "It could've been anyone."

"Who?" Mattie asks. "Who else could've done it?"

"Your brother, for one," Cam says. "Ruth."

"My brother? Are you serious? Why would he do something like this?"

"I'm just saying," Cam says. "We don't know it was her. It could've been anyone."

"Not anyone," Blair says. "Right? Only someone who could've gotten into your house."

"It's not like we leave the front door open," Mattie says dryly.

"Do you have an alarm?" Cam asks.

"Yeah, but half the time nobody bothers to turn it on. Not during the day, anyway."

Cam turns the book over in her hands again, thinking. "Why would she do this?" she wonders aloud.

"She doesn't want me asking questions, because she's a fraud," Mattie retorts, impatient. "We're getting closer. She's getting scared."

"But this is so obvious," Cam says. "She would know she'd be the first person you'd think of. That you'd assume it was her."

"Of course," Mattie says.

"I don't know," Cam says. "That's pretty bold. I thought you said she's been kissing up to you."

Mattie snatches the book from her hands, clutches it to their chest protectively. "What are you saying? Do you think I'm lying? Do you think *I* did this, to make it look like it was her?"

"No," Cam says, although the thought has just occurred to her. "I don't think you'd do that, Mattie. I just don't think we should assume it was her."

"It wasn't my brother," Mattie says again. "I know him. Anyway, why would he do something like this? He thinks that girl is Lola."

"I don't know," Cam says.

"Mattie," Blair says. "I think maybe it's time to tell someone else about this. This is . . . this is scary."

Mattie shrugs again. "Who?" they ask. "Who am I going to tell? Who's going to help me, besides you?"

"At least tell Luke," Blair says.

"Absolutely do not tell Luke!" Cam protests.

"Everybody thinks I'm crazy," Mattie says. "He's just going to think I'm crazier than he already does."

"I'm sure he doesn't think that," Blair says.

"You don't know what my brother thinks," Mattie says. "I don't want to tell him. I didn't want to tell you, except that it's evidence. Please."

"But—" Blair tries.

"If anything else like this happens," Cam says, "you have to tell us. Promise."

"I'll be fine."

"Please," Cam says. "Promise."

Mattie scuffs at the floor with the toe of their Oxford shoe. "I promise," they say dully. "But *she* left it. And now I know you don't believe me either."

"Mattie—" Cam begins.

But Mattie turns away from Cam and Blair, the book still held to their chest, and trudges away from them down the hall.

BLAIR'S BOOK PROPOSAL:
ADVENTURES IN AFTER-SCHOOL BOATING

Dear Meredith Payne-Whiteley,

Luke's boat is called the *Rorqual*. Thanks to *Spying on Whales*, I know this is a general word for any member of the baleen whale family, which I said, and which definitely impressed him. It's small, with a tiny cabin and kitchen and a tinier toilet inside and a hollowed-out place behind the cabin where you can sit outside and steer and put the sails up and down.

These are not the technical boat terms you're supposed to use. So maybe I should do some more research before we send this to any editors. Do editors know about boats? That's your area of expertise, not mine.

Anyway.

Luke told me the kitchen is called a "galley" and the hollowed-out place is called the "cockpit," like on a plane, and he also told me the names of the sails and all the ropes, but I forgot them immediately.

Oh, and the toilet is called the "head," and you have to flush it with a kind of crank. Luke blushed when he showed me how to use it, which was cute.

"This whole boat is *yours*?" I asked.

"It was Dad's," he said. "It's mine now. Well, and

Mattie's. But I don't think they want it." He looked
the same way he had when he'd showed me his model
ship. The expression of a small boy: defiant, sad, almost
ashamed. I wondered, not for the first time, what it
feels like to have your father walk out on you forever. I
don't imagine it feels very good.

I didn't know what to say, so I didn't say anything.
Luke loosened lines, turned on the motor. I asked if I
could help, and he gave me that smile that turns me
right into a sucker.

"Later," he said. "Later" is a big word, Meredith. It
could mean five minutes from now.

It could mean five years.

I feel easy around Luke in a way I never felt with
my ex-boyfriend. Luke doesn't seem to care what I'm
wearing or how I did my makeup. When I talk, he
listens. When I'm quiet, he doesn't mind. When I write
it down like that, I sound pathetic. What basic things to
find extraordinary in another person. That's what Cam
would say. Maybe that's true. But for me, those things
are new.

Once we were out of the harbor, Luke put up one
of the sails. I did help, then. He said again that I didn't
have to, but I wanted to know what it felt like to pull
on the lines as the fabric unfurled. It's harder than it
looks, I can tell you that much, and I'm in good shape.
But there's something so satisfying in tangible action.
Pull a rope, the sail goes up, the wind fills the sail, the
boat goes forward.

"Too bad we didn't come out earlier," Luke said.
"It'll be dark soon."

"Next time, I'll skip school," I said.

He turned and smiled at me again. "Sounds like a plan."

It was freezing, and the wind was picking up, and the sky was threatening rain. I could've stayed out there forever anyway, the two of us on the rising waves, a tiny white dot in all that gray-blue water. An easy place to pretend the rest of the world was a universe away.

But I hadn't forgotten what I was supposed to be there for.

I waited until Luke took the sail down, turned on the engine again, pointed us back toward home.

"Does your sister like sailing?" I asked.

He shook his head. "She used to, when we were kids. But then she started getting seasick." A beat. "She hates Dad," he said. "After he left, that's when she started saying being on the water made her want to puke. I think she doesn't like anything that reminds her of him."

"Fair enough," I said. "Mattie says you and Lola were close."

His face was turned away from me. I would've had to move to see him as he spoke.

"We were," he said. "Not so much anymore."

"Do you remember the night she—" I didn't know the right word. I don't know what Luke believes. If she ran away, or if she was kidnapped. Which option would be worse for him.

"Not really," he said. "I said good night to her. She was still out on the back patio when I went to bed. I had this dream that someone was walking through the house. Someone I recognized in the dream, but when I woke up, I didn't know who I'd seen. And she was gone. Just like that."

"Like your dad," I said.

"Pretty much," Luke said. "Except my dad never called me back after he moved to Hawaii. And Lola couldn't not call me back, because I had no way of calling her."

"Were you angry at her?"

"I don't know what I was," Luke said.

"What about Becca?"

Finally, he looked directly at me. I don't know what reaction I expected to see, but his face was impossible to read. "What about her?"

"You guys were, like, a thing, right?" As soon as the question was out of my mouth, I regretted it.

You guys were, like, a thing, right? A baby question, phrased like a baby. *Holy shit,* I thought. *I'm* jealous.

"We were kids," he said.

"But you stopped talking to her after—afterward."

He stared at me. "Did *you* talk to her?"

"Cam and I did, yeah."

"Why would you do something like that?"

I clearly hadn't thought this one through at all. "We, um . . . We thought it might help Mattie. I don't know. They're so—you know."

Some of the alarm faded from his face. "Yeah," he said. "I know. Look, I didn't do a very good job of handling things after my sister disappeared. I'm trying to make it up to Mats now, but Becca . . ." He sighed. "She must hate me," he said simply. "I don't blame her."

"I don't think I would've done much better in your shoes," I said. "Not when I was fifteen. Probably not now, for that matter."

He shook his head and looked away from me again. "I'm sorry, but can we talk about something else?"

"Of course," I said. I could hear Cam in my head: *You idiot! Don't drop it* now!

But I couldn't do it to him. Couldn't keep pushing him. The whole thing was such a black hole of pain: for Mattie, for Luke, for Becca.

For Lola and Darren? Who knows.

There was one thing I was sure of, though: Whoever had left that book for Mattie, it hadn't been Luke. Which left only three people.

Ruth? Unlikely.

Mattie was right. The obvious choice was Lola. I couldn't imagine why she'd done it, but that didn't mean it wasn't her.

And the third option was, of course, Mattie. Desperate to make us believe. Could they do it? Sure. But would they? I tried to put myself in their shoes. With their impossible story. Their need to believe their sister would never have left them.

I should tell Luke, I thought. He should know. But Mattie hadn't, and I couldn't break their trust any more than I already had. Not until I knew for sure who'd left the book.

Luke and I were both quiet for a while. We'd only been out on the water for an hour, but already the world of mysteries and school and homework and my future—even you, Meredith—seemed like a distant country I had visited once but could barely remember. Nothing was real except the cold wind coming off the water and soaking into my bones, the slap of the waves against the boat's hull, the harsh cries of gulls carrying across the sharp air.

"Why didn't you go to college?" I asked him suddenly. I don't know where the question came from. So much for moving the conversation to light topics. But he didn't seem to mind.

"Partly because of Mattie," he said. "I didn't want to leave them alone with Ruth. But that's not the whole reason." He shifted his hands on the wheel, moving us toward the stone jetty that marked the entrance to the harbor. "I was good at school, but it was like . . . It didn't mean anything, you know? Just some boxes I was checking off. And I couldn't imagine doing that for another four years, and then going to work in an office somewhere and just . . . checking boxes for the rest of my life. When Mattie graduates, I'm going to sail to Mexico, and then we'll see. I have enough money saved from the restaurant to last me for a while."

"Ruth didn't care?"

"She cared," he said. "She's not happy about it. But she wants a perfect family, and we haven't been that for a long time. We never were, but when my dad was around and me and Lola were little, she at least had pictures of one to show her friends." He laughed, but the laughter was forced. "Now, she can't even do that. My dad's gone, I didn't turn out to be what she wanted, Mattie didn't turn out to be what she wanted, Lola—" He cut himself off. "Me not going to college—we had some fights about it when I graduated, but now it's just one more thing on the list of what Ruth chooses not to see."

"Do you regret it?"

He shrugged. "Sometimes. Not really. My life here is so small, but I know this isn't forever."

"Four more years," I said. "That's a long time."

He's frozen, I thought. He and Mattie are frozen, stuck forever in the place they were when Lola disappeared. Like flies trapped in amber. I wondered if he'd ever really sail away, or if that was just something he told himself to pass the time. I thought of what Mattie had said about Luke: *Girls always like my brother. They think they can fix him.*

But maybe he just needed to get out of Oreville.

Maybe the person he needed to get him out was me.

"I don't think I'm going to go to college either," I said. I hadn't been sure of it until that moment, the first time I'd said it out loud. But out there, on the water, just me and Luke—it was so obvious.

"Why not?" Luke asked. There was no judgment in the question, just curiosity.

"Because that's not the kind of thing I need to learn," I said. "Not right now. I want to take—a year. At least. Maybe more. I want to see something bigger than Oreville."

"You can see something bigger than Oreville pretty much anywhere you go," Luke said, smiling. "Definitely at college. Well, maybe not at Wazzu." Washington State University is an infamously rural college in eastern Washington. The kind of place you could go to watch football games and tip cows, if that's your thing, and not much else.

"I know," I said. "But you know what I mean."

"Yeah," he said. "I know exactly what you mean."

"My parents are going to kill me," I said. Their ambitions for me might not be high, but that doesn't mean they don't assume I'll do what's expected of me.

"The best thing I ever learned from my sister," Luke said, "is that adults can't actually stop you from doing what you want."

"I don't have any money," I said.

Luke shrugged. "Sailing is cheap," he said. "And so is Mexico."

I stared at him. "Is that . . . are you inviting me?"

"Sure," he said, smiling down at me where I sat in the cockpit with my legs tucked up underneath me, my heart thumping in—what? Elation? Terror? Hope? His eyes were warm, intent. He was looking at me as if he saw something he liked very much.

"You look like you're freezing," he said. "Want a blanket?"

After that, we stopped talking about anything serious. We stopped talking about much of anything at all. Luke was quiet as he moored the boat. Quiet as he held out a hand and helped me onto the dock. I didn't need it, and I think he knew it. I think it was an excuse to touch me. At least, I hope it was. But he didn't say anything as we walked back toward our cars.

"I'm sorry," I said finally, when we reached mine.

"Sorry for what?"

"Sorry I keep asking you questions about your sister," I said.

"It's okay," he said. He was facing me, his hands shoved in his pockets. "But I don't think it's going to help."

"Help?" I didn't know what he meant.

"Mattie," he said. "Whatever it is they're going through, they're going to have to work through it on their own."

"I know," I said. "I want to help them."

"You're a good person," he said. "I like that about you."

I'd done nothing but lie to him since the moment we met. I wanted to throw up. I wanted to run to Mattie then and there. Insist they drop this whole thing with their sister. *Let it go,* I would've said.

Let her back into her life.

Let her tell you where she's been when she's ready.

Let me have this.

Let Luke go.

Please.

"Thank you," I said instead.

And then Luke kissed me. Light and easy, the way you'd kiss a child.

Except he kissed me on the lips.

"I should go," he said.

"See you soon?" I asked.

But he was already walking away.

If he heard me, he didn't answer.

Meredith, please help me. Now what do I do?

Sincerely,
Blair Johnson

Day 13: Thursday

The Second Interrogation of Becca Conrad

MATTIE is tense and quiet as Blair navigates the dark, rainy streets after school. Their fingernails are bitten down to the quick, and their eyes are huge and wild in Blair's rearview mirror.

"You okay with this?" Blair asks.

"Yes," Mattie says.

Downtown Oreville is strung with Christmas lights, but the spotlit blow-up Santas and tinsel-bedecked reindeer are struggling to convey cheer on this sodden, pitch-black early evening.

"Fascism," Cam mutters, glaring foully at a leering plastic elf holding aloft a plastic hammer.

"What?" Mattie says from the back seat.

"Christian heteropatriarchy is the basis of fascism!" Cam says more clearly, gesturing out the window.

"Oh," Mattie says. "Yeah. That's too bad."

"I like the lights," Blair says. "They're festive."

"Lights can be nice," Cam concedes. "But all that plastic crap is going to end up in the ocean."

"I think the lights are pagan originally," Mattie says. "You should check with Sophie, though."

Blair's smiling as she pulls into the parking lot of the strip mall.

They wait for Becca on the sidewalk a few feet away from the real estate office door. Lurking in the shadows, like vampires, Blair thinks. Mattie shivers and stamps their feet. They aren't wearing a coat, just their elbow-patched grandpa detective sweater. Cam shrugs out of her feather-shedding old puffer and drapes it around their shoulders without asking.

Becca's the second-to-last person out. Tonight, she has a wool beanie pulled low over her dark hair. They almost don't recognize her.

"Let me talk to her," Mattie says, stepping forward. "Hi, Becca."

Becca turns, sees Mattie standing with their arms crossed, Cam's bedraggled coat around their shoulders like a sad mockery of a superhero cape. They should look silly. Instead they look calm, fierce, determined.

They look like Cam, Blair thinks, when Cam's facing down a hostile adult.

Becca squints. "*Mattie?*" she says. "What are you doing here?" And then she sees Blair and Cam in the shadows behind Mattie. "What the hell?"

"I want to ask you a few questions about my sister," Mattie says.

"Don't ask me. Ask her," Becca says.

"Becca?" One of the other girls from her support group has turned around. "Everything okay?"

"I'm fine, Jess," Becca says. "See you Sunday."

The other girl wavers. It's obvious to all of them that Becca is not fine. "All right," she says. "Call me later?"

"Sure," Becca says, her eyes on Mattie.

Jess stands for a second longer. Looks at Blair and Cam, and then at the phone in her hand. "Okay," she says again, turning at last and heading for one of the cars in the lot.

"You know what happened to my sister," Mattie says, when Jess is out of earshot. "Don't you?"

"Mats," Becca says. "Listen. I—" She takes a step toward them, stops.

"Please," Mattie says. "You were her best friend. She trusted you." Becca flinches, her face going white. "I know you know what happened to her."

"She ran away, Mats," Becca says hoarsely. "She ran away, and then she came back."

"You were still there," Mattie says. Cam moves forward, letting Mattie do the talking but standing firm at their back. Blair's right behind her. Becca's eyes move from the two of them, back to Mattie again, out to the parking lot.

"We watched the security footage from the driveway," Mattie says. "You told the police you left with Mark and Jake in their truck. But that was a lie, Becca. You didn't go home when you said you did. You were in the house the whole night."

Becca shakes her head. "Not the whole night."

"When did you leave?"

"I told you," Becca says.

"You lied," Mattie says, relentless. "To *me*, Becca. The day after my sister went missing. I called you, and you lied to me. Why?"

"We were so messed up that night," Becca says. Her eyes are filling with tears. "I didn't know what time it was. I don't know who was there. I loved her, Mats. You know I loved her. I can't talk about this. I'm so sorry."

"I loved her too," Mattie says.

"I promised."

"Who did you promise?" Mattie takes a step forward, their

intensity carrying them. "Darren? Lola? Did you promise my sister? Did she leave on purpose? *Did she leave me?*"

"Go to hell," Becca says. But not to Mattie; to Cam and Blair. "Both of you." She's crying openly now. "What's wrong with you? Why are you digging this up? Do you get off on this?"

"Where is my sister?" Mattie's composure breaks. They're yelling now, their voice as ragged as Becca's. "Where is she?"

"At your house," Becca says. She wipes away tears with the back of her hand, leaving smears of black eyeliner. "At your house, Mattie. In her little princess room, in her little princess world. She doesn't care about either one of us anymore. Leave me alone. Please, leave me alone."

Mattie's fists tighten, and for a moment Blair thinks they'll hit Becca. She puts a hand on Mattie's shoulder, feeling the tense wires of their muscles contracting.

"You're a liar," Cam says. "You're a liar, and you owe Mattie the truth."

"I don't know what the truth is anymore," Becca says. "I'm begging you. Leave me alone."

"I can't," Mattie says brokenly. "Becca, I can't."

"How can you do this?" Cam asks angrily. "Can't you see how hard this is for Mattie? How would you feel if someone you loved disappeared overnight and nobody told you anything?"

"Do you think I don't know how it feels?" Becca's voice rises. "Lola was my *best friend*. Luke was—Luke and I were—I was in love with your brother, Mattie, like completely in love with him, and I thought he felt the same way. I thought it was going to be the three of us together, forever—we had this big plan, we were going to move to Seattle together after graduation, get an apartment, Lola was going to work at that big bookstore she loved on Capitol Hill and start writing a book, Luke and I were going to sail your dad's boat to—"

Blair looks like she's going to be sick.

"She never told me that," Mattie interrupts. "She wasn't going to move anywhere with you. She would've told me."

Becca snorts softly, but her face is sympathetic. "There was a lot Lola didn't tell you, Mats. I think you've probably figured that much out by now." She shakes her head. "Luke ghosted me after that night. Just completely ghosted me. At first I thought, okay, Lola's missing, I get it, maybe he's trying to deal with Ruth, with the police, with you—I tried to understand, I really did. But he never talked to me again. It was like I stopped existing. I was so desperate I called *Darren*. You don't even know—" Her voice cracks, and she starts to cry again.

"What did he say?" Cam asks sharply.

"What do you think he said? He told me to never call him again."

"When? When did you call him?" Mattie demands.

"A few months after Lola—does it matter?"

"What about now?" Cam says. "Did you call him after we talked to you the first time? Did you send Mattie that book?"

"What book? What are you talking about? I haven't talked to Darren since then. It's been years."

"And Luke?" Blair knows Becca's not telling them everything, but she also knows how close to the edge Becca is. Cam pushed her too hard the last time. But Blair wants to shake Becca too.

She might not know everything. But she knows *something*.

"Luke," Becca says, her voice savage. "Luke is— Luke could die tomorrow, for all I care. Mattie, I'm sorry. I'm sorry Lola left. But she came back. Just—be glad. Go home and watch scary movies with her and forget all this shit."

"No," Mattie says. "I can't."

Becca stares at them, her face white and bloodless.

"Then leave me alone," she says. She pushes past them, into

the rain-heavy night. Mattie lurches toward her. Blair holds them back, gentle.

"She's a liar," Mattie sobs. "She knows. *She knows.*" Cam and Blair enfold them in a hug, and Mattie weeps in the shelter of the embrace.

"I know," Blair says. "I know. Let it out. We're here."

They stand like that, the three of them, on the empty sidewalk, in the brutal night, until Mattie's tears slow to a trickle, until Mattie scrubs at their face with the sleeve of Cam's jacket and stands up straight again.

"Sorry," they say.

"There's nothing to be sorry for," Cam says. "But I don't know what to do next."

"I do," Blair says. "Let's go to McDonald's."

Blair's parents gave her a credit card long ago to use for emergencies.

This, she is confident, qualifies as such.

She buys them a feast, over Mattie's protests. French fries and burgers and a vegan burger for Cam, who wants to try it, and McNuggets for herself with three kinds of sauce, and three flavors of milkshake—vanilla, chocolate, and strawberry—which they pass around in the brightly lit McDonald's.

Cam picks at the last of her fries.

"She doesn't believe me either," Mattie says. Under the harsh glare of the fluorescent overheads, it's clear they've been crying, but the massive infusion of carbohydrates and fat has had the anesthetic effect on them that Blair was hoping for.

"Becca?" Blair asks.

"Nobody believes me," Mattie says. "Even you don't believe me." They push their hands through their short hair. Their eyes are dull. "She's going to be there forever," they say. "She killed my sister, and she's in my house, and she's never going to leave."

"I believe you," Cam says.

Mattie looks at her for a long time. And then they look away. "No, you don't," they say.

"What do you want us to do?" Blair asks.

"What can you do?" Mattie says. "You can't do anything. At least you tried."

"We could talk to Ruth," Cam says.

Mattie snorts and doesn't bother to answer.

"We promised you a slumber party," Blair says. "Still want to come over?"

Mattie shrugs. "Sure," they say.

PUTTANESCA

All three of them are silent on the drive to Cam's. Mattie stares sightlessly out the car window. They're not crying, but Blair isn't sure if that's a good thing or a bad thing.

Everything about them suggests a person who has given up completely.

I did try, Blair thinks. *We both tried, me and Cam*. She wonders what Meredith Payne-Whiteley will have to say about that.

This is not the ending Meredith Payne-Whiteley was hoping for.

And she realizes—to her surprise—that she doesn't care. She hasn't thought of Meredith Payne-Whiteley all day.

The person she's thinking of is Mattie. Mattie, alone in that terrible house, with a person they're convinced is a stranger, with a mother who's indifferent at best and malevolent at worst, with a brother who can't do anything to protect them.

What is Mattie going to do now? Blair and Cam can't drop this because they didn't find an answer. Blair feels responsible for Mattie now, in a way she's never felt responsible for another person.

Mattie isn't a story to her anymore.

They're a friend.

"That's weird," Cam says, as Blair parks in front of her apartment.

"What?" Blair, deep in her own thoughts, takes a second to register what Cam's said.

"The light's on. Irene's still up."

"It's not that late," Mattie says.

"It's late for Irene when she's working," Cam says.

A seed of misgiving sprouts in Blair's heart. She wants to turn the car around and drive away very fast.

To where?

New York?

"I'm sure it's fine," Blair says.

It isn't.

Irene has been waiting up for them for a while, which Cam can tell because the kitchen reeks of cigarette smoke and there are several butts stubbed out in the ashtray in front of her. She's sitting next to Brad, whose expression is inscrutable.

Kitten has made himself scarce, which is also a bad sign.

"You," Irene says to Cam. "And you," Irene says to Blair. "And who the hell are *you*?" Irene says to Mattie.

"This is—" Cam begins, but Irene holds up a hand.

"I don't want to know, Cameron. I don't want to know anything about this podcast. Whatever you're putting on the internet. I can only imagine what you're going to put us through this time. What I *do* want to know is why in god's name you spent your night *harassing my patient outside her support group meeting,* putting *her* health in danger, putting *my* job in danger—" Irene's voice gets louder as she talks and she's rising out of her chair.

Brad puts a hand on her shoulder, gentle, and she sinks back into her seat.

"How did you—" Cam begins.

"We can explain," Blair says.

"I think you'd better," Brad says.

"Are you upgraded to doing discipline now?" Cam asks.

"*Cameron*—" Irene shouts, standing up so fast her chair falls over backward.

"Wait," Mattie says, stepping forward. "All of this is my fault. You must be Irene. Cam's mom, right?"

Irene stares, her mouth open mid-shout.

Mattie keeps going, fast, before Irene can yell again.

"My name is Mattie Brosillard. I found Cam and Blair because of the podcast about Clarissa. That's true. They're not making a podcast now or anything. They're helping me to be nice." Blair makes an embarrassed noise, but Mattie doesn't stop. "My sister disappeared from a party in the middle of the night five years ago. Her name was—is—Lola. Like Clarissa. The disappearing, I mean. Lola wasn't anything like Clarissa, I don't think. She was—is—really beautiful too, but she, uh, kind of hung out with some people she shouldn't have. And I know she did drugs. And—other things. Even though she was really young. She was a year older than me when she disappeared, but I don't do drugs or anything like that. So you don't have to worry that I'm a bad influence.

"And then this girl came back two weeks ago. She said she was Lola and that she had been kidnapped and finally escaped. My mom believed her and so did my brother. But I didn't, because she wasn't. Normally I would take care of things on my own. I read a lot of detective stories. I have a good idea of how to do it. And where to look for clues and that kind of thing. But I'm only fourteen. I don't have a car or anything.

"I needed help, and Blair and Cam seemed like the obvious choice. Because they found a missing girl already, so I thought they could help me. But we still don't know what happened to my sister. We talked to Becca—your patient—because she was my sister's best friend and lied about what happened the night she disappeared, and I'm really sorry, and I hope you're not in trouble, but please don't get mad at Cam, because basically I made her do it."

For once, Irene is speechless.

Even Brad looks as if someone has hit him over the head.

"What?" Irene manages finally.

"It's true," Blair says. "All of that. It wasn't Cam's fault. But we never, ever should've bothered your patient. That's true too. It was wrong."

"Extremely wrong," Mattie seconds. "But also totally necessary."

"I—" Irene seems to turn over several possible avenues of inquiry. "All right," she says, pointing at Cam and then to the remaining kitchen chairs. "You. Cameron. Sit. You too, Blair. And you—Mattie? Do your parents know where you are?"

"No," Mattie says. "But they don't care. My dad has a new family in Hawaii, and my mom is with a bunch of other fascist moms trying to rescue fetuses."

Irene puts her head in her hands. "Sweet baby Jesus on the cross, give me strength," she says into her palms.

"You sit down too," Brad says, taking over and righting Irene's chair for her.

Irene sits.

Brad looks at Blair and Cam in a stern manner. "This is serious," he says.

"No shit," Cam mutters.

"Cameron P. Muñoz!" Brad says sharply.

"Sorry," Cam says, not very apologetically.

"Why did you think it was acceptable to harass Irene's patient, Cam? Did you not think about the fact that she could have lost her job if this girl reported her?"

"*Did* she?" Cam asks, alarmed. "Wait, how did she find you?"

Irene takes her head out of her hands. "I got a call from someone else you went after," she says. "Some guy named Darren? Friend of Becca's? She called him in a panic after two girls harassed her outside her support group. Not once, mind you. Twice. He's the one who put two and two together and called me. You, Cameron P. Muñoz, and you, Blair Johnson, are not particularly anonymous these days."

"But did she report you?" Cam asks anxiously.

"Does it matter?" Irene says, her voice rising dangerously again.

"Kind of," Cam says.

"So if I don't get in trouble, it's ethical to go around hounding my patients in recovery?"

"That's not what I mean," Cam says. "I swear. I—please say you're not in trouble."

Irene glowers at her. "He figured out I was your mother, because we're famous," she says finally. "That's why he called me. He didn't put together how you found her. He doesn't know I worked with her. Thank god."

"We really weren't doing this for a podcast. Or to get famous," Cam says.

"That's not true," Blair says. "But Cam didn't do anything wrong. I'm the one who wanted to get famous."

"What?" Irene and Brad say at the same time.

"This literary agent called me a couple of weeks ago from New York and told me I need a new story for a book. That she—that I—that I could, um, be a real writer. And sell a book. That a lot of people would read. And I said yes. And then Mattie showed up in Cam's kitchen and all of this happened. We really did want to help them. I didn't tell Cam about the literary agent either. Not at first. I'm the one who did something wrong.

I pressured Cam into helping because I wanted a story. Irene, I'm really sorry."

"On the *cross*," Irene says, and puts her head in her hands again.

"I'm not sure I'm totally following here," Brad says.

"But it's my fault too," Cam says. "All of this. Because Blair *did* tell me eventually about the literary agent, after I caught her with Mattie's brother—"

"*What?*" Irene shouts—

"—and I kept it a secret for her too, because I wanted something good to happen finally for somebody I love, and I didn't think about the consequences—"

"You never do!" Irene yells, stabbing one forefinger into the air—

"—and everything that happened last year was so hard, and sometimes it was really scary, and I still have nightmares about that guy and being in that basement and the gun, like really bad nightmares where I wake up screaming, and I keep getting panic attacks—"

"Wait, what?" Blair says—

"You do?" Mattie says—

"*Panic* attacks?" Irene shouts. "Cameron, you didn't tell me about *panic attacks,* we are getting you back into therapy *immediately*—"

"And I wanted to have a good ending for somebody"—Cam raises her voice over all three of them, finishing in a rush—"and I want something good to happen for Blair after last year and all those people calling us and bothering us and doxxing us and sending us hate mail and saying we're stupid and racists and should all go to hell and get raped and also I know it's really hard to love me and I don't want to lose anyone that does."

This monologue is followed by a brief silence.

"Cam, you're not hard to love," Blair says. "Why didn't you tell me you were having nightmares?"

"What is this about *rape threats*?" Irene demands.

"It was a lot," Cam says. "I didn't want you to worry. Just a lot of emails. Message boards."

"Whole forums," Blair says. "About how we were too political and what does abolishing the police have to do with anything and what does Clarissa being white have to do anything. And then some other stuff about how we should get raped and that would fix us."

"Jesus Christ," Brad says.

"Racists?" says Irene.

"Against white people," Cam says.

"You can't be racist against white people," Irene says automatically. "Racism is a structural—"

Cam cuts her off. "*I* know that. But try telling that to the internet. I'm really sorry about Becca. That was a big mistake. I should never have done that. Especially after—after everything we put you through last year. Everything *I* put you through. You, and Blair and her family too. None of the podcast stuff was Blair's fault. That was all mine. I think I thought I was making it up to her somehow. Or maybe I wasn't thinking very well."

"Making it up to Blair, or to Clarissa?" Brad asks.

"I meant Blair," Cam says. "But none of this seems very fair to Clarissa either."

Irene reaches for her pack of cigarettes.

Brad clears his throat.

Irene gives him a dirty look.

"The great thing about quitting," she says, lighting a cigarette and blowing the smoke toward the open window, "is that I can do it again tomorrow. Do we have any wine in this house?"

Brad gets up immediately. "I'll find you some," he says.

Irene finishes her cigarette in luxurious silence.

Mattie fidgets uncomfortably.

Cam stares at her hands, folded neatly now in her lap.

Blair wishes that she, like Becca, had a lip piercing to chew on. Just for this particular occasion.

Brad brings Irene WORLD'S #1 DAD and a half-empty bottle of red wine. Irene stubs out her cigarette and fills WORLD'S #1 DAD to the brim.

"All right," Irene says. "Let me get this straight. *Your* sister disappeared," she says to Mattie. "And recently a girl turned up and said she was your sister and had escaped kidnappers, but you don't believe it was her. And you enlisted my child and her friend in this puzzle because last year they made a podcast and found a missing girl."

"Clarissa," Brad says.

"Sorry," Irene says. "Clarissa."

"Yes," Mattie says.

"And *you* helped this stranger out, even though that's a totally ridiculous story, because you felt bad you almost ruined all our lives last year, in particular Blair's," Irene says to Cam.

"Yes," Cam says.

"And *you* helped this stranger out because somebody called you from New York and said she will make you rich and famous," Irene says to Blair.

Blair wavers. "I really liked Mattie." Irene snorts. "Yes," she says.

Irene turns to Brad. "What would *you* do?"

"I don't have kids," Brad says with alarm.

"I wouldn't recommend it," Irene says. But she doesn't sound quite as angry as she was before. "What would *you* do, Cameron?"

"With me?" Cam asks.

"Yes," Irene says. "With you. These two"—she points at Blair and Mattie—"are not my problem. I have enough problems."

Cam thinks for a while. "You could ground me," she says.

"You never go anywhere," Blair and Irene say at the same time.

Irene sighs. "Do you remember your grandparents, Cam?"

Irene moved back to Oreville after Cam's dad died so her parents could help her; single motherhood in a punk squat in New York City was, in Irene's words, "unsustainable." But Cam's grandparents died within a few years of each other not long after that.

Cam's memories of them are blurry and vague. Colors, smells. The soft skin of her grandmother's cheek. Her grandmother's lullabies in Spanish. Her grandfather's pipe smoke. Irene brings up her parents even less often than she talks about Cam's dad. Which is to say, basically never.

"Tamales," Cam says.

"Yeah, tamales. Your grandmother was a hell of a cook. But we never really got along, me and my parents. Typical second-generation immigrant stuff. They wanted a good Mexican daughter and I wanted what I thought was American freedom. They were so strict, so traditional.

"When I was your age, it made me so angry. I thought they were pathetic, clinging to a life that was long gone. I thought I left all of that behind when I moved to New York. And when I got pregnant—I didn't want any of that for you, Cam. Any of that pressure. Any of that confusion, about what world you belonged in. What language was yours.

"Maybe I went too far in the other direction. Definitely threw the baby out with the bathwater when it came to cooking and teaching you Spanish. I really should've learned some of Mom's recipes before she passed. I don't know, Cam. I'm so proud of the person that you are. But you still don't understand when to stop, and that scares me. That's all me. Maybe I did a bad job—"

"You didn't!" Cam protests.

"It was just me," Irene says. "This whole time. Your dad gone, my parents gone. I had no idea what I was doing. I have no idea what I'm doing now."

Brad reaches over and takes Irene's hand.

Somebody is going to start crying any minute now, Cam thinks in a panic. Will it be her? Will it be Irene?

Please, god, don't let it be her.

Or Irene.

"It's totally different for me," Mattie says. Irene blinks, as if she's forgotten Mattie and Blair are still sitting there. "I'm white. My mom's not strict because she's trying to hold on to her culture. My mom thinks the government is being taken over by communists."

"If only," Irene murmurs wistfully.

"Ruth tried so hard to make my sister into a person she wasn't. I think it broke something inside her. I think that's what happened to her, why she had so many problems. I don't know where Lola is. I don't think she would have left me behind. Not on purpose." Mattie's voice breaks.

It's Mattie, Cam thinks. *Mattie's the one who's going to cry.*

But Mattie keeps going. "The scariest thing I can imagine is never knowing what happened to her. And Cam and Blair took that seriously. Even when they had so many reasons not to. Even though they think I'm making it up, they still took me seriously. Nobody's ever done that for me before except my sister.

"So I understand why you think that Cam did something bad, but like I said, that was my fault. And I'm really grateful she did. I think you did an amazing job, because Cam is one of the bravest people I've ever met. And Blair too. Even if you *are* going to put me in a book," Mattie says to Blair.

Blair flushes but doesn't look away.

Mattie stops talking rather suddenly, shrinking back slightly in their chair as if overwhelmed by their own loquaciousness.

A long pause follows this series of disclosures.

"Well," Irene says. "Well, I." She clears her throat, as if she's about to say something else. But she looks as though she's at a total loss.

"Mattie's right," Cam says fiercely. "You *did* do an amazing job. Anything that's wrong with me is the fault of, um . . ."

"Violent video games," Mattie offers.

"Violent video games," Cam agrees.

Irene, at last, smiles. "Heavy metal," she says.

"Romance novels glorifying problematic relationships," Blair suggests.

"No, that's what's wrong with *you*," Cam says.

"Ouch," Blair says, but she's smiling too.

"N.W.A," Brad says.

"What?" Cam asks.

"Those are oldies now, sweetheart," Irene says. "These infants have never even heard 'Fuck tha Police,' let alone been led astray by it."

"Sure we have," Blair says. "That's, like, an anthem."

"Wonderful," Brad says, his face lighting up. "I'm so glad." He squeezes Irene's hand and gets up. "I don't know about the rest of you, but I'm starving. Anybody else up for spaghetti alla puttanesca?"

"I don't know what that is," Blair confesses.

"Late-night pasta snack invented by Italian hookers," Brad says cheerfully. Irene clears her throat. "Sex workers," he amends. "Who are also workers, like any other workers, to be clear. Deserving of the same protections and rights and, uh, health care?" He glances at Irene. "Did I get it all?"

"It's late," Irene says. "That'll do."

"I still don't know what kind of pasta it is," Blair says.

McDonald's seems like a very long time ago. And all this talk of feelings leads to feelings of great hunger. "Say yes," Cam says. "It's Brad cooking."

"Yes," Blair says.

Mattie nods vigorously.

Humming to himself, Brad sets a pot in the sink to fill with water.

"You're still in trouble," Irene says to Cam, back to stern. "But we can détente until after snacks."

"Can we détente until tomorrow?" Cam asks.

"Fine," Irene says. "Détente sleepover. Blair Johnson, if you put my child's name into your *New York Times* bestseller, I'm going to skin you alive over a very hot fire. And if the police come looking for you"—this to Mattie—"I am *not* going to be happy. Are we clear?"

"Yes," says Blair.

"Yes, ma'am," says Mattie.

"I'm using the last of the garlic," says Brad from the stove. "In case anyone else might need some later."

Day 14: Friday

A DAY OFF

BLAIR wakes up to Kitten's increasingly insistent meows. He's spent the last several hours in what must be absolute Kitten heaven, snoring and drooling rapturously across not one but three entire warm humans nested in a pile of musty sleeping bags and extra blankets on Cam's bedroom floor.

He shoves his hard little skull under Blair's chin and meows again. Then he waddles across her stomach and stands by Cam's door, looking at her in a significant way.

"You have to feed him," Cam says sleepily from the other side of Mattie. "Or he'll come back and meow in your face again."

"*You* have to feed him," Blair says. "He's your cat." She checks her phone, sits up in shock. "Oh, no! We're going to be so late for first period."

"Hnnnnph," Cam groans into her pillow. Mattie's still dead to the world. No wonder; it was after three when they went to bed. Blair is a spaghetti alla puttanesca à la Brad convert for life.

Blair struggles to her feet, follows Kitten into the kitchen.

Irene and Brad are both gone—to work, Blair assumes—although Irene's left them a full pot of coffee. A Post-it on the oven reads INSIDE: TREASURES in Brad's sprawling hand, with a surprisingly convincing sketch of Smaug settled on his hoard. Blair opens the door, finds scrambled eggs keeping warm in a Dutch oven.

Brad, the gentle domestic goddess, preternaturally thoughtful of others, soother of Irene, constant provider of delicious foodstuffs: who would've guessed, last year, when she and Cam confronted him in his sad and lonely exile surrounded by guns.

We all contain multitudes, Blair thinks, *but some of us contain more multitudes than others.*

Cam yawns her way into the kitchen, rubbing sleep from her eyes and nearly tripping over Kitten, who surges to his feet to twine around her ankles. His meowing increases to a frantic pitch.

"Let's skip," Cam says.

"The whole day?" Blair asks.

"First period," Cam says. "I haven't had an absence all year. And it's social studies. I could do with a break from the discussion of current events."

"It's important to remain aware," Blair says.

"I'm aware current events are very bad," Cam says. "Plus, Mattie's still asleep. Young people need a lot of rest."

Even after all the years of their friendship, Blair has absolutely no idea at times like this if Cam is joking or in absolute earnest regarding, for example, the sleep needs of young people, a group to which she herself indisputably belongs. But Blair doesn't have much use for first period either, and she's not going to college anyway, so who cares if she misses it.

"Okay," she says.

Cam opens a can of wet food for an ecstatic Kitten. Mattie comes into the kitchen. Their eyes are ringed with dark circles, their face pale and ghastly. Their hair is sticking up at odd angles. Blair's heart twinges in her chest.

"Hi," Mattie says, trying and failing for a brave face. "I think we're missing first period."

"We made an executive decision," Cam says. "While you were asleep. Unexcused absences all around."

Mattie grins devilishly. The smile transforms their face. "Unexcused? Seriously? You found a whole entire missing girl, got into MIT, and still never learned how to forge an excuse note?"

Cam looks at Mattie with respect. "Goodness," she says. "In that case, let's skip the whole day."

So they do.

Pillar Point is a beach about an hour west of Oreville that Lola tagged often in her public Instagram. Blair drives them there along Highway 112, a winding and beautiful road that slides in and out of heavy forest to offer mist-shrouded views of the Strait of Juan de Fuca.

This time of year, the beach is empty. The tide is halfway out, the driftwood-strewn rocky beach giving way to seaweed-dotted mudflats along the water's edge.

Cam raided the apartment before they left, filling Blair's back seat with a mismatch of old raincoats, a pair of galoshes of mysterious origin that fit neither her nor Irene but are somehow the perfect size for Mattie, a thermos (Brad's) full of coffee, and half their sleeping-bag nest for good measure.

Cam and Blair wrap a sleeping bag around themselves and sit on a bone-white length of wood, trading the coffee back and forth, while Mattie ranges along the beach, their head bent.

"Now what?" Blair asks. In the distance, Mattie squats down, picks something up, holds it to the light, drops it again. Moves down the beach.

"I don't know," Cam says.

"They're not going to let this go," Blair says.

"I know," Cam says. "Maybe we can talk to her."

"Lola?" Blair asks.

Cam nods. "Whatever happened that night, she has to tell them. No matter how bad it is. Whatever Darren did . . ." Cam trails off. "If he did something," she says. "If Becca did something. If Lola did something."

"You think it's her," Blair says.

"It has to be her, Blair. Don't you think?"

"Yes," Blair says.

"Do you think Luke—"

"No!" Blair says.

Cam is quiet.

Blair sighs.

"Maybe," she says. "Maybe he knows something. Maybe that's why he stuck around. But there's no way he left the book. He loves Mattie."

"You think you can solve this and fix him," Cam says.

"I do not!" Cam gives her a stern look. Blair sighs. "When did *you* get perceptive?" she mutters.

"I learned it by watching you, Dad." Cam smirks. "But if he's been lying to Mattie this whole time, that's too big of a project even for you."

"He's not a project!"

"Fine. You're the boss. But he knows something. 'Of course I don't fucking know what she wants,' remember?"

"I know," Blair says. "I . . ." She shrugs helplessly. "I think he's torn. I think if he knows where Lola went, he's trying to protect her *and* Mattie."

"How noble of him," Cam says.

Blair ignores this. "Let's say he *was* talking to Darren. If Darren and Lola planned something together, and she came back—does that mean Darren thought she was going to black-mail him?"

"Maybe it wasn't money," Cam says. "It could've been the drugs. If Darren was selling them, and Lola knew—maybe she was selling drugs too. And whoever was selling *them* drugs got pissed about it. So Becca and Darren had to help her hide, and make it look like someone kidnapped her. Isn't that what happens when people sell drugs? That's what happens on television."

Blair laughs.

"It's not funny," Cam says.

"I'm not laughing at you," Blair says. "I'm laughing at this whole mess. The heroin kingpin of Oreville, whoever that is, putting out a hit on Lola so that she has to flee the state is as good an explanation as anything else."

"What are you going to tell Meredith?"

"I don't know," Blair says.

"Rich people have problems too," Cam says. "That could be your book title. *I Had No Idea: But Really, They Do.*"

"Meredith will flip," Blair says, smiling.

"A novel angle," Cam says. "Bud-dum bum."

"You are not allowed to make puns," Blair says. "Not at a time like this. Honestly, I'm more worried about what we're going to tell Mattie."

Cam watches Mattie's small figure, stooping once more to look for treasure amid the gray stones. "They're not going to forgive us," she says.

"That's why I'm worried."

"But we have to do it."

"I know," Blair says. "It would be easier if we had an answer."

"This is Lola's fault, not yours. Ours. She's the one who lied to them. She's the one who's still lying."

"That's not going to make them feel any better," Blair says.

"No," Cam says. "That's going to make them feel worse."

Cam and Blair fall quiet as Mattie makes their way back to them. A lone seagull wheels above the water, shrieking invectives at the cloud-strewn sky.

"Today," Blair says when Mattie is almost back to them but still out of earshot. "We'll go home and tell them today."

"Okay," Cam says.

"I'll do it," Blair says. "I'm the one who started this."

"We'll do it," Cam says. "Together."

CHEWING GUM

On the drive back, a deer wanders out into the road while they're still far out into the county. Blair sees her in plenty of time.

She stops the car. The deer stands in front of them, unconcerned, for a long time, before turning and leaping gracefully back into the woods.

It's late in the afternoon by the time they're back inside Oreville city limits. Blair and Cam are bantering idly about which of Brad's dishes is the finest when Mattie makes a strangled noise from the back seat.

"Are you all right?" Blair asks.

Mattie's pale. The hand holding their phone is shaking.

"Pull over and look at this," they say.

Blair does. Mattie hands their phone forward. Cam leans over Blair's shoulder to read.

It's some kind of a table, charting letters and numbers that make no sense to Blair.

"What is this?" she asks. "An email?"

"Scroll down," Mattie says.

She does.

Reads:

Statement of results: The siblingship index is calculated by multiplying the sibling index values for each DNA locus. The siblingship index represents how many times more likely it is that the tested individuals are full or half-siblings than not related. Based upon the genetic data, siblingship index is calculated at .01 and indicates that the genetic evidence is not supportive of a sibling relationship. These results should not be considered to supersede any other testing involving the biological parents of the sampled individuals.

"Mattie," Cam says. "What *is* this?"
"I told you," Mattie says. "I *told* you."
"Oh my god," says Blair.
Cam takes the phone from her and reads the email.

Biological specimens corresponding to Lola Marie Brosillard (Alleged Sibling 1) and Mattie J Brosillard (Alleged Sibling 2) were submitted by Mattie J Brosillard for confirmation of sibling relationship . . .

"Holy shit," Cam says. "This is—is this *her*? Are you sure this is right?"
"How did you—" Blair begins.
"Chewing gum," Mattie says. "Whoever she is, she used to smoke. She goes through like a pack a day. Yeah, I'm sure. It was her gum. And she's not my sister."
They take their phone back, slumping in the back seat. They run a trembling hand through their hair. "I was starting to think I was losing my mind," they say. "Like I was in some kind of horrible alternate universe. Nobody believed me. You didn't believe me."
"We—" Blair begins.

"You didn't," Mattie says. "I'm not mad about it anymore. I wouldn't have believed me either." They look down at the phone in their lap. "Take me home," they say.

"What are you going to do?" Blair asks.

"Find out what that bitch did to my sister," Mattie says. Their voice is cold and absolutely calm.

"We should call the police," Blair says.

Mattie laughs. "Seriously? Who? Detective Bradshaw? The police don't care. They didn't care when she ran away. They're not going to care now. I doubt this is legal." They hold up their phone. "You think they're going to arrest that girl because of an email? I can't prove it was her gum. They're not going to take the word of a crazy fourteen-year-old over my entire family."

"They'll listen to us," Blair says. "Me and Cam."

"No, they won't," Mattie says. "They didn't listen to you last time until somebody held you at gunpoint."

"Mattie, this could be really dangerous," Blair says.

"What's she going to do?" Mattie asks. "Murder me?"

"She might," Cam says. "But she's not going to murder all three of us."

"What?" Mattie asks.

"You're not going back to that house alone," Cam says. "We're coming with you. Me and Blair. Right, Blair?"

Blair takes a deep breath.

This is such a bad idea, she thinks.

"Right," she says. "Let's go."

LOLA, INTERRUPTED

They drive. The twilight is gusty and disordered with stars, patches of constellation gleaming briefly through scraps of cloud.

Mattie's house is dark and silent. Luke's car is gone. So is Ruth's.

"I don't know where my brother is," Mattie says. "Ruth has pro-life circle on Friday nights."

"Pro-life circle," Blair echoes.

"They make a lot of posters," Mattie says. "It's the only time she gets her hands dirty. You really don't have to come in with me."

"Shut up," Cam says.

Inside, the house is quiet and still. A lone light on in the immense kitchen, motion-sensitive night-lights flaring to life along the halls. The air smells of Lysol.

If this was a horror movie, Blair thinks, *we'd be about to die.*

Lola's door is closed, as always. But a line of light, as always, gleams along its base. Mattie knocks.

"Mats?" Lola says from inside. "Come on in."

Mattie opens the door. Lola—whoever she is—is sitting on her bed, a laptop open in front of her. From the sound of it, she's watching *The Vampire Diaries.*

"Slumber party?" she asks, her eyes on Cam and Blair. "Am I invited?"

"Who are you?" Mattie asks. "What did you do to my sister?"

"The cute one's here," says a vampire from Lola's computer. She closes it mid-quip.

"Mattie," the other Lola says. "We've been over this."

Mattie brandishes their phone. "Yeah," they say. "But now I have a DNA test. *Who are you?*"

The other Lola laughs. "Seriously? Pulling hairs out of my hairbrush?"

"Your chewing gum," Mattie snarls.

"And?" Lola is calm, smiling, but her eyes are fixed on

Mattie's face. It's as if Cam and Blair aren't even there. This showdown is just for Mattie and Lola. "What do you think that'll change? You dug someone's gum out of the garbage, and you think that means I'm not your sister?"

"It was your gum." Mattie's voice is a howl. "I watched you take it out of your mouth. I know you're not Lola. *Who are you? Where is she?*"

Blair is afraid Mattie is going to assault this girl. She puts a hand on their shoulder, both for support and as a check.

But Lola—the fake Lola—whoever she is—is implacable. So calm, Blair feels doubt creeping in. How *does* Mattie know for sure the gum was Lola's?

"And your little podcaster friends are here to back you up?" Lola says, amused. "I thought your whole thing was how true crime was a bogus suburban-mom obsession? Are you changing your minds now? DNA evidence leads to wrongful convictions all the time."

"Sometimes it also exonerates innocent people," Cam says. Like Blair, like Mattie, she's watching the other Lola like a hawk. But somehow, the balance of power in the room has already shifted—to Lola. She is so calm, so in control. Cam feels almost foolish, standing there in the middle of her room. The three of them accusing her of something so wild it's barely plausible. It's barely *possible*. Gum or no gum. DNA or no DNA.

"I know what you are," Mattie rasps. "I'm not afraid of you. You thought you could scare me off with that book, but I'm not stopping until the whole world knows you're a fake."

For the first time, Lola looks surprised. "What book?"

"Don't you dare pretend—" Mattie lunges forward. Blair's hand tightens instinctively on their shoulder, the only thing holding them back.

"The book you left them," Blair says. "The threat."

"I don't know what you're talking about," Lola says.

Mattie takes a deep breath and rears backward, bringing themselves under control with a visible effort. They dig through their backpack with shaking hands, pull out the mutilated copy of *The Big Sleep*. They throw it at Lola where she sits on the bed, hard enough to hurt if they'd hit her, but missing her deliberately. Lola picks up the book and pages through it, her expression unreadable. Finally, she looks up.

"I didn't do this," she says. She smiles, a hard, merciless predator's smile. "If I wanted to get rid of you, this isn't how I'd do it."

"Oh, no?" Mattie says. "You think you can hurt me? You can't hurt me."

"I could get Ruth to send you to a conversion camp tomorrow if I wanted to," Lola says, her voice absolutely flat. "She's halfway there on her own."

"You wouldn't," Cam says. Rage is flooding through her like a drug. "You wouldn't do something like that. You can't do that to them. You *can't*."

"You don't know anything about what I can do," Lola says to her. "You don't know anything about what I've done already." The three of them stare at her, at a loss for words.

"You killed her," Mattie whispers finally. "You killed my sister, didn't you?"

To all of their astonishment, Lola laughs. Clear and bright. "Of course I didn't. I am your sister, remember?"

"No," Mattie says. "I don't know who you are. I don't know what you did to her. But you're not. You're *not*." Their voice is almost desperate now. Pleading.

This, Blair thinks, *is not how I thought this was going to go*. But how *did* she think it was going to go? Lola, confronted with Mattie's barely there proof, reduced to a tearful confession?

No way. Whoever this girl is—the real Lola, an evil twin—she's never lost a game in her life.

Lola sighs, the laughter gone. She runs one hand through her long, silky hair. Leans back against the wall, crosses her legs on the bed. Settling in. The way she's been settling in all along. Into this house, into this life, into this skin.

"I'll make a deal with you," she says to Mattie. "You drop this. All of it. Your little investigation, your little friends. Give me a month or two, and I'll be gone again. All I really need is some money and a new ID. A passport. The car, the house, the credit cards . . ." She shrugs. "Nice if you can get them, but I don't really like it here. I never did."

"A *deal*?" Mattie says in utter disbelief.

"And if you keep your end, I'll get Ruth to leave you alone. You know I can do it. I've got her eating out of the palm of my hand, Mats."

"Are you out of your mind?" Cam blurts.

Mattie shakes their head. "I'll never—I would *never*—*where is my sister?*"

Lola looks at them for a long time, debating some question Cam and Blair can't parse. "Conversion therapy for minors is illegal in Washington," she says. "But Idaho is right next door. Or she could send you pretty much anywhere in the South. Or Montana. Wyoming—"

"Stop it!" Cam shouts. "Just—stop! What kind of monster are you?"

"You wouldn't," Blair says suddenly. Even as she says the words, she knows they're true. "Because you actually aren't. You're trying to be a monster. Maybe you *want* to be a monster. What you've done, coming here, pretending to be someone you aren't—that's a monstrous thing to do. Maybe you did hurt the real Lola, or—or kill her. Or you know where she is. I think you're a person who's done a lot of awful things. But you're not a monster. I've seen the way you are with Mattie. You care about them"—Mattie makes an awful noise—"I know, Mattie, but it's true. She does. Don't you?"

Lola breathes in hard, her eyes widening, as she looks at Blair.

"You *do*," Blair says, triumphant.

Lola looks away. "Oh, hell," she says tiredly. "You wretched little bitch."

"I'm right," Blair says. "And you owe Mattie the truth." Cam and Mattie, next to Blair, are speechless.

Something strange moves across Lola's face as she looks at Mattie, as though she is processing some new emotion for the first time. And then her expression resolves into stoicism, and she seems to come to a decision.

"Sit down," Lola says to the three of them, gesturing to the floor.

"I—" Cam says.

"Just sit," Lola says. "I'll tell you the truth. I'm not going to hurt you." She looks at Mattie. "She's right," she says in rueful wonderment, as if she can hardly believe it herself. "I would never hurt you. Sit."

Mattie's shaking so hard they can barely stand anyway. Blair and Cam sink to Lola's bedroom floor, holding on to Mattie.

This is insane, Blair thinks. *Is this happening?*

"A few months ago, I did something that wasn't entirely legal," the girl says easily. "It seemed like a good idea for me to go away for a while. I read a story in a magazine years ago about a man who made a habit out of pretending to be other people. He'd search online for boys who'd gone missing, boys who looked like him and who'd disappeared long enough ago that any differences could be explained by the passage of time. That's where I got the idea."

"You . . ." Mattie says. They're having trouble forming words.

"It took me a long time to find your sister. But when I

did—she was perfect. Mysterious disappearance. Police gave up right away. We were almost the same age. Same height, same size. She looked so much like I did that it seemed like a sign. So I thought, *Why not?* I didn't want to be the person I was anymore. I wanted to be someone else. It was worth a try. It's not that hard to figure out what it is other people want from you, and give it to them. I've been doing it all my life. If I couldn't pull it off . . ." She shrugs. "I'd already disappeared once. I could do it again."

Cam finds her voice. "For money? You did it for the money?"

"I had no idea about the money until I got here," the girl says. "The money doesn't hurt. I wasn't thinking that far ahead when I ran. I wasn't sure it would actually work—it couldn't possibly work, right? It was a completely insane idea. In that police station—god, I was terrified. Once I started it, I couldn't take it back. But I was so sure the three of you would show up and see I was a fraud in seconds. I thought I'd have to crawl out the window. Cops chasing me with guns, or dogs, or something." Lola shakes her head. "But it was so easy. So easy, to be her. The prodigal daughter, miraculously returned a better version of herself. Ruth never wanted the Lola who disappeared. All I had to do was be the daughter she wished she'd had. Nobody asked questions. Except for you," she says to Mattie. "You knew. I thought, with enough time, I could convince you. I guess not. Which is funny, in the end, because you're the reason I wanted to stick around."

"But my sister," Mattie says in a tiny voice.

"I don't know," the girl says. "I never met her. I never heard of her before last month. I don't know anything about what happened to her."

"But you knew," Mattie says hoarsely. "You knew about the time we went to the hot springs."

"I found her journal," the girl says. "She really loved you, Mattie. She really, really did."

Mattie chokes on their sobs, buries their face in Cam's side. Cam and Blair put their arms around Mattie, hold them tight as they cry.

The girl watches them, her expression hard to read.

"I can see why she did. You're an easy person to love, Mattie Brosillard," she says.

Cam wants to hit this girl. Tear her to pieces. "Don't you dare," she snarls. "Don't you—don't you dare say things like that to them after what you did. You're evil."

"Ruth was going to send your sister away," the girl continues, ignoring Cam. "To one of those wilderness places that kidnap you in the middle of the night. Boot camp for troubled teens. Lola found out. I don't know if that's why she ran away."

"Boot camp?" Mattie echoes.

"It's the last thing she wrote in her journal," the girl says. "A few days before she disappeared. She was staying up all night, waiting for them to come and get her. She hadn't slept in days. She told Luke about it, and he told her not to worry. Looking the other way seems to be standard operating procedure for your brother."

"But Luke . . ." Blair says, pleading. "Luke thinks you're his sister."

"No, he doesn't," the girl says. "He asked me what I wanted on the second day. He asked me if I was here for money. He said he'd do whatever I asked. If he wanted me out of here, he could side with you, Mattie. But he's terrified of me."

Mattie lifts their head, their eyes bloodshot. "What?"

"He knows I'm not your sister," the girl repeats. "But he hasn't done anything about it."

"Why?" Mattie whispers.

"You'll have to ask him that," the girl says.

"And the book?" Cam asks.

"I'd ask him about that too," the girl says.

"He wouldn't," Blair says sharply. "He didn't."

"Well, someone did," the girl says. "And it wasn't me."

"Darren," Blair says.

"No!" Mattie protests, their voice breaking. But they sound unsure. Blair doesn't blame them.

They were right all along, and now everything is worse. Their whole world is collapsing around them.

"Luke would never," Mattie croaks. "Not Luke."

The other Lola only shrugs.

"I'm calling the police," Blair says, taking out her phone.

"What do you think the police are going to do? I've read all about you. I looked you up as soon as Mattie brought you to that awful party. Two teenybopper podcasters at the end of their fame, trying to dig up a new story? The police aren't very fond of you, are they? You made them look bad. They're not going to admit they were wrong about another missing girl."

"Ruth," Cam says.

The girl laughs. "Ruth? Are you kidding? You've met her. You know better. Ruth won't back you up. Luke won't back you up. The police will laugh you out of the room."

"The DNA test," Mattie says.

"You say it was my sample," the girl says. "You can't prove anything. It'll be your word against mine. Ruth's not going to make me take an official one."

"Do you think you're going to stay here?" Cam asks incredulously. "Just . . . keep being Lola? After all this?"

"I could," the girl says.

"Why are you doing this to us?" Mattie cries.

The other Lola's perfect face is uncannily serene.

"You were there," she says. "And look how easy it turned out to be."

"Except for me," Mattie says.

The girl smiles. "Except for you," she says.

There's something like affection in her voice.

Something like a wry respect.

"How can you live with yourself?" Mattie asks. "How can you do something like this, and—" They're struggling for words. "What *are* you?"

"We know what you are," Cam says, ferocious. "We won't let you do this. We'll—we'll—"

She falters while the girl watches her struggle.

Because the truth of it is, the girl is right.

What are they going to do?

Who are they going to tell?

Mattie's been telling the truth all along, and no one's listened.

Cam and Blair didn't believe them until an hour ago. And only because of the proof Mattie can't prove is real to anyone else.

The adults in Mattie's life have already signed off on this version of Lola. The police. Their mother. Their brother.

The adults in Mattie's life have watched them suffer this whole time, and done nothing.

Because it's easier for this girl to be the Lola everyone wanted than for the real Lola's family to admit this Lola doesn't exist.

Mattie comes to a decision. They stand, tugging Cam and Blair to their feet. "You're sick. You do whatever you're going to do," they say to the girl. "I don't care. Tell Ruth whatever you want. Tell her I'm staying up all night shooting heroin and having sex with strangers. Get me put in jail, if that's what makes you happy. I'm going to find out what happened to my sister. And we will never, ever have a deal."

"Mats—"

"Keep that name out of your mouth," Mattie snarls. "That name is for my *sister.*"

Mattie pushes Cam and Blair out into the hallway.

The last thing Cam sees, before Mattie slams Lola's bedroom door, is the other Lola's huge green eyes.

Gleaming with tears.

"We have to find my brother," Mattie says when they're outside. "He'll know—he'll know what to do. Text him, Blair. Tell him—I don't know. Tell him you want to go on a date. Tell him anything."

"Mattie," Cam says. "I don't think—"

"Just do it," Mattie says.

Mutely, Blair obeys.

> hey, you busy tonight? want
> to hang out?

"Tell him we know," Mattie says. "Tell him—" Their voice breaks again.

Blair looks at her phone. Actually—got some news about your sister, she types. Thinks for a while. What can she even say?

> Mattie has questions. They're
> with me and Cam right now.
> Can we talk?

She sends the message.

The three of them stand in Mattie's driveway for a long time, staring at Blair's phone. The screen stays dark.

"Let's get out of here, at least," Cam says. She looks up at the house, looming over them like a bad dream. At its heart, still, the other Lola, weaving her spider's web. How can Mattie ever go back inside? How can any of them stop this from happening? What is she supposed to do now? She hasn't felt this powerless since the basement.

"Do you want me to call the police?" Blair asks Mattie.

Mattie scoffs. "She's right about that much," they say. "What would you even tell them?"

"I don't know," Blair admits.

"Let's just drive," Mattie says. "Somewhere. Anywhere. I don't care."

Blair hands her phone to Cam. The three of them climb into her car. Blair drives.

Maybe she'll drive them to California. Keep going south, to Mexico. As far away as she can get them. Anywhere but here.

A pair of headlights on bright devour her windshield, blinding her. A car roars past in the other direction, speeding.

And then the road is dark again.

"Is Luke at work?" Blair asks.

"No," Mattie says. "Not on Fridays. Sometimes he hangs out at that dive bar on Water Street."

Blair, numb, drives them to Water Street, loops the block to check for Luke's car. She parks. Cam hands back her phone.

Luke's read her message, but he hasn't responded. For a moment, she sees a text bubble spring to life, the three dots flickering. He's typing something.

"Hold on," she says.

But the dots disappear.

No message.

"I'll check the bar," Mattie says. "Wait here." They're out of the car before Cam or Blair can say anything, running down the street. Disappearing into the bar. A moment later, they pop out again, shaking their head as they lope back to Blair's car.

"Where else?" Blair asks. "Friends?"

"My brother doesn't have friends," Mattie says.

Blair's phone buzzes in her hand.

Hey Blair, sure, we can talk.
last minute but tonight is
parade of lights in the harbor,
i'll take you out in the boat.
it's cheesy but pretty. bring
cam & mats too

"Is it him?" Mattie asks.

"Yeah. He wants to take us all sailing," Blair says.

"Now?" Mattie asks. "Are you serious?"

"Parade of lights," Blair says. "I don't know what that is."

"Ask him when," Mattie says. "No. Don't ask him. Tell him we're coming."

"I think this is a bad idea," Cam says loudly.

Mattie gives her a bewildered look. "It's my *brother*," they say. "He's not going to hurt us. I just want to talk to him. I just want to— She was lying," they add. "She was *lying*. He never asked her that. He thinks she's the real Lola. When we tell him—when we prove she isn't—he'll help us. He *will*. He just needs to see the proof."

Cam sighs. "Right," she says. "Knight in shining armor, your brother."

"He'll *help* us," Mattie insists. "Text him," they order Blair. "Tell him we'll meet him there."

in the car, Blair texts. should we come to the harbor?

A moment. Then: perfect see you in a few

"What's the parade of lights?" Blair asks, pocketing her phone.

"Boat parade," Mattie says. "Everybody puts Christmas lights on their boats and sails around in a circle. All the rich people try to outdo each other." They frown. "Usually it's the day before Christmas."

"Maybe it's early this year," Blair says.

"I guess," Mattie says. "I'll do the talking."

"Are you sure you want us there?" Cam asks.

Mattie gives her a withering look from the back seat.

"Just making sure," Cam says.

PARADE OF LIGHTS

For once, there's no rain. But a cold, wet wind is blowing in off the water, and the stars are blotted out with clouds. Blair parks in the harbor lot. Mattie's out of the car before she turns off the engine, stamping with impatience.

"How often do boats sink?" Cam asks.

"Not often," Mattie says curtly.

"That's good, because I can't swim," Cam says.

"Doesn't matter, this time of year," Mattie says. "The water's so cold you'll freeze before you drown."

"Thanks," Cam says. "That's very reassuring."

Mattie's so tense they're nearly vibrating as they half walk, half run along the network of jetties toward the *Rorqual*.

Luke's out on deck waiting for them, a steaming travel mug in one hand. He's wearing a wool fisherman's sweater with a complicated knit and a beanie pulled low over his ears. His expression changes when he sees them, but it's not enthusiasm.

It's fear, she thinks.

But that doesn't make sense.

"You made it," Luke says, helping Cam and Blair step off the dock onto the boat. Mattie stays on the dock, loosening the lines from their cleats. When the boat is free they leap agilely onto the deck as Luke starts the motor and pulls deftly out of the slip.

Blair watches the dock slide away before it occurs to her they're out on the water alone.

"Where's the parade?" she asks.

Luke is busy with the wheel. "We're early," he says.

Misgiving is rising in Blair's belly. "But there are no lights," she says.

"We must be really early, then," Luke says without conviction.

"Did you get the date wrong?" Mattie asks. "Isn't parade of lights always the day before Christmas?"

"Maybe," Luke says.

Cam's eyes flick from Mattie, who's not worried yet, to Blair, who clearly is.

Surreptitiously, she slides her phone out of her back pocket, sets it next to her butt.

But who is she going to call if something goes wrong?

Does 911 get you to the coast guard?

Does Oreville *have* a coast guard?

"If it's the wrong day, let's go back," Cam says. "I'm cold. I think I might not like boats very much."

"We have to talk," Mattie says. "I found out something, Luke. I have proof. It's not her."

Luke glances at his sibling, his mouth tight.

"Oh, Mats," he says. His voice is heavy with weariness.

"I don't *see anyone else*," Cam says, enunciating.

"Just a few minutes," he says. "We'll see everybody else moving out in a second. We can talk then, okay?"

They are moving farther and farther away from land, out into the bay.

"Luke," Mattie says, "I need to ask you something. And you have to tell me the truth."

"Not now, Mats," Luke says.

There's a noise from inside the boat. A loud thump, and then footsteps. And then Darren comes out on deck.

"*Darren?*" Mattie is bewildered, not frightened. They're looking from their brother to Darren and back again, confused. Even Blair looks surprised. After all this, Cam thinks dourly, after everything. She's so distracted by her feelings for Mattie's brother that she still can't see it.

The three of them are in trouble, now, for real.

I knew we shouldn't have gotten on this goddamn boat, Cam thinks. Mattie and Darren and Luke and Blair are all looking at one another, waiting for someone to speak first. Cam reaches for her phone. RORQUAL BOAT HELP Cam texts with her thumb, as fast and as covertly as she can.

But Darren catches the motion, is across the deck in one long stride, snatching Cam's phone and pitching it over the side of the boat over Cam's squawk of protest.

Did she hit "Send"?

She really, really hopes she hit "Send."

Does she have a signal this far from shore?

Please, no, Cam thinks. *Not this again.*

She should be panicking, she realizes. She should be reduced to a shivering mess. But here, in this moment, when the danger is real and right in front of her, she is astonished to find herself calm. *This is it,* she thinks. *I have to get us through this. I have to take care of my friends.*

I'm strong enough to take care of my friends. The knowledge moves through her, sure as weather, as the turning of the earth.

"Darren," Mattie says. "What are you doing here? Why are you—"

"Phones," Darren says. "You too, Mats."

"Darren," Luke says, an unconscious echo of Mattie.

Darren holds out his hand.

"Please turn the boat around, Luke," Cam says. Her voice is steady. "I would like to go home now."

"Not yet," Darren says.

"Yes," Cam says. "Now."

But in the faint glow from the boat's running lights, Blair can see the bulk at Darren's waistline.

She's spent enough time at Brad's range to know what it is. Cam hasn't seen it yet. Neither has Mattie.

"Cam," Blair says, handing over her phone. "Mattie. Listen to me. Just do what he says."

Mattie looks at her, at Darren, back at her.

Wordlessly, Mattie reaches into their pocket, digs out their phone, gives it to Darren.

Blair is trying to think how to transmit *gun* to Cam without scaring Mattie. Or Cam, for that matter. But for all Cam's mighty brainpowers, telepathy has yet to number among them.

"Luke," Darren says. "Phone."

"Darren, come on," Luke says. "This isn't what you said. You said we were just going to talk."

"I'm changing the plan," Darren says, and reaches for his waist.

"Give him your phone!" Blair says. "Please. We can figure this out. Everybody take it down a notch. Let's see what Darren wants. Right, Darren? We're just talking. That's all."

Luke glances at Blair, uncertain.

"Just do it," she pleads. He shakes his head, but hands the phone over.

"That's right," Darren says. His voice is tight with tension. "We're just talking. We're just going to talk, and nobody needs to get hurt."

"Who's getting hurt?" Mattie barks. "What's going on? Darren? *Darren?*"

"Mats," Luke says, warningly. "Calm down."

"Somebody tell me what's going on!" Mattie yells. "That girl—"

"Mattie," Blair says. She remembers the voice Irene used last year, when everything fell apart and Cam was locked up in a basement and Blair was pretty sure they were all going to die. Irene's magic talking-people-down voice. "Mattie, we're just having a conversation. It's okay. Everything is going to be okay. Darren, what did you want to talk about?" Blair says, doing her best Irene. Calm, authoritative, reasonable. "Did you have something you needed to say to us? We're listening, Darren. We're right here."

Darren's hands are shaking, Blair notes. There is a part of her brain hovering above the boat, watching, detached, taking notes.

"I want to talk about Lola," Darren says.

Darren's hands are shaking, Blair thinks.

Darren has a gun.

Darren needs to talk to us. Luke and Darren had a plan, but Darren changed the plan, and now Luke doesn't know what's going on.

"That girl isn't Lola," Mattie says.

Blair thinks *MATTIE NO SHUT UP,* but it's too late.

Darren starts to laugh. "No shit," he says. "You had to go and be a detective, huh, Mats? Couldn't leave it alone? Let your brother be happy? Let me live my life?"

"What happened to my sister?" Mattie says. Their voice is low and hoarse and their eyes are huge and they are gazing up at Darren with horror. "Darren, what did you do?"

"Darren, I really think we should—" Luke begins. He's turning the wheel back toward shore.

"Shut up, Luke, and give me the wheel," Darren says.

That's when he pulls out the gun.

"No," Cam says, a small awful sound that cracks Blair's heart in half.

"Darren, you don't need a gun," Blair says, still trying for Irene. But Irene is a grown woman with years of experience talking down drunk skinheads at punk shows and punk friends freaking out on bad drugs and who knows what else, a person with the dense weight of authority and confidence behind her, and Blair is a teenager, and she knows her words don't have the same force.

So what's she going to do? Shoot out Darren's kneecap with eyeball lasers?

Darren's holding the wheel with one hand and the gun with the other, and even from here, in the dark, Blair can see the hand with the gun is shaking harder than ever.

What happens if you shoot a gun on a boat? Blair thinks. Do boats have gas tanks? In the movies if you shoot a car in the gas tank the car explodes immediately, but Blair is pretty sure that might not be scientific.

"I would like you to put the gun away now," Cam says, loud and clear and calm, and now *she's* the one who sounds like Irene.

"Darren, man, come on," Luke says.

"I'm not going to jail," Darren says. "I'm not going to jail. Not now. Not after all this time. I have a life. A real life."

"We don't want anybody to go to jail," Cam says. "I know you're not a violent person, Darren. Darren, I know you don't want to hurt us."

Where did *this* Cam come from? Blair wonders in awe. Has she been *practicing*?

"We all know that, Darren," Blair agrees. "We know you just want to talk. We're listening, Darren."

"*Where is my sister?*" Mattie screams.

Darren starts. He jerks the wheel hard, and the boat lurches.

Blair crashes into Cam.

Luke loses his balance, falls into the two of them.

And then Luke is crying, still half sprawled on Blair's lap.

"Lo's dead, Mats," he says. "I'm so sorry. I'm so, so sorry. Me and Darren killed her and buried her in the woods. She died that night. She's been dead this whole time."

A DÉNOUEMENT

"Luke, no," Darren says, slumping forward over the wheel. The gun is still in his other hand, but the meanness has gone out of him. He looks like what he is.

Darren was a loser, Blair thinks.

Becca had called it, all those years ago.

"What did you do?" Mattie cries. "What did you do to her? Luke? *Luke?*"

"What are you going to do, Darren?" Luke begs. "Shoot them all and throw them overboard? You gonna kill me too? Put the gun down, man. It's over. It's time to tell Mattie the truth."

Darren's eyes are wild. "I was thinking about killing myself," Darren says.

He means it, Blair thinks. *And if this guy shoots himself in front of Cam, it will mess her up for the rest of her life.*

And then she thinks, *If this guy shoots himself in front of me, it will mess* me *up for the rest of my life.*

"If you shoot yourself in front of Mattie, it will mess them up for the rest of their life," Cam says calmly. Maybe she is telepathic after all. "We can all get out of this. Put the gun down, like Luke said. Tell us what happened. Tell Mattie what happened, if you don't want to tell me and Blair. They deserve to know."

"I can't," Darren says. "I . . . I can't." The hand with the gun wobbles harder, and then he's flipping on the safety, putting it back in his waistband.

If this was a thriller movie, we'd all be tackling him to the deck, Blair thinks.

But none of them move.

"Please," Mattie says.

Darren looks at Luke, and then away. "I can't," he says again thickly.

"It was the end of the night," Luke says. "Just me and Darren and Becca and Lola, out on the back lawn. Everybody else had left. Me and Becca were—uh. You know. Messing around. Darren was passed out. We were all so high, Mats. After a while, me and Becca passed out too. When I woke up it was four in the morning. Lola was lying on her back in the grass. I thought she was asleep." His voice cracks. "But then I saw that her eyes were open. There was—she had—I think she choked. I don't know. I was still high. And then Becca was there behind me, screaming her head off—"

"I slapped her," Darren says. "We were outside, Becca was making so much noise, I could barely think— Becca started sobbing, but at least she quieted down. I knew we had to get her out of there before she freaked out again."

"Why didn't you call an ambulance?" Mattie asks, pleading.

"She was dead, Mats," Darren says. "She was—she was cold. Like ice. There was nothing we could do. If we called an ambulance—it would've been—I mean, for me, it would've been over, can't you see that? It would've been the end of everything. I brought the drugs. I was over eighteen. It was *heroin.* I would've gone to jail for the rest of my life. I didn't want to do that. Come on. Who would that have helped?"

"You just—" Mattie's mouth is working, but they can barely get the words out. "You just . . . you just did *nothing*?"

"I wasn't thinking at all," Luke says. "Darren was saying we had to get Becca out of there. I had no idea what I was doing. But somehow I remembered I had left my car by the side of the house so people had room to park. Darren was asking about the cameras on the driveway." He looks up at Darren. "I don't know how you had it so together," he says.

"I was on autopilot," Darren says. "I was as high as you were, Luke."

"Yeah, well," Luke says bitterly. "You seemed pretty okay to me."

"I wasn't okay," Darren snaps.

"He told me to bring the car around," Luke says to Mattie. "So I did. To the backyard. Must've only been a hundred feet or so, but I could barely drive. Darren took over. Pushed Becca into the back seat. She was in shock. I mean, obviously. Darren disappeared for a few minutes and when he came back"— Luke's voice cracks again—"he had a shovel. I don't know where—I didn't know you knew the house that well," he says, talking to Darren again.

"I was her boyfriend," Darren says. "Of course I knew the house."

"Right," Luke says dully. "Her doting boyfriend. 'We have to put her in the trunk,' you said."

"You asked me who I was talking about," Darren says.

"I guess I was in shock too," Luke says. "I don't—I don't really want to talk about the next part, Mats."

"You," Mattie says. "*You* don't want to—"

"She didn't feel anything," Darren says. "She was already gone."

"We got her in the trunk," Luke says. "I couldn't—I was—Darren drove. We took Becca home first. Darren said some stuff about how we had to keep quiet. We could all go to jail. I don't know if that's true, now. We were minors. I don't know if Becca understood him."

"She understood him well enough to stay quiet for your sake for the next five years," Cam says savagely. "Even though it almost killed her. She was *fifteen*, Darren. Her best friend had just died in front of her and you told her she was going to *jail* if she talked about it?"

"It wasn't like that," Darren says.

"No?" Cam says. "What was it like, then, Darren? Please tell us what it was like for Becca when her best friend's adult boyfriend told her she was going to jail for the rest of her life for something she didn't do if she didn't stay quiet."

"Nobody did anything," Darren says. "It was an accident. An *accident*. Nobody hurt her."

"Nobody hurt her?" Mattie shrieks. "She *died*!"

"Everybody was scared," Luke says. "Darren was the only person thinking straight."

"You call that thinking straight—" Cam's so furious she almost chokes.

"Then what?" Mattie asks. They're crying, the tears running down their cheeks unchecked without their noticing, as if they're in a trance. "What did you do after that?"

"Darren drove us out to—I don't know where we were. Somewhere in the Olympics. We, uh. We buried her," Luke says.

"She's in the trees, up in the mountains," Darren says to Mattie, pleading. "She's in a place she loved with her whole heart. I wanted her to have a special place to rest. I loved her, Mats. I loved her. You know how much I loved her."

Mattie's fist is against their mouth, as if they're trying not to throw up.

"It was past dawn by the time we were done," Luke says. "I don't really remember what happened after that very well. Darren drove us back to the house. We came in the back door. He said we had to do something to explain why she was gone. He broke the glass in the patio door from the outside, so it would look like a burglar got in. It was so loud. 'Go to bed,' he said. 'We'll deal with the rest of this tomorrow.'

"But then Ruth came into the living room. We didn't hear her until it was too late. She stood there and looked at us. We were covered in dirt and broken glass. 'Where's your sister?' she said to me. And I said, 'I'm not sure.' And she said"—his voice breaks a third time, and tears are running down his face, but he doesn't stop—"'What has she done now?' And I said, 'I don't know.' She was—we were yelling. 'What did your sister do?' she kept saying. And Darren said, 'We don't know where Lola is.' He just kept saying that. 'Did she run away?' Ruth screamed. And I couldn't take it anymore, I just—"

"You put your hands over your ears like a child," Darren said.

"He *was* a child," Blair says quietly.

"I did what I had to do," Darren says. "I told her Lola wanted to leave town. That she hadn't wanted us to tell anyone, but since Ruth was her mother, she deserved to know. I said we took her to the bus station."

"And she *believed* you?"

"I don't know what she believed," Luke says. "But that's when you woke up, Mats. You came into the living room and we were all standing there and you asked what was happening. Where Lola was. You saw the broken window and you started crying. And then you grabbed Ruth's phone—she had left it on the sideboard when she came out to see what was going on—"

"I didn't do that," Mattie says. "I was asleep."

"No, you weren't, Mats," Luke says. "You woke up. You just don't remember."

"I didn't," Mattie says, shaking their head. "I didn't. I would remember. I would!"

"It was you," Luke says. "Not Ruth. It was you who called."

"I would remember," Mattie says hoarsely. "I would . . ." They falter, looking at Blair and Cam, back at their brother. "I thought I remembered everything perfectly. I always remember everything perfectly."

"Nobody remembers everything perfectly," Luke says. "Ruth tried to stop you. She didn't want to call the cops any more than—than Darren did. I don't think—" He pauses. "I don't think you could have lived with her," he says finally. "If you remembered it the way it really happened. I think that's why you forgot."

"I remember her yelling at me," Mattie whispers. "I remember . . ." Their eyes fill again with tears. "She slapped me," they say. "I forgot . . . She slapped me, didn't she? I remember the phone. I had her phone." Their voice cracks. "I . . ."

Luke presses his lips together, looks away.

"It would've been fine," Darren says heavily. "Everything would've been fine. Ruth was handling it. But you had to go and call the police, Mattie. Jesus."

"You want to blame *Mattie* for this?" Cam is incredulous. "You think this is *Mattie's* fault? What is *wrong* with you?"

"Ruth sent me home," Darren says, ignoring her. "Like I was—like I was nothing. Nobody. 'Don't show your face around here again.' Unbelievable." He shakes his head.

"We had to tell the police something when they showed up," Luke says. "They came so fast. There was the broken window, dirt everywhere. You couldn't stop crying. Darren was gone by then—I couldn't even think straight. Ruth said that her daughter had vanished in the night and someone had broken into the house. She said we had all been home, the whole night. She told them that I was asleep and didn't know anything. She told them I had a dream that someone came into the house, but that maybe I hadn't been dreaming. That it was real, and I'd been half-asleep and not understood what was happening. But she knew they wouldn't push it too hard. Lola had a record. Nothing was missing from the house."

"Did she know?" Mattie whispers. "Did she guess what you did?"

"I don't know," Luke says. He can't meet their eyes. "I don't know how much she guessed. She was just trying to protect us, Mats."

"Not *us,*" Mattie says. "You."

"We never talked about it again," Luke says, still not looking at them. "Not after that night. It was like it had never happened. I started to think—maybe it hadn't. Maybe it had just been a bad dream. Maybe I was . . ."

"But she was gone," Mattie cries.

"I know," Luke says. "I know. I'm so sorry, Mattie. I'm so . . ." He can't finish the sentence.

"It was better for you this way, Mats," Darren says. "Wouldn't it have been so much worse if you knew? If you thought she ran away, she could still be alive for you."

If Mattie doesn't kill Darren, Cam thinks, as if from a great remove, *I might.* She feels as though she will be ill.

"Mats, we were trying to do our best," Luke says. "Don't be like this. Please."

"And then she came back," Darren says. "I thought I had lost my mind."

"We all did," Luke says. "Me. You. Becca. You should've seen her at the welcome-home party, Darren."

"She had to go to the hospital," Cam says. "You did that."

"I didn't do that," Darren says, holding up his hands. "I wasn't there."

"Yeah, you weren't much help," Luke says bleakly. "You wouldn't talk to her. You didn't want anything to do with us."

Blair remembers the night of their first date. Luke's phone call.

Of course I don't fucking know what she wants.

"You thought she was trying to blackmail you," she says.

"I didn't know," Darren says. "I had no idea. It wasn't possible. None of it was possible. Lola was dead. I knew that. I saw—" His voice cracks. "She was dead," he says again.

"The book," Mattie says. "That was you."

"I just wanted you to drop it," Darren says. "Everything would've been fine. She was back. She *came back.* Ruth was happy. Luke was happy. But you wouldn't let it go. You wouldn't stop asking questions. You couldn't leave it alone. I wasn't really going to hurt you. I'm not a bad person, Mattie. I swear."

"Did you give it to him?" Cam asks Luke. "Did you give him the book?"

"What book?" Luke asks. The confusion on his face is genuine.

"He didn't have anything to do with it," Darren says. "I still have a key, from when Lola and I were together."

"You were never *together,*" Luke says under his breath.

"But it wasn't fine," Cam says. "It wouldn't have been fine, Darren. Because you thought the fake Lola was trying to blackmail you. You were going to hurt her too, weren't you?"

"No," Darren says weakly. "I didn't hurt anyone. I'm not that kind of person. I wouldn't."

"You know what's funny?" Mattie asks savagely. "She had no idea what you did. She wasn't trying to blackmail you at all. But you . . ." Mattie looks at the gun in Darren's waistband. "You went to the house first," they say. "Before you came here. You passed us on the road. Before you told Luke to text us. Did you kill her?"

"No," Darren says. "I swear."

"Darren," Luke says. "Jesus, Darren, what did you do?"

"I didn't do anything," Darren says. "She wasn't there. She's gone."

"She was there an hour ago," Cam says.

"She's not there now," Darren says. "She left the front door unlocked. I went in. Her room looks like a tornado went through it."

"You went there to kill her," Mattie says. "That's why you have the gun."

Darren's mouth opens. Closes again. He looks at Mattie, beseeching. "Mats, what happened to your sister was an accident," Darren says. "I have a life now. I have a girlfriend. We're getting married. We're talking about having a baby. Please don't screw that up for me. *Please.* We can keep going the way things are now. The past is just the past."

"You think you deserve to have a life now?" Mattie can't hold it back anymore, gun or no gun. "You think I should *pretend this never happened?*"

"Someone's coming," Luke says.

"What?" Darren's head snaps up. The roar of a motor is building across the dark water, a blaze of light heading directly toward them.

"Who did you tell?" Darren demands, bringing the gun up again. "What did you do, Luke?"

"I didn't do anything!" Luke protests. "I swear to god, Darren, I didn't tell anyone!"

"I did," Cam says. "Put the gun down, Darren. It's over. If you shoot us in front of my mom's boyfriend, I guarantee he'll tear you apart with his teeth."

Darren's hand with the gun goes up.

Cam moves faster than Blair has ever seen anyone move in her life, lunging straight for his chest. She hits him hard in the torso with both fists and he shouts in surprise and yanks at the wheel again, trying to keep himself upright.

The boat spins hard and Darren goes flying over the side and into the water.

Mattie's on their feet almost instantly. "Blair!" they shout, their voice full of authority. "Point at him! Don't take your eyes off him! Hold out your arm and point!" Blair obeys without thinking, jumping to her own feet, arm outstretched, pointing at where Darren is crying out in the black water, sliding away from them as the boat moves forward. "Luke, kill the engine!" Mattie yells, hurling themself across the cockpit at a fluorescent-orange life preserver.

"Cameron, we're here!" Brad's huge voice rings out over the motor of the approaching boat.

"Kill your engine!" Mattie bellows. "Kill it now! We have a man overboard!"

The heavy roar of the motor cuts out immediately. "Where?" Brad shouts.

"Follow Blair's arm!" Mattie yells. "Luke, bring the boat around! Blair and Cam—"

But Cam's already standing next to Blair, pointing her own arm. Is that still really Darren? The darkness is thick as ink. The boat is turning as Luke pulls hard at the wheel. A white light flares to life as Mattie throws the bright circle of the life preserver out as far as they can, the harsh glow of the safety beacon arcing through the air.

Blair can't see Darren anymore, but she can hear him shouting in the dark—a funny, high-pitched noise that barely sounds human. And when the life preserver lands on the water, the light illuminates his pale, desperate face. Mattie's aim was true. He thrashes toward the life preserver, frantic.

Blair drops her arm. *If it was me,* she thinks, *I'd let him drown.*

But Mattie pulls on the line, bringing him in. Brad's deftly using the speedboat's momentum to bring it alongside the *Rorqual,* and even in her state of shock Blair is capable of marveling at how he handles it—surely it's much, much harder than he's making it look to parallel park a speedboat next to a moving sailboat while someone on the sailboat is carrying out a nautical rescue.

"Cam!" Irene shrieks. "Cam, are you okay? *Cameron, where are you?*"

"I'm here!" Cam yells. "I'm here. We're all here. We're all fine." No, she thinks, they're not fine. But they are whole. Unshot. Un-tied-up-in-basements. They are alive. Even Darren, wailing in the frigid water, is alive.

"Help me get Darren into the boat," Mattie shouts, snapping Cam back to the situation at hand. "Cam! Blair! Come on! He's going to pass out!"

"You!" Brad barks at Luke, who's standing at the wheel, dazed. "Put out a fender and tie us up!" Luke moves automatically to help, catching the line Brad tosses him and wrapping it around a silver cleat on the *Rorqual*'s deck. Brad doesn't wait for him, leaping the gap between the boats neatly.

Mattie and Cam are trying to pull Darren out of the water. His sodden weight drags them under with him. Blair moves quickly to help. Between the three of them, they manage to drag him onto the sailboat's backboard. His lips are turning blue, and he's shivering so hard he can't talk anymore. His eyelids slide closed.

"I think he's unconscious," Cam says with alarm.

"Irene, we need you," Brad says. Irene's already clambering aboard the sailboat, though rather less gracefully than Brad.

"Call 911," she orders Brad. "Right now. He's going into hypothermic shock. You!" She snaps her fingers at Luke. "What do you have for first aid on this boat? I need an emergency blanket, *now*! We need to get his clothes off."

But Luke isn't moving. It's as if tying the boat off was all he could do. He's just standing there, swaying with the motion of the boat.

"I'll get it," Mattie says, pushing past him and diving into the cabin. They emerge seconds later with a first aid kit. Blair and Cam help Irene haul Darren the rest of the way into the sailboat, pull off his sopping clothes. Mattie digs a foil blanket out of the first aid kit, and together they and Irene wrap Darren tightly.

"Is he breathing?" Cam asks in a low voice.

"Barely," Irene says.

". . . at the harbor," Brad's saying into the phone. He looks at Mattie, and then at Cam and Blair. "Boating accident," he says. ". . . No, I happened to be in the area. I didn't see what happened . . . Yes, in the water for several minutes . . . Thank you." He hangs up. "We need to get him on the speedboat," he says. "The ambulance is on its way. You"—this to Luke—"you're in shock. The water is too deep here to drop an anchor. Irene, can you drive the speedboat back to shore? I'll help him bring the sailboat in."

"I can do it," Luke says numbly.

"No, you can't," Mattie says. "I'll do it."

"I'm not leaving you on this boat alone with him," Cam says.

"I'm not leaving either of you alone on this boat until somebody tells me what's going on!" Irene shouts.

Across the water, the sound of sirens.

Mattie shakes their head. "There's no time," they say. "Just go."

"But—"

"Come on," Blair says, pushing Cam toward Brad's boat. "Mattie can do this."

Brad climbs back into the speedboat. "Move him to the edge," he directs. "Give me his feet. This is going to be tricky."

Mattie holds the line connecting the two boats, keeping

them pressed together, as Irene, Cam, and Blair half drag, half push Darren up against the cockpit wall. Brad leans over from the speedboat, grabs his legs. "Ready? Watch the gap. Mattie, hold tight. Now push him over."

Darren's a dead weight, but the four of them manage it. He tumbles into the speedboat, Brad catching his upper half so that he doesn't hit his head. Irene climbs into the boat, helping Brad haul him into one of the seats.

The sirens are closer; Blair can see whirling lights now, flashing toward the harbor.

"Come on!" Brad shouts. "Cam! Let's go!"

Cam topples into the speedboat, her crisis-prompted coordination abandoning her. Blair climbs cautiously after her. "Loose the lines! He's clear!" Brad directs Mattie. They undo the ropes binding the boats together, toss the speedboat's line to Cam.

Irene hugs Cam and Blair tight to her chest as Brad pulls away from the *Rorqual* with a burst of speed.

Blair turns as the boat roars away to see Mattie at the wheel, their face set. Luke is slumped next to them in the boat's cockpit.

He's not moving, not helping.

Mattie's handling the boat entirely alone.

And then Mattie's just a pale point in the darkness, fading fast into the night.

Cam is soaked from pulling Darren out of the water. "You're going to freeze to death," Irene worries. "Blair, help me look in these compartments. There's got to be another emergency blanket here." She glances in the direction of the sailboat. "We need two," she says. "We shouldn't have left Mattie alone."

Blair and Irene ransack the boat; Irene tosses aside pristine lifejackets, fishing rods, and a Yeti cooler. She cries out in triumph as she unearths another space blanket. "Here," she says. "Cam, take off your jacket, you're wet."

"I'm fine," Cam says.

"Don't you argue with me right now!" Irene barks. Cam starts, and then meekly pulls off her bedraggled jacket. Irene wraps her up in the emergency blanket like a burrito, checks on Darren, moves back to Cam, efficient as a nurse in a field hospital.

The gun, Cam thinks suddenly. The gun is gone, lost somewhere in the dark water. And she's still here. The worst happened, and she and Blair and Mattie got through it, and now Irene and Brad are here, and everything is going to be okay.

They might not all live happily ever after. But they're here. Together.

"Maybe I *will* try therapy again," Cam says to no one in particular.

Brad catches it over the roar of the speedboat's engine and smiles.

"How did you know where to find us?" Blair asks.

"Cam texted me the name of the boat," Brad says, as if this explains everything. He sees Blair's confusion. "It's a requirement for boats of a certain size to have an automatic identification system. A lot of smaller sailboats have one too. I found the *Rorqual* with a marine traffic app. Luckily."

"Lucky you knew what to do," Blair says.

"That's why I texted him and not Irene," Cam says, her teeth chattering. "No offense."

"I can take the blanket away," Irene says dryly.

"I'm glad you came too," Cam says. "Mom."

"I didn't know you had a boat," Blair says to Brad.

"I don't," Brad says, slightly embarrassed. "I hot-wired this one."

"Irene," Blair says, "I think you should probably marry this dude."

BLAIR'S BOOK PROPOSAL:
THE AFTERMATH

Dear Meredith Payne-Whiteley,

In the end, it came down to spaghetti alla puttanesca à la Brad again.

That was after we'd handed Darren over to the EMTs, who'd whisked him away in the ambulance in a blare of noise and light.

After Brad tied up the stolen speedboat—he had, I noticed, managed to pick the most expensive-looking one in the whole harbor—and we stood on the dock, watching Mattie moor the *Rorqual* with a level of skill that startled all of us. Calm and assured, despite everything that had happened.

After Luke walked past the four of us, without a word, heading for the parking lot. He didn't look back at us—at me—once.

After Mattie started to follow him, their face set.

"What are you doing?" Cam asked as Mattie trudged past.

Mattie stopped.

"Going home," they said. Their face was blank with shock and grief, their eyes like dark pits. My heart contracted.

"That's not your home," Cam said.

"Come on," Brad said. "It's freezing. Let's get out of here."

And he was the one to reach for Mattie then, to fold them into the shelter of one big arm, and Cam and me into the other.

Irene flung her arms around the whole bundle of us, holding tight.

"Somebody," she said, her voice muffled by Cam's shoulder, "had better tell me what the hell happened here."

"Yes," Brad rumbled. "Over pasta. Let's go."

And now, we're all at Cam's kitchen table again. Kitten purrs lasciviously in Mattie's lap, kneading his way to heaven. Irene wrapped Mattie in a pile of blankets, but they're still shivering in their chair, one hand numbly stroking Kitten's fur.

I want to ask them if they're okay, but I don't. Because that's the stupidest question I could come up with, under the circumstances.

I don't know if Mattie will ever be okay.

But I know if anyone could be okay after something like this, that person will be Mattie.

It's Cam who tells Irene and Brad the rest of the story, so Mattie doesn't have to talk.

She doesn't mention the gun. Or the mutilated book.

She doesn't mention that Darren went to the Brosillards' before he waited for us on Luke's boat.

That the first time, he became a murderer by accident.

The second time, he was ready to become one for real.

Brad's clanking around at the stove while Cam talks, and the kitchen smells increasingly incredible. He mutters to himself as he pulls mismatched plates and bowls from the cupboards, loads them full of pasta.

Just as Cam finishes, he sets the food in front of us, and nobody talks for long moments after that because we're too busy shoveling in food. It's the most delicious thing I've ever tasted. Nothing like a brush with death to whet a person's appetite.

Irene pushes her empty bowl away with a deep, satisfied sigh and sits back in her chair.

"I should go home," Mattie says dully. They've barely touched their pasta. Cam's eyeing the almost-full bowl, and I know she's weighing the horrifying rudeness of stealing a grief-stricken person's meal against the magnificent benefit of more Brad pasta.

For once, she decides to be her better self.

"None of that," Irene says matter-of-factly.

"What?" Mattie looks up.

"You're not going anywhere," Irene says. "You're staying here as long as you want."

"I can't do that," Mattie says.

"Why not?" asks Cam.

"Because—" Mattie stops. "Because you're not— you don't have to—" They can't finish the sentence.

Irene gets up, finds WORLD'S #1 DAD and her bottle of wine, pours herself a mug, sits back down. "Being an adult is a pile of shit most of the time, but every now and then you get a chance to do whatever you want, which almost makes it worth it," Irene says. "Now is one of those times. You are welcome in this house, Mattie. If problems arise due to that decision, we will solve them. Do you understand?"

Mattie nods mutely.

Brad puts one arm around Irene's shoulders, and she leans into him. "Together," he says. "We will solve them together."

"Thank you," Mattie says.

"Do you want to call the police?" Brad asks. "I mean, about your sister?"

"I thought about that," Mattie says. "I've been thinking about it for a long time. When I thought it was—her. The fake Lola. What I wanted to happen to her, if she killed my sister. But the truth is so . . ." Mattie trails off. "The truth is so much more complicated," they say. "I don't think Darren is a very good person, but he didn't mean for Lola to die. Even if the cops did do something, even if he went to jail . . . It wouldn't bring her back. It wouldn't change anything. I want him to hurt like I'm hurting, but he never will. He could go to jail for a thousand years, and he wouldn't know what this feels like." Mattie starts to cry. "I want my sister back," they say, choking. "The only thing I ever wanted was my sister back. And I'll never have that. I don't even know where they—buried her. And I don't really care about anything else."

"I know how that feels," Brad says. Mattie looks at him, and I can see them see it in his face: He *does* know. He knows what Mattie's going through in a way Cam or I or even Irene don't. Can't.

He knows what it's like to wait for someone who's never coming back, and find out the truth far too late.

He knows what it's like to wish for a killer to suffer, and to know that nothing, no punishment ever devised, will equal the suffering that person has already inflicted.

He knows what it's like to go over and over and over the last thing you ever said to someone you love, the last moment you ever spent with them, when you had no idea that was all you'd ever get.

He knows what it's like to carry around all the things you'll never be able to say.

I don't know anything about any of that. I've only

ever seen someone else go through it. I know I'll find
out one day; I'll lose someone I love, and have to enter
a world I've only witnessed from the outside. I'll have
to learn to live with grief the way most human beings
do.

But I have learned something about stories in the
last year, Meredith. I've learned about what happens
when I walk into a story that isn't mine and make
myself a part of it. I've learned what happens when
I try to take the words out of other people's mouths.
I've learned that good intentions don't lead to better
consequences.

And this time, with this story, I can't even say my
intentions started out good.

I'm not sure if I believe in fate. I don't know if I
would've had the conviction to talk Cam into helping
Mattie if you hadn't called me. I don't know if Mattie
would've found out the truth about their sister on their
own. I don't know if they needed me and Cam at all. I
don't know if we helped, honestly.

And Luke—

Yeah, I still have a lot of learning to do, it turns out.
I'll deal with that part later.

Not that that's any of your business either, Meredith.

I don't mean that to be rude.

It's the truth.

But tonight, after everything, we're safe.

And looking at Mattie and Brad in Cam's kitchen,
at the understanding moving between them—a connection so strong it's almost visible, like a living thing
taking shape in the steamy air, among the empty plates
and bowls, Kitten purring in Mattie's lap, the winter

night storming against the windows, Irene lighting a cigarette—looking at that, I think:

Mattie and Brad were meant to find each other.

Cam and I helped with that. That's what I mean about fate. Mattie and Brad would've been strangers forever if Mattie hadn't come to me and Cam. If you hadn't called me and asked for a book. If I hadn't talked Cam into this.

Mattie and Brad were meant to find each other.

And their story, both of their stories, belong to them.

One day I'll come to you with a story that's mine alone. I don't know yet what that story will be. If it'll be true, or something I made up, or something that's a bit of both. I don't know if it will be any good. I guess you never do, until you're done telling it. And even then, it's probably hard to be sure.

Maybe it'll be a story that you think people want to hear.

Maybe not.

That part's not up to me.

I know you were hoping for serial killers, Meredith. Something flashy, at least. The real Lola tied up somewhere, tortured and terrified and eventually murdered in some slow, horrific way.

You wanted gore and survival against the odds. Me and Cam trapped in a basement again while the killer advanced, chewing through our bonds just in time to fight for our lives or rescued at the last minute by heroic police.

You wanted the fake Lola to be a monster with a

thirst for blood. Maybe a manhunt, a body count, a sea of dead girls.

Their blank eyes, their ravaged bodies. Until, in the final pages, justice prevails and everybody is happy and the film rights go for millions.

I'm not stupid; that's what sells.

But that's not my story.

And Mattie's story isn't mine to tell.

For that one, the one that is?

I'm afraid you'll have to wait.

Respectfully,
Blair Johnson

DAY 17: MONDAY

MR. PARK ENTERTAINS A NOTION

IT'S hard to imagine that Monday will dawn like any other morning, a perfectly ordinary day on which they will be obligated to get out of bed and dress themselves and attend school. And yet, Blair thinks, time has a habit of progressing, regardless of how one might feel about it.

The day passes in a haze, teachers' voices blurring together in a staticky fuzz. When the bell rings, signaling the end of Journalism, Blair and Cam exhale in simultaneous relief.

"Blair, Cam," Mr. Park says from the front of the room. "Please stay after class. The rest of you, thanks for all your hard work today."

Jenna the irritating junior gives them a malevolently triumphant look as she slinks out of the classroom.

Blair has no trouble recognizing the essay sitting on Mr. Park's desk as she and Cam approach. She's the one who wrote it, in a feverish spurt over the weekend, desperate to meet their deadline. Cam helped.

Sort of.

If you count delivering irritating monologues clearly cribbed from Sophie while Blair frantically typed as helping.

"Did you like our editorial?" Blair asks anxiously, shifting her weight from one foot to the other.

"Sit, sit." Mr. Park gestures to the empty front row of desks.

Blair's heart sinks. This conversation, apparently, is going to take a while.

Not good.

"The editorial," Mr. Park says. He gives her a Mr. Park look over the rims of his round glasses. "It has a few more grammatical errors than I am accustomed to seeing in your work."

"Our work," Cam says hopefully.

"And it's a bit on the short side," Mr. Park says. "Despite the page count." He looks down at the printout on his desk. "I am an old man, Blair Johnson, but I do notice when my students attempt to disguise brevity with a font the size of a diner menu."

"Right," Blair says.

"Perhaps the two of you will consider spending a bit more time on revision than you did in generation," Mr. Park says.

"Sure," Cam says. "Whatever you think. That sounds great. Can we go?"

"No," Mr. Park says. "I'm not interested in talking to you about your editorial. Your worst work, Blair, is significantly better than the best of what most of your peers have to offer, but that is no reason to be lazy. I'd appreciate it if you fixed this. But I'd much rather hear what the two of you were actually doing in my class for the last two weeks, since it clearly wasn't working on your editorial."

"Ah," Blair says.

"Mmm," says Cam. "We were. Um. You know, I'm not very good at writing, so Blair was helping me. With writing."

"You didn't write a word of this," Mr. Park says to Cam

mildly. "Though I recognize the influence of Sophie. How is she, by the way? Tell her to email me if she has a moment. I'd be delighted to hear from her."

Cam's eyes are wide. If Blair herself were not terrified, she would be enjoying the sight of Cam stunned into speechlessness.

"We," Blair says. "We, uh."

"I had the most fascinating conversation with my colleague Karyn on Friday," Mr. Park continues.

Karyn? Blair thinks.

And then she thinks, *Oh, no.*

Ms. Lackmann's first name is Karyn.

"The two of you went to see her last week, did you not? And then, over the weekend, I received an equally fascinating email. A transfer request, from a freshman. Most unorthodox at this time of year, don't you think? I believe you know this young person. Mattie Brosillard?"

Cam glances at Blair. "We, uh, know them. A little bit. From around."

Mr. Park folds his hands on his desk and gazes at them with a pleasant ruthlessness.

"Mattie's sister went missing five years ago, I'm told."

"We did hear something about that," Blair manages.

"And briefly returned two weeks ago before going missing again? On Friday?"

"I don't know," Blair says. "Anything. We don't, I mean. Know anything."

"*Very* interesting," Mr. Park says. "A story that seems almost familiar."

"No," Cam says. "No, nothing familiar. I don't think."

"*I* do," says Mr. Park.

He waits. Silently.

It's the oldest trick in the journalism book: Let the silence get so big it takes on a personality of its own. Most people can't stand to let it sit there.

Being on the other side of that silence, it's no wonder why.

"We can't tell you," Blair blurts.

This time, it's Cam who kicks Blair's ankle.

"Cam, he's not stupid," Blair says.

"Why, thank you, Blair," Mr. Park says.

"Mattie is our friend," Blair says. "Yes. Obviously. I think you should let them into Journalism. Not that it's my decision. That's your decision. Of course. But we can't tell you what we were doing."

Mr. Park raises an eyebrow.

"Because it's not our story," Cam adds, rallying to Blair's side. "It's Mattie's. We were just sort of—there. That's what we learned last year. That's what you were trying to *get* me to learn, Mr. Park, and it worked. Because you're such a good teacher."

"What did you learn, exactly?" Mr. Park asks.

"The difference between a good story and a story that's ours to tell," Cam says. "That's what I learned. I think. Mostly."

Mr. Park sits back in his chair and looks at them for a long time.

"Okay," Mr. Park says at last.

"Okay?" Cam asks.

"Okay," he says, nodding. "Explanation accepted. I don't normally allow freshmen into my class, as you know, but this Mattie is quite talented. They sent me a few samples. A bit imaginative for Journalism, but we can work with that. I trust, Blair, that you're willing to act as a writing mentor if they join the class?"

"Me?" Blair asks, startled.

"Yes, you," Mr. Park says. He's not doing a good job of hiding his smile.

"But I—" Blair stops.

But I'm not any good at writing, she was going to say.

Why was she going to say that?

That's not the kind of thing she's going to need to say in New York.

"I'd be glad to," she says.

"Then that's settled." Mr. Park picks up their—her—ridiculous editorial and drops it in the trash. "I'm looking forward to your revision. By Friday."

"Yes, Mr. Park," Blair says.

"Now go home," Mr. Park says, waving a hand at them regally.

"Yes, Mr. Park," Cam says.

"I'm going to miss you both next year," Mr. Park says. "I'm afraid things will be awfully dull."

"Oh, I think Mattie will keep you on your toes," Cam says.

"Wonderful," Mr. Park says. "See you tomorrow."

THE DEPARTURE

Sophie flies in on the second night of winter break. Irene offers to take Cam to pick her up at the airport, but Sophie goes instead to her parents', for what she says will be a few days. To see how it goes, she says.

How it goes lasts six hours, and then she's at Cam's door.

"Hi," she says.

Cam flings her arms around Sophie without a word. Sophie buries her head in Cam's shoulder.

"I came out to my dad," Sophie says, her voice muffled by Cam's sweatshirt.

Cam leans back, looks at her. "How did it go?"

"Can I stay here?"

"Obviously," Cam says.

Sophie is looking up at Cam, her perfect face still. "For a while?" she asks.

"Obviously!" Irene shouts from the living room.

"Don't be a dummy," Cam says. "Come in."

Mattie moves from Cam's room to the couch. Blair has been over all day, hopefully eyeing the oversized pot in which Brad boils spaghetti noodles, and the day before that. So has Brad. Irene tells a long, boring story about her time in Williamsburg squats—"Thirteen people and six cats, and for a while we didn't have running water," she says, with a gleam in her eye that looks alarmingly like nostalgia. Kitten is beside himself, elated by his new, lap-abundant life.

It is a kind of cozy, cheerful chaos that Cam has never experienced in all her tenure in this tiny apartment.

To her great surprise, she likes it.

That night, she goes into the bathroom to change into her pajamas. Which is silly, she knows; it's not like Sophie hasn't seen her naked before. It's not like Sophie hasn't spent the night at her house before, for that matter.

But this feels different.

"This feels different," Sophie says in Cam's room. She's sitting on Cam's bed. She's here, where Cam desperately wants her, back in Cam's world, back in Cam's life at last, and Cam doesn't know what to say.

"I don't know what to say," Cam says.

"The last three months were hard," Sophie says. "We can start there."

Three months? Has it really only been three months?

"The last three months felt like ten years," Cam says.

"I know," Sophie says.

"Do you want to break up with me?" Cam blurts. "You can still stay here. Of course. For as long as you need to. But if you want to break up with me, that's okay. I mean, it's not okay. With me. But it's your decision."

Sophie looks at her. "Come here," she says.

Cam sits next to Sophie on her bed. Takes Sophie's hand. Thinks, *Let me keep this.*

Please.

"No," Sophie says, and at first Cam thinks Sophie is saying *no* to what she's begged for in her head. But Sophie is still talking. "I don't want to break up with you. I don't want to lose you. But I don't know how to do everything I want to do and still have enough time for us. And I understand if that's—if you can't."

"Can't what?" Cam asks, confused.

"Can't do it," Sophie says. "If it's too much."

Cam thinks about this.

"You could text me twice a day at noon and six p.m. your time," she says.

Sophie is taken aback. "Is that what you want?"

"No," Cam says. "Blair said that was something I could ask for, though."

Sophie smiles. "Was that all she said?"

"No," Cam says again. "It was more complicated. It was about how I have to figure out what I want."

"Have you?"

"I want you around all the time," Cam says. "I want to go to college and think even more interesting things than I think now and learn about the structure and formation of galaxies. I want to be an astrophysicist. And have my own lab. And I want you to be there every day."

"I could unionize your graduate students," Sophie says.

"You won't have to," Cam says. "I'll unionize for them. Give them a union. Whatever."

"I can't be there for you every day, Cam," Sophie says. "There are a lot of things I need to do. There's so much work."

"I know," Cam says. "I know you can't. Can we keep trying?"

"Yes," Sophie says.

"Will you call me more?"

"Yes," Sophie says.

"Okay," Cam says, absurdly happy.

"It's not going to be easy for us," Sophie says.

"Easy is for the little people," Cam says.

Sophie smiles. "I love you," she says. "So much."

"I know," Cam says. "I love you too."

"I know," Sophie says. "Turn out the light. I haven't gotten laid since I left Oreville."

"Good," Cam says, and does.

In the morning, Brad comes over with a Christmas tree. "Fascism," Cam says sorrowfully, as he and Mattie stand it up in a corner of the living room.

"Tell Irene to get out the ornaments," Brad says.

"We're communists," Cam says. "Communists don't have Christmas tree ornaments."

Brad gives her a long, level look, decides she's not joking. "I guess I'll have to buy you a stand too, then," he says. "Costco's going to be a nightmare."

"Ruth's probably out somewhere," Mattie says. "We can raid my garage."

Brad gives them a fist bump, points a stern finger at Cam. "If you take that tree hostage while we're gone, I'm coming after you," he says.

"She won't," Sophie says, coming into the living room. Cam looks over at her girlfriend, her heart surging with love.

"I guess we can have a tree this year," Cam says, putting her arms around Sophie. Sophie leans into her side. "Since Mattie wants one."

"Good girl," Brad says, and hugs all three of them. His arms are long enough to reach.

True to her word, Irene takes them out to Olive Garden on Christmas Eve. Cam and Sophie, of course, but also Blair, and Mattie, and Brad, and Jenny and her girlfriend, Ellie.

My family, Cam thinks.

Brad, she knows, had to fight the impulse to protest her choice of location. But he lets Cam have her joy.

After all, even Brad cannot provide her with a bottomless breadstick basket.

Her heart is full.

Cam and her chosen family, secure in the warm glow of faux-rustic lighting, sit at a massive fake wood table in front of a massive fake wood fireplace in which a gas fire merrily burns. Outside is December, cold and wild with storms, and inside is everyone she loves.

Irene puts her head on Brad's shoulder, and he wraps one brawny arm around her. Irene is violently and vocally opposed to the patriarchal institution of heterosexual marriage, but last night Cam caught her discussing Brad's need for the robust spousal health insurance coverage provided through her work.

It's the closest Irene will ever get to admitting she wants to put a ring on him.

If Brad and Irene get married, does that mean she will have two parents? Will she have to call Brad *Dad*? This thought is unimaginable.

She looks over at Brad, whose chin rests now atop Irene's sleek dark hair.

No, she thinks.

Brad's not going to ever make her do anything she doesn't want to do.

Unless it's something like eating more salads.

"How's the book coming?" Brad asks Blair.

"Oh, the book," Blair says, shifting in her seat. "It's, uh, on hold."

"What?" Cam asks. "What does 'on hold' mean? What did that Meredith person do? I'll kill her."

"No, no," Blair says, laughing. "It was me. I wrote her." Blair glances at Mattie. "I said that it wasn't my story to tell and I was pulling the proposal. And she would have to wait until I found another idea. One that was really mine."

"What did she say?" Cam demands.

Blair flushes. "She said, um, that she totally understood." She flushes harder.

"And?" Cam demands.

"And that I was so talented she could wait for whatever I came up with next," Blair squeaks.

"Well, you are," Brad says.

"Blair Johnson," Cam says, radiant with pride. "Are you telling me you actually stood up for yourself?"

Blair, beet-red, smiles. "Yeah," she says. "I guess I did."

"What are you going to do?" Irene asks.

"I'm going to move to New York," Blair says. "And then we'll see what happens."

"You *are*?" Irene is delighted. "You're moving to *New York*? Oh, I will make you the *longest* list of where to go and what to eat and what to do—you have to take the Staten Island Ferry and go to Kalustyan's to buy spices and sit in the Temple of Dendur—you know, that's the best place in the entire world to cry—and most of the great show venues are closed now, but I can still give you some places—"

"The dinosaurs," Cam interrupts. Once Irene gets started about the greatness of New York, she will keep going until everyone around her is asleep or dead.

"I'm saving the dinosaurs for when you come visit," Blair says.

"New York's a four-hour train ride from Cambridge," Irene says.

"I am *aware* of that," Cam says.

"You'll have to start out in some roach-infested apartment with forty-three roommates and no working hot water," Irene says dreamily to Blair. "God, I'm so jealous."

"Move back," Cam says.

"Too late for me," Irene says dismissively.

"Why?" Brad asks.

Irene turns in the circle of his arm to look at him. "You would hate New York," she says.

"How do you know that?" Brad asks. "I've never been there."

Irene stares at him.

"See," Cam says. "People are surprising, Irene. And it would be much more convenient for *me* never to have to come back *here*." She gives Blair a piercing look. "What about Luke?"

"Cam," Sophie says.

"No, it's fine," Blair says. She looks at Mattie. "Is it okay if we talk about this?"

Mattie nods.

"Ruth sent my brother to rehab," they say. "Somewhere in Colorado. With horseback riding and coloring."

"Art therapy," Blair says.

"Sounds a lot better than state detox," Jenny says wryly.

"Did you talk to him?" Irene asks Mattie.

They shake their head. "He called me a bunch of times, but I haven't called him back. Maybe I will one day. But not for a long time."

"Have you talked to him?" Cam asks Blair.

"No," Blair says. She reaches for one of Cam's breadsticks. "I got so wrapped up in the story that I missed the person," she says.

"My brother can be charming," Mattie says.

"You were right," Blair says ruefully. "About the project thing. I can't fix anybody. I don't want to fix anybody. I think it's time for me to focus on my own story for a while."

She looks up from the breadstick. Cam is gazing at her in wonder.

"I'm proud of you," Cam says.

Blair blinks. "You are?"

"Yes," Cam says. "I am."

"Becca called me too," Mattie says. "She left a message. She wants to talk to me about . . . about Lola. She said she understands if I don't want to talk to her."

"Do you?" Jenny asks.

"I think so," Mattie says. "It wasn't her fault. It wasn't Luke's fault either. I know Darren told them they would both go to jail if they told anyone. They were really young and really scared, and here was this older person, telling them what to do. I'm not excusing them, but I understand it. Once you start lying like that, it must take over your whole life. But I don't know if I can ever forgive either one of them for not telling me what happened."

"That's fair," Brad says.

"That's more than fair," Irene says. "It's wise."

"Becca loved my sister," Mattie says. "We can talk about that, and see where it goes. Luke . . . I don't know. We'll see."

A thoughtful silence falls. Cam, beneficent, passes around her breadstick basket.

"So, what now?" Sophie asks, taking Cam's hand. Mattie watches with hungry eyes. "Can you stand a life out of the limelight, Cam?"

"*Yes,*" Cam says.

"No internet stalkers this time around," Blair says.

"No forums calling for our death," Cam agrees.

"Nobody saying you're reverse racists," Brad says.

"There's no such thing as reverse racism," Sophie says.

"He knows," Irene says, gazing at Brad in a loving manner. Jenny catches Cam's eye, mimes sticking her finger down her throat behind Irene's back.

"Is it weird?" Mattie asks. "You were so famous last time. And this time, nobody knows what you did."

"What you did too, Mattie," Cam says.

"It isn't weird at all," Blair says. "It's your story."

"We did learn *something* last year," Cam says. "Whether we wanted to or not."

"Speak for yourself," Blair says placidly. "I haven't learned a thing." She sits up suddenly. "Wait a minute. Mattie—the DNA test. You said when we first talked to you that you never tried that, because you don't have a credit card. How did you figure out how to get one, in the end? Who paid for it?"

"Oh, that," Mattie says. They shift awkwardly in their chair. "Technically, you did."

"I did?" Blair asks, startled.

"I stole your credit card the night you came over and looked at the security footage. The rush fee for the test was kind of expensive. I'll pay you back. I'm sorry."

"No, you're not," Cam says.

"No," Mattie agrees. "Not really."

Finally, Mattie smiles.

Blair smiles back. "It's okay," she says. "I think I deserved it."

"Blair took me by the house today," Mattie says to the rest of them, serious again. "Ruth's house. To pick up some clothes. And I found— Can I tell you this?" They glance around the table. "I don't want to ruin Christmas."

"You won't ruin Christmas," Irene says gently. Mattie gives her a grateful look.

"This came in the mail a couple of days ago," Mattie says.

They slide a thick, battered manila envelope out of their bag and hand it to Cam. It's addressed to Mattie in block letters and postmarked from Moab, Utah. There's no return address. Inside, there's a black notebook, the twin of Mattie's own, and several sheets of paper.

"What is this?" Cam asks.

"Lola's journal," Mattie says.

"Which Lola?" Brad asks.

"Both," Mattie says. "The first half my sister wrote. The rest, *she* did. She found it in my sister's room when she moved in. That's how she knew what to say. Who to be. She pretended we had all these memories in common. But I looked for this every day for months. Everywhere in the house. And she's the one who found it. She wrote . . ." Mattie trails off.

"Wrote what?" Jenny prompts gently.

"She wrote me letters," Mattie says. "And yesterday, I got this text. It's a location. I tried calling the number the message came from, but it doesn't work."

"Location for what?" Cam asks.

"It's in the park. It's where my sister is buried," Mattie says.

"How does she know that?" Cam asks.

"She made Darren tell her," Mattie says, almost awed. "She called him and told him she'd watch him for the rest of his life and if he ever did anything to hurt me, she'd hunt him down and kill him. That's what she wrote me, anyway. You can read it if you want."

"I don't think it's any of my business," Cam says.

"No, I want you to," Mattie says. "Maybe it will help. I don't know."

Cam takes the notebook from them. It takes her a while to read through the pages covered in the other Lola's bold scrawl. When she's done, she looks at Mattie, who nods.

Cam hands the book to Blair.

One by one, they pass it around the table.

The waiter brings shrimp scampi, fettuccine alfredo dripping with a cream sauce that makes Brad wince, fried mozzarella, a frightful appetizer called "Lasagna Fritta" that Blair is at a loss even to describe.

Jenny's the last to read the other Lola's book, Ellie looking over her shoulder. "Wow," she says finally when she's done.

"And this," Mattie says, unfolding a printout of an online article. "She sent me this too."

"Read it out loud," Blair says.

WOMAN SOUGHT IN CONNECTION WITH ARMED ROBBERY OF PINE OAK BANK

August 17, 2022
Pine Oak, Iowa

Police are searching for a woman captured in a surveillance video in connection with the armed robbery of the Pine Oak branch of Iowa Savings and Security Bank. No one was harmed during the robbery, which police have described as "very well-planned, almost methodical," but police reports indicate the thieves stole over $500,000. Two people have already been arrested as suspects in the robbery: Earl Sticklin, 18, of Pine Oak, and Marcus Hayes, 20, also of Pine Oak. The third, female accomplice is believed to be Shari Ross, 18, of Pine Oak. Her identity is not confirmed and she remains at large.

The article is accompanied by a grainy security-camera photo of a young woman in a black stocking hat looking directly into the lens with a mocking smile.

"That's her," Cam says, taking the printout from Mattie.

"No wonder she needed a new passport," Blair says.

"She sent me this too," Mattie says, showing them a book. A mint-condition copy of *The Big Sleep*, the same edition Darren destroyed.

"Why did she leave me all this?" Mattie asks. "I could go to the police. Tell them she was here." They shake their head. "Not that they would believe me. Believe any of it. And not that I could find her now."

"I think it's her way of apologizing," Blair says. "She's trusting you with the truth."

"And she found out where Darren buried your sister for you," Cam says. "So you didn't have to ask him yourself."

"Why?" Mattie asks again.

"Because she cared about you, Mattie," Blair says. "Cares. In her own way."

Mattie sits with this for a moment, their face a wash of emotions.

"Yeah," they say. "I guess she did. Does."

Blair can't imagine the feeling.

Mattie, all alone in that gaudy mansion with a brother who knew the truth and lied to them for years and a mother who didn't care. A mother who'd been ready to send away their sister. A mother who the other Lola could've easily convinced to send them away too.

And the other Lola. A liar, a thief, a grifter—and, despite everything she'd done, the one person who'd fought for Mattie in that house.

The other Lola could've stayed. Blair has no doubt about that. She was ruthless, and clever, and fearless. But staying would've meant getting rid of Mattie. Getting Mattie sent to a place no better than jail. A place that could easily have destroyed them.

And, no matter how many lies she'd already told, the other Lola couldn't do that.

Instead, she'd run.

And then she'd given Mattie the truth.

Mattie laughs softly through their nose. "Funny," they say. "She's the only person in my family who turned out to have a backbone. Other than my real sister."

She's the only person in your family who loved you enough to protect you, Blair thinks.

Mattie meets her eyes.

Mattie, Blair knows, is thinking the same thing.

"We'll take you to your sister," Blair says.

Cam nods. "Tomorrow, if you want." She clears her throat. "You have us now, Mattie. For life."

"Tomorrow's Christmas," Mattie says, their voice shaky.

"We'll come too, if you want us to," Irene says. "Or not. If you'd rather be alone. That's totally up to you."

"I'd like it if Cam and Blair came with me," Mattie says.

"I'll pick you both up around noon," Blair says.

Christmas Day is clear and sharp and cold. A pale skin of frost glitters on the dark earth as Cam and Blair and Mattie walk through the woods to the place where Darren and Luke buried Lola.

Five years is a long time in the forest. And a location point looks small and easy to find on a screen, but out here in the wild? Surrounded by feral green and dripping leaves and half trails left by deer darting through the undergrowth?

The point the other Lola sent them, the place that Darren gave her, could be anywhere. Or nowhere. It could be under their feet, or a dozen yards away. There's no clearing, no telltale patch of trampled earth. No place free of growing things where pale bones show themselves.

Just the heavy smell of sodden wood and sleeping trees, of coming snow, of clouds.

We'll never find her, Blair thinks. *Not if we come out here with a backhoe and cut down every tree for a mile.*

Just thinking about cutting down trees here, in this place, feels like sacrilege.

As if they can hear her, Mattie looks down at the phone in their hand, checking one last time. And then they put it away in their pocket, turn their face to the dripping emerald canopy above. They close their eyes, listening.

Cam and Blair listen too.

If you hold still enough here, Cam thinks, *I bet you can hear things growing.*

"There was a nurse log there once," Mattie says, opening their eyes and pointing to a row of massive firs growing in a straight line, their roots entangled at their bases. "So long ago that it's rotted away now. But that's how they grow. Seedlings take root in the fallen tree. They don't all make it. But the ones that do grow up strong, because the old tree fed them."

They look around one more time.

Cam and Blair are silent.

"She would've loved it here," Mattie says. "But she's gone now. Let's go home."

Dear Mats,

The last time we saw each other, you asked me how I can live with myself. It's a funny question, if you think about it. The answer is: easily. Breathe, eat when I'm hungry, sleep when I'm tired, drink when I'm thirsty, get drunk when I want to forget. The body manages itself, when you give it what it needs to survive.

I know that's not what you meant. But that's your answer. I think your sister and I were more alike than you might want to admit. It was easier than it should've been to live inside her skin. You loved her, but I understood her. Those are different things.

Anyway. A bit of business: You're wondering how I knew what happened to your sister, in the end. I was still in the house when he showed up, the night you confronted me. Though I was already packed. I heard the key turning in the lock, and I knew it was him. You weren't coming back. And Ruth and Luke always come through the garage. So I hid under the bed and waited. He came crashing in, screaming her name. *Lola, Lola, Lola. I buried you.* I don't know the whole story, but I can guess. I saw the gun. I know he left you that book. It's not hard to see the kind of man Darren is. Not if you know how to look.

Sorry, Mats. I know you loved him. I wish he'd earned it.

I called him from the road. Our conversation was short, but I said a few things he'll remember for a long time. Darren's very afraid of the police, Mattie, but now he's much more afraid of me. I told him I would watch him until the end of his life, and if he ever did anything to hurt you I would pull out his tongue with pliers and fill his mouth with molten lead and boil him alive in oil and leave his bones on Ruth's lawn to rot. But I'd start with his baby, if he ever has one, and then I'd move on to his girlfriend, and I'd make him watch what I did to them before I got around to him. You don't need to worry about Darren. I hope you never think about him again. Some people don't deserve our memories. Keep your sister in your heart, where she belongs, and let everything else around her go.

Do you think about me as much as I think about you? I never had a sibling. If I did, I would've wanted them to be someone like you. Smart and brave and funny and resourceful. A person solid at their center, sure of themselves. You might not know it yet, but you are. I wish I could be there to see the world welcome you. I know you're going to do great things.

This is the last time I'll write you, but I'll carry you with me for a long time. And maybe, one day, we'll find each other again. Somewhere unexpected, out on the open road. We'll recognize each other, the way you do when you find someone familiar in a dream. I'll tell you where I've been, and you'll tell me what you got up to after I left. That's the happy version of the story. That's the one I prefer.

I'm in the desert now, on my way to somewhere new. Another family, another story. Another chance to be a different person. To write the first line on a blank page and see how far it carries me.

But I'll never forget what it was like to be your sister for a while, no matter how many other girls I become.

Good luck, Mats.

I'll be seeing you.

Love,
the other Lola

ACKNOWLEDGMENTS

Thank you to the amazing team at Wednesday Books: Sara Goodman, Eileen Rothschild, Olga Grlic, Lauren Hougen, Soleil Paz, Rivka Holler, Brant Janeway, Zoë Miller, Eric Meyer, Melanie Sanders, Diane Dilluvio, Elishia Merricks, Maria Snelling, and Amber Cortes. Particular thanks is due to the eagle-eyed Vanessa Aguirre. Thank you as well to Andrea Morrison, Hayley Burdett, and Greg Ferguson. Nick Pyenson's wonderful *Spying on Whales* should not be judged by the foibles of its fan in these pages. I remain indebted to the work of Mariame Kaba. For more about the Bundy occupation of public lands in the West, start with Leah Sottile's podcast *Bundyville*.

Thank you to Maik Lübke—I'll write the real one soon—and to Bennett Madison, whose fault all of this technically is. And to you, dear Reader, with love.

—Ripley

ABOUT THE AUTHOR

© Maik Lübke

RIPLEY JONES is a person of interest.